# The North Star

# The Third and Final Book of the Star Saga

Warning: book contains scenes of physical abuse, sexual content, violence, adult content, and foul language. Some scenes may be triggers to some and are not appropriate for all ages. Thank you for reading- S.E Dymek

Dedication

To Aaralyn, Ivy, and Caiden. My biggest inspirations for everything I do.

To my husband, Aaron, who is my biggest support.

Acknowledgments

I'd like to thank my parents, close family, and all
my inner, dearest friends who listened to me
babble about ideas and were willing to read them.
I love you all. Thank you to all my readers!

About the Author

S.E. Dymek is an upcoming author who is published on several ebook platforms. She has a passion for writing romance novels including paranormal romance novels and historical. All of her works include twists and turns, keeping her readers on their toes. She is a mother of three and loving wife. When she is not writing; she is working as a veterinary technician. Born and raised in Rhode Island, she has found her second home in Texas.

# Chapter One

## Tomatoes

The rotten tomato she held in her hand was black and mold ridden. She was angry as she ducked behind the boxes, hiding. She poked her head out and looked about to see if anyone might notice. She smirked seeing no one around. She launched the tomato towards the building. The tomato hit with a thud and busted into pieces on impact all over the sign. The wooden sign swung back and forth as pieces of the rotten tomato slid off. She reached into her sack finding another tomato. She aimed again at the sign that read " Smith and Brothers Trading". The second tomato spirals towards the sign, following the same pattern as the first. Exploding all over the sign. She stifled a chuckle this time. She quickly reached into her bag again and was holding the third in her hand. She let it fly, each tomato flung; she felt a little less mad. As the third tomato was headed to its destination the door of the building opened up and out stepped an older  man. He was dressed perfectly right down to his shoes. He adjusted his collar pausing in the doorway as his salt and pepper hair blew lightly in the breeze. Seeing him she ducked behind the boxes peeking out just as the tomato erupted all over the sign. Pieces of the rotten vegetable splattered all over the man's white shirt. She couldn't help herself, it was too good to be true, her laughter rang out in the alley she had been hiding in. The man's eyes shot her way and his face frowned, spotting her.

"You wretched creature!!" He bellowed.

"That's what you get Smith! You thieving bastards!" Danica yelled back no use in hiding since she had been spotted.

Just you wait!" He yelled back.

"Father?' Another voice coming out behind the man came.

This man was a younger version of the man splattered with tomato. His chocolate brown eyes studying the scene in front of him. Realizing what had happened, part of him wanted to laugh.

"Well don't just stand there!" His father yelled angrily at him.

The man shrugged trying to figure out what his father wanted him to do. Danica was now almost doubled over laughing at the scene.

"Go get her, boy!" His father yelled, slapping him in the back of his blonde head.

Hearing that she paused locking eyes with the man who was probably only two years older than her. He smirked after recovering from the wack in the head, starting across the road towards her. Fine she thought, come and catch me then. Laughing she took off running down the alleyway. Her raven black hair flew out behind her as she did. She rounded a corner running down another alley way. She could hear him catching up. She was fast but he was gaining on her. Her footsteps pounding on the cobblestone street as she ran across a busy road ducking in out of people walking by. She glanced back seeing his blonde head pop out just on the other side. She quickly ducked into another alleyway. She just needed to make it two more streets and then she would be home. Looking back and not paying attention she slammed into a fence. She blinked, stumbling back. This was new. When did this go up? She studied it, she could climb it. Being in the stupid skirt was going to make it hard. She heard footsteps stop at the top of the alleyway she was in.

"Hey! Girl!" The blonde man yelled down the alleyway to her.

Danica grumbled why was he so fast? She thought, glancing from him to the fence.

"Come on now, he'll probably just want you to clean the sign that's all." He said to her walking slowly.

"Yeah, I don't think I will be doing that." Danica grumbled back to him.

"Seriously, what's your problem?" He said as he was approaching her.

"Really? What's My problem. My problem is you and your family." Danica said, backing herself against the fence.

"Who are you? What did my family do?" He asked, confused, pausing.

Danica rolled her eyes at him. She glanced down at the bag she was still holding. She reached inside pulling out a rotten tomato. She smirked as she sent it flying at him. The tomato hit him square in the forehead. The rotten juices running down into his eyes and mouth.

"Are you kidding me!" He yelled, wiping his eyes.

Danica used this opportunity to climb the fence. By the time the man was done whipping the tomato out of his eyes, the girl was gone. He shook his head, not sure what any of that was about.

"Who the hell was she?" He muttered to himself turning around and going back the way he came

Danica laughed to herself as she crashed through her front door. Closing it breathlessly she straightened herself up before continuing into the kitchen. Ariadne raised an eyebrow at her as she entered. Ariadne was hovered over paperwork upon paperwork that she had scattered about the kitchen table. She didn't have enough room on the desk in the office.

"Danica, I could use some help here." Ariadne said frustrated as she tapped the paper.

"All right, what are you looking for exactly?" Danica said, walking over to the table.

"A loophole, a miss print, a flaw, anything at this point that we could use against those bastards." Ariadne muttered.

Danica frowned; she knew exactly what her sister was feeling. Ever since her parents left and their brother Orion went off to secure their trade business in the east, everything had been falling down around them. Most companies don't want to work with a woman and with the new trading company underhanding their offers. The only thing that they had going for them right now was they had more ships and still had the queen's favor. The queen though was getting up there in age and she knew Smith and Brothers trading company was buddying up to the queen's son.  Danica buckled down, taking a stack of paper and began reading through it. Not too long into researching there was a knock on the door. Ariadne glanced at Danica who raised her eyebrow looking at the direction of the door. Before either one of them could move a more forceful knock followed.  Ariadne grabbed a pistol from behind her that she had casually sitting on the counter. Danica went and grabbed a sword. She nodded for Ariadne to go to the door. Being alone, just the two of them, they were prepared for anything and unfortunately the town had become noisy and everyone knew each other's business.

Open it, Danica mouthed to Ariadne as she held the sword ready to attack. Ariadne tucked the pistol into the door slightly as she cracked the door open. A man was standing outside. He had blond ruffled hair and deep chocolate brown eyes. He was tall and looked strong, his shoulders and stance said he could hold his own against anything. He smiled politely at Ariadne as she waited for him to say something. After several seconds Ariadne became frustrated.

"Can I help you?" Ariadne said her tone annoyed.

"Aye sorry, I was looking for someone...I guess. This is Abner's trading correct?" He asked, his voice had warmth as he spoke.

Danica perked up at the sound of his voice. The words seriously what's your problem echoed in her head. She let out a small gasp as Ariadne shot her a funny look.

"Aye it is but I don't have any appointments today so kindly state your business." Ariadne said frankly to him.

Close the door, Danica mouths to her. Ariadne was so busy studying the stranger that she didn't see Danica trying to get her attention.

"Aye my apologies. I could come back at a later time and talk to your boss whenever he is available." The man nodded his head as he spoke.

Fire lit in Ariadne's belly at his statement, like he was looking down on her. This wasn't the day she thought.

"Well unfortunately for you SHE will most likely not want to speak to you. You can send a letter to HER, with whatever it is your wanting." Ariadne said making sure she was overly loud as she used the feminine pronouns.

Danica snickered and then went back to trying to get Ariadne's attention. The men cleared his throat realizing he had offended her, Danica leaned closer and poked Ariadne gently with the tip of her sword. Ariadne swatted the blade away as she locked eyes with the man burning a hole in him.

" I am so sorry madam. I didn't mean to offend." He began to apologize.

Danica went to poke her again, this time Ariadne didn't see it coming and winced as the blade poked her.

"Aye, most men don't think that a woman could possibly be running a business, never mind being in the world of trade." Ariadne said trying to recover from the awkward motion Danica was making her do.

"No ma'am, that's not what I meant to imply at all. I am from-

Danica had enough of this. She was done. She made her way over to the door and grasped the door pulling it open wide. Ariadne stumbled slightly.

"Yeah we're not interested in anything you have to say or offer. If I were you I would walk myself back down our walkway while you can.' Danica said sword still by her side and her eyes narrowed with intent.

"Tomato girl?" The man said, confused.

"Aye and you better be going before I throw more than just a tomato at you this time." Danica threatens him.

Ariadne looked confused as tomatoes were brought up but she quickly recovered going back to being composed and firmed as her sister was about to chase this man off their property.

"Dani." Ariadne said softly.

"Dani?" The man said almost by accident as he tried to remember her name.

"Danica and you are-" Danica went to say as she was cut off

"Patrick." The man said, holding out his hand to her.

"You are leaving...leaving" Danica said continuing.

"Ladies, I think we've gotten off on the wrong foot. I am Patrick Smith, from Smith and Brothers trading company across town-

"We know...bye now" Danica said, still glaring at him.

Ariadne nudged her lightly, she wanted to hear what he had to say. Danica sighed, rolling her eyes as she waved her hand telling him to continue.

"Anyways, My father wanted to make an offer to you. He knows the recent competition between our two companies are..taking its toll on your business

and he wanted to make an offer to buy you out."
Patrick continued.

"Can I kill him now, Ari?" Danica growled as
she tightened the grip on her sword and she stepped
forward.

"Mr. Patrick, how kind of you to think of us poor
women here and offer a buyout in our time of need.
We will be declining. You can tell your …..charming
father to take his offer-

"And shove it." Danica finished for Ariadne who
cracked a smile.

A smile cracked across Patrick's face as he
looked in amazement at these two very strong and
very capable women. He threw his hands up in
defense as he tried not to chuckle.

"All right I will let him know." Patrick said with a
smile dancing on his lips.

"Goodnight." Ariadne said, walking away from
the door.

Danica stood there continuing to glare at
Patrick. If looks could kill, Patrick was sure he would
have died over and over again in the short amount of
time he had been standing there. He nodded slightly
at Danica as he began to make his way away from
the house.

"Another thing Mr. Patrick. If your father wasn't a lying, cheating low life we wouldn't be in any situation. There is enough world out there that there is no use of us fighting over it!" Danica yelled at his back.

Patrick paused this was the second time she had brought up his father being a liar and a cheat. He wanted to go ask what she meant but chose to keep going. He had been away for so long that he really didn't know exactly what was going on but his father had always been an honest man. He shook his head slightly as he began making his way further away from their property.

"Ari, give me a tomato." Danica said loud enough so Patrick could hear it.

Patrick heard her but chose to ignore her as he heard her laughter at his back, the whole situation made him want to find out more. He thought hard about this whole scene as he began to make his way home.

Danica came inside and slammed the door. She was still angry as she turned to look at Ariadne who had already gone back to work.

"Tomato girl?" Ariadne asked her.

"Yeah don't worry...how bad are we?" Danica asked her.

"We haven't made any real profit in almost two months. We are barely keeping afloat and that's just because of Orion making his contracts out east. We are just lucky enough Smith and Brothers haven't found a way to head east yet. I don't know how long we can keep this up. Even if Da and Ma  cut their time away short I think they would be falling victim to this as well." Ariadne said a tinge of hopelessness in her voice.

"Ari go rest a bit, you've been doing this for hours. I'll take over and maybe by tomorrow we will have a solution. But staring at the same pieces of paper forever isn't going to help and you need a break." Danica said, going over to her and nudging her as she spoke.

"Fine but the same goes for you. Don't be up all night." Ariadne muttered, feeling the exhaustion from it all.

"Aye I won't." Danica smiled as she watched Ariadne make her way upstairs and she took over.

## Chapter Two

## Treasure map

Danica paced the floor of the kitchen reading document after document. She glanced up to the ceiling and she finally heard Ariadne stop moving about, she hoped she had fallen asleep. With the deadline three weeks away if they didn't have the money they would lose a ship and a major contract. Danica felt defeated. Smith and Brothers were going behind each of their contracted partners and offering "better deals". Always just a little less than what they were offering. Danica became frustrated and found herself missing her parents. She knew this wouldn't be happening if they were there. She wandered into her father's office. She loved the smell in there. All the old books and maps. She inhaled, finding peace among it all. She sat down at her father's desk and smiled, running her hands over it. She remembered sneaking in there late at night when she was supposed to be in bed. She would sit up on the desk as her father would talk to her about his adventures, the ocean, and the stars. He would show her maps and point out places he had been. She couldn't wait to be older and have her own adventures. She smiled at the memories.

"Oh Da what would you do?" She grumbled into her hands as she propped her elbows up on the desk.

She yawned slightly, folding her arms downwards as she rested her hands on them. They need a miracle. She quickly drifted off to sleep.

Patrick walked home completely confused. He wasn't sure what just happened or why the two girls were so angry with him. He reached the concrete front steps of his fathers home, he shook his head seeing the rotten tomato still on the steps. A small smile came to his face. The girl...Dani. she had such fire, he had never had a woman speak to him like that. He thought, shaking his head as he walked inside.

"Patrick, I am in the study." His father called him when he heard the door.

Patrick removed his coat and hung it on the rack by the door before heading to his father's study. Walking in the room it was dim, his father sat in a tall red chair in front of the fireplace. He was smoking a cigar and had a small glass of brandy next to him. Seeing Patrick come in he motioned to the chair next to him. Patrick walked over and sat in it. The fire dancing in the fireplace caught his eye.

"So how did it go?" His father asked as he took a drag off his cigar.

"It didn't." Patrick said shortly.

"What?" His father asked as he placed the cigar down in the ashtray and turned to him; like facing him he would get a better answer.

"It didn't, I barely got a word out. Those woman are -

"Wretched, that's what they are. Children, spoiled brats. They need to let go of that company. I need them to do it before their parents come back too." His father cut him off, becoming frazzled.

"Not interested." Patrick mumbled and finished his sentence.

"Why before their parents come back?" Patrick asked as he stood walking over to his fathers small bar.

"Because they might be able to fix it." His father mumbled to himself, taking a sip from his glass.

Patrick poured himself a glass of brandy and walked over to the fire place, leaning against it as he took a sip. His fathers words seemed to click as he glanced over to him.

"Fix what?" Patrick asked.

"Never mind. Never mind. We will just have to wear them down. That's all and in three weeks it might not matter. If everything goes well they will be begging me to buy them out." His father chuckled to himself going back to his cigar.

"Why did they call us thieves?" Patrick asked with an eyebrow raised.

"They were just upset." His father said, waving his hand at the comment.

"Are you not telling me something Father?" Patrick said, making a face not sure if he believed what his father was telling him.

"There's nothing to tell. You just need to follow my instructions. You may be grown but you're still my son and this is my house. You may have been away at that fancy business school but this is my business and I am running it just well. You do what I say." His father said becoming very defensive.

Patrick nodded slightly and poured his brandy into the fire. The alcohol sizzled and made the flames brighter. He set the glass down and started to walk out the room.

"Night Father." He muttered leaving the room.

His father made a noise and went back to his drink and cigar. Patrick was frustrated. He knew there was something else going on. He just didn't know what and wanted to find out. He climbed the stairs to his room and shut the door a little too loud.

Danica stirred in her sleep, the moonlight dancing across the desk, hitting her in the face woke her up. She rubbed her eyes with the palm of her hands and then ran them down her face. She sighed deeply. She stretched slightly to stand. She hadn't found a solution but she was too tired now. Standing a glimmer of moonlight bounced off something in the book shelf. Danica began walking to it with a puzzled look on her face. Reaching the book shelf, the books looked like ordinary books.

One stood out as the moonlight danced over it. The book looked like an old book. It was a deep navy blue cover but there was a piece of silver peeking out from the binding. Danica pulled the book carefully from the shelf. It was much heavier than a normal book.  Danica ran her hand over the cover and opened the book. It was a normal book. She frowned, running her hands over the pages filled with words telling  a story. The cover was so thick, she turned it over in her hand trying to figure out what was going on. As she did she accidentally fumbled it and the book crashed to the floor. As the book made impact with the floor the cover popped open revealing a secret compartment inside the cover. Danica bent down picking up the book as an old looking piece of paper fell out of it. It floated to the floor unfolding slightly.

It was a map. The moonlight danced across it as Danica knelt down to look at it. She recognised her dad's handwriting as she read it. She traced his coordinates and followed the route. An X was marking a spot. Danica looked at it closer and read the small handwriting next to it. It read "The Hollow" and it was written in her father's handwriting. She looked at the map puzzled. Why would he have this? She thought. She knew her father had a captain's log for each of these voyages. She needed to find them and see what this was. She knew all the trade routes and this was not one of them. The place seemed to be a random island in the middle of nowhere. She stood up and went to a small bookcase in the corner. She kneeled down going through all the old bound books that were her father's journals. She picked up what looked to be the oldest one and began skimming through it. She didn't see anything about The Hollow so she moved on to the next. She sat criss crossed on the floor with his journals spread out around her. Her eyes grew heavy as she looked through one after another. She leaned back into the bookcase nodding out. A dark blue journal in her lap.

"Dani! Dani! Danica!" Ariadne yelled from the doorway of her father's office.

Danica stirred slightly, opening her eyes. She groaned, stretching her legs out in front of her. She could feel the numbness running up and down them; as pins and needles set in.

'What are you doing?' Ariadne asked her.

"I thought maybe Dad's journals might have something in them. Something that could help us." Danica sighed, wiggling her legs trying to get them to wake up.

"I got breakfast on the table and then I'm going to send an update to Orion. Then maybe go try to speak to that tyrant." Ariadne said, her voice sounding almost sad.

"I'll keep looking for something here. Don't worry Ari, we will figure this out." Danica said to her hating to see her older sister feeling defeated.

Ariadne smiled weakly to Danica before walking out from the doorway. Danica groaned softly as she went to stand. The dark blue journal flopped open on the ground in front of her. Danica shook her head bending over to pick it up. Her eyes scanned the page as she did.


The Hollow, it is said that a Spanish conquistador left his fortune there. It is buried under the trees marked like an X. Travis will be excited to find that I actually have the map. I couldn't believe I tracked it down but now we have it. We can set sail on The Morning Star tomorrow.

Danica's eyes read her father's passage. She stared at the words on the page for several minutes letting them sink in.

"It's a treasure map." She whispered to herself out loud.

She closed the journal reaching for the map. She held it in front of her face as she studied it once more. Her mind was trying to understand what her mouth had whispered.

"It's a treasure map!" She yelled.

"A treasure map." She laughed while repeating it.

She ran into the kitchen with the maps and journal tucked under her arm. She scanned the kitchen for Ariadne did not find her. She went to the front door and pulled it open. Again Aridane was nowhere in sight. She sighed. She needed to tell her. This might be what fixes everything. If they could get the treasure their money issues would be gone. She thought calmly. She could go find her, what did she say again? Oh right she was trying to get a message to Orion and then she was heading to Smith and Brothers. Danica thought about trying to think of what to do next.

She grabbed a bag and headed back into the study. She grabbed the book with the secret compartment that she had found the map in. She placed the map back in there and closed the book. She then placed the book and dark blue journal into the bag. She was going to try to meet Ariadne before she went to Smith and Brothers. She locked the door to the house and headed out hoping she reached Ariadne in time.

Ariadne had found a man on the dock that was heading east. She handed him her message for her brother. He had agreed to take it to him for her.

"So I will pay you half now and half when you get back." Ariadne said, waiting for the man to agree.

"Half when I get back?" The man asked, raising his eyebrow.

"Aye to ensure you actually take the message. My brother will send you a letter back in return and when you show that he actually received the message, I will then pay you the rest." Ariadne said to him.

"Aye but-

"Sir not to be rude but there are other sailors here heading east. If you do not wish to enter this agreement then I can move on." Ariadne said, folding her arms across her chest.

"Aye fine sounds good." The man mumbled taking the letter and then waiting.

Ariadne almost rolled her eyes as she handed him a small bag of coins. The man took the pouch of coins and looked through it. He nodded slightly before heading to his ship. Ariadne rolled her eyes.

"One task down now, one more nuisance to deal with." Ariadne muttered to herself  heading in the direction of the town where Smith and Brother's were located.

Danica rushed down to the docks. If Ariadne needed to get a message to her brother she would pay a sailor to bring it to him. Scanning the docks she didn't see her. She frowned realizing she missed her. She didn't want to go to their business. She all but stomped her feet as she walked away from the dock.

Ariadne stood across the street staring at the brick building. She couldn't bring herself to cross the street yet. She fidgeted looking at the building. She shouldn't have to be doing this. If they were good people they would make their own way instead of stealing what wasn't there. She groaned trying to get her feet to move. Just then she heard loud footsteps coming up fast behind her. Her hand went to her hip where she had hidden a small knife. As the noise got near she spun around holding out her knife.

"Stop there." Ariadne orders the person coming towards her.

"Ari, it's me." Danica said, putting her hands up.

Ariadne shook her head and put away her knife, she gave Danica a look and asked why she was there. Danica smiled bright.

"We don't have to do this, come home I have an idea I want to tell you about. I found an old map for dads." Danica said excitedly.

"Map?" Ariadne asked, confused.

"Aye and it will fix all of our problems." Danica smiled, motioning for her sister to follow her.

"How will a map-

"Can you please just come home and see what I am talking about?" Danica said, cutting off Ariadne.

Ariadne sighed and motioned for Danica to lead the way home. She really didn't want to go talk to Edward  anyways. She thought, glancing back at Smith's and Brothers building.

Patrick was on his way home when he spotted the girl in the alley way across from his home. He thought that it was going to be another tomato attack so he went around to sneak up on them. As he approached them he stopped hearing their conversation. Map? He thought.  He was intrigued by it. He wondered if his father knew what kind of trouble or problems they had. And how would a map solve it? He did not approach them as they turned around to leave. He wanted to know more. He moved out of the shadows of the alley and headed to his home.

His father was in his study once more, this time standing over his desk. Maps rolled out in front of him as he muttered to himself. He didn't even hear Patrick walk in.

"Damn Abners." He muttered, throwing his pen against the map.Patrick cleared his throat to get his father's attention.

"Patrick. My boy come, come and brainstormed with me. It might be what I need. A fresh new pair of eyes." Patrick's father called him waving him over.

"Now look here. Tell me what you see." He said pointing at a spot on the map.

Patrick looked over at the map. He saw several trade routes. They were the most frequently used. He ran his eyes over it. He noticed his father had marked off their contract trading points with red. There were several others in blue. If they obtained this one in particular they would have a majority of the north west. He then saw why he wanted that spot in particular. It would open him up for trading further north. Like most parts of the world no one has traveled too far in any directions. The Abners had made it the furthest now making trade deals with the east.

"What are the blue markers?" He asked softly.

"Abner's contracts, these here in the northwest used to all be blue. I've been slowly wearing them down and weeding out their weaker contracts. Making deals with them that underhand the Abners." His father chuckled proud of himself.

"I get why we are thieves now." Patrick said, shaking his head, now fully understanding the girl's anger.

"We are not thieves, we are opportunists and if you don't get your self righteous chip off your shoulder the world will eat you alive boy." His father said angrily at him.

"There's nothing wrong with doing things the right way." Patrick said, shaking his head in disgust.

"Well lucky for you and this company I can bite that bullet. How do you think I've made all this? Why do you think you've had an easy life because I did what I had to do." He said, slamming his fist in anger on the desk.

"Abners left themself wide open when Gavin and Morgan thought they could take a vacation. Opportunity doesn't wait for anyone. In this world no one is safe. Learn it and learn it quickly." He continued staring down at his son.

Patrick could only shake his head as his fathers rant continued.

"Those girls don't stand a chance and soon you will be thanking me. I am going to leave you a company that will leave you very well off." His father said, waving him away.

"I wouldn't underestimate those "girls" father. They have more fight and fire than you know." Patrick said quietly.

"What could they possibly know? Get out of my sight." He growled at Patrick.

A small framed woman came to the doorway. Her hair was placed neatly above her head in curlers due to the late hour. She hugged her night robe around her as she softly cleared her through.

"Ed, what is all this yelling about?" She asked softly but her voice held authority.

"Nothing sweet heart." Ed said to his wife.

Patrick shook his head and began leaving the room. As he got to the doorway he leaned over and kissed his mother's cheek.

"Goodnight Mother." Patrick smiled as he left the room.

# Chapter Three

## The Plan

Danica pulled Ariadne into her fathers office and carefully shut the door. She walked over to the window and closed the shutters. The room instantly got dark. The sunlight spelling in from the window cracks as Danica blindly makes her way to the desk. Feeling around she found a candle on the desk and lit it. The amber glow lit the room and Danica motioned for Ariadne to come over. Adriane raised her eyebrow at her.

"This seems a little over the top, what do you got going on Dani?" Ariadne asked as she walked slowly over to the desk.

"Ok but you need to be open minded." Danica said to her, making a face at her.

"Ok ok, just tell me." Ariadne said wanting to know what exactly was going on.

Danica frowned and then began pulling the book and journal out of her bag. She set them both down in front of Ariadne. Ariadne looked down at them and back to Danica confused. Her face asked Danica what was this? Danica sighed, rolling her eyes.

"This is Dad's old journal. Before he started the trade business with Ma." Danica explains.

Ariadne waved her hand in a "get on with it" motion. Danica waved her hand back at her. As she pulled out the book.

"So this isn't an ordinary book. Look, see here." Danica explained as she opened the secret compartment in the book.

Ariadne stepped forward looking at it. Dancia then pulled out an old style map. Ariadne looked at the paper. It was stained with age and creased over and over again. Ariadne didn't know how it was still intact. Danica unrolled the map and Ariadne immediately noticed her father's hand writing. She saw his marking and followed the route with her eyes.

"The Hollow?" She asked, running her hands over her father's handwriting.

Danica slammed open his journal and showed her the entry mentioning The Hollow. Adraine skimmed it and glanced back at her sister trying to piece together what Danica was trying to tell her.

"Treasure...it's a treasure map." Danica said, spelling it out for her.

"And.."Ariadne said, her forehead creasing with confusion.

"Oh for the love. Treasure map Ari as in money, as in gold. As in we need money." Danica said, rolling her eyes at her sister.

"You want us to go treasure hunting." Ariadne said, getting frustrated.

"Are you not here? Am I not speaking english?" Danica asked sarcastically.

"Or maybe I am talking to a child. Dani we cannot leave to go after some treasure that may or may not be real. While Mom's and Dad's hard work disappears." Ari said, becoming angry.

"Ari, this might be the solution. It's Dad's handwriting, it's Dad's map. His journal he thought it was real." Danica said, trying to not get angry at Adriane.

"Dani, I'm not talking about this anymore." Adriane said, starting to walk to the door.

"Fine, go cower to those bastards. Go strike a deal. Mom and Dad would be so proud." Danica said in anger.

Ariadne froze in the doorway, her hands clenched by her side. She was starting to shake from being angry. She forced herself to walk through the door holding her tongue. She wasn't going to say anything to her sister she was going to regret. Danica instantly felt bad as she watched her sister leave. She put the map back into the  binding of the book. Stuffing them back into her bag. She looked around the room before storming out too.

Ariadne had stormed up to her room, Danica knew by the way the door slammed as she made it out to the kitchen. Danica's aggravation kept growing and she decided to leave. She stomped out the door and kept walking. She didn't know where she was going but her anger kept growing the more she replayed the conversation her and Ariadne just had. How could she not think it was a good idea? She was the only one that had an idea? Ariadne seemed like she just wanted to give in to the Smiths. Danica thought as she walked harder and faster. Her feet pounding on the pavement as she went along.

Before long she found herself down by the docks. The sea air was refreshing as she paused watching the men come and go from the ships. Her eyes wandered over the boats. The Crown was sitting proudly waiting for its next voyage. Her parents had taken The Morning Star and auntie Claire and uncle Jack had been gone for a little bit now with The Evening Star.

"I would need one of the ships that they wouldn't miss right away but that would be strong and had all the quirks of the others." Danica said out loud looking over the other ships of the companies.

Most of them had started to become just trade ships, there were very few that packed a punch when they began transiting them over to trading ships. Her father's pride and joy was The Morning Star and the Crown fell second. She couldn't take The Crown

Ariadne would notice right away. Her eyes scanned the ships more carefully.

"The North Star." She whispered

She began walking to it ignoring everyone on the dock. She made her way up the walkway to it and began studying it. She walked about the ship mentally taking notes of things. The men on board moved out of her way as she did. Three masses, equipped with cannons, and it had all the little details her father liked. The ship was made from a darker wood, it had a tint of rich brown in it but the color  also wanted to be grey.

She walked up the stairway sliding her hand over the railing as she did. She smiled seeing the detail her father put into this ship. A blue turquoise line went up the side of the handle rail, looking about this turquoise color was etched into the ship. Across the rails, out lining the cabin doors. As she reached the upper deck she made her way to the helm.

Standing in front of the wheel, she stepped forward, taking the wheel in her hands. It felt like it was meant to be hers. The wheel had the same turquoise blue lines down each side of it. She smiled. She glanced up at the sails, they were gray in color but the very top sail was a dark grey sail and in the middle of it a turquoise color star. This was her ship, she felt it in her gut, felt it in her bones. It was meant to be hers.

"Can I help you with something Miss?" One of the crew members came up to her asking.

"Aye, prepare the ship to be ready to sail. We're leaving tonight." Danica said with authority.

The man looked at her a little confused but nodded and went to gather the crew. Another man approached her, he was older, his hair just starting to become salt and pepper. He smiled at her as he approached her. Danica could see the crow's feet at his eyes as he smiled.

"Dani! What brings you on the ship?" Adam asked as he approached.

"Adam! I almost didn't recognize you." Danica laughed.

"I came to let the crew know we are leaving tonight...late." Danica smiled brightly.

"Leaving? Late?" Adam asked, raising an eyebrow at her with a small smile on his lips.

"Aye." Danica said with a nod.

"Dani, what's going on? I've known you since you were a babe. I can tell when you're up to something." Adam smirked.

"Oh fine but follow me. I don't need Ari finding out." Danica said, shooting him a look as she made her way away from the helm.

Adam followed Danica across the lower deck and out to the docks. He paused looking at the ship as he waited to hear what was going on. He glanced back at Danica and motioned for her to start talking. She sighed and let a big breath out.

"So you probably know that Smith and Brother's have been underhanding all of our contracts. We are losing money. We need a good sum of money for everything to work. The deadline is three weeks." Danica said frustrated thinking about the whole situation.

Adam frowned slightly and motioned for her to continue.

"I found one of my father's old journals and a map. The map is marked for treasure at a place called The Hollow. If we can find this treasure and get back in time we can settle everything." Danica explained.

"Dani, how do you even know if it is real?" Adam asked her, his tone not condescending but concerned.

"My father's journal entries. It's all there and the map isn't just marked. The voyage is charted." Danica said to him trying to become upset with him.

"I just don't know lass." Adam said quietly.

"You have your father's journal?" Jacob asked quietly, coming up from behind the two as he walked by on the dock.

"Jacob. Aye that she does." Adam smiled at Jacob as he nodded saying his name.

"I only heard a piece of it. What are you doing with the journal Dani?" Jacob asked.

"Jacob, you're one of the few that have known my father the longest. Have you heard of the Hollow?" Danica asked him softly.

"How do you know about the Hollow?" Jacob asked her.

Adam raised an eyebrow at him and turned to studying him as Danica responded.

"So you do know it...I have the map." Danica said quietly.

"You found his map?" Jacob asked, repeating her.

"So it's true?" Adam asked Jacob.

"Aye, it's real. Gavin had one heck of a time with that map. The only good thing about it was that's how he met Morgan. It's real all right but no one has tried to go after it." Jacob said.

"I am." Danica said with certainty.

Jacob studied her, he recognized that look. He had seen it before in Morgan and in Claire. Danica had their fire and there was no telling her no when she set her mind to something.

"Allright lass but I'm steering." Jacob nodded.

"All right?" Adam repeated.

"We're leaving tonight. We can't tell Ari. when it's dark we will meet here." Danica said to both of them.

"Aye, I will find a few more men that can handle this type of voyage." Jacob said to her.

"So it's settled, we leave tonight." Danica said to both of them.

Adam stood there confused but if this was what was happening he was being left behind. He watched Danica leave the dock, he shook his head softly and went to speak to Jacob. Jacob laughed and shook his head at him. He patted him on the back before heading off down the dock as well.

"Well I guess I'll make sure the ship is taken care of." Adam muttered going to the ship.

Patrick happened to be walking by the docks when he overheard the whole conversation. He debated with himself what to do. He should go tell his father but everything his father was doing was wrong

and he disagreed with it. He watched Danica walk
back towards her home, her long raven hair moving
back and forth as she did. She was something else he
thought. He could go for a good adventure.

## Chapter Four

## The North Star

Patrick wandered back home thinking about what he had overheard. He day dreamed as he walked about sneaking on board and going off. He couldn't, they already knew what he looked like. They need someone else. He thought walking into his home.

"Well that's just wonderful Kaleb. I am so glad you are home. Sound the alarm. My wayward son has returned." Ed shouted sarcastically.

"Ed, stop it dear. The neighbors will hear you. Darling Kaleb, why don't you take your stuff up to your old room and get settled. Dinner is at five." Their mother said sweetly.

"Anita he isn't staying here." Ed said to his wife.

"Now Ed. He might not live the life we wanted but he's still our son. At Least he's not a criminal." Anita said, walking to Ed and patting his hand sweetly.

"Fine...go." Ed said, waving Kaleb off.

Kaleb rolled his eyes to himself as he walked out of the kitchen. He leaned over and kissed his mother's forehead before walking out.

"You! You're perfect!" Patrick said, excitedly meeting him in the hall.

"Well thank you! Best compliment today brother. You're not too bad yourself." Kaleb chuckled, slapping his brother on the shoulder.

"No, no no. Come." Patrick said, motioning him to come with him upstairs.

Kaleb shook his head at his older brother as he started up the stairs after him. He had his small amount of belongings strapped over his shoulder in a bag. His dark auburn hair tied back in a short ponytail that went to the nape of his neck. Patrick looked very much like his father, where Kaleb looked like his mother. He had her same sapphire blue eyes. Walking into his old room he scanned it. He smiled his mother had left everything the same as when he left a year ago. He never got along with his father. He didn't care for the business. He wanted more out of life. So he spent the last year traveling from place to place, living life. He ran his hand over his old desk as Patrick shut the door quietly. Kaleb set his belongings down on the bed and then looked curiously at Patrick.

"So what's with the welcome?" Kaleb laughed as he sat down on his bed.

"Ok so long story short i'm pretty sure father is illegally stealing contracts from the Abners and I need you to sneak aboard the Abner's ship tonight, they're leaving." Patrick said as he leaned against the door focusing on if anyone was coming.

"Ok well that story was a little too short and I just got home." Kaleb said, looking at Patrick like he was crazy.

"Father is stealing all the contracts out from under the Abners. The two daughters are left in charge. They have no funds coming in and need funds. The youngest is sneaking off tonight to go after some treasure. I can't go, one father would notice and the two daughters know what I look like so….you go." Patrick said as quickly as he could.

"Treasure...like pirates and all that?" Kaleb said, trying hard not to laugh at his brother.

" I don't know. There's a map...maybe." Patrick said, shrugging , starting to give up on convincing his brother on going.

"Dad would be pissed." Kaleb smirked.

"Probably seeing how we're going behind his back." Patrick said, shrugging.

"Ok." Kaled said with a smirk on his face.

"Ok?" Patrick repeated.

"Yeah I'll do it." Kaleb nodded with a shrug.

"Really?" Patrick said not believing him.

"Aye, I came back to see mom not dad and if it will make him love me more why not." Kaleb said, throwing him a wink.

"That's great." Patrick said coming over and wacking him on the back.

"When do they leave?" Kaleb said, laughing at his brother's response.

"Late tonight, she's sneaking off with a crew and a ship called The North Star." Patrick explained.

"She?" Kaleb asked, confused but intrigued.

"Aye the youngest daughter is going. I think her name is Dani. She doesn't want the oldest to find out." Patrick said, shrugging.

"Alright then." Kaleb laughed.


Night fall came pretty quickly but not fast enough for Danica. She spent most of the day pacing around and avoiding Ariadne. Danica sighed watching her sister from the doorway. She was still up studying papers and contracts. Danica gave in  and went to see her. She was still going through with her plan but she didn't want to just sneak off on her sister.

"Hey." Danica said softly coming over to the table.

"Hey." Ariadne replied back just as quiet.

They sat in silence for a few minutes. The silence quickly turned into awkwardness. Adriane cleared her throat to break the silence.

"Dani it's not that I thought your idea was a bad one, I just dont think it;s the right one right now. I'm sorry I said things the way I did earlier." Ariadne said softly.

Danica wanted to tell her how it was and that they didn't have a better one but with her leaving soon, she wanted to leave on good note.

"It's alright Ari, I'm sorry too." Dani said, draping her arm across her sister's shoulder and squeezing her lightly.

Ariadne reached up and squeezed Danica back, leaning her head against her shoulder. She yawned slightly as she did.

"If you keep going like this Ari, you're going to burn yourself out and get sick." Danica said to her frowning.

"I know but it's got to be done. We need to find a way out of this situation." Ariadne said quietly.

"Well there's nothing more you can do tonight why don't you go get some sleep. I'm sure things will be better once we hear from Orion." Danica said to her, stepping to the side.

"Aye your right Dani. I can barely see the words right now." Ariadne said, starting to stand.

Danica stopped her from going and scooped her into a big hug. Ariadne was startled at first but quickly squeezed her back.

"Dani you ok?" She whispered, still hugging her.

"I'm ok. I just want you to know you're doing your best and you're the best sister ever." Danica said, tightening her hug just a little bit more.

"Thank you. You're the best little sister anyone could ask for. You should get some sleep too. The stress is getting to you too." Ariadne said to her as they stepped back from the hug.

"Aye I will. Night Ari." Danica said to her as she watched her start walking up the stairs.

Danica listened to her sister walk about upstairs for a while before settling tino bed. She heard her toss and turn a few more times and then was quiet. Danica waited until she could hear a light snoring. A smile came across her face listening to her sister snore. She then walked to the door picking up the bag she had hidden with her stuff before ducking out.

The path to the ship was dark but she knew it by heart. She had walked this way over a million times. She loved watching the ships come in and out of the harbor. She looked up at the dark night sky, it looked cold as the stars twinkled in it. The moon was bright and round lighting up the path she took. Reaching the dark she could see lanterns on The North Star and shadows moving about. The ship was being made ready. She wrapped her hand tighter around her bag she had over her shoulder as her foot hit the wooden dock. Her feet took her to the walk away of the ship fast.  She was caught up in looking at the ship. Her nerves and excitement are getting the best of her. She didn't see the man standing at the end of the walkway. Danica walked right into him. She stumbled backwards and almost over into the water. Strong arms wrapped around her waist pulling her back. She was pulled against a very firm chest and the hat she was wearing toppled over behind her. Her long raven hair fell out cascading down her back. She blinked trying to regain her thoughts.

"You all right, miss?" A warm voice asked.

"Aye, I wasn't watching where I was going." She said softly, bringing her eyes up to the man's face.

Bright sapphire eyes stared back at her and a lock of auburn hair fell out from under his hat. Danica got lost in the moment.

"Are you going on this ship?" The man asked, still holding on to her.

Ship? At the sound of the word her brain stopped scrambling. She smiled, stepping back away from the man. She straightened herself out before answering him.

"Aye, that I am; sorry about this" Danica said moving her hands in front of her as she talked.

He smiled and nodded as if to say don't worry about it. Danica then motioned for him to go ahead up the walkway. He shook his head and motioned for her to go first.

"Ladies first?" Kaleb smiled at her holding a hand out to help her.

"What's your name sailor?" Danica asked him not moving from her stop and ignored his hand.

"Kaleb and might I ask yours?" Kaleb said, flashing her a charming smile.

"Danica." She said holding her hand out for him to shake.

He took a hold of her hand gently and was surprised when she squeezed and gave a pretty good hand shake.

"Well I hope you're ready for this, see you on board." Danica smiled at him as she let go and started up the walkway.

Kaleb was taken back a bit by her statement and a smile crept onto his lips. He watched her walk away in almost a trance. She was definitely different. He looked after her as if staring at her would let him know what exactly it was. He shook his head trying to gather his thoughts as he began to walk up the walkway.

He made his way across the lower deck trying to blend in. thankful he was not very known around here. At Least not anymore, he didn't think anyone would recognize him. A man was walking about giving orders. He spotted Kaleb and started to make his way towards him. Alarms were going off inside of Kaleb's head but there was nothing he could do. He was spotted. If he ran or tried to make himself unnoticed it would make just the opposite happen. He stood there waiting for the man to reach him to see how things would go.

"You there." The man said, pointing to Kaleb and motioning for him to come over.

Here we go Kaleb thought as he walked over to the man. Although he was worried that he was caught, his exterior remained calm and cool. If you were to look at Kaleb you would have never believed he was the slightest bit worried.

"Aye?" He said approaching the man.

"Your new correct?" He asked him as he looked him up and down.

"Aye." Kaleb answered.

"Ok you're going to be in charge of getting the mass going right now. We will give duties as we go but right now I need these masses to start getting unrolled. Captain wants to take off as soon as possible." The man said painting to the sails as he spoke.

Kaleb nodded and headed over to the first mass and began helping the men unroll the sails. Something caught his eye, he glanced in the direction of the helm. He saw the girl from earlier up there. The way she was moving and how the men she was speaking to were acting, it looked like she was giving orders. Captain, the man said earlier She can't be captain? Kaleb thought as he watched her. As he watched the helm the sails quickly came down on the mass. He heard the sound of the anchors coming up.

"Walkway." Danica's voice echoed down over the top rail.

The men quickly rushed to follow her order. The walkway was pulled in as quickly as they could. Kaleb  inched closer to get a better look at Danica. He watched her head to the helm gripping the wheel in her hands. He watched her look up at the stars and studied them for a moment before pulling the ship out of the harbor.

"I know what you're thinking lad. A woman captain. The Abner women are no ordinary women." A man standing by him chuckled.

"You'll be alright." The man laughed again walking away.

He watched her navigate the ship, not ordinary echoing in his head.

## Chapter Five

## Constellations:

Danica stood at the helm and a yawn escaped her lips as she steered the ship. She watched the stars dance across the ocean current. She sighed happily. She was always fascinated with sailing and the ocean. She remembers trying to sneak on each ship her father would take to go on a trades deal. One time she even got out of the harbor with them. A small smile crept on her lips as she thought of the memory. How angry her father was that he had to turn around because six year old her had gotten past everyone. She remembered when she could finally go on her first voyage with him and the excitement she felt. Her smile grew thinking of the memory.

Kaleb wandered up the stairs to the helm and most of the crew were asleep. He couldn't sleep. There were too many thoughts and what ifs running through his head. He stopped pausing on the upper deck. He found himself staring at Danica. Her long Raven black hair shimmered blue in the moonlight. The smile on her face was warming. His brows came together when he realized what he was doing. He shook his head at himself going to leave, he couldn't get involved like that he thought to himself.

"Kaleb." Danica called to him, seeing him staring down the stairs.

Kaleb froze his hand gripping the railing of the stairs. Could he just pretend he didn't hear her and continue? No you paused, she knows now. He made a face at his thoughts.

"Kaleb." Danica called to him again this time a little louder.

Kaleb sighed and looked over at her with a smile before turning around and heading back up the stairs to the upper deck and to the helm.

"Aye Miss?" Kaleb asked softly.

"I'm so glad someones awake. I was getting sleepy. Stay awhile and chat with me?" Danica asked with a sweet smile.

Crap he thought he couldn't have just gone and pretended to sleep. He responded by just nodding.

"So what do you want to chat about?" Kaleb asked her as he walked over to the rail of the upper deck and leaned against it. His arms folded across his chest.

"Oh I don't know anything...everything. Just something." Danica said with a small laugh.

"Ok, um where did you learn to steer?" Kaleb asked with a small smile growing on his face.

"My father. I used to try so hard to sneak off with him when I was little. All the adventures and voyages he went on. He finally let me go with him when I was old enough and I set out to learn everything I could about the ship and what it took to run one." Danica said her smile growing as she thought of her father and past memories.

"It sounds like you had a great childhood and good relationship with your father." Kaleb said with a short smile as he began to think about his own overbearing father.

"What about you? What brings you on the ship?" Danica asked him, looking forward as she spoke.

"I am a little bit of a wanderer so when an opportunity comes up to see something new; I don't even think about it. I just go." Kaleb shrugged and said shrugging he wasn't lying that's how he did live his life.

"What about your family? Don't you miss them?" Danica asked.

"Well my mother and brother aye but my father...Lets just say I am not his favorite son or person for that matter." Kaleb chuckled.

"How come?" Danica asked curiously.

Kaleb laughed out loud this time, this woman had no filter and said whatever she thought.

"He doesn't agree with my decisions about my life. He owns a business and I personally have no interest in it. It makes him upset. He had this picture of his two sons conquering the world, being all powerful. I'm ruining that dream for him." Kaleb shrugged.

"Well he sounds like he needs someone to help him reevaluate his thinking. He needs to understand that he can't hold you to his dreams when you have your own. I'm sorry...that sounds tough." Danica said with a sympathetic look to him.

Kaleb was a bit taken back by the guiness of her statement.  Even the look she gave him wasn't pity but heartfelt. He wasn't sure what to say in response. He just nodded. He tried to think of something to change topics.

"My sister and I are very different. She is beautiful, smart, well spoken, mature, classy, and has a softness to her. Almost the perfect child. I am nothing like; that My father calls me his wild flower. Regardless of the headaches I caused because i wasn't like Ari. They never stopped encouraging me to go for what I wanted. They accepted me for me. Your father needs to do that." Danica said to him.

"Thank you." Kaleb said almost speechless.

He never had anyone say anything like that to him. It was more Kaleb why do you keep doing this, Kaleb you're going to put your father into an early grave. He shook his head as he thought. He turned his focus onto the stars because he wasn't sure what to do with himself.

"Do you know anything about them?" Danica asked him with a smile on her face as she looked up to the dark night sky.

"Bits and pieces, I know where the north star is." Kaleb said his eyes were studying the sky.

"Well that is one of the most important ones." Danica smirked.

"I feel like you  want to teach me something." Kaleb said, smirking.

"Aye! Can I tell you?" Danica laughed eagerly.

"Aye go ahead." Kaleb said, watching her light up.

He watched her search the sky and then spotted something. She motioned for him to come stand next to her.

"Ok  so each part of the sky has constellations that stay in that section. In the northern section you can find Draco. See it here." Danica said, running her fingers along the shape in the sky.

Kaleb nodded, waiting for her to continue.

"Draco is usually one of the easiest to find in the north part of the sky because he's the biggest. Now Draco was said to be a Titan that fought with the gods for ten years. Until the goddess Minerva tossed him into the sky where he froze around the north pole." Danica said grinning.

Kaleb watched her face light up as she spoke his own smile following suit. He loved how she truly enjoyed everything she was telling him. It made him want to hear more and know more.

"I'm sorry. I love this stuff." She chuckled.

"No, don't say sorry, tell me more." Kaleb said as his eyes went to the sky.

Her smile grew bigger if it was at all possible. She looked around the sky searching for one.

"So you see the very bright star in the sky, it's called Hadar and it's the brightest star in the southern sky. It's in the constellation Centaurus. Centaurus is for Chrion who tutor Hercules and they became great friends. Hercules accidentally took a sacred wine from Chiron home to his friend's home. Once the wine was opened the scent drew several centaurus to the home. A fight broke out and Hercules killed many centaurs. Chiron had came to stop the fight but sadly was struck by a poison arrow. Due to him being immortal he could not die but lived in agony and pain.

One night he begged Zeus to let him end his life because the pain had become too much to stand. Zeus did and to honor him made the constellation Centaurus." Danica said his eyes shifted from the horizon to the stars in the sky.

Kaleb watched the magic in her eyes as she told the story. He was taken back by her passion for it and that she knew so much. Most women were still taught to be seen not heard. Too cook and take care of their home and husband. She was different, she was...captivating he thought. She caught him looking at her odd and smiled.

"My father and mother love the stars as much as they love the sea. My oldest sister's name is Ariadne and my brother's name is Orion which are both constellations. " Danica smiled.

"And Danica means?" Kaleb asked curiously.

" Danica means morning star. Danica was the sun's younger sister." Danica smiled.

The sun began peeking up over the ocean, the sky going lighter as they sat in silence for a moment. Danica glanced at the sun as the tops of the water began to turn golden.

"You didn't sleep. You should probably go try before the crew is up and moving." Danica said a small frown on her face.

"It's fine, I'm used to not sleeping." Kaleb said softly as his eyes went to the sky.

Behind them the first mate's cabin door opened and Jacob walked out. He wasn't the first mate on this ship but he was second in charge to Danica. He wasn't letting one of Gavin's daughters do this on their own. He stretched walking out the door. He frowned seeing that Danica had steered all night.

"Dani." He said quietly approaching her.

Seeing Kaleb there he switched his tone from fatherly to respectful.

"Captain, you should have called me. I would have taken over steering in the middle of the night for you." Jaob said.

"It's fine Jacob, I enjoyed it. I was too excited that I wouldn't have been able to sleep. Although sleep now sounds good. You can take the wheel." Danica smiled.

Jacob smiled and stepped to her side allowing her to pass the wheel to him. Danica stretched as she stepped away from the wheel.

"Don't let me sleep too long. We should be going past Siren Gulley. From my fathers notes we will be taking the long way around it. I don't feel like tipping the ship to get through it." Danica said, starting to walk away.

"Tipping the ship?" Kaleb said as she walked past him.

"Aye." She laughed starting down the stairs.

Jacob watched Kaleb and how his eyes followed Danica down the stairs as she walked away. Was he out here all right with her? Who was he? Jacob thought becoming protective.

"You lad what's your name?" Jacob said to him his tone was almost threatening.

"Kaleb." Kaleb answered with no expression in his voice, his eyes studying the man wondering if he was going to be trouble.

"Kaleb, go start waking the crew and then clean the cannons." Jacob orders his eyes going from Kaleb to the horizon letting Kaleb know he was dismissed.

## Chapter Six

## Gone


The sun rolled across Ariadne's bed and she groaned slightly shifting trying to get away from it. She wasn't ready for another day. She didn't want to dive into the stress and the papers upon papers. She didn't want to have to think about the fact she was failing her parents. She groaned again, kicking the covers off of her. She thought it was too late. She had already begun. She could feel the tightness in her chest from her thoughts as her feet touched the wooden floor of her bedroom. She stretched before standing. Maybe she could just take some time off from her thoughts and work today, she missed Danica and how she always seemed to make everything feel lighter. They hadn't spent much time together recently. She walked to her bedroom door and stepped out into the hall. She glanced at her sister's door which was shut. She approached it and knocked softly.

"Dani. Dani are you up yet?" Ariadne called softly through the door.

No answer came, Ariadne shrugged and headed down stairs letting her sister sleep more. Getting into the kitchen she felt her chest tighten as she looked at the piles of paper. She shut her eyes and took a deep breath in. Holding it for a second she slowly released it. She did that once more and then opened her eyes. She frowned seeing the papers. She went to the chair in the corner of the room. She took the light weight blanket off the back of it and walked over to the table. She very carefully unfolded the blanket and placed it on top of the papers.

"There!" She smiled hoping it would make her feel better.

Not seeing the mess she felt better but in the back of her mind and heart she could feel the nagging painful feeling trying to sneak up. She rolled her head back and forth trying to get rid of the headache trying to form in the base of her neck. She needed air. She went to their door shutting her eyes as she reached for the handle. She could feel the invisible string the paperwork had on her pulling and tugging at her. Trying to pull her back so she couldn't leave. She felt frozen as she gripped the handle tighter. The pain in her head started to creep up the back of her neck. She turned the handle and her chest tightened. She was feeling shaky and light headed as she tried to open the door.

A loud two knocks on the door startled her and interrupted her descent into a panic attack. She blinked a few times thinking she may have made it up. A third knock occurred and Ariande slowly pulled the door open. She stared confused looking at the man who stood ignorant of her. Dani had chased him off the other day...his name was Patrick she thought.

"Can I help you?" She asked him.

"Are you ok? Do you need something? You look very pale and like something is wrong." Patrick asked concerned.

"I..I..no I am ok. Can I help you?" Ariadne said regaining herself.

She then realized she was still in her night dress. A sense of panic flashed over her as she slammed the door in Patrick's face. Patrick stared at the door confused as he wasn't sure whether he should leave or stay there. He waited several minutes as he debated knocking again. He heard a bunch of moments inside and he decided to just wait. A few minutes later Ariadne reopened the door fully dressed.

"Can I help you?" She said as if nothing happened before.

"Um I...I.."

"You?" Ariadne asked, confused, cutting him off.

"Sorry, I guess I didn't think this far ahead. I got to the part of coming here but then I didn't really know what to say." Patrick said, rubbing the back of his neck.

"Ok well let me let you know that we are not interested in whatever your father and you are thinking about offering." Ariadne said, starting to shut the door.

"Wait." Patrick said, sticking his arm in the way of the door closing.

The thought of slamming the door on his arm passed through her mind and a small smirk came onto her face. Danica would definitely have approved. She sighed looking at him waiting for him to continue.

"I came to help." He said shortly.

"Help?' Ariadne said, opening the door slightly.

"Aye. I don't think what my father is doing is right." Patrick said quietly.

"Right and I'm just supposed to believe you." Ariadne said.

"I don't know how to convince you. Believe me I would love to have the business but I believe in doing things right and fair. I don't want to steal and take things out from under others. That business will be mine one day and I want it to stand for something and not just be some mindless machine that does whatever it takes to make a dollar." Patrick said passionately.

Ariadne studied him while he spoke. She wasn't sure why but she felt  like she could trust him. She studied him for a moment but couldn't bring herself to listen to her gut. She thought it was crazy that she wanted to trust him. He just wanted to see the insides working of how they were planning on stopping them. She gritted her teeth and shook her head.

"Thank you for the offer but you should go." Ariadne said firmly as she waited for him to move his arm.

Patrick frowned at her and slowly took back his arm. He stared at her for a moment before slowly moving his arm away from the door opening. Ariadne's stomach felt sick as she slowly shut the door on him. She stared at the back of the door unmoving as she waited to hear his footsteps walking away. Patrick for some reason felt hurt as he stared at the door. He wanted her to trust him but he understood. He was the enemy and why would she trust him? He sighed deeply as he walked away from the door trying to figure out what to do next to prove that he was in fact trustworthy.

Ariadne let out the breath she was holding as she heard him start walking away. She couldn't believe that. Why would he want to help them when his  father was doing everything he could to destroy them. She shook her head. She had to go tell Dani. She needed to see what she thought. She headed back up stairs and to Dani's door. She opened the door and stepped in starting to talk as she did.

"Dani, you would never believe what just happened. The Smith-" She started to say as she realized the room was empty.

She glanced about, Danica's bed didn't look like she had slept in it at all. She turned about the room her closest door was left open. Ariadne walked to the closest door confused. Getting to the closest she realized a good portion of her clothes were gone. Her stomach dropped.

"Danica, I swear if you did what I think you did." Ariadne growled walking into the room.

She quickly turned on her heels and raced down the stairs. She didn't stop as her feet reached the lower floor. She walked across the kitchen heading to the door with intent. She flew open the door and marched down the path leading to the docks. She was almost running as her feet hit the rocky path. She almost tripped and fell as the dock came into view. The dock seemed empty as Her eyes scanned the ships as her foot hit the word. She began counting in her head. The Morning Star was gone with her parents, Auntie Claire and Uncle Jack had The Evening Star, Orion had Andromeda, The Crown was sitting in the dock, along with Ophiuchus. She walked down the dock. She knew one was missing, she counted the ships. Which one was gone? She thought grumbling as she did to herself as she walked down the dock nearing the end of them.  Seeing the empty spot she gritted her teeth. The North Star was gone. She clenched her hand in fist at her side. Several different emotions rolling through her, anger how dare she leave her! Worried that she would be ok. She felt herself shaking.

"Miss?" A man's voice said coming up behind her.

"Aye." She said angrily as she turned to see the man.

She recognized him as one of the men from the crew of Ophiuchus. He stepped back a little bit taken back by the amount of anger in her voice. He cleared his throat before speaking again.

"I have something for you. Two notes, one from your brother and the other is from your sister." He said quietly holding them before out to her.

She nodded slightly and took them. She stared down at the paper swallowing hard. She was almost worried about reading both of them. She glanced at the man and smiled weakly. He nodded and walked off. She inhaled opening Orion's note first, taking the one she could probably handle the best.

"Dearest Sister, I have good news and bad news. I received your message about The Smith's and I am returning home as quickly as possible. The

good news is the deal went through and the bad news
is I had to negotiate down very much due to the
Smith's reaching them as well. They are also trying to
go east. Lucky are standing relationships with the
east trading post held out. Although the amount I am
bringing back is not enough. I will see you soon. -
Orion."

Ariadne sighed, her heart sank a little bit, she
had hoped the Smiths wouldn't dare venture east, It
was uncharted territory for most. How were they
getting all this information ? She gritted her teeth.
There had to be someone telling the Smiths all of their
plans and moves. She shook her head staring down
at the note in her hand from Danica. She closed her
eyes, taking a breath in before unfolding the paper.

"Ari, I'm sorry. I had to do this. I can't sit by any
longer seeing you work so hard. This is the only thing
I could think of. Please don't hate me. I have taken
Jacob and Adam with me so I have good men who
have been out to sea several times. Don't worry we
can do this. I will return with what we need. You keep
doing what you're doing. I know you will find a way to
stop them. You are the smartest person I know. In the
meantime I will find a way to find us funds. I love you-
Danica"

Danica sighed deeply, running her hand over
her face. Her first instinct was to take a ship and go

after her sister. She couldn't, she was the only one left here. She shook her head looking  towards the horizon. Her family was going to be the death of her. She shook her head. She took another deep breath in as the ocean air rushed over the dock. The wind on her face and running through her hair felt. Part of her wanted to run away. She wished she could do just what Danica did, hop ship and just leave.

She was slightly annoyed and almost angry that her parents left. She didn't blame them, they didn't know this was coming and no one had sent them word that they were in trouble. They did deserve the getaway. She sighed once more before starting to leave the dock.

## Chapter Seven

## Notes

Danica stretched her eyes still shut as she let out a groan in the middle of her stretch. The stretch felt good as she opened her eyes and stood up. Shifting to the edge of the bed she dangled her feet over the edge of it placing them on the floor. Aloud yawned her lips as she stretched once more.

"Sleep well?" Jacob laughed as she was standing over at the desk reading the map.

Danica laughed and stood walking over to Jacob. She stood next to him seeing what he was looking at.

"How are we doing so far?" Danica said, looking down at the map with him.

"Well we've started to take the long way around like you said to. The gulley would have saved a day and half time but we will try to make up for it somewhere down the line. I was looking at the map to see if there was a way too." Jacob said, still looking at the map.

Danica's eyes followed the route they were going. Her fathers notes stopped after Siren Gulley. Before The Hollow there was another passage called the Sailor's Right. She was cautious of short cuts. Her mother was good at finding them but Dancia seemed hesitant since she read her fathers journal. They could make up for time lost and save on time back if they took it. She studied the passage as if it would speak to her. Jacob was still searching the map, she was quick to scan and find things. She had watched her mother help her father so much it was second nature for her to have things stand out on maps. The passage basically jumped off the map and waved at her. She waited a few more moments before tapping the passage, pointing it out to Jacob.

"Here." Danica nudged Jacob as she said it.

He glanced down at the stop she pointed to. She saw him frown studying it. He traced the route with his finger.

"Does your father's journal say anything about it?" Jacob asked.

"No, his notes end after Siren Gulley. There was some battle and then he and my mother began working on building the trade business. From what I can tell he hasn't been out this way again." Danica said, shaking her head no as she spoke.

"Well I guess we can judge it when we get there." Jacob said with a nod.

Danica paused, staring at the map. She  had read in her father's journal about Siren's Gulley but all passages couldnt be like that one. Her father's ship and crew almost didn't make it out of the gulley. She didn't want to risk anyone's lives. She couldn't risk not returning home empty handed ethier. She sighed.

"Dani, it will be fine." Jacob said to her, squeezing her shoulder.

"One step at a time, let's get there first." He continued.

She smiled weakly at him and nodded, taking her eyes off the map. She looked about the room and then back to Jacob.

"Whose steering?" She asked.

"Adam." He answered her.

"Good I'm glad we don't just have two people who know how to steer. I understand my fathers reasoning but we are not really into pirate ships anymore." Danica laughed

Jacob just shook his head with a smile. Danica looked about the room once more and realized that the small area that had light coming through was dark. Had she slept all day? She looked from the door to Jacob.

"Is it night time already?" Danica said quietly.

"Aye lass, it seems that you haven't slept well in a while." Jacob said with a small smile, he knew the inner workings of the Abner's and how much stress the girls have been under.

"It's crazy that I am still tired. How far have we gotten?" Danica said slowly walking to the door.

"Stress will do that. We made it around Siren Gulley and headed for Raven's peak. I have been there once before several years ago. You were still a bun in the oven. After Raven's peak it's uncharted territory for me." He smiled.

"Well then it will be an actual adventure for you." Danica said with a smirk going to the door.

She turned around looking at him and seeing the tiredness across his face. For the first time Jacob actually looked his age to her. He wasn't the young man she had met as a child. That would chase her up and down the docks with seaweed. She could now notice how he was leaning ever so slightly on the desk to support himself as if something hurt. Danica raised an eyebrow at him. She knew better than to point it out. He was very much like her father; he would just ignore her.

"Hey get some sleep, I am going to need you to steer in the morning." Danica said to him, giving him an order rather than asking him to take care of himself.

"Yes Ma'am." Jacob chuckled.

Danica laughed quietly to herself as she walked out the door leaving Jacob. As she walked outside the cool night hit her. She smiled as it ran through her hair that was very ruffled from sleeping. She looked up at the sky and a small sad feeling passed through her. She felt a tug on her heart as she looked at the stars. She hoped Ari was ok. She hoped that she wasn't under too much stress and that she didn't feel like she abandoned her. Most of the crew was already settled in. She made her way down to the lower deck. A small group of guys were playing cards. She watched them for a second.

"You want to play captain?" One of the younger men said with a soft smile.

"Maybe later boys." Danica said as she began walking past them and started up the stairs to the upper deck.

"Evening Captain. Sleep well?" Adam called her as she got up to the helm.

"Aye still sleepy but good. How are you holding up?" Danica asked him, going to the upper deck rail and leaning on it.

"I'm doing well captain. We are actually making good time with the wind on our side." Adam smiled.

Danica nodded in agreement looking out over the horizon. You could barely tell where the deep blue sky ended and the dark ocean began.  She got lost in the dark swirls of it. She studied the swirls of the  dark water as it reached up to the sky calling to it. Off in the far distance she could see cliffs and large peaks that stretched out into the water. She squinted trying to study it. She couldn't because everything was too dark and the dark cliff only stood out in the slightest against the sky. She began to humm as her eyes went to the horizon to the men below. She recognized Kaleb. He made his way slowly to the group of men playing cards. She saw him smile as a man shifted over so he could join them. He smiled sitting down at the group. The man holding the cards dealt him in. She watched all the men carefully pick up their cards and study them. She smirked seeing their reactions. She watched them place bets and then everyone showed their cards. The smallest man laughed and began collecting his winnings.

"They play almost every night. Even back home." Adam said knowing what Danica was watching.

"I know a little bit of how to play but not enough to actually sit in a game." Danica said back to Adam.

"They would gladly teach you." Adam said reassuringly.

"Maybe some other time. Did you want a break?" Dancia asked, taking her eyes from the group of men.

"Maybe in a little bit but I am ok for now," Adam said.

Danica nodded and then spotted a chair leaning up against the first mate's cabin. She went over and took a seat.

"I'll be here when you're ready then." She smiled as she sat although her eye slides felt heavy.

She shifted slightly and leaned her head back against the wooden wall. In seconds her eyes were closed. Adam glanced back at her and laughed out loud.

Ariadne sat at the kitchen table, she reluctantly gave in and discarded the light blanket she placed over it. There had to be something she was missing in the contracts. She had brought everything up to the courts and they had interviewed Edward Smith. The only response she got from the courts was what he was doing was legal. She didn't understand how he was getting around it or how he knew their every move. She sighed letting her head drop onto the table. She groaned into the table, frustration getting to her. She wanted to take and toss the papers off of them. She lifted her head from the table and rubbed her brow. She didn't know how long she had been sitting there. It felt like hours, her head throbbed and her eyes hurt. She stood going to the counter and grabbing herself her glass of water. She took a long sip shutting her eyes as she did. A loud thump on the door made her almost drop the glass he was holding and she started to cough on the water. She glanced at the door, it was so late. Who would be coming to her home at this hour. She pulled open one of the kitchen drawers. Reaching inside of it she grabbed her father's pistol. She waited looking at the door as another single thump was heard. She gritted her teeth as she walked slowly to the door. Before reaching the door she checked the pistol quickly making sure it was properly loaded. She inhaled as she prepared herself to open the door. She grabbed a hold of the handle and turned the door slightly. She counted to three in her head and flung open the door pistol aiming for whoever was there.

Ariadne found herself staring out into the night. No one was there. She paused her hand still ready with her pistol just in case this was some sort of trapt. She scanned her surroundings not going out of the door way. There was no noise other than the crickets chirping away. She bit her lip waiting anxiously. She heard the noise twice, it was definitely a knock both times. She shook her head and backed into the house. The gun is still pointing outwards. She used one hand to start closing the door and that was when she saw it. A piece of paper tacked to the door. Ariadne cautiously took the paper, still watching as she stepped back inside. She locked the door before beginning to unroll the note. She unwrapped the paper slowly, not sure what to expect.

"The Smith's paid off the courts."

Ariadne blinked looking at the note. Who would have sent this to her? She thought.  It made a lot of sense now that she thought about it. They never told her exactly how everything Ed Smith was doing was legal and she never got to see any paperwork. Her wheels started spinning as she started down at the note. She would go to the courts tomorrow or the constable and see what she could do. She wasn't sure who would send this to her but she was thankful….skeptical but thankful. She looked at the stack of papers. Maybe she just needs to focus on one contract that they lost. Maybe if she could break it down and see exactly what loophole the Smith could use to get out of the contracts. She grabbed a stack of paper and went to the bottom. The first trade contract was with  the Mullins in the northwest port. She grabbed the contract pushing the other papers aside.She then reached behind her grabbing another candle, lighting it as she sat down.  She felt a little hope since receiving the note maybe there's something she was missing. She began reading the contract carefully.

# Chapter Eight

## Return

Ariadne woke up, drool seeping out of her mouth as she sat up. She fell asleep face planted in contracts. Sitting up one of the contracts was stuck to her face. Ink smearing as she tried to remove it. She groaned as she looked around. The house seemed empty without anyone here. Her stomach grumbled letting her know she didn't remember the last time she actually had a meal. She stood going over to the bread box and pulling out some bread. She grabbed some jam spread on it and took a bite. She needed to write a letter to request an audience with the judge. She needs to find proof as well in order to present to them. She needed to go survey the ships as well. She couldn't wait for Orion to be home so he could attend to those things. She sighed, taking a second bite of her brown bread with raspberry ram. Her stomach curled inwards happily like it couldn't wait for the food to reach it.  She finished the piece of bread and started for a second when she heard noise at the door again. She frowned, grabbing the pistol off the table and started for the door. She was more annoyed this time. She didn't want to play any games. She grabbed the handle and yanked the door open.

"Woah woah woah."

"What the hell are you doing Noah?" Ariadne yelled at the young boy.

Noah was Robbie's son and spitting images of him. He was eleven years old and entering the awkward stage in a boy's life, where he was mostly all legs and his voice was starting to crack. Ariadne smiled at him after a few seconds to soften the blow of her yelling at him.

"I thought I checked on you. Dad said to make sure you girls had everything you needed." Noah said to her his hands still up in the air.

"Sweetie, that's very kind of you but be careful down here by the docks. The men aren't always ….sweet." Ariadne said.

"Dad said if you need anything to come to the Inn and he will help you out." Noah said with a smile.

"Tell your Dad I said I will and thank you. Noah, is this the first time you came by?" Ariadne said to him ruffling his hair up.

"Hey leave it alone! And aye this is the first time why?" Noah said, struggling to get away from her.

"I can't help it, your hair is adorable when it's all messy. I was just wondering." Ariadne chuckled.

"You should talk, you got blue all over your face." Noah said, laughing and pointing at Ariadne's cheek.

She blinked a few times before wiping her cheek. Pulling her hand back there was ink. She shook her head as Noah held his belly laughing. Ariadne rolled her eyes at him, swatting him lightly.

"Allright run along and send my thanks to your family." Ariadne laughed.

Noah  took off down the path. Ariadne hung in the doorway waiting for him to get out of sight before going to shut the door. She paused, seeing another note stuck to the door. She felt her stomach turn. She appreciated the help if that was what this was but the sneakiness of it all was kind of creeping her out. She snatched the note from the door and rushed back inside. She quickly opened it.

"There's someone on the inside leaking information to the Smiths, reevaluate your circle."

She felt sick, her family had trusted each of their employees and knew most of them personally. There wasn't one person who she felt would betray them. She looked at the note. What if this was some game someone was playing. She felt more confused now than ever.


Danica felt warmth spread over her, she wanted to reach out and grab ahold of it. She sighed as tried to get it closer to her. She sighed happily as she snuggled against it. She then realized that she was moving. Her eyes shot open. She began flaying as she realized she was being carried.

"Woah woah easy." A warm calming voice said to her.

Danica instantly felt ok and recognized the voice. She stopped flaying and looked up to the face. His auburn hair had fallen loose from his pony tail as he continued to walk across the lower deck with her in his strong muscular arms. His deep sapphire eyes shot down to her.

"Morning sleepy head." Kaleb smiled, his smile was almost perfect, she found herself liking that his eye teeth were just a little off set then the rest of them giving his smile this devilish charm.

She blinked at the relaxation of him carrying her setting in. She cleared her throat awkwardly.

"You can put me down now." Danica said softly.

Kaleb wanted to ignore her and keep her close but he couldn't justify it. He set her lightly down on her feet, his hands lingering on her just a little too long before he stepped away.

"Sorry but you almost fell off that chair twice, Adam suggested I carry you to bed." Kaleb said, rubbing the back of his neck.

"Oh well thank you. I don't usually sleep this much just haven't been lately and I guess it's all catching up to me." Danica said apologetically.

"No, don't worry about that, are you ok?" Kaleb said, his own ears not believing the words that came out of his mouth, he never cared about others' issues.

"I will be once we complete our mission and we're back home." Danica said with a bright smile.2

Jacob grumbled as he looked down at the sight in front of him. He didn't know this lad and him getting close with Danica was making his nerves tingle. He sighed he promised Gavin he would look after the girls and he planned too.

"Kaleb crow's nest." Jacob yelled down from the upper deck to them.

Kaleb's eyes shifted upwards meeting Jacob's. They stared at each other one long moment before Jacob spoke again.

'Timmy needs to stretch his legs before he loses them and you're awake so go be useful." Jacob growled.

Kaleb wouldn't normally let any man growl at him, his hand twitch at his side but he gritted his teeth.

"Jacob-

Kaleb cleared his throat as Danica went to speak which stopped her in her sentence. He smiled at her before nodding and heading to climb up the mass. Danica frowned slightly as she looked up to Jacob. Jacob was too busy following Kaleb with his eyes. Danica's frown deepened as she stared for the stairs.  Jacob was still glaring at Kaleb as he watched him climb the mass. Jacob didn't even notice Danica coming to his side. She pinched him sharply under his arm, which caused him to jump.

"Hey lass what was that for?" Jacob said, rubbing his arm fat.

"Captain, and you know exactly what it is for." Danica said glaring at him.

"Do you know him?" Jacob asked Danica.

"No, I thought you did." Danica said watching Kaleb begin his climb up to the crows nest.

"No." Jacob said him watching Kaleb as well as he began thinking to himself.

He needed to know how Kaleb found out about this voyage, how he got on the ship, and who exactly he was. He ended up glaring at him again as Danica shoved him lightly. Jacob scowled at her. She laughed and shook her head at him before heading back to the helm.

"I'm going to steer." Danica called back to him as she made her way across the lower deck.

Danica didn't give him time to answer as she made her way back up the stairs to the upper deck and to the helm. She could see that Adams eyelids were heavy  and he was starting to nod out. She smiled, walking over to him and tapping him on the shoulder.

"Go get rest." she said softly.

"Aye Captain." Adam said gratefully, stepping away from the wheel as he passed it off to her.

Danica gripped the wheel in her hands as she began to steer. She glanced upwards watching Kaleb get settled in the crows nest and Timmy's feet hit the deck floor. She could tell by the way he walked away from the mass what Jacob said was true, his legs were killing him. She took note of it and would need to make a better schedule for crow's nest duty with more rotations. She focused on the horizon seeing Raven peak coming into view. Jacob's voice echoed in her head, after Raven's Peak it was uncharted territory for him. She glanced to the upper deck across the way Jacob was still leaning against the rail studying everything. She didn't know why but she felt like something was coming. She shook the dread from her thoughts and focused on the horizon.

Ariadne had spent the day writing her request for an audience with the court. She wanted to at least speak to someone about what was going on and have an actual conversation. She had attempted to talk to anyone but everyone was busy today. Or so they said. She also needed some type of proof to go with the audience she was requesting. She had spent the last two hours going through and outlining contracts and trying to find loopholes she may have missed.

She stood going over to the kettle she left on the stove. She pulled it off of it and began pouring the hot water into her tea cup. She grabbed some tea bags from her silver tin can next to the stove. She took the tea bag and dunked into the tea. Getting lost in the slow way the water slowly turned a warm amber color. A small noise was heard at the door from the outside. Ariadne dropped the tea bag into the cup and it sank into the amber water. She had been carrying the pistol now on her. She retrieved it from her side. She quietly but quickly walked to the front door. She quickly pulled open the door gun pointing at her enemy.

"Woah woah easy." A voice shouted.

She knew the voice and it took her a second to process as she stood there, her gun inches away from her brother's nose.

"Orion?" Ariadne whispered.

"Aye, sorry I know it's late and I wasn't supposed to be back this early but I'm here." Orion said with his arms out.

Without a second word or look Ariadne wrapped her arms around her brother. A small amount of relief washed over her. She didn't realize how much she missed him. Orion felt the stress and worry roll off his sister as he squeezed her back.

"Here, here come on in." Ariadne said letting go of him and starting back in the house.

Orion chuckled scooping his bag off the ground and followed Ariadne in. He stretched lightly entering. He took in the giant heap of mess his sister had out on the table. He quickly realized it was paperwork for the company, old contracts. She smiled happily while getting her brother a drink.

"Orion, how long are you staying this time?" Ariadne asked him,

"For as long as it takes." Orion said, reaching out and squeezing his sister's hand.

Ariadne smiled and began walking over with hot tea for Orion. Orion cleared a space for him at the table moving the paperwork out of the way as he did. Ariadne sat the cup of tea down in front of him. She then sat down herself with her own tea.

"Ori tell me about how everything went. You said you had to fight to keep the contract with the east trading post." Ariadne said, taking a long sip.

"Aye I  did. The Smiths sent a vessel to the post as well. They had to have left just after us because their ship arrived less than a day after we did." Orian began telling Ariadne.

"That's strange, I need to know how they knew." Ariadne said more out loud then to Orion.

"Aye they are getting information somehow." He said quietly.

"Oh here I meant to give you this. It was stuck to the door when I walked up." Orion said, pulling out a folded piece of paper from his front pocket.

Ariadne stared at the paper as Orion held it out to her. How? She had been in the kitchen for hours. She didn't hear anything, not one sound came from the door. The person was getting better at leaving them or she was much too involved with her work. She took the folded up piece of paper from Orion and unfolded it slowly.

"Andromeda"

## Chapter Nine

## Raven's Peak:

Ariadne masked her expression; she didn't know yet if she was going to tell her brother about her "friend" leaving her notes. Orion motioned to her asking with his eyes and hand what the note was about. Ariadne shook her head with a smile.

"Nothing, just Robbied making sure we have everything." Ariadne said quickly, making something up.

"They are good people. I will go down there in the morning and thank them." Orion said, taking a sip from his tea.

Ariadne looked from the note to her brother and then crumpled into her hand. Andromeda the word echoing in her mind, what did it mean? Could it mean that the traitor was on andromeda? Could it mean there was something about the ship or the recent contracts it made? She sighed frustrated, the note fairy could leave better hints. She grumbled thinking.

"Orion, do you have the signed contract with the east post?" Ariadne asked him.

"Aye it's in my luggage." He said standing and going over to the bag he left by the door.

"Before this contact what was the last one made on Andromeda?" Ariadne said as her brother searched his bag.

"Isles." He said not looking up as he searched.

"Isles." Ariadne whispered as she began searching the far right pile of paper.

She pulled the contract out and set it aside. What if it wasn't about the contract for the last trip Andromeda did. She looked at Orion, her face puzzled.

"What?" Orion said, looking at her with his brows scrunched in confusion.

"Do you have a list of crew members?" Ariadne asked him, her voice sounded like she was unsure.

"Aye. What's this all about Ari?" Orian asked not to move from his spot.

"Just a hunch." Ariadne said to him.

"Well how about we revisit this all in the morning. I'm exhausted and you look like the dead." Orian said playfully.

"No its ok-

Orion didn't take the no for answer; he began shoving her towards the stairs. Ariadne swatting at him as he shoved her along.

"The contracts, stress, and hunch will all be there in the morning." Orion said, pushing her up the first step.

"Fine if you will stop shoving me!" Ariadne said, shoving him back as she stepped up the first step.

She laughed at him shaking her head as she continued up the stairs. Orion watched her head to bed before going back over to the paperwork spread out everywhere. What was she trying to find? He thought looking at the mess. He curiously looked for the note. There was something off about the way she had said things. Not really the way she said it but the way she looked when she did. She was hiding something he thought.  He shifted things around but not too much, not wanting to make more work for his sister. He couldn't find it. He yawned, he was exhausted as well. He headed down the hall towards his old room.

Danica yawned at the wheel. The dark cliffs slowly approached, Raven's peak the name echoed in her head as she stirred the ship slowly past them. Dark vines stretched down over the slate black cliff, running down into the ocean. At the very top was a tree, its dark limb stretched out over and the leaves looked black as well. She caught herself staring at the tree. They weren't leaves. She thought as she watched one of the leafs shift. She then saw its beak, she could now make out the black feathers on each of the birds. They covered the tree at the top of the cliff.

Looking like little tiny undercover leaves. She was mesmerized by them and seemed lost looking at them. As if sensing her one floated down to her landing neatly on the wheel. It's dark feathers shimmer blue in the moonlight, as it turned its head looking at her from side to side. Its eyes were jet black and almost lifeless. Danica froze, staring at the bird inches from her. She had a feeling like she needed to back away from it and another of wanting to reach out and run her fingers down its back.

"Cliff!" Kaleb's voice rang out catching her attention.

The bird took off at the sound of Kaleb's voice. Danica snapped out of it and just in time. The ship barely brushed the cliff side. She took a deep breath in and out as she straightened the ship. Kaleb leaned over the edge of the crow;s nest to try to see who was stirring. He watches Danica pull the ship away from the cliff side. He shook his head;  what was that woman thinking, he thought shifting his legs.

Danica glanced back at the tree as they continued by the cliff. The tree was now bare, not one of the birds were nestled in their branches. The tree looked haunting as its limbs reached up into the night sky. Did she make the birds up? Was she that tired? She looked about the ship  as she steered the ship away from the cliffs. It seemed to be taking forever like time had slowed down. A dull whistling noise or whooshing noise seems to be coming from somewhere. She glanced up to the crow's nest wondering if Kaleb heard it too. She saw him shift but couldn't tell. She shook her head wondering if she was making it up. The whistle became louder and louder.  She rubbed her ear. She glanced about the ship. No one was acting like they heard it. There were only a few of them up but still how could they not hear this. Her eyes searched for a source. It was coming from behind her, She glanced over her shoulder to see a black swarm coming for her. She ducked just in the nick of time. A mob of black birds swooped over the top of her head. She could feel the wind from their wings as they passed over her.  The bird swooped down onto the lower deck, she heard yelling as she stood up on her tippy toes trying to see over the ledge.

The birds swarmed a sleeping man and began to peck him violently. He was screaming, flapping his hands trying to get them off of him. She watched a man grab a mop and began swatting at them. The mob of birds turned on him. They left the sleeping man and began to attack the man with a mop. They swarmed around him. The man was being lifted off the deck floor in a blur of black as they began carrying him away. Danica couldn't believe her eyes as she watched. The birds carried the man away up to the tree top. She blinked, disbelieving what she just saw. Seconds later a loud scream was heard as the man's body was dropped from the sky. His body hit the deck floor shattering. The whistling started coming again.

"Danica!" Kaleb yelled to her trying to get her attention.

His voice snapped her out of the shock and she reached over to her left ringing the bell to let the crew know there was trouble. Adam came rushing out behind her from the first mate's cabin and across the way Jacob appeared on the upper deck looking confused.

"Sails need to be completely down now!" Danica yelled.

"What's going on!" Adam yelled going to her side.

"We're being attacked." She told him quickly.

"Sails now!" She yelled out over the ship.

As the men started to come out they paused seeing the bodies. The sleeping man was gone as well. The birds had peeked his eyes out along with his throat. Gaping holes were left in both areas. Blood seeping from them. The same happened to the man that was taken. His body inches away from the sleeping man.

"Sails!" Danica yelled again.

"They're coming back!" Kaleb yelled down.

Jacob nearly jumped to the lower deck shoving the men he passed out of their trance. He raced to the ropes that were holding the few sails partly open. He grabbed a hold of one and began to untie it. Another man began helping loosen the sails. The whistling is coming back.

"Captain, what are we being attacked by?" Adam asked, confused.

"Birds." Danica said as the whistling started coming back,

"Birds!" Adam yelled.

His voice caught the ears of the rest of the crew that seemed to pause. As if they were not sure what they heard.

"Aye, they killed both of the men below. We need to get out of here as soon as possible." Danica said to Adam.

The crew seemed to pause not sure what to think, Adam was looking at her like she was crazy. She rolled her eyes at him.

"Why in the world would I lie about that?" She growled at Adam.

Adam put his hands up defensively. As he looked around he wasn't sure what he was looking for. He could hear a whistle noise in the distance he looked around trying to pinpoint it.

"It's them, it gets louder as they get closer."
Danica said as the whistling increased

Within minutes the mob of birds were back and
began circling the ship. The crew stopped in their
tracks as they watched the black blur whip around the
ship. Dania's mind raced with what she could do to
stop it. They were blocking her view and she couldn't
see past them. A small bunch of the birds emerged
from the black blur, They seem to be looking for a
target. They floated effortlessly just inside the ship.
They then attacked in a sweeping motion towards the
lower deck. They flew past Jacob, their beaks and
claws reaching out. Scratches appeared on Jacob's
arms as they passed him. Another man was clawed at
it as the small group of birds sped around the ship.

"Adam take the wheel." Danica said her voice
was almost a whisper.

"What the heck are you thinking?" Adam
whispered back.

"Fire." Danica whispered as she began slowly
backing away from the wheel as Adam took it.

If she could get to the lantern in Adams cabin
she would have fire. The small swarm of birds seem
to be looking for someone in particular. Growing
frustrated you could tell by the harsh movements it
was making. The man on the lower deck had armed
themself. One man swatting and slicing at them with a
sword. His blade made contact with a bird and it

flopped to the ground injured. The swarm turned on the injured bird. Attacking and ripping it apart before it turned on the man. Danica took this opportunity to duck into the cabin without making any noise.

She quickly grabbed the three lanterns in there. She rushed to Adam's closest and grabbed a few of his shirts. She needed something to wrap the shirts around. She was making torches. She looked at the chair. She set the lanterns and shirts on the desk. She inhaled as she grabbed ahold of the chair and brought it up over her head. Slamming it down with all her might onto the floor. Two of the legs broke off. She flipped the chair over so that when she brought it down again the two remaining legs would hit the floor. As she brought the chair down and the legs impacted on the deck floor they shattered away from the base of the chair. She smiled in relief as she saw four pieces of wood. She grabbed them quickly and rushed back to the desk.

Kaleb looked down at the birds beginning to attack. He needed to do something. He glanced at the helm Adam was steering blindly. They could crash any minute if the large mass of birds did not leave. He then heard several large crashes coming from the first mate cabin. His eyes began searching for her. Where did she go? Without thinking he began climbing down the crows nest.

The men began to swing their blades frantically at the birds. Each time one was killed another bird from the outer swarm would replace it and the outer swarm didn't seem like it was getting smaller. Kaleb dodged the swarm of birds as they targeted a single crew member, they engulfed him and he could hear his scream as he ran past them. He raced up the upper deck and to the sound of where he heard the large bang happened. He didn't even give Adam a second look as he went to the door of the cabin and just as he reached for the handle the door opened.

"Kaleb! Great! Here take this!" Danica yelled as she thrusted a wood stick with cloth wrapped around it into his hand.

"What is this?" He asked, confused.

"It's a torch We're going to set fire to those winged things!" Danica said quickly walking past him.

Kaleb gripped his torch and followed her. He watched her pause by Adam and squeeze his shoulder before heading down quickly to the lower deck. Kaleb raced behind her barely keeping up. She avoided the birds who were too occupied attacking another crew member as the rest of them tried to fend them off with their swords. Jacob was fighting off a swarm of birds that had split from the pile and was now attacking him.

"You catch!" Danica yelled to a crew member before tossing him a torch.

She saw Jacob fighting and was becoming worried. She walked to him striking a match as she got close she lit the cloth on fire. Stepping in front of Jacob she thrusted the torch into the middle of the swarm of birds. They quickly went up in flames as they tried to fly out of the ship. She quickly lit the second torch she was holding and handed it to Jacob.

"Burn them." Danica said quickly with a nod before turning to walk the other way.

Kaleb rushed to herside holding his torch out to hers. She placed hers against his, his quickly ignited. He looked at her as if to say now what? Danica didn't say anything but pointed to the man she had given the last remaining torch to and then the second small swarm of birds. Kaleb nodded and headed off to follow her instructions. Danica looked at the large swarm outside the ship circling it.

"Jacob you get the portside and I'll get starboard. On three, place your torch into the swarm!" She yelled to him rushing as quickly as she could across the ship.

Jacob nodded and headed to the left side of the ship. Kaleb and the young crewman took care of the small swarm still on the ship. He looked up in time to see Danica approaching the larger swarm. His stomach crunches inside of him in fear for her. He was worried about her safety. He gritted his teeth starting to go for her.

"One, Two, Three!" Danica yelled and held her torch out into the darkness.

Jacob followed suit, It was like the birds couldn't stop in their flight pattern. They were all quickly going up inflames and the ones Danica was missing Jacob was catching on the other side. Kaleb went to  Danica's side, seeing the force of the birds flying was starting to push her back. He went behind her and helped steady her, his arm going around her waist ever so slightly. He saw her flame starting to dim and he handed her his. She grasped and placed both torches into the remaining darkness. Within a few minutes all the birds were on fire. They were dying and falling into the sea.

As the last bird died and fell into the ocean, the moonlight danced across the lower deck. Danica laughed leaning back into Kaleb. A cheer went up around them from the crew. She chuckled in relief.

"Brace yourself!" Adams' voice came down from the helm.

As the sky opened up they were heading straight for a cliff. Adam held tightly to the wheel and pulled as hard as he could away from the cliff. The North Star skimmed the wall of the cliff. Kaleb pulled Danica back away from the rail, the torches they were holding falling into the ocean.

As the North Star skimmed the wall debris began to fall. Kaleb wasn't quick enough to move out of the way. He pushed Danica away from him with all his might as a rock came tumbling into the ship. He watched Danica land on her butt and slide far enough away from him. Thank god he thought  seeing her safe. He then felt the impact, searing pain shooting through him as he tired stepping forward. The rock hit Kaleb hard, the last thing he remembered before the world turned black was hearing a beautiful voice shout his name.

# Chapter Ten

## Wounds

"Wake up! Wake up! Ari. What is this?" An angry Orion said, shaking his sister.

Ariadne began hitting whatever was attacking her. She threw a fist as she sat up towards her attacker. Orion blocked and grabbed a hold of her fist. He then second guessed about waking her up like this.

"Ari it's me! Stop!" Orion yelled.

"What the hell are you doing?" Ari said, yanking her fist back.

"I could ask you the same, what is this?" Ori said, holding another note in front of her face.

Ari went to grab but Orion pulled back his face looking like their father right now when they would be intolerable.

"Orion I don't know what it is or who they are from but they seem helpful." Ariadne said, holding out her hand for the note.

"How do you know that Ariadne? This could be some big goose chase to get us off path, this could be a trap from the smiths." Orion said, tossing the note on to Ariadne's bed.

"It could be but right now it's all we got and they make sense." Ariadne said becoming angry and it reflected in her tone.

She unfolded the note and looked at it in her hands.

"Ariadne's Crown."

She groaned reading the note, did it mean The Crown the ship or did it mean her. She was named after the story of Ariadne. She became frustrated. She needed to know who was putting these notes on her door.

"Orion, while you were gone I went to the courts for help. The Smiths have to be doing something illegal to help the trade post out of contracts with us, they said he wasn't. The first note said that he paid the courts off. It would make sense Edward seems like the type of man to throw money at his problems and there's no way he's not doing anything illegal. Second note said we have an inside man spilling our business plans. Which makes sense because no one knew we were going east. You left quietly and we had no real announcement about it other than in our circles. How did the Smiths know about it and get there? The note before this said Andromeda which I don't know what that means and this note now says Ariadne's Crown. I figured Andromeda was referring to your ship but I don't know

if this note means The Crown ship or something else."
Ariadne said frustrated.

Orion looked at her, clearing his throat. He
didn't know what to say. The first two parts made
sense. They did all of sudden know how to go east
and they had to be doing something illegal to steal
their contracts. This is all way too fishy for him
though.

"Who do you think is leaving the notes? I think
that will tell us if we can trust them or not." Orion said
quietly thinking.

"I honestly don't know.I think we need to start
somewhere though. Maybe get me the list of the crew
members on Andromeda when you went east. Maybe
we can find a clue amongst the crew." Ariadne said
softly, still looking at the note.

"Aye but we should also do something about
our note fairy as well." Orion said his tone was very
harsh as he started out the door.

"Aye you're right about that we need to
know...I'll think of something." Ariadne said to Orion's
back as he nodded leaving.

Ariadne got out of bed as soon as her brother
left her room. She quickly got dressed. She needed to
go over the Isle's contract and see what could be
there. She also needed to go over the list of crew
members as well as set a trap for their note fairy. She

sighed deeply looking at herself in the mirror. She could feel the dull pain of a headache forming in the base of her skull. She told herself she could do it and to suck it up. With a nod to herself in the mirror she left her room.

Kaleb groaned as he turned slightly. His head and shoulder were killing him. He could feel pain shooting down from the top of his head to the tips of his finger tips. The searing tingling, throb pain made him grit his teeth. He kept his eyes shut trying to focus himself before he went to move. He went to move and he felt someone press lightly on his chest.

"Hey now. It's ok, don't move." A very sweet voice said to him.

He was very foggy and couldn't even tell if this was real. His head hurt too bad to open his eyes. Something warm lightly touched the top of his head and he felt water run down his neck. He reached out to grab a hold of the person. His fingers gripped around the softest skin he had ever felt. The warmth of the skin matched the warmth in the voice he heard.

"Hey it's ok I need to fix you up." The voice said softly again.

Kaleb opened his eyes and found himself staring into the most beautiful brown eyes he had ever seen. They had depth to them and sent warm tingles through him as he stared. He lifted his good hand and brought it to the cheek of this woman. Her dark cascading her framed her face as a small smile was placed on her perfect pouty mouth. Kaleb thought he clearly had died. This woman is an angel.

"You're so beautiful." He said his voice was weak, as he ran his thumb down his angel's cheek.

"Shh Kaleb you need to rest." Danica said to him, patting his hand softly.

"Can I have you? Stay with me?" Kaleb said with a goofy smile coming on his lips.

"Well the rock really hit you hard." Danica laughed, taking his hand from her cheek and placing it on his chest.

"Beautiful, so beautiful." Kaleb said as his eyes drifted close and he passed out once more.

"Thank god if he said one more thing to you I would have knocked him out anyways." Jacob said from behind her.

Danica laughter filled the cabin as she reached for more clothes. The rock had grazed the side of Kaleb's head from what she could tell there were just scrapes there, the rock continued down into his shoulder which received most of the impact. There was a large wound and more scrapes going down the rest of his arm.

"Knife." Danica said, holding her hand out to Jacob.

Jacob raised an eyebrow as he unsheathed his knife and handed it to her. She then stood over Kaleb and one swift motion she ran the blade up the middle of his shirt exposing his chest.  Danica paused for a moment trying to recompose herself seeing Kaleb's chest. Her eyes wandered over his very firm chest that matched how strong his shoulders looked. His stomach was defined and she found herself wanting to run her hand over them. He must work hard for a living, she thought. Jacob cleared this throat as if he was going to yell at her as he peered over to see exactly what she was doing.

"Jacob, I don't think I need to remind you that my father nor my mother is on this ship. I would also like to say I am the captain." Danica said her voice was very firm as she spoke. She was done with Jacob fathering her.

"Yes Captain.' He said softly.

"I am looking for more wounds." Danica said to him, waving him off.

There was bruising on his ribs. She frowned and wanted to see if there were any broken but she decided to do that last incase he came to. She wanted to clean up all other wounds before getting to the most painful. She rinsed and cleaned the wound on his head, the blood almost fading into his auburn colored hair. She brushed some caringly out of his eyes as she moved on to his shoulder. She rinsed and cleaned the biggest wound. There was a small bit of debris from the rock inside of it. She carefully pulled pieces of the rock out of his shoulder. The wound itself would have to heal and close on its own. There was no way of suturing it, she could try but she would have to cut away too much good tissue and then closing it would be more of a mess. She then moved onto the scrapes on his arms. The muscles on his forearm were just as defined as his chest. She could imagine him carrying heavy things. She shook her head. Stop it. She told herself.

"Jacob I am going to need something to bandage his shoulders and possibly his chest." Danica said finishing up.

Jacob nodded and began moving about the cabin gathering different materials. He brought over a roll of what look like cotton and then a wider material. She nodded, taking the cotton material and began wrapping the wound on his shoulder. Securing it with a cloth like material she wrapped on top of it. She then sighed preparing to feel his chest. She didn't want to hurt him, she hoped she would stay asleep. She started at the top ribs and pushd on them lightly, they felt in place. She then began to slowly make her way down the remaining of the ribs. Kaleb would flinch slightly and it became more present as she got closer to the bottom of his ribs. Reaching the bottom

Kaleb flung his arm forward trying to stop whatever was hurting him.

"Stop." He groaned, still asleep but in pain.

"Bruised, not broken." She said to herself out loud, she heard Jacob make a grunt noise in agreement.

"I might need your help in holding him up right while I wrap his chest. Just be careful of his shoulder." Danica said motioning for him to come here.

Jacob grumbled to himself going over and lifting Kaleb upright. Danic sat next to Kaleb on the bed and began wrapping his ribs. She passed the bandage material around his front and then leaned into him to wrap it around his back. She passed it between her hands and brought it back up to the front. She did this several times before Kaleb started to wake. Danica attempted to go fast leaning into him, passing the bandage material between her hands behind his back. As she leaned over him, her head pressing into his chest. Kaleb slowly opened his eyes and was looking at the top of her head. He wasn't sure what was happening but he without thinking cradled her with his arm.

"Are you ok?" He said not realizing what was going on.

Danica froze as Kaleb's arm wrapped around her. The warmth radiating from his chest made her want to curl into him more. She almost let a happy sigh escape. She pulled back slowly from him. His hand falling away from her. She brought the bandage material around his front.  Jacob stepped away letting go of his shoulders so Kaleb could support himself

"Kaleb, do you know who I am?" Danica said as she wrapped the last piece of material around him.

"Aye captain." Kaleb said with a confused look on his face, his head began to spin, he had to close his eyes before he became nauseous.

Danica saw his face grow pale and he squeezed his eyes shut. She gently placed her arm around the back of his neck, her other hand going to his chest, and then slowly helped him into a lying position.

"Better? " She asked quietly not taking her hand off his chest.

"Aye." He whispered softly not evening meaning to  but his hand covered hers that laid on his chest keeping it there.

Danica felt warm tingles spread through her as she stared at her hand trapped between Kaleb's hand and his chest. She could feel a smile creeping onto her lips. She cleared her throat trying to regain her thought process.

"Good, ok so a rock fell onto the ship and hit you. You're going to be very sore for the next few days and I need you to take it easy. You have a wound that is bandaged on your shoulder, a wound on your head, and your ribs are badly bruised but not broken." Danica smiled at him.

Kaleb blinked, taking the information in. An image of him shoving Danica away from him flashed through his mind. He grabbed her arm quickly and he moved away from Jacob who he didn't realize was holding him up. He began looking Danica over.

"Did it get you? I remember it was coming for you." Kaleb said not letting her go.

"No, you saved me. Thank you." Danica said, squeezing his hand gently.

He nodded and then the rush of pain hit him. He winced as he shut his eyes trying to within stand the wave of pain he was experiencing. He let air out of his mouth in a slow outward breath.

"Do we-

Danica began to ask Jacob about pain medicine. Jacob must have read her mind. He went to the closet and pulled out a bottle of rum. He walked over to Kaleb and handed him the bottle. Kaleb looked down at it, his face turning sour as he did.

"Thank you but I will be alright." Kaleb said, turning down the offer.

"You should get some more rest." Danica said to him softly, looking him over once more.

"No, I'm good." Kaleb said going to sit up but the head rush he got he had to lay back down before he was even upright.

"Laid down and rest. That's an order." Danica said going to sit in a chair nearby and she was exhausted.

Kaleb grumbled but physically that was all he could do. He really did need to listen to Danica and take it easy till his head stopped hurting.

"Jacob, I need you to check on Adam.that may have taken a lot out of him. Also check on the other crew members. I know we need to bury some at sea. I still can't believe what just happened, happened. Birds. That's absolutely crazy." Danica said thinking out loud as she talked to Jacob.

"Aye captain. I hope this isn't a bad sign for us." Jacob answered, saying the last part almost to himself.

"There's no such thing as bad luck or good luck. You're in charge of your own outcome." Kaleb muttered from the bed.

Danica smiled at Kaleb's muffled response. She liked it. Everyone was also so caught up in signs and bad luck, superstition. It was nice to hear someone say that all that was nonsense and you're in charge. She smirked at Jacob who just rolled his eyes.

"Clearly you've never met sailors or pirates." Jacob said, walking to the door.

"Pirates?" Kaleb said his voice a little louder.

Jacob did not respond and walked out the door, Danica leaned back in her chair and a chuckle escaped her lips.

"What's funny?" Jacob asked, his voice sounding a little painful.

"I can't remember but Jacob may have been a pirate. My father was before he met my mother." Danica said her parents' story was adventurous and romantic to her.

"Hmm well that's something." Kaleb said, almost sounding thoughtful.

Danica wasn't sure how to answer so she stretched out a little bit trying to get comfortable. Her eyes started to grow heavy. She heard Kalebs breathing change and get heavier. She knew without looking at him he drifted back to sleep. His breathing made her tired. She wants to curl up in bed as well.

She yawned once more shifting in her chair and she gave into her heavy eyelids.

# Chapter Eleven

## Buried at sea

Ariadne spent all day focusing on the isle contact; she couldn't find what she was missing. It was frustrating she knew it was there but it wasn't standing out to her, Orion was now overlooking it as well. He was becoming just as frustrated. Ariadne had come up with a list of men who were on the Ariadne's Crown and Andromeda. So far she had five names. It wasn't uncommon for men to swap ships. Especially if they were in the business of making money. Many times men would hop off one ship and jump on the other with no breaks just to continue earning money. She rubbed her forehead as Orion came through the front door.

"Any luck?" He asked her as he sat more papers down.

"I have five names that were on both ships." Ariadne said, sighing deeply.

"Ok let me have them, I'll go get them and see who the rat is." Orion said fire in his eyes as he took a step towards the table.

"No, we need to be clever about this Ori. I think we should feed each one of these men false information but differently and see what gets back to the Smiths. I feel like I need one more thing or something to reference these men with to really determine who we should be looking at. But I can't find it!" Ariadne said the last part was so frustrated, she was on the verge of wanting to rip all these papers up or cry.

"Ariadne, you're doing the best you can. You need to breathe and take a break. Let's go out and get you out of the house for a while. Away from these papers." Orion said to her as he walked over and squeezed her shoulder.

'Aye, that would be nice." Ariadne nodded.

"Ok well let's go then." Orion said with a laugh.

"Ok but first I need to rig the front door with my trap. Until it goes off and we catch our note fairy we need to use the back door." Ariadne said with a smirk, Orion looked at her interested with the same smirk on his face.

Ariadne walked out the front door and Orion followed. She motioned for him to stand away from the door towards the path away from the house. Orion chuckled and stood with his arms folded across his chest watching his sister work. She bent down over the cobble stone path and pulled a long fishing wire across the walkway of their home. It was right outside the doorway. If he didn't see her place it there he wouldn't have even noticed it was there. He followed the fishing wire with his eyes. There was a bucket hanging above the door that was triggered but someone tripped the fishing wire. His eye brows folded as he tried to figure out the bucket. He then spotted another fishing wire that went off to the side, it connected to a fishing net. The bucket being pulled downward would trigger the net to come flying from the side. He was very impressed. He looked at his sister tying off the last piece of invisible wire. He watched her stand with her hands on her hips looking very accomplished. She looked back at Orion and laughed seeing his expression. She walked over to him carefully stepping over the wire.

"So in a nutshell tripping on this wire triggers the bucket which is filled with water to fall. The weight of the bucket falling triggered the fishing net to come flying at our victim. Which then gets tangled in the net and if we're lucky trips on the bucket for added fun." Adriane laughed at the end of explaining her trap.

"Remind me not to prank you ever." Orion said with a laugh.

"Ok so where too?" Ariadne smiled.

"Sunflowers?" Orion said with a shrug.

"Sure I haven't been there in a little bit and I wouldn't mind catching up with Joyce and Robbie." Adriane said as she began walking.

Danica watched the men prepare the body for burial. Three men in total were killed by the Raven peak attack. They had wrapped them in white cloth and now were setting them on platforms that they would lift up over the side of the ship and lower the bodies into the sea.  She stared at the three bodies, she didn't even know their names, if they had families. Her stomach pitted and turned on itself. Jacob came up next to her and squeezed her shoulder.

"Henry, George and Leon." Jacob whispered into her.

She inhaled with a nod. These poor men, she could feel the guilt and blame attacking her stomach. There was a silence about the ship as the men waited to send their brothers to their final resting place. Danica cleared her throat stepping forward facing the platform, her head hanging slightly lower in respect.

"We are here to honor these poor men whose lives were cut short. We honor their sacrifice as they gave their lives for us. As we commit the earthly remains of our brothers Henry, George, and Leon to the deep, grant them peace and tranquility until the day we all meet again. May they rest easy." Danica said.

A grumble of agreement went through the crowd as the man began to pull the platforms up. Danica stepped forward to help the platform up over the side of the ship steadying it as it started to descend. She stood at the rail tall watching as the platform sunk into the sea. After a few minutes the men pulled the platform back out of the sea. The bodies of the men started to sink away from the platform. Several minutes later Danica was helping lift the empty platform up over the side rail. She stared at its emptiness for several minutes before she turned back to the crew.

" I do not know what the journey ahead lies. I know you all knew this was not a trading voyage. I did not think we would be facing life or death but now I am not so sure. The path ahead no one on this ship has journeyed past this point. If you would like to leave at the next docking point I will not hold that against you." Danica said strong.

"Captain there is always the chance of death when at sea. You never know what lies out here. This is not your fault." A man from the center of the crowd called out to her.

Danica recognized him as Kyle, he was one of the younger crew men but the sea had aged him, She smiled thanks to him.

"Aye captain if it wasn't-

"If it wasn't for you we wouldn't be in this mess." An angry man said, beginning to move through the crowd.

Danica felt Jacob stiffen up next to her wanting to go to her defense. She patted his arm to tell him to stand down.

"This journey was supposed to be simple, a treasure hunt, get some extra earnings and go home. Not have your eyes and throat ripped out by birds." The man yelled, stepping through the front of the crowd.

Danica did not respond; she was letting this man have his moment. He clearly was afraid and needed to vent. She stood there emotionless, hands collapsed behind her back waiting for him to continue. When he didn't she went to respond to him.

"Luke, I did not know that birds would attack us. Nor did  I think we would be facing life threatening things. I understand being upset or frighten-

"Frighten, whose frighten. Do I need to show you frightened!" He screamed, stepping towards her, his hands clenched in fist at his side, his body sending off threatening messages as he started to get closer to Danica.

Danica remained unphased by this, she did begin preparing herself for  a fight, her mind playing what seranio this would take. She began thinking about where she should hit him first. He grew closer, his face turning red, spit forming at the side of his mouth. Danica shifted her stance so if she needed to throw a punch she would use her body and throw her weight into it.

"If it wasn't for you-

"IF it wasn't for you captain none of you would be alive." Kaleb's voice was soft but powerful as he appeared to the side of the man

"I don't know who you think you are but-

"I am going to be the person who rips out your throat  if you don't back away from the captain and take your place back in the crowd." Kaleb said his voice was so calm as he threatened Luke it sent terrifying chills through the air.

Luke went to step towards Danica testing Kaleb and in a blink of an eye a blade was pressing into Luke's neck. A small red bead of blood began to appear against his neck.

"Kaleb." Danica whispered.

"I am going to let go and if you so much as breathe wrong, you are a dead man," Kaleb whispered letting Luke go.

Luke's whole demeanor changed. He nodded to Danica and then to Kaleb before shifting slowly back into the crowd. Danica was staring at Kaleb  in amazement. He was quick and fast and terrifying. It drew her to him even more. She looked at him confused at how he was able to recover so quickly from his injuries. Injuries the word bounced off the walls inside her brain until it registered. Kaleb was hurt.

Danica went to him with a frown on her face. She didn't even say anything to him, she put her hand on top of his that was still holding the blade out and gently pushed it down. Kaleb's chilling presence softens Danica's touch. She smiled gently at him as she then looped her arm through his and began leading him away from the crowd.

"Get back to your duties or the next person we bury at sea will be my fault." Danica called over her shoulder as she led Kaleb towards the captain's cabin.

Jacob blinked several times trying to process everything that happened. He felt that he had underestimated Kaleb and him standing up for Danica earned him respect in his eyes. He had a small smile on his lips as he heard Danica threaten the crew. She in that moment reminded him of her father, although her threat to toss someone over board was much more elegantly put.

"Back to work, if you wish to be off the ship at the next docking point like the captain originally started to say please come see me. Until then business will resume as normal and without any further interruptions." Jacob called out also threatening the crew.

As soon as they entered the cabin Kaleb's tough guy demeanor seemed to fade away. Danica could immediately see he was in pain. She led him over to the bed. His head was starting to spin again. He groaned frustrated as he sat down very slowly on the bed.

"What's going on?" Danica asked him softly as she sat next to him studying his movements.

"The world keeps randomly spinning and when it happens my head hurts. It's the worst headache I've ever had," He said, propping his arms up on his legs and leaning his head into his hands so they cradled his head as he spoke.

Danica nodded, there was nothing she could really do for that, it was because he got hit so hard in the head. She placed a hand on his back and began to rub it slowly. Kaleb didn't know why but her touch made him feel instantly better. He found himself subconsciously leaning towards her as she rubbed his back. She smiled at the reaction but didn't say anything.

"You should lay down and try to sleep this off the best you can." Danica said softly to him,

Kaleb wanted to argue but couldn't find anything that would justify arguing with her. He groaned softly and then began to lay back. The world spinning quickly as it did the pain rushing into his head faster and fiercer. He tried to do anything to stop it. He thought he was going to vomit from it, it was hurting so bad. He heard movement behind him but he couldn't focus on what was going  on. He felt the weight in the bed shift and then something cold was on the back of his neck. The pain eased up slightly. Danica put a wet rag on the back of his neck and began to rub his back. He felt slightly better.

"Thank you." he managed to whisper through gritted teeth.

"You're welcome." Danica said through a yawn.

She was exhausted. It was still the middle of the night and the energy she spent with the birds and then the crew was catching up to her. She could see Kaleb relaxing more. He hand began to slow rubbing his back and she saw him stiffen again. She raised an eyebrow and replaced her hand on his back, rubbing it slowly. He relaxed. She smiled at the sight of her touch actually helping. In a few more minutes she could tell he had finally drifted to sleep. She went to pull her hand away and get up off the bed. Kaleb's warm hand grabbed hers.

"Stay." He barely whispered.

The plea in his voice was so filled with need and pulled at her heart. She couldn't deny him, she was exhausted as well. She didn't need to be asked again. Kaleb felt the weight in the bed shift once more as he felt her lay next to him. Danica began rubbing his back once more and he drifted back to sleep. Her eyes grew heavy as well and before she could think about sneaking away she too was asleep.

## Chapter Twelve

## Bucket:

Ariadne stumbled up the walkway to their house every now and then clinging to her brother. Orion laughed as he steadied her.

"Why don't you just lean on me the rest of the way." Orion said, trying not  to laugh as he tried to grab Ariadne before she stumbled again.

"No, I am just fine." She said, drawing out the last word, swatting her brother away.

"Oh I bet you think you are." Orion laughed letting her wander from the path a little.

"I am! I am just great!" Ariadne said, stopping and looking at him as she flapped her arms about as she spoke.

"Mhmm. Your head is going to feel really great in the morning." Orion laughed walking past her.

"It's gonna be just fine, I'm fine, my head's fine. Everythngs fine." Ariadne said straighten herself out and walking after him.

"Six drinks for someone who doesn't drink is not gonna be fine in the morning." Orion laughed.

"It was five.....ish." Ariadne said followed by several giggles.

She caught up to Orion still laughing and grabbed his arm. She tugged on it, getting him to stop. He laughed looking at her waiting for her to explain herself.

"Let's not go home. What if we just go? What if we go?" Ariadne asked him, her voice bordering on sadness almost.

Orion was taken back by this, he hadn't really thought about what his sister might be going through. He inhaled softly trying to figure out what to say or ask.

"Where do you wanna go Ari?" Was all he could really come up with.

"I don't know. Anywhere somewhere. You just came back from the east. Dani's on some wild goose chase. I've been stuck here. Mom and Dad are having their own adventure. I've been here." Ariadne said her voice boarding between being sad and angry.

Orion felt that statement tug at his heart. She was always the oldest, always the most mature and responsible. It never crossed his mind that maybe she didn't want to be. Orion scratched the back of his neck trying to find the words to say. If they really did leave now they would lose the business. What if he just let Ari go? He thought.

"Ari why don't you-

"Oh I know! Let's just go break into the Smith's. Then we could just find out what they're really doing. Oh let's go tear all their ships' sails! " Ariadne said, walking past Orion and getting closer to their home.

The wheels in her head were spinning with ideas she could do to the Smiths' business or ships. Orion laughed, passing her getting the key out as they neared the front door.

"Or we could get something really sticky and cover their deck floors with it. That would slow them down." Orion said, adding to it as he stepped into the doorway of their home.

"Orion there's something i'm suppose to remember-

Ariadne said as Orion tripped the fish wire trap. The bucket came flying down and as it hit the walkway the fishing net was launched towards Orion. It enclosed around him knocking him to the ground in a tangled up heap. He groaned struggling to try to find a way out of it. Ariadne rushed over to her brother as quickly as she could, leaning down she couldn't help but look at the trap in amazement.

"Holy shit it worked!" Ariadne said, putting her hand over her mouth as she watched her brother struggle.

"It sure did." A voice said from directly behind her

Ariadne nearly jumped out of her skin as she heard a voice she didn't know behind her. Without even missing a beat, she grabbed the bucket  and spun toward the man. The bucket swung out as she spun around. The bucket made a hard impact with the person's head and without blinking or making a noise they fell back onto the ground. Ariadne squeezed the bucket handle in her hand.

She slowly walked over to the person laying on the walkway to their home. Stepping over to them and ready to whack them again she squinted at them, she recognized him, his blond hair that the moonlight was making shimmer. His slender but fit build. Patrick Smith. She groaned looking down at him. She nudged him lightly with her foot and he didnt move. She knelt down to make sure he was still breathing and he was. She got up quickly and rushed over to Orion. She quickly unraveled him from the fishing net.

"What the hell is going on?" He yelled standing up, throwing the remaining part of the net off of him.

"Well my trapped worked and I knocked out Patrick." Ariadne said with a shrug.

"Patrick? Whose Patrick?" Orion said, trying to look behind her.

"He's a Smith and I don't know why he was here but can we just get him inside?" Ariadne said, grabbing Orion and bringing him over to Patrick.

"Oh god did you kill him?" Orion whispered, seeing him not moving on the ground.

"No! Shut up! He's still breathing. Come on, be useful." Ariadne said, bending down and grabbing one of Patrick's arms.

She tried to pull him but almost fell over herself. The world was starting to spin and she felt like she was standing on a ship.

"Get out of the way drunky. I will get him; Just go hold the door open." Orion said with a half laugh.

Ariadne stumbled to the front door opening it and then leaned against it as she watched her brother grab Patrick underneath his arms and begin carrying him towards her. She couldn't help but laugh, she wasn't sure what she found funny exactly but she found herself laughing anyway.

"Really funny Ari." Orion said a little out of breath as he continued to pass her.

He half carried, half dragged Patrick to the small couch they had in the very corner of their sitting room. The couch was placed right under a window. Their mother would sit in it and read to them or herself. Orion remembers many nights before sitting by this couch listening to his mother read about far off places and adventure. He plopped Patrick down onto it and he groaned as he did. Orion felt a little relieved when he heard him make a noise. The last thing they needed was to have a Smith's blood on their hands. The whole it was an accident most likely wouldn't work. Ariadne stumbled in behind them carrying some warm water and clothes. She thought for sure he should have some type of wound from how hard she hit him with the bucket.

"Do you see a wound?" She asked coming closer, trying to make herself sober as she did.

Orion sighed, turning around to light the lanterns that hung on either side of the window so he could see. The moonlight coming in through the window wasn't enough. He then bent down and began checking Patrick's head. He moved the blond hair out of the way so he could see. There was a small gash on the right temple.

"Yeah there is a small one right-

The next thing he knew he was wet. He was wet, the couch was wet, and Patrick was wet. Orion wiped his face, sighing once more as he turned to see his sister holding an empty container.

"Sorry." She said trying to be sincere but then began laughing hysterically.

"I am never taking you out drinking again." Orion grumbled.

"Oh Ori stop it. It's just water." Ariadne said, putting down the container and walking over to the couch.

"Says the person that's not wet. Can you just sit, just sit here. I'm going to go change and I'll be back to check on him. Just let him be for now. The cut is not that bad. Just sit and stay still" Orion said, pointing at the chair in the corner.

"I'm not a dog." Ariadne said glaring at him.

"No, a dog would actually listen." Orion said, walking out of the sitting room.

Ariadne kneeled down next to the couch looking Patrick over. She brushed a lock of blonde hair away from his forehead, trying to find the cut. She took note of how handsome he was. She smiled a little bit and for some reason ran her finger down his nose. She chuckled lightly as she did it. She shook her head.

"Get it together Ariadne." She told herself trying to get the silliness that kept creeping up on her to stay away.

She looked over at the container that was once filled with water and a clean rag. The rag was still in there and was wet. She leaned over grabbing it and then brought it to the cut on Patrick's head. She began to carefully clean it up. It was not bad at all she thought once she cleaned up the blood from around his forehead and the little bit that ran down towards his ear. There she thought.

"Orion, bring him one of your shirts! We can't let him stay in the wet one." Ariadne called to him.

She heard Orion mimicking her and then items being moved around. She knew he was searching for something for Patrick to wear. Patrick shifted a little bit and Ariadne put her hand on his chest to steady him. She then noticed a piece of folded up paper in his shirt pocket. She reached up carefully pulling the folded piece of paper out of his pocket. Before she could open it. He groaned again, his hand going up and grabbing hers. She inhaled as he grabbed her. She wasn't sure what to do. His eyes opened slowly. She was about to rip her hand away when the warmath from his eyes caught her.

"What happened?" Patrick asked.

"You scared me." Ariande said without thinking.

Patrick blinked as if realizing who was talking. He went to sit up but Ariadne shook her head and applied a little press on his chest to tell him to stay there.

"I scared you?" He repeated back to her as if trying to understand.

"Sorry." She said quietly.

"She hit you with a bucket." Orion said, coming up from behind them.

"A bucket?" Patrick asked.

"Great, you broke him." Orion signed frustratedly handing the shirt down to Ariadne.

"Yeah. I hit you in the head with it and you lost consciousness. This is my brother Orion...I'm Ariadne. I don't remember if you know my name or not." Ariadne explained to him.

"Why am I wet?" Patrick asked his surroundings to start to come together.

Ariadne busted out laughing, she couldn't help it. She put a hand over her mouth trying to make herself stop. It was actually all pretty funny to her right now.

"Ms. Graceful over here was trying to bring water to tend to the cut she gave you on your forehead." Orion explained.

"But here's a new dry shirt." Ariadne said, shoving the shirt at him trying not to laugh again.

Patrick looked at her strangely as he slowly sat up. He looked at them both a little confused. He took the shirt from Ariadne who was still kneeling in front of him. He scooted himself a little over before pulling the wet shirt up over his head.

"Woah!" The words fell out of Ariadne's mouth as Patrick exposed his very well defined chest and abs.

Patrick looked confused and looked down at his bare chest trying to see if maybe he had another wound. Before he could actually get a look at his chest. Ariadne ran her hand down it. Her fingers then ran over his abs tracing them slightly.

"Well goodness." She said a little breathy, her eyes looking up into Patrick's warm brown eyes.

He inhaled sharply as his heart began to sped up in his chest. He looked down at her as she was kneeling in front of him. Her red hair falling down around her in waves, her very full, very perfect lips begging to be touched. The way her finger tips sending tingles throughout him, he felt himself stiffen. He knew he should move away from her. A gentleman would, he was telling himself to but his body had other plans.

Orion started choking as he began to move towards his sister.

"Ari!." Orion said, snatching her up away from him.

"Ori its fine! Do you see his chest?" Ariadne said as he pulled her away from Patrick.

"Out! Get out! Go to your room. Never again Ariadne i swear. Never again." Orion said, guiding her out of the sitting room.

"But but-" Ariadne saif protested but the way the world had started rocking again she couldn't really fight Orion.

"No, you're gonna go sleep it off now." Orion said, shoving her into his room.

"This isn't my room." Ariadne said like a child.

"No but I am not having your stumbling ass go up the stairs right now. Sleep here." Orion said lighty shoving her into the room before closing the door behind her.

Orion sighed, running his hand through his hair. He took a deep breath before making his way back into the sitting room. Patrick was dressed sitting on the couch. He was holding his head slightly. Orion studied him for a moment before walking in.

"Ariadne is not herself right now. However I'm not sure why you're at our home this late in the evening though." Orion started out apologetic but then quickly turned to threatening in his tone.

"I was-

"He's the note fairy!" Ariadne announced from the doorway holding up the piece of paper that she had taken from his pocket.

## Chapter Thirteen

## Note Fairy

Danica stretched, warmth radiated from the side of her. She wiggled closer to it curling into it slightly. She felt it tighten around her. At that moment her brain woke up. Her eyes shot open and she found herself tangled up with Kaleb. His arm draped across her pulling her tightly to his chest. He was still asleep.

She got lost in the moment, a small smile came across her face as she watched him. His face was originally scowled but as his grip tightened he seemed to relax. She watched the small amount of sunlight dance across his auburn hair and fall across his face. He had a stumble forming on his chin and lower jaw she reached out and ran her finger down the length of his jaw, the stumble tickling her finger. If at all possible it made him even more handsome. He responded to her touch by wrapping his other arm around her. He nuzzled his face into the nape of her neck, sending shivers through her body. She mindlessly curled her fingers into his hair trying to keep him close as a small sigh escaped her. He groaned in response and then she felt small kisses being placed along her neck. Her heart sped up in her chest. As more shivers ran like electricity through her. She curled into him more, closing her eyes as her grip tightening on his hair. Her mind melted just focusing on what her body was feeling.

Kaleb pulled back slightly his blue eyes, studying her face. He at first had thought he was dreaming but now with his eyes open and seeing her in his arms; he couldn't deny that this was real. Danica's face was filled with pleasure and want. He felt himself building seeing her reaction to him. He hesitated but brought his face closer to hers. As he debated kissing her she opened her eyes slowly, her honey brown eyes stared into his, the cloud of lust fogging them. He wasn't sure what he should do, he knew what he wanted to do. Before he could decide Danica tugged on his hair that she had her fingers still woven in, bringing it closer to her lips. He watched her lick her lips in anticipation.

He couldn't resist any longer he brought his lips to hers. He slowly pressed his lips against hers and she quickly responded. She mimicked his actions following suit, warmth spreading over her as she kissed him back. She felt him apply more pressure with his lips as he kissed her. He captured her bottom lip with his and he tugged on her lower lip, When she opened her mouth slightly he slipped his tongue into her mouth. This excited her and surprised her. She felt him rub his tongue against hers and she felt chills in her core. She wanted to be closer to him. She began to follow him and brushed her own tongue against his. A small groan escaped him as he pulled her even closer to him. She felt something hard press against her hip as he moved her closer, his own hand slipping in her hair. He kissed her deeply, wanting and needing to radiate through the kiss. She moved slightly and felt it again. Alarms went off in her head, that what she was feeling was his member. She felt excited, nervous, and even a little scared. He reluctantly pulled his mouth from hers and buried his face into her neck, groaning as he did.

Danica was confused by him stopping but her mind was foggy to begin with. Kaleb pulled away from her neck and kissed her forehead lightly. He saw her confused look on her face and he smiled. He brushed her cheek with his thumb.

"We need to stop." He whispered almost out of breath.

Danica felt hurt and it flashed across her face as she began to shift away from him. He stopped her pulling her closer.

"Danica...was that your first kiss?" He asked softly,

She narrowed her eyes at him, not sure what he was getting at. aye it was her first kiss, if he's asking because she is bad at it she would kill him. She was almost glaring at him before she could even think of how to respond.

"I'm just asking because i don't want to push things further if-

"You don't need to be asking anything. Aye it was and it's none of your business and don't worry it won't happen again!" Danica said, shoving herself away from him.

Kaleb went to grab a hold of her but she was already up and off the bed. He tried to follow suit but the pain in his shoulder stopped him from moving as quickly as he wanted to.

"Danica wait!" He called to her as she began walking to the cabin door.

"Captain and no I won't." She said to him, opening the door and walking out, the door slamming behind her.

"Note fairy?" Patrick asked, confused.

"You! Your the-

"Note fairy!!!" Ariadne yelled again walking into the room this time.

Orion waved at her telling her to be quiet as she stumbled again. Orion sighed, his hand going to rub the side of his forehead. Patrick had shifted slightly and put his hands up defensively. Ariadne wobbled past Orion and poked Patrick in the chest.

"I still caught you haha fairy." She said sitting down next to him laughing.

"Ok you, you're never drinking again and you better start explaining why the son of our rival is sending us tips." Orion said frustrated.

"I tried telling your sister a week or so ago but they wouldn't listen. The other one threatened me with a sword. I thought this would be the ebay way to help-

"Oh you would have been kind of proud of Dani, she really wanted to get him with the sword." Ariadne laughed and poked Patrick again.

"You wouldn't have stood a chance! What the heck did you do before you came here-

"That's a good question, yeah where have you been? We didn't even know Edward Smith had a son." Orion said.

"You're very….fit." Ariadne said, poking him again.

"Ariadne, I am going to strangle you. Don't touch him again." Orion threatened his sister.

"The oldest is now a toddler." Orion groaned, they were leaving such a great impression with their enemy right now.

"I was away at school for the most part studying business, sailing, and negotiating. I want to take over my father's company and make the best of it. However, on my first day back I saw a lot of concerning things that I didn't agree with. I tried to make friends but your sisters had their guard up. Which is completely understandable. I think we can help each other. I want to have a solid business that is fair and my father has been doing alot of deceitful things to yours." Patrick patted Ariadne's hand and gently put it in her own lap as he spoke.

Orion was analyzing everything he said, could they actually trust him. What about the information he had been feeding them, how was he getting it and why not just come out with it. Ariadne was starting to nod out. She leaned against Patrick as he tried to respectfully steadied her. He looked at the note that fell from her hand.

"The North Star." The note read.

Orion's face turned to worry, his gut clenched in on itself. Danica's on that ship. He stood up, his fist clenched at his side as he stared down at Patrick.

"What does that mean? The north star. My sister is on that ship, start talking now or else.' Orion said through gritted teeth his hazel eyes burning into Patrick.

"Hold on, hold on." Patrick said defensively as he carefully placed Ariadne who was now passed out on her side on the couch.

"Talk now." Orion said if his jaw clenched any tighter he probably would break it.

"All I know is the person who is spying on you for my father is currently on The North Star. They were also on Ariadne's Crown and Andromeda. That's all I know. I don't think there's any harm or foul play in the works, just spying and reporting back." Patrick said, trying to show respect but also preparing himself to go rounds with Orion if he went to attack him.

Orion could feel his body shaking even if it wasn't visible. He took a deep breath, he wanted to trust Patrick. He seemed true to his word. The passion when he talked about his fathers company and wanting to right wrongs seemed real.

"When were they on these ships, do you know how many men we have that bounce from ship to ship." Orion said angrily, running his hand through his red hair.

Patrick began trying to think, it had to be all recently. Ariadne groaned behind them. Orion looked at Patrick and motioned for him to follow him into the kitchen. Patrick nodded and followed him, still thinking.

"It had to be recent, was there anything recently that my father knew about that you were sure he couldn't have known?" Patrick asked, folding his arms across his chest trying to think.

"The east. Your company did not know we were trading with the east. That was my last voyage. I don't know how the person would have literally jumped off my ship and then got on to The North Star, Danica snuck off in the middle of the night according to Ari. I don't think we were even docked yet." Orion said, trying to think out loud.

"Or was there anyone who knew about your voyage to the east that maybe backed out at the last minute?" Patrick said his face lighting up as he told Orion.

"Aye, I remember three men backing out. I need my ship logs. He said going over to the kitchen table and began looking through papers.

"What does it look like?" Patrick asked coming over to help.

"Simple note paper, it will have Andromeda on the top of it and it will start  listing off men's names and possible positions." Orion said, shifting through more papers.

"Here I got it." Patrick said, rounding the table and handing it to Orion.

Orion scanned the names on the paper, he saw three names crossed out Bruce Johnson, Timmy Barnes, and Luke Wrenfield. He grabbed another piece of paper and jotted the names down. He glanced up to Patrick who seemed to be waiting for him to say something.

"It's still late. Every part of me wants to go right now and knock on doors to integrate these men but I also don't want to show any commotion to bring more attention to us right now. If word got out we could lose our chances right now." Orion said, sitting down trying to form a plan.

"Aye your right it would draw attention. We need to do this thoughtfully." Patrick said leaning back against the counter,

"We?" Orion said, shifting in his chair to look at him.

"Aye, I am telling you the truth. Everything I said I mean." Patrick said with a firm nod.

"Aye, I think I believe you. I promise if this is just a scheme you and your father have planned out, you better run and hide. Abner's have a side of them you don't want to see." Orion promised him.

"Aye I believe you and I give you my word." Patrick said.

"All right then." Orion thoughtfully looked at the table.

"I think what I will do is I will make up a voyage and call men in to interview for spots. I don't always do this but for big voyages I do. I will purposely call these three men in and whichever one does not show then we know." Orion said planning out loud.

"Aye that sounds solid and it's not suspicious at all." Patrick said, agreeing.

"The other thing needing to be done is you need to look through your contracts. My father hasn't let me in on exactly how he's getting the trade post out of their contracts with you but there is probably the tiniest detail that you're missing." Patrick said thoughtfully.

"I know Ari's been killing herself trying to find it." Orion said a hint of sadness in his voice.

"I can help." Patrick said with a small smile.

"That would be appreciated, a fresh set of eyes might be what we need." Orion said with a nod.

"Aye, I'll find a way over here tomorrow." Patrick said, beginning to make his way to the door.

"Are you sure you're alright?" Orion said, pointing to his head.

"Aye, even though she's….not herself. She's got good form. I would hate to see what she would have done if she was sober." Patrick laughed, reaching for the door handle.

"You better hope you never find out." Orion laughed, meeting Patrick at the door.

"Be safe." Orion said to Patrick as he headed out.

Patrick nodded and began making his way home. Orion closed and latched the door. He sighed, pausing for a while at the door. He ran his fingers through his hair trying to gather himself and push away his frustrations. Tomorrow would be better, he told himself before going to check on Ariadne.

# Chapter Fourteen

## Error

The door slamming behind her drew the attention of the crew. They all seemed to pause and look her way. The glare was still on her face as eyes fell on her. Several of the crew members looked away quickly and the ones still looking wished they had followed suit. Danica narrowed her eyes at them and it was chilling. The men quickly went back to their duties. She walked away from the door and began walking down the stairs. The cabin door flew open behind her.

"Dan- Captain." Kaleb said, catching himself as Danica spun on her heels facing him, her eyes burning holes into him.

"Watch  what you say." Danica said, taking a step towards him.

"I was just, can we go talk -" Kaleb began trying to find the right thing to say but not draw attention which was already on them.

Danica threw her hand up, telling him to stop speaking. He begrudgingly listened, he began to match her stare.

"Crow's nest." Danica said, looking at him.

"What?" Kaleb said, almost confused.

"Crow's nest." Danica said again.

He glanced up at the crows nest and back at her. His face emotionless as he began walking by her. He wasn't going to try anymore. He didn't say a word as he passed her. She watched him walk down the stairs and across the lower deck. Reaching the center mass he began to climb the ropes using one arm, his shoulder on fire as he did.

"Dani,  I don't think that's the best idea for him. He is still injured." Jacob said in a whisper coming up behind Danica.

Danica felt instant regret as she watched him struggle. She couldn't back down now, she glanced sideways to Jacob and frowned slightly.

"Aye, I wasn't thinking." Danica said to him.

Jacob smiled softly at her. " It's alright Lass. Sometimes things cloud our mind, that's why there's a team."

She nodded, it's true Kaleb was clouding her mind and she didn't need him to. Right the crew was counting on her, her family was counting on her. She straightened up.

"I am going to go relieve Adam. Go stop him before he kills himself. Have him go below deck and do something." Danica said walking away from Jacob.

"Aye aye captain." Jacob said with a smile.

Danica made her way silently to the helm. She didn't look at anyone who she passed. Most of them could feel the anger rolling off of her and moved quickly out of her way. She reached the wheel and quietly Adam stepped aside.

"Morning Captain." He said quietly, one of the few that was brave enough to talk to her right then.

She smiled at that while she nodded her response. Adam stayed off to the side as she took over steering. She stayed silent for a minute before looking back to Adam. He was politely giving her space. She really liked him, he was a good man.

Her eyes were focused on the center mass. She watched Jacob call Kaleb down. Guilt pitted in her stomach as she watched him struggle. Jacob clapped him on the back before sending him off below the ship. Kaleb didn't even look her way. She grinded her teeth fidgeting as she stood at the wheel. Her hands tighten on the wheel. She inhaled and exhaled trying to get a handle on her emotions. She glanced back at Adam who didnt even act like he noticed. She's sure he did but didn't act like he did, which she greatly appreciated.

"Mr. Adam, I'm ready to be updated." Danica said calmly to Adam who smiled and took a few steps back to her.

"We are about a day and half from the passage, assuming you still want to take it Captain." Adam said shortly.

"Aye we will judge it when we get there. It will save us a day if not more in time but I don't want to risk any more lifes."Danica said, her eyes focusing on the horizon.

A day and half just to get to the passage and then the Hollow is just on the other side of it. She sighed, she didn't know how far into the land the treasure was. The map didn't make it seem like it was far but she knew it would be dangerous.

"Something wrong Captain?" Adam asked sincerity in his voice as he did.

"Just thinking that's all Adam. You can go rest now, I promise I am fine." She said to Adam with a smile.

He nodded and headed to the first mate's cabin. As the door shut Danica was left alone with her thoughts and the open sky.


Adriane groaned as she rolled over in the bed. She felt super nauseated and her stomach was so upset with her. She sat up and she did it way too quickly. Her head wasn't all happy with her either. She grabbed a hold of it as it began to throb. She was going to puke. She felt her body becoming warm and she began to feel shaky.  She panicked trying to get out of the room. She realized she was on the bottom floor and in Orion's room. She rushed by the kitchen table and threw open the front door. Before she could even make it just outside the door her stomach wrenched forward and she vomited all over the walkway. A hand reached out and quickly pulled her hair back for her. She was thankful but couldn't say anything as she wrenched forward again vomiting the remaining contents of her stomach. Sweat beads were across her forward as she stood up, shaking as she did so. A hankerchief appeared at her side and she took it gratefully. She wiped her forward head and then her mouth. She needed the fresh air, the cool breeze made her feel instantly better.

"Ori, I am so sorry." Ariadne began to say as she turned towards him.

"Patrick actually. Your brother left an hour ago to go let crew members know of your next trade voyage. Here, come inside and I'll explain everything. I also will make you something that will heal your headache and cure your stomach." Patrick said, offering her a hand.

She blinked at him several times trying to prove that it was not her brother and that the son of their enemy was being nice to them and helpful. Patrick reached forward and took her head gently and guided her back into the house. She followed like a senseless robot but she was still so puzzled that she was almost on autopilot.

"Here, sit." Patrick said, pulling out a chair for her and motioning her to sit.

Ariadne sat down but she watched him carefully. He began to rummage through their cabinets setting down some herbs and tea. He mixed a few things together and put them into a warm tea. He brought it over to her and offered it to her. She eyed him not taking the cup. He then realized she was quiet because she didn't trust him. He sighed and took a sip of the tea showing her he wasn't poisoning her. He then held it out to her. She carefully took, she looked at it for a moment, smelt it and then took a sip. She waited for something to happen but nothing did. She sighed and took another. By the third sip her stomach had settled and she could feel the throbbing in her head starting to wane.

"Thank you." She said softly to him.

"You're welcome." Patrick smiled back at her.

He sat back down at the kitchen table just opposite her and began looking through the papers once more. Ariadne cleared her throat trying to not jump across the table and attack him.

"Excuse me who said you could look over our contracts." Ariadne said, alarmed.

"Your brother did. I know you...you weren't yourself last night but when you had gone to bed your brother and I talked. We are going to help each other. He thought a fresh pair of eyes looking over the contracts might find a minor error that is allowing my father to help trades post out of their contracts with your company." Patrick said, explaining.

Ariadne took a long sip and listened. If Orion trusted him then she would. It took alot for Orion to trust people and he was very good at following his gut. If Orion thought it was the right thing or even way to go and his gut told him, he was always right. The words not yourself suddenly crept its way into her head. She looked up from the cup, her eyes wide as she looked at Patrick. He was too busy studying another contract. An image of her running her hand down his chest and abs flashed through her mind. She prayed she dreamt it up and that she had not really done that. She was cringing. He however was acting like nothing happened.

"So." Ariadne said out loud trying to think of something to say to him.

She knew the standard conversation questions. Oh this is some weather we're having, Isn't it nice? Do you think winter will come early and other nonsense small talk questions. She hates small talk. She really just wanted to blurt out  and ask if she really did run her hand down his chest. She prayed that she dreamt it up. She already felt embarrassed.

"About last night I am sorry, I have not been out in a long time, and this whole thing is a mess and stressful. I guess I just wanted to forget for a few hours. " Ariadne said not looking at him.

"Don't worry, I completely get it." He smiled and reached over and squeezed her hand lightly.

"I've had my own moments that I was trying to escape and they ended a lot worse than yours." Patrick said, letting go of her hand and laughing at a memory that crossed his mind.

Ariadne smiled and watched him bring his gaze back over to the contracts. He seemed to have read several of them already. He was holding one in his hand as Ariadne shifted closer to him and began reading over his shoulder. He shifted and brought the contract in the middle between them. He smiled at her. Ariadne could feel the heat rising in her cheek as she tried hard not to look at him. His leg brushed against hers and he swallowed hard.

"I think we need to be looking at the Isle contract." She said out loud a little too rushed.

"Isles...that actually sounds familiar. I think I've heard my father talking about it." Patrick said, standing and leaning over the table.

Ariadne got up quickly too and began shuffling through the papers. She did have everything sorted the way she wanted then but she guessed now that

Orion and Patrick were looking through them they shifted things about. She was frustrated at that, she had been working day in and day out and they took one morning and decided to touch everything. She began to shift through the papers with frustration as she thought about it. She then saw what she was looking for, the Isle contact. She reached for it and was excited that she found it first.

"I got it." She called out as she spun around quickly to face Patrick.

Patrick turned to meet her half way but she stumbled into him. She fell into his chest. He wrapped his arms around her to steady her. She froze slightly as she tried to shift away but fell back into him, she couldn't get her footing. Patrick laughed softly. His warm laughter rolling off his chest made Ariadne's heart flutter. She inhaled his scent as he tried to help her stand. He smelt of warm spice, it reminded her of fall. She shut her eyes enjoying his warmth, she didn't mean to but her hand slowly crept to his shirt and wrapped her fingers around it keeping him close. He glanced down at her, his hands wrapped around her waist, her fingertips brushing the skin as his shirt bunched slightly in her hand sent a shiver through him. He cleared his throat as he looked down at her, he watched her nervously bite her lip and he wanted to know at that moment what her lips felt like.

" I found it." Ariadne whispered slowly, raising her head to meet his eyes.

His eyes studied her face as his hands let go of her waist and went to her cheek. His eyes made the thoughts in her head stop for once. The nagging noise that told her she wasn't doing enough, that she was failing was gone. She instantly leaned into his hand. She wanted to be closer to him, he felt peaceful and calm but at the same time he excited her, he was different. She let go of his shirt and placed her hand on top of the hand that was on her cheek.

"Woah!" Orion said entering the room.

Patrick cleared his throat and stepped back away from Ariadne. Ariadne turned and shot her brother a glare. She ignored him as she handed Patrick the contract,

"We need to start with this one." Ariadne said, still ignoring Orion.

"We need to start with what the hell was going on." Orion said, coming around the table, his eyes threatening Patrick.

Ariadne stepped in front of Patrick and put her hand out stopping her brother. Her eyes narrowed at him as she stared at him down. Daring him to move.

"I was rushing trying to find the contract for Isles. I became frustrated and when I found it I spun and fell. Patrick caught me. Which by the way if you didn't touch all my hard work I would have found it much quicker and been less frustrated. " Ariadne said her stare as she spoke was deadly.

Orion flexed his jaw as he looked at Patrick. He threatened him once more with his eyes before stepping away. He went and leaned against the wall, his gaze still locked on Patrick. Patrick chose to ignore Orion and began reading the contract.

"Well, are you going to tell us anything that you found out while you were holding whatever meeting you forgot to tell me about?" Ariadne said still angry,

"Well for one you were drunk and then asleep so I couldn't run the plan by you and secondly it's either timmy or luke. Both are on the north star, both were supposed to be on andromeda and both were on the crown." Orion said being just as harsh as Araidne was.

Ariadne went to step towards him but Patrick caught her hand. At the sight of Patrick touching Ariadne again Orion stood up, his hand going into fist as he went to cross the kitchen. Patrick placed his hand up to Orion telling him to stop.

"Here is your error." Patrick said, pointing to a spot on the contract.

The two siblings stopped and looked at each other before going to see the spot Patrick was pointing out. Orion looked to Ariadne asking her with his eyes if she understood what exactly Patrick was pointing out. It was the last sentence of the contract saying that it would hold true and nothing would void it. She was just as confused as Orion.

"Explain." Ariadne said to Patrick.

"There's no time frame. It is just assumed by you and the trade post that the contract lasts indefinitely but there's no mention of that. It's the smallest loophole but it's one my father could use. Without saying an exact time frame the contract is up for determined by said party. Which means they can ultimately end the contract whenever they feel like it." Patrick explained.

"Holy shit." Orion said almost in shock.

"We need to begin rewriting our template and we need to get all current contracts to sign updated ones with a time frame" Ariadne said flustered as she began to move towards her fathers study.

She paused in the doorway looking back at Patrick, a small smile spread across her lips as she looked at him. Patrick felt his heart speed up slightly.

"Thank you." Ariadne said with a small nod before walking into the study.

## Chapter Fifteen

## Fall

Danica stood at the helm, her hands firmly on the wheel, the sun beginning to set. Jacob had come by several times to take over but she was still too annoyed with Kaleb to leave the wheel just yet, Jacob came by offering food and a quick break just before sunset, Danica threatened and chased him off. The sky was beautiful shades of red and orange with hints of pink streaks as she shifted her foot slightly. She felt awful but she told herself it was because she had been so annoyed today. Her headache and she felt shaky but she pushed it to the back of her mind, enjoying the sun set.

"Captain, I know it's not my place but you really should switch out. I think  you  might hold the record for staying at the helm the longest." Adam said coming up behind her with a small smile on his face, trying to keep the mood light.

"Aye I know." Danica said she couldn't be mad at Adam, he was always so genuine and never came off as fatherly or bossy like Jacob; even though Jacob just cared.

"Have you even ate or drank anything today Captain?" Adam asked, leaning against the top rail, his eyes on the sky as well.

Danica wanted to answer but she couldn't think of a time where she had actually eaten or drank. Now that he brought it up her stomach turned angrily in on itself. It was starving and it now felt like her stomach was trying to eat her back bone. The shakiness was returning as well.

She didn't say anything but sighed and waited for Adam to come to her side. He smiled politely at her as she stepped away.

"Go get something to eat Captain, I can hear your belly from here." Adam laughed as he grabbed the wheel in his hands.

Danica nodded to him as she began walking down the stairs to the lower deck. Each step she took she could feel her legs wanting to buckle. Her head began throbbing.  She grabbed a hold of the railing as she felt her legs starting to cramp. She just needs to get to the Captain's cabin, get something to eat and drink and she would be ok. She hurried down the last remaining steps and to the best of her abilities rushed across the lower deck. She stumbled and bumped into someone.

"Captain?" The familiar voice said but Danica didn't stay too long to find out who it was.

She regained herself the best she could and began climbing the steps to the upper deck. She thought she heard someone calling after her but she chose to ignore it. She could feel the sweat beading on her forehead and the shaking in her knees made her legs feel like jello. She finally made it to the top step but something was blocking them.

"Going somewhere Captain," The voice snickered as if they realized she was in trouble.

Danica squinted her eyes at the person trying to make out how it was. Her vision cleared and she saw Luke standing in front of her blocking her way. She went to order him to move but the world was starting to tunnel.

"Move." She whispered.

"Make me." Luke said leaning over to her and whispered to her.

She went to tell him to move once more but she was losing her footing. She was going to drop any minute. She felt someone push her shoulder and that's all she needed. She stumbled backwards and the lights went out.

Kaleb made it up the stairs just in time to hold his arms out and catch Danica. He wasn't sure what just happened or what was wrong with her but he felt relieved that he caught her and she didn't stumble all the way down the stairs. He looked up to the top of the stairs and seeing Luke standing there he glared at him.

"Hey don't look at me like that. I was just offering her help and she refused it before she tumbled backwards." Luke said defensively.

Kaleb shifted slightly and brought Danica closer to his chest as he adjusted holding her. He cradled his chest and finished climbing the stairs. He didn't say one word to  Luke as he passed him and headed to the cabin. Jacob was in there staring at the desk as Kaleb entered carrying Danica.

"What's going on?" Jacob said, alarmed as he dated and started walking towards them.

"I don't have the slightest idea. She was stumbling across the lower deck so I tried to see what was wrong but it was like she couldn't hear me. I followed her up the stairs and she collapsed." Kaleb said, trying to mask the concern in his voice.

Kaleb placed her on the bed and touched her forward. She was clammy, her breathing was ok, why did she pass out he thought. Jacob came over and started looking over Danica. He had watched Morgan for years help people with illness and wounds. He motioned for Kaleb to move. Kaleb shifted slightly but did not move completely from Danica.

"Stubborn ass." Jacob muttered.

Kaleb raised an eyebrow at him asking about the comment he made.

"She didn't eat or drink all day. Her body crashed." Jacob stood up frustrated.

He began to rummage around the cabin muttering to himself. Kaleb went to the door and yelled for water to drink and water to place on her head.  Kaleb waited impatiently at the  door for someone to bring him what he ordered. A small framed man rushed up the steps carrying a basin of water and a bottle in his hand. He handed both to Kaleb. Kaleb said nothing to the man but took them shut the door and quickly walked back over to Danica. He set the basin of water down on the nightstand next to the bed. He dunked a cloth he had grabbed into the water. He rang it out to put it on her forehead. Danica shifted slightly a small noise escaping her mouth. Jacob came back holding something in his hand.

"We need her to get something into her." Jacob said shortly.

Kaleb grabbed the water and handed it to Jacob. Kaleb glanced at Jacobs' hand trying to figure out what exactly he had. Jacob saw him looking and showed him an amber bottle. Honey. Kaleb understood. He saw Jacob debating with himself on how to do it. Kaleb went behind Danica and lifted her slightly.

"Hold her, I am going to sit behind her to support her sitting up, that way when you try to give her something it wont choke her." Kaleb said as he held Danica's shoulders.

Jacob took hold of Danica after placing the bottle of honey down on the nightstand. She was like Jello and was basically flopping everywhere if he so much as moved. Kaleb sat down on the bed behind her and scooted up behind her. Jacob leaned her back into Kaleb. Kaleb cradled her head, his body supporting hers. Jacob picked up the honey and glanced around.

"Put it in the water, stir it up some and then give her some." Kaleb suggested.

Jacob nodded as he grabbed the drinking water and began to mix the honey into it.  Jacob walked over to Kaleb and Danica looking at Kaleb to position Danica better before bringing the cup of water to Danica's mouth. He slowly poured some water with honey in her mouth. Her body luckily instinctively swallowed the water.

Jacob paused for a moment before giving her more. She stirred lightly, Jacob then grabbed the honey and squirted some into her mouth. She made a face but her mouth began to eat it. He then helped her chase it with some water. Kaleb watched her color start to come back to normal after several times of Jacob feeding her water and honey. The anxiety Kaleb felt was slowly going away with each small movement Danica was making. Kaleb shifted slightly and she stirred. Jacob was going to put some more water into her mouth when he hand caught Jacob's. Jacob paused for relief rushing over him.

Kaleb shifted his grip slightly on her and tightened a little bit as she began to move. She shifted her head back and moved into him more. A small groan escaped her mouth. Kaleb studied her face trying to figure out what was wrong. Her honey brown eyes fluttered open and she was staring at him. The confusion written on her face. He hadn't realized he had been holding his breath until he went to talk.

"Danica. It's ok we've got you." Kaleb said softly to her.

She squinted some more as if trying to understand what he meant. She looked over to a very relieved but annoyed Jacob. She groaned when saw him and turned her head into Kaleb's chest. She buried her face into his chest as if she was hiding from Jacob. A small smile crept across Kaleb's lips. He held his hand out for the bottle of water.

"Danica, you need to drink this." Kaleb said softly to her, holding out the bottle of water.

"I am going to go get some food for her. Try to get her to drink all of it, if not most of it." Jacob said heading to the door.

Danica brought the bottle to her lips and took a big sip. She was still a little shaky, her hand shook as she held onto the bottle. Kaleb saw and helped steady her hand. She took a long sip and then let Kaleb move the bottle.

"Danica, have you ate or drank anything today?" He asked her not sure if she was ready to have conversations yet.

She groaned and shook her head slightly no, Kaleb sighed as a response to her. She curled into him more as she was starting to feel a little bit better. Kaleb helped her drink some more water, which each sip she seemed to be getting better. Kaleb was enjoying holding her like this although he was trying to tell himself to ignore the feeling. Jacob came back with a plate of bread, cheese and salted meat. He placed it down next to them.

"Kaleb, do you have her? There's an issue on board that I need to take care of." Jacob said even more annoyed.

"Aye go, I got her." Kaleb said, leaning over and taking the plate of food.

Jacob nodded his thanks and headed out the door quickly. Kaleb glanced at the door wondering what could be happening. His focus quickly shifted back to Danica who was reaching for the bread on the plate. Kaleb smiled as she bit into the bread. Mid chew it was like she realized she was starving. She reached for the cheese and salted meat.. Kaleb laughed at her which caused her to slow down.

"Easy here, let me show you something." Kaleb laughed as he went to take the plate from her.

She looked like a wild animal as he went to take her plate, he swore she was going to growl and attack him. He couldn't help but laugh again.

"Woah I'm not going to take any of your food, just let me show you something." Kaleb said laughing.

Danica swallowed the chunk of bread she had in her mouth before letting him take the plate. She watched him crack the piece of bread in half. She raised an eyebrow at him as he did. He then took the piece of cheese and meat, placing it on the bottom bread. He then placed the remaining piece of bread on top. He then passed the plate back to her. She picked up the sandwich he made and looked at it like she had never seen one before. He laughed again and then with his hand made a motion on how to eat it.

Danica picked up the sandwich and took a bite out of it. Her eyes lit up, she enjoyed every piece of the sandwich as she chewed. She leaned back into Kaleb's chest as she finished chewing. Kaleb looked down at her as she continued to eat it. Each bite she took she felt better and better. She was completely engrossed with the sandwich, ignoring Kaleb completely. By the time she was done she felt herself again. She sighed happily as she snuggled back into him. She was doing all of this absentmindedly.

"Better?" Kaleb asked, his voice soft and tired.

"Aye thank you. The last thing I remember was trying to get to the cabin." Danica explained her voice was also sleepy.

"You didn't make it. You passed out. You need to make sure you're eating and drinking throughout the day. The sun is strong out here on the sea." Kaleb said softly, not trying to lecture her.

"Aye I know. I guess I was just so wrapped up in my thoughts. I completely forgot about anything else." Danica whispered.

Kaleb shifted slightly, adjusting himself behind and that's when it all hit her. She realized that she had curled herself into Kaleb and was nestled nicely between his legs, her back and head resting on his chest. She felt her face growing warm. She felt his hand wrapped around her waist, all too close to her bare skin. She tried to slow her breathing.

"Danica, are you ok? Your face is flushing again and you look like your breathing is off?" Kaleb said becoming concerned.

"Yes, I am fine, just. I need some more water, that's all." Danica said quickly, making up an excuse.

Kaleb nodded, handing her the remainder of the water Jacob had mixed up. She finished it quickly and handed it back to him. Part of her didn't want to leave his lap, she loved how it felt to curl into him. It felt like she was meant to be in his arms.

She scrolled herself and reminded herself of his comments earlier, trying to make herself mad. But thinking of earlier only made her think of their kiss. She could feel her face burning. She felt sparks starting to flare up on her skin wherever he was touching. She needed to escape but didn't want to.

"Dani, are you sure? Are we getting really red?" Kaleb asked shifting her slightly so he could see her face, he placed his hand on her forehead.

"You're calm. No fever but there could be one coming." Kaleb said, trying to hide the concern in his face.

"I'm ok, just tired. I think I am going to lay down. Thank you for helping me." Danica said, starting to scoot away from him.

Kaleb reluctantly let her scoot away. He watched her for a second and realized the face she was making meant she was feeling slightly nausea. He then helped her lay down and propped her up with a pillow. Kaleb tucked her in and was about to leave. The world was spinning slightly and Danica didn't want him to go.

"Kaleb, could you stay? The world is spinning and I don't want to be alone right now." Danica said slightly.

She felt the weight of the bed shift and she felt Kaleb lie down next to her. She felt so much better knowing he was going to stay.

"Thank you." She yawned her eyelids growing heavy and closing,

# Chapter Sixteen

## Mutiny

Screaming, loud angry screaming. Danica shifted in the bed. She couldn't have been asleep long. Checking her surroundings he realized that Kaleb was gone. She stood quickly heading to the cabin door. The yelling becomes louder and clearer.

"She's not fit to be captain!" An angry slur came across.

"She is Gavin and Morgan's daughter, it hers right." Jacob's voice said calmly.

"She has no fucking right being on this ship, never mind commanding it." The voice yelled back.

"Watch your fucking mouth." Kaleb snapped back, the anger and rage in his voice making him sound deadly.

"Listen boy, I'll run my sword through your gut so fast you won't even know you're dead till you're talking to the big man." The angry voice yelled back at him.

"I dare you to try." Kaleb said his voice was not even raised but sounded sinister.

Danica sighed, straightened herself out and pushed open the door of the cabin. She walked out head held high, confident in every step she took.

"That's enough of this bullshit gentlemen." Danica said, stepping out into the middle of the group of men that formed.

The men stood still not sure how to proceed with their previous conversation. Danica looked at the men. It seemed she had stepped right in the middle of the two sides. Luke of course was the angry voice challenging Kaleb and Jacob behind him a few more men stood, only a handful seem to be with Luke, the rest seem to just want to watch. Behind her stood Kaleb, Jacob, and some of the most loyal men to her family.  She crossed her arms across her chest. Her face looked displeased as she studied the men in front of her.

"Well!" She yelled at them waiting for some type of response.

Many of the men seemed to flinch as she yelled out at them. Luke didn't back down and smirked at her. She glared at him daring him to step out of line.

"Well you see…..Captain. The crew thinks you're not fit to be captain." Luke said the word captain sarcastically.

"So who would like to be captain then." Danica said a playful smile on her lips as she exaggeratedly looked at the crowd of men.

All the men seem to shuffle back and forth; looking from one to another. Not one man moving forward nor knowing how to respond.

"Anyone? Really now? All this noise and nonsense is for nothing then?" Danica said, rolling her eyes.

"Lass you really think you're fit to be Captain? You spent one day staring all day and passed out. Come on now sweetheart it's a man's job and this is a man's world. Just pass on the title and you can spend the rest of the voyage enjoying yourself." Luke said and at the last part nodded to Kaleb.

Kaleb immediately drew his blade and moved forward. Danica threw her arm out in front of Kaleb, stopping him. She smiled sweetly at Luke and then looked at Kaleb.

"Sword please." Danica said to Kaleb her voice was very sweet.

Kaleb raised an eyebrow at her but did not question her. He quickly turned his sword handle to her and let her take it. She nodded her thanks to him. She then turned her attention to Luke.

"You're lucky I am a woman. Men are rash and are all action. No thought process. No offense boys. You know if I was my father you would be drowning in your own blood right now. Your entrails scattered about the deck floor from a gaping hole in your belly.

While I order your buddies to scoop up what's left of you and toss you overboard to the fish." Danica said chillingly as she walked towards him, her sword moving as she spoke.

"Mutiny is a very serious offense." Danica whispered, placing the tip of her sword under his chin.

Luke stiffened and swallowed hard, Danica watched Luke's apple dance up and down as she burned a hole through him with her eyes.

"Sword." She yelled.

The men shuffled about her and one overly eager man ran forward handing her a sword. She gripped the sword and her current sword still under Luke's chin as he pretended that everything happening was not bothering him. Danica looked at Luke once more before stepping back. She thrust the sword into his hand and stepped away.

"If you can beat me. You can name whoever you want Captain." Danica said standing firm.

Luke grinned looking at the sword in his hand. He stepped forward a little bit as if debating which each step he took. He stopped short just in front of her. Kaleb didn't like this and had moved up to Danica's side. Jacob caught him by the collar and yanked him back.

"Show her your support. She isn't in need of rescuing." Jacob whispered to him as he pulled Kaleb back to his side.

"You can't be the serious sweetheart you want to duel?" Luke said laughing.

"Aye I am. You win, you can name whoever you want Captain. I hope you stand down and get off my ship at the next port." Danica said nonchalantly.

"All right then." Luke said with a nod.

"Agree?" Danica said, holding out her hand.

"If he so much as grazes her I am gutting him," Kaleb whispered to Jacob.

Jacob gurnted his response to Kaleb as he watched Danica and Luke shake hands. They both stepped back away from each other and it began. Luke didn't waste any time engaging in battle; he came running at Danica with a full force sword drawn. Danica stood still waiting. As he ran at her it looked like she was not even aware of it. Kaleb shifted at Jacob's side. Jacob nudged him and Kaleb ignored him shifting closer. Danica shifted slightly as Luke came towards her. She brought her blade up her center and grasped the handle     tightly.

As he approached and looked like he was going to run through her Danica stepped to the side and as he ran by she smashed the handle of her blade into his face. He dropped to the floor instantly. His nose broke, blood rushing down from his nose. He landed on the ground with a thud. He groaned rolling over to the side grabbing his nose. Danica stood off to the side waiting. Some men in the crowd cracked up laughing as Luke rolled around on the ground. Kaleb blinked and looked at Jacob; he didn't expect that. Jacob smirked as if to say I told you so.

"Give?" Danica said, waiting.

He groaned loudly and got to his knees and then slowly to his feet.  Luke's eyes filled up with rage. He wiped the blood from his nose on his forearm. He held his sword tightly in his hand and stepped towards Danica. She tightened up her stance and waited for him. Luke lunged at her, Danica swiftly blocked him. After blocking him she launched a counterattack and swung her sword hard at him. He blocked and the two proceeded to dance about the upper deck.

The crowd would shift as they went about. Luke began slashing violently at her. She had to use all her strength to block each attack, She was getting out of breath quickly from this. She went to block and failed. Luke's sword sliced her forearm. A long laceration ran diangle across her left forearm where the blade met her flesh. Her skin peeled open slightly as blood began to ooze out. She blinked, staring at it like she didn't believe it happened.

"I'm killing him." Kaleb's voice caught her ear snapping out of the trance.

"Let me go!" Kaleb said frustrated as Jacob caught him by his arm, with a nod from Jacob two other men had to help hold Kaleb back.

"Need your little boyfriend to come save you? Luke said laughing seeing the blood leaking from her arm.

"No but you might need saving soon." Danica said, adjusting herself, erasing the pain and image of her arm out of her mind.

Luke growled hoping she would just fold. He came running at her. A loud cling was heard as their blades locked and they became stuck. Luke grinned knowing that he was stronger then Danica. He pushed on his sword causing her to step back. Danica had to use both hands to help hold on to her sword. He was backing her up into a corner. His grin getting wider with each step back Danica had to take. She smiled at him as they approached the corner. He looked confused, giving Danica the split second she needed. She slipped one of her hands off of her sword handle and brought her fist back. She threw her fist through the two entwined swords and punched Luke in his broken nose.  He dropped his sword and fell to his knees. Danica shoved her sword under his chin.

"Give." Danica said firmly.

"No." Luke said, his voice cracking from being in pain.

Danica moved her sword from underneath his chin and pointed the tip of it at his nose. She applied a small amount of pressure.

"I could cut it off, that might help." Danica said, flashing a charming smile.

Luke groaned, the pain was unbearable. Blood had poured down over his mouth, down his chin, and all over his chest. It looked like someone had slit his throat, there was so much blood. His nose was now very much crushed.

"Whose Captain?" Danica asks, turning the sword slightly.

"You are." Luke groaned, wanting everything to stop so he could do something to help his nose.

Danica almost smirked as she walked by Luke, as she did she kicked the sword towards the crowd. She walked back over to the center taking her stance in front of Kaleb and Jacob. She ripped a long piece of cloth from the bottom of her shirt and wrapped it around her arm. She made sure it was tight enough to stop the bleeding. She placed her hands on her hips as she looked over at the crowd.

"Anyone else?" She asked, pointing her sword towards them.

Several men shook their heads no and they all grew quiet.

"Good! Get back to work." She yelled out so all could hear her.

The men nodded and quickly shuffled back to their stations as quickly as they could. Danica looked back at Kaleb and Jacob and her smile grew. She shrugged lightly at Kaleb who seemed to be a bit taken back.

"Underestimated me Kaleb?" Danica said with a smirk lingering on her lips.

Jacob caught Danica's eyes and with his he asked her about her arm. She shook her head lightly at him, letting him know not to ask and she was fine. She didn't want to make it seem like she needed any help right now in front of the crew. She didn't want to be seen as weak. She made herself seem like that earlier when she fell out. Jacob understood and let it go.

"Careful how you answer, son, you want to keep your nose." Jacob laughed, clapping Kaleb on the back before walking off.

"No. Well I mean I was worried for you and you did surprise me but I didn't think you would lose." Kaleb said with a small smile on his lips.

"Good answer. Get back to work." Danica said her smirk still on her lips as she threw a wink at him walking down the upper deck stairs.

Kaleb frowned and looked at her arm. He went to take a hold of it to look at it. Danica withdrew her arm, placing it behind her back. She gave him a stern look

"Back to work." She said her voice echoing her look.

Kaleb gritted his teeth as he struggled fighting with himself but he nodded. He took a step closer to her. Leaning in to whisper into her ear.

"I know right now is a big moment so I'm listening respectfully but I am going to fix your arm later." He said as he started walking away.

"Crow's nest." She yelled at his back a huge smirk and laughter in her voice as he walked away.

## Chapter Seventeen

## Kiss

Ariadne slammed the last bit of paper down. She had redone all current contracts. She was exhausted and had an awful headache. She didn't know when the last time she ate was. She heard a soft knock at the door of the office. She looked at it wondering who it could be, Orion would just walk in.

"Come in." She called to the door, she was holding her head in her hands.

The door opened slowly and Patrick popped his head in. He smiled at her as he pushed the door open the rest of the way. He then held up a plate of food and a glass to her. She smiled widely at him. Her stomach grumbled immediately seeing the plate.

"You've been here so long, I've left and came back twice. I thought you might be hungry." He smiled and brought the plate over.

"Starving, thank you so much!" She said almost excited.

Patrick set the plate down in front of her. There was chicken, small cut up potatoes and green beans. Her mouth instantly watered. She looked up at him and her eyebrows came together slightly.

"I have two questions: one did you make this and two where's yours?" Ariadne asked, picking up her fork before she asked it.

"Aye I did make it and I have a plate out there for me. Orion scoffed his down and said he had to go check something with one of the ships." He said with a shrug.

Ariadne picked up her plate and came out from behind the desk. Patrick looked at her confused as he started walking to the door.

"Well come on, you're not going to eat alone are you?" Ariadne asked, shaking her head at him with a playful smile on her lips.

"Company would be great." He smiled following her out the door and into the kitchen.

Ariadne sat down at the kitchen table, her belly grumbled again as her mouth watered at the food. Patrick sat down across from her, his smile growing hearing her stomach. As soon as he sat she picked up a fork full of potatoes, she couldn't get them into her mouth fast enough.  He laughed watching her close her eyes and chew.

"Good?" He asked, his voice still full of laughter.

"Amazing, I am so hungry." She smiled, scooping up some green beans.

"Good." Patrick smiled, taking a bite of his own food.

They ate in silence as Ariadne enjoyed the food. She then quickly realized that she had been just shoveling food in her face and the silence. She took a napkin and wiped her mouth slightly and glanced at Patrick. He didn't mind the quietness and thought her actions were cute. He liked that she was enjoying her food.

"Sorry everything tastes so good and I guess I haven't eaten since yesterday." Ariadne smiled.

She realized that they didn't have drinks and she stood to get some. Patrick stood and motioned for her to sit back down. He went to the cupboard to get glasses. He filled both cups and returned to the table placing one in front of Ariadne and the other infront of his plate.

"You know it's actually refreshing to see a woman actually act human." Patrick said with a small laugh.

"Human?" Ariadne asked him taking a sip of her drink.

"Aye, all the women my father tries to make matches with me, they are all prim and proper and god forbid they act like they are hungry or messy or have feelings." Patrick said, rolling his eyes as he thought about it.

"So I am not prim or proper?" Ariadne said a smirk playing on her lips as she baited him.

"No, that's not what I meant. I meant you don't pretend to be this mindless unrealistic person." Patrick said, fidgeting with his fork.

"We were raised to be true to ourselves. If me being myself is too much for someone then they're not right for me." Ariadne smiled.

"I like that." Patrick said simply and took a sip of his drink.

"I do too." Ariadne laughed going back to eating her food.

"So doesn't your father question about where you've been?" Ariadne asked, raising an eyebrow towards him.

"Aye and it's becoming hard to come up with excuses. I originally told him I was trying to gather intel from you. I then told him I was scooping out the ships. I even made up a mystery woman who comes from money I am trying to court. It's really starting to be a headache." Patrick said almost all in one breath as if it was something he was bottling up.

"Well they're all believable." Ariadne said with a shrug she didn't like any of those answers.

"I guess but when you're not coming back with any information or a woman on your arm it starts to seem suspicious." Patrick said, taking a bite of his food.

"I can see that." Ariadne said but she was studying him, it was hard to believe that the son of their enemy was actually helping them.

"So these other women that your father tried matching you with what he was looking for?" Ariadne asked curiously.

"Money ultimately and my mother wants cute grandkids." Patrick laughed while taking a sip.

Ariadne shrugged, she hadn't found one thing she liked about Ed Smith. Even now trying to find someone for his son, he only cared about what it would bring him.

"What about you? Any potential suitors?" Patrick asked her like he was asking something simple, like how was the weather.

Ariadne coughed on her drink as she set it down. Her hand patted her chest as she cleared her throat.

"No." Ariadne answered softly.

"So No as in none." Patrick said with a raised eyebrow.

"Aye there have been some but I wasn't interested." Ariadne said fidgeting slightly in her chair, the conversation of her future making her uncomfortable.

"That's good." Patrick said softly.

"Uh? What's good?" Ariadne asked, confused.

"No, I mean it's good that your parents don't push people on you." Patrick recovered with a smile, he was actually glad she didn't have someone actively pursuing her.

"Oh, yeah. My parents just want us to be happy and healthy with whatever we do or whomever we choose to be with." Ariadne said with a shrug.

Ariadne stretched her back moving slightly in her chair. She could feel the dull nagging headache in the base of her neck. She sighed standing, she did not need another headache. She reached up and pulled her hair out of the lower ponytail holding it. Her red hair fell down around her in waves. She groaned lightly, letting her hair down. Patrick's eyes widened as he took in the sight of her. Red soft curls fell down around her face framing it. The way the candle light about the room flicked in her eyes. She smiled at him getting up. Her eyes with her smile, her full pouty lips. He watched her walk around the table and come towards him. He shifted in his seat but then stood. She tilted her head at him as she reached him, a confused expression crossed her face. She smiled again, stepping just past him and placing her plate in the sink behind him. Patrick let out the breath he was holding in.

He wasn't sure what he had expected but that wasn't it. He smiled silly at himself shaking his head. He went to grab his plate and his hand hit something warm. He glanced down Ariadne had snuck around him and was reaching for his plate, her body just inches from his in front of him. He had reached down and accidently caught her hand.

"Sorry." He said softly but didn't let go of her hand.

"It's ok, I'm sorry I thought you were finished." Ariadne said thinking he was stopping her.

"Oh I am, I was trying to grab the plate too." Patrick said his other hand was going to the back of his neck but his left was still holding Ariadne's.

"Oh I'm sorry, go ahead." Ariadne said she could feel the warmth in her cheeks as she let go of the plate and stepped back.

She took a step back, her back pressed against the counter behind her. Patrick stood and turned, reaching into the sink behind her. Ariadne felt her cheeks flushed as she realized she was trapped between the sink and Patrick. Her stomach flipped nervously and excitedly inside her. Patrick placed his plate down and paused a second. His eyes tracing her. She inhaled, holding her breath nervously. Patrick placed his hand to the side of her cheek. The warmth radiating from his hand made her smile. His thumb traces a line of freckles running from her nose across her cheek. He instantly fell in love with their speckled trail. He leaned closer to her, Ariadne heart sped up in her chest as she nervously licked her lips. He stepped closer to her, his other hand going to her hips as his mouth came towards her. He brought his lips to hers and kissed her gently.

Fireworks went off inside of Ariadne's body. Patrick placed slow kisses over her lips and then pushed his tongue gently past her lips and found hers, Ariadne's body shivered with his touch. She followed his motions kissing him back, her hand going to his cheek as well. Patrick deepened the kiss, backing her up against the counters more. She didn't even mind the counter top digging into her lower back. She wanted more of him and she didn't want this to end. Patrick's hand circled around her waist pulling him against him. She wrapped her fingers around his pant loop keeping him close to her. His touch sent sparks of electricity through her skin.

"What the hell is going on here!" Orion bellowed, walking into the kitchen and seeing his sister tangled up in the arms of the enemy.

Ariadne didn't even hear him, her mind was putty and the only thing working was her sense of touch. Patrick pulled back quickly, his attention going to a very angry Orion standing in the doorway of the kitchen. Ariadne was confused and almost hurt as she watched Patrick back away from her.

"Are you drunk again?" Orion asked, his voice bouncing off the walls.

Drunk who the hell was yelling at her. She blinked looking at Patrick and then to where he was staring. She saw Orion standing arms crossed across his chest, feet planted, and face turning shades of red. She rolled her eyes at him, She would be embarrassed but she was now angry with him. She smiled sweetly to Patrick and then walked over to orion. She stepped towards him and her expression became even more angry. Orion was taken back by this. He unfolded his hands off his chest and looked at her confused although he was trying to keep the angry face on. Ariadne walked past him as she pinched him fiercely under his arm and motioned him to follow her. Orion blinked and followed her but not before sending another glare toward Patrick. Patrick shrugged it off and egan cleaning up.

"Ari what the hell was that?" Orion said, following her out the back door.

"That wasn't not any part of your business." Ariadne said, narrowing her eyes at him letting him know she meant it.

"He's Ed Smith's son. You can't trust him. Nevermind locking lips with him." Orion fired back just as angry.

"I understand that Ori but you understand me. I am the oldest sibling, I am in charge here and I will not have you be involved in any of my personal business. Understand." Ariadne said angrily at him.

Orion blinked, going to argue some more with her but Patrick walking out the door stopped them.

"I am going to take my leave now. I'll see you tomorrow sometime as soon as i can get away.`` Patrick smiled mostly at Ariadne.

She smiled back and nodded, stepping out of the walk way so he could go by. Orion refused to move, locking eyes on him. Patrick didn't seem frazzled or phased by Orion. Patrick nodded to him as he stepped around him. He got why he was mad but at the same time he wasn't going to crave. He didn't regret the kiss at all.

"Good night Thank you for dinner." Ariadne said to him as he walked away.

Orion watched him leave as he clenched his hands in fist by his side. His eyes went back to Ariadne glaring. Ariadne took one look at Orion and waved him off with a giant sigh before walking back into the house.

Orion followed her huffing and puffing his whole way in . He was acting very much like a child who had not been given a snack yet. Ariand turned to face him, folding her arms across her chest.

"Ariadne I just want you to be careful. We can't fully trust him yet." Orian sighed trying to explain his concern.

"Aye leave that to me. What's with the papers?" Ariadne asked, looking down at Orion's hand.

"I sent Dean and some men to visit the remaining post on the west that we can get to. I am taking these and heading east, hitting the few I can before getting to the east trading post. Although now I don't want to go." Orion said, almost pouting.

"Thank you. I will be fine here and don't worry about Patrick. When do you leave?" Ariadne asked.

"Tomorrow afternoon." Orion sighed.

"Have you packed?" Ariadne asked quietly.

"I never unpacked." Orion smiled.

"Ok well I guess you better get some sleep then." Ariadne said suddenly becoming sad, when he leaves she will be alone here.

"Why don't you come read the book mom used to every night. I miss her voice." Orion smiled at her.

Ariadne nodded and they both headed to the sitting room.

## Chapter Eighteen

### Never

Danica sighed as she walked into the captain's cabin, her arm was throbbing. She was ignoring  the pain the best she could. She walked over to the desk and sat down. She glanced down at the piece of cloth she had tied over her wound, that was once white now bright red. She sighed again, her hand was starting to ache the pain radiating down into her finger tips. She pulled open the drawer to the right of her. Reaching, she grabbed some bandages. She frowned and she needed something to clean it with. She stood going to walk to the door.

The door opened up and Kaleb walked in holding a basin of water in his hands. She frowned instantly seeing him. She went to fold her arms across her chest to emphasize how displeased she was that he was here but the pain in her arm made her wince instead.

"I thought you were manning the crow's nest." She glared at him.

"Nope, Timmy's got that. I wasn't needed.  Sit." Kaleb said firmly to her.

"Well I guess you're not needed anywhere." Danica said being stubborn still standing.

"Sit down." Kaleb said, setting the water basin on the desk and glaring at her.

Danica locked her jaw, who did he think he was just telling her what to do. He walked around the desk, his eyes locked on hers, matching her glare. Why was she being so difficult?

"You can stop the act, your arm needs to be mended. You can't do it yourself." Kaleb said, stopping inches from her.

"I can do it." Danica said almost childishly.

"Do you like your arm?" Kaleb growled at her.

"Aye do you like yours?" Danica said, stepping towards him challenging him.

Kaleb sighed and straightened his shoulders, standing up in a way to almost show her how much bigger he was than her. A small shock of surprise passed through Danica's eyes but she quickly regained herself, straightening herself up as well.

"Ok prove those idiots right. Prove to them you're incompetent." Kaleb said to her through his teeth.

"Excuse me." Danica basically yelled at him.

"You heard me. Try to mend your arm yourself. It won't get done properly, you'll get an infection, lose your arm or die. You'll really show them how independent and strong you are that way." Kaleb said, sounding like it didn't matter one way or another.

He shrugged and began to walk away from her shaking his head. Danica frowned deeply, he was right. She hadn't thought about it that way. She bit her lower lip watching his broad shoulders walk away.

"Damn it." She muttered to herself.

"Wait." She said reluctantly.

"Hmm?" Kaleb said, turning around annoyance written all over his face.

"Well." She motioned to the water basin and then her arm.

Kaleb crossed his arms across his chest facing her from across the room. They were locked in dead silence. He wasn't helping unless she asked him.  He continued to stare at her waiting.

"Seriously." Danica said to him, rolling her eyes.

He grunted and made a face at her as he turned, reaching for the door handle. He was about to walk out when he heard a huge groan come from Danica.

"Will you help me?" Danica asked through her teeth.

"Help you…." Kaleb said, turning around trying to fight off the smirk on his face.

"Help me with my arm?" Danica asked, her face drenched in confusion.

"Help you with your arm…." Kaleb said the smirk breaking through his stone face.

"What the hell are you looking for Kaleb? I asked if you could help me with my arm. Damn it. Please just come over here and help me without all the games." Danica said, flapping her arm downward.

Danica's arm bounced off her leg and pain shot up it. "God damn it!" She yelled, grabbing ahold of it and bringing it to her chest.

Kaleb instantly felt bad and walked over to her. He could see tears bubbled up in her eyes, that she was fighting back.  He slipped his hand around her shoulders and gently pulled her into his chest. She wrapped her good arm around his waist as she buried her face into his chest. She loved the way he smelled. He bent forward and kissed the top of her head.  He loved the way she seemed to fit perfectly against him. He swallowed trying to change his thoughts.

"All right love, let's look at your arm." Kaleb said, squeezing her shoulder slightly.

She sighed softly, reluctantly moving away from him and going to the chair and sitting down.

Kaleb followed behind her. Going to her side he took her arm in his hand and untied the piece of cloth she loosey managed to tie around it. He dipped the cloth he had brought into the water and ran it down the wound cleaning up the wound. Once He got the wound cleaned he looked at it. A small frown coming on his face. Danica watched him a little impressed. Not because of the way he cleaned the wound but the way he was looking at it, she knew he knew some medical stuff. She knew right away looking at it that she was going to need sutures. She was going to find a way to do it herself but now watching him she wondered if he knew how.

"What's wrong?" She asked watching him.

"The wound is deep in some spots, it's going to need to be closed." Kaleb said, his frown deepening.

"In the drawer to the right of you there is a small medical kit. In there you'll find suture and a needle. If you can do it." Danica said softly, starting to prepare herself mentally.

"How-

"My mother and Aunt knew a lot about different medical stuff due to their travels. They loved to learn so whatever they learned they taught us. I knew the wound was going to need suturing but  I was trying to figure out a way to do it myself."  Danica explained.

Kaleb nodded slightly as he searched the drawer for the medical kit she described. Once finding it, he took it out and set it out on the desk. For the first time in a long time his heart was in his stomach. He didn't want to hurt her. He knew the pain of having your skin sutured shut, although it wasn't the worst thing he's ever felt it sure wasn't pleasant.  He glanced at Danica as he opened the case. She seems to be zoning out. He got the suture needle and suture along with the tools needed to close the wound. He felt sick but shook it off. He wasn't sick at the fact of the blood or doing what needed to be done. He was sick at the thought of causing her pain. This feeling was new to him and he wasn't sure what to make of it yet.

His foot captured a nearby stool and he dragged it over to him. He sat down and looked at Danica's arm once more. He inhaled and exhaled and then looked at her.

"Ready?" He asked Danica.

"Always." Danica said her voice was mellow and calm.

He wasn't ready. He looked over the wound once more before deciding he was going to put one stitch in the widest most middle part of the wound first to help keep a center and hold the skin together as he worked. He pinched the side of her skin with the forceps and pushed the need through the skin. The

needle piercing her skin and the thickness push back
of it on the needle made him cringe. He glanced up to
study her face but there was nothing. It was like
Danica had shut everything out and she wasn't there
right now. He brought the needle and suture across
the wound and pierced the skin on the opposite side.
He pulled the suture through and grasped the end of
the thread. He then made his knot. One stitch down
he thought.  His hands were beginning to shake, get
yourself together Kaleb. He mentally yelled at himself.

He shook his thoughts out and his body lose
before moving onto the end of the wound. He began
working on it getting quicker with each stitch. His eyes
glanced at Danica as he worked trying to judge her
pain and discomfort but she remained blank and
expressionless. He worked quietly and quickly as he
could, he wanted to get done before the pain became
too much. He could feel the sweat beading across his
forehead and running down his back as he finished
the last stitch. Twelve sutures lined her arm. The long
wound came together nicely. Kaleb let out a sigh of
relief as he finished and looked at Danica. He didn't
notice but a small tear had seeped out of her eye and
ran down her cheek. It was already wiped away but
he could see the tear stain mark. How did he miss
that he thought to himself?

"All set." He said quietly, his face studying hers.

"Oh thank god that was awful. My arm is killing me, it is throbbing so bad." Danica said moving her arm towards her chest, cradling it lightly.

"I'm sorry I tried to go as quickly as I could." Kaleb said softly.

"No you did great, I don't think I would have been able to suture that fast even if I was doing it on someone else. You're very good at it." Danica said, leaning back in the chair and closing her eyes.

"It's amazing how you just seem to have left yourself. I didn't even notice you were in pain." Kaleb said, looking at her in a different light.

He knew she was stubborn, that she possessed skills most women didn't have; like sword fighting, sailing, and reading but to be able to block out pain the way she just did. Or to withstand it the way she just did was astonishing. He knew some men that would break down and cry if you so much as poked them with a needle. He watched her study his sutures once more before wincing slightly. Kaleb looked around in the drawer some more and found a bottle of rum. He looked at it and held the bottle up to her.

"Might help with the pain." Kaleb said with a shrug.

She just shook her head no. She did need something to take her mind off her arm. She went to stand and stood too quickly. She wobbled backwards. She felt Kaleb capture her waist to help steady her.

"You all right, you gotta go slow." He said softly, his breath tickled her ear and a shiver went through her, she felt flushed.

"Aye, I stood up too fast." She said, shaking her head at herself and going to step forward.

Kaleb's hand slipped away slowly from her waist, hesitating to let her go.  He watched her walk over to the book shelf and pulled out a book. He watched how her body moved, his eyes wandering over her hourglass shape, her perfect hips and bottom. He grew uncomfortable as his mind wandered to thoughts of wanting to touch her.

"We are coming up on the passage and I need to decide if we go through it or around it. It would be faster to go through it then around it but everything tells me it might be safest. My father's journal recalls a passage they went through and my uncle almost drowned. The ship almost wrecked. I just don't know, I need to get home as soon as possible." She said her eyes locked on the journal as she turned around.

Kaleb didn't realize when he had started moving to her but as she turned around his face was inches from hers. He had heard all her worries and he just wanted to make them go away.  Danica's breath caught in her throat as she looked up from the journal and found his eyes staring into hers intensely. She felt her body grow warm with anticipation.

"Kaleb." She said her voice just above a whisper.

Kaleb moved closer, his nose brushed hers as his lips met hers. She stepped into him as he kissed her; following the motion of his lips with hers. His hand wrapped around her waist pulling her closer. His other hand travelinging down to the small of her back. Danica dropped her father's journal out of her hand. The sound of it hitting the floor echoed throughout the cabin. She wanted more and all the nagging thoughts were completely gone from her mind. Danica's hand traveled to the back of his neck and wove her fingers into his hair as she kissed him back harder. The bookshelf pressed into her back but she didn't pay attention to it.  He pulled back from the kiss, placing soft kisses along her jawline down onto her neck. As his lips touched the skin of Danica's next an intense shiver went through her. Her head immediately moved to the side allowing him more access to her neck. She dropped her hand away from his hair as he placed more kisses down toward her collar bone. Her arm swung down into the book shelf and pain shot through her as her wound rubbed against the shelfs. She let out a small yell and Kaleb immediately stepped back trying to see what happened. Seeing her bring her arm towards her he reached out catching with his hand; his eyes studied it. Luckily nothing broke open.

"Are you ok?" He whispered almost as if out of breath, his other hand cupping her cheek.

The way he looked at her like she was the only thing that mattered and the concern in his eyes melted her. She smiled softly and nodded, stepping towards him. Kaleb flashed with uncertainty as he looked from her arm to her face. She put her hand to his face and pulled him closer. She placed a soft kiss on his cheek  and then one on his jaw. He frozed slightly, as she moved her mouth from his jawline to his neck.  When her lips hit his neck, shivers passed through him, she placed kisses down his neck towards his shoulder, his head tilted backwards her touch driving him crazy. Images of her mouth on more intimate places flashed through his mind. A growl escaped him as he pulled back and captured her mouth with his. His hand circled around her bracing her bottom as he scooped her up. Her legs wrapped around him as he began moving. He carried her towards the bed kissing her deeply.  Reaching the bed, he sat her down in one motion, his lips never leaving hers. He laid her back on the bed, his mouth moving from her mouth to her neck. Chills swept over her, her mind completely gone, the only thoughts racing through it was how good everything felt.

Kaleb's mouth placed a trail of kisses down her neck and to her collar bone, his hand pulled her shirt loose from her pants, with one quick motion he pulled on the shirt and the buttons came loose exposing her chest and stomach. She inhaled sharply as the rush of cold air sent goosebumps over her. She shut her eyes in anticipation. Kaleb studied her face before moving his mouth down over her chest. Danica let out a small moan as he neared her breast. His hand cupped it, squeezing it firmly as he took her nipple into his mouth. The sensation of his warm mouth over her breast was so intense she arched into him craving more. Her body was shaking from the feelings rushing through her, her toes curling into the bed as he began kissing down her stomach. Everywhere his mouth touched sent sparks of cold fire through her. She let out a small moan as his mouth ran over her pants line. His fingers found the button and quickly undid it. He lifted his mouth from her skin, hands on either side of her pants wanting to rip them off.

"Tell me to stop." He whispered his voice husky and wanting, he was tethering on the edge as well.

"No." She said fiercely to him, shaking her head as she lifted her hips.

That was all he needed, he was fighting with himself this whole time but he couldn't hold back anymore. He looked at her face that was filled with desire with  her hips  lifted and caved. He ripped her pants out from under her, taking her underwear with them. She was exposed to him completely. He hesitated looking at her, his mind screaming at him that this was her first. He could see her body responding to his touch. She let out a small groan and moved her hips slightly. The sight drove him insane.

He wanted to taste her. He began to place soft kisses on her, his tongue playfully playing over her slit. She inhaled sharply letting a small pleasure noise out of her mouth as she once again arched into him. He pushed his tongue past her slides and began playing with her bud.

"Oh my god." She whispered as the sensation overwhelmed her.

Her hand immediately found its way into his hair as if to keep him there. He began making small circles with his tongue over it, she time she tensed up and released enjoying the rush she was getting from it. His fingers found their way into her entrance, he slowly pushed one inside of her. She laid still at first getting used to the feeling. He felt her hesitation and sucked on her bud. The action sent her over the edge with pleasure. He began to slowly move his finger inside of her allowing her to get used to the feeling. She moaned, arching against him, the feeling of ecstasy coursing through her. After several minutes he knew she was ready, seeing her wet with desire. He moved away from her for a second, undoing his pants quickly discarding them. She didn't even notice he had moved from her, she was too lost in everything her body was feeling. She felt something large at the entrance of her core, her breathing quickened. She was ready but she wasn't sure what to expect. Kaleb saw her tense up, his fingertips found their way to her bud and began rubbing small circles on it.

She immediately relaxed and was lost in the sensation of it. He slowly pressed his way into her. The sharp rush of pain coursed through her but left just as quickly as it came as Kaleb made sure to tend to her. He allowed her to get used to the feeling of him before he slowly began to move. The movement hurt at first but it quickly was replaced with intense pleasure. It felt like she had been missing something and now was full. The tingles and waves of pleasure made her start moving with him. She wanted more and needed him. A pressure was building inside of her, like she had been climbing a mountain and her body was about to give out. She wrapped her legs around him, locking him into her. He could feel herself tightening around him and he throbbed with need. He could feel his release coming. A warm feeling washed over her as all of the muscles in her began to contract. She let out a moan clinging to him as a wave of intensity rushed over her. He felt her orgasm and it instantly made him release. Her body twitched in the aftermath of everything Kaleb burying his face into her neck. She relaxed, running her hand mindlessly up and down his back enjoying the euphoria of it. He rolled to the side of her pulling her into him.

"Are you ok?" He asked as he kissed her shoulder.

"Mhmm." She said, sounding tired, her finger tips running over his forearm that laid across her naked torso.

He waited a few more seconds just enjoying holding her. He went  to ask her again just to make sure but noticed that she had passed out. He smiled looking down at her beautiful face. He grabbed the blanket to the left of him and brought it over her. He stood up and quickly walked over to the cabin door. He slid the dead bolt locking it.

"Don't leave." He heard her sleepy voice say.

Kaleb smiled as he made his way back to the bed. He slid in next to her, taking her in his arms.

"Never Love." He whispered to her as she sighed happily.

## Chapter Nineteen

## Caught

"I can't do this anymore!"Patrick shouted, slamming his fist down onto the desk causing the various items on it to shake.

His father sat on the other side of the desk staring him down. He grabbed a hold of his glass of wine that was shaking tightly. He watched Patricks shoulders move up and down as he took  deep breaths trying to calm himself down. Patricks fist was still resting on the desk as he matched his father's stare. Their eyes locked burning into each other. Not one of them budging.

"What do you mean can't!" Ed shouted back at him, breaking the silence.

"This,...this whole scheme. I can't do this. It's wrong." Patrick said, throwing his arms about as he talked.

"You haven't even done anything. You haven't even given me one useful thing. You've been useless." Ed growled through gritting teeth.

"Well good because I'm done. I'm out." Patrick said, nearly knocking the chair over that as he shot up out of it.

"You're out when I say you are!" Ed yelled, standing just as hard and quick as Patrick.

"Whatever you say Father." Patrick said sarcastically walking to the study door.

"It will be whatever I say boy! Don't you dare walk away from me!" Ed yelled, slamming his fist down on the desk, knocking over the wine glass.

The sound of the glass hitting the wooden floor and shattering stopped patrick. He turned slowly to look at his father. His complexion was bright red, his hair looked like he had been thrown into a wind storm, and his fist was clutched. Patrick glanced from the disheveled man to the floor of the broken glass.

"You're wrong Father. This is wrong. And I am not having any part of it." Patrick said softly but his voice held its stance.

"Get out and don't come back." Ed said mono toned.

Patrick turned and finished his way to the door. He reached for the handle as he heard his father take a deep breath in.

"Don't come back." Ed said sharply.

Patrick gritted his teeth as he pulled open the door. He walked through it, slamming the door behind him. The sound of the door slamming echoed throughout the house. Patrick headed to the front door. Reaching the door, he felt a small fragile hand grasp his.

"Pat. He doesn't mean it. Don't go. I'll talk to him." His mothers voice said, reaching out holding him in place.

"I am just going to get some air mother. No worries. He can't chase me away." Patrick said, patting his mothers hand softly.

"Kaleb is hardly ever here. I don't want him to run you off too, my son." She said, squeezing him.

"Just some air mother. No worries." Patrick said, leaning forward and placing a kiss on his mothers forehead.

She nodded as he pulled away. Patrick smiled at her before heading out the door into the night air.


"Be safe." Ariadne said to her brother as he walked up the walkway to Andromeda.

"Always." He smiled brightly as he stepped onto the ship.

She smiled and nodded to him as he gave out orders. The walkway was quickly drawn up and the men ran about the deck to their stations. She watched Orion walk to the helm and take his post to guide the ship out of the harbor. It seemed like seconds and the ship was already heading out to sea. Ariadne stood at the dock until she could no longer see the ship in view. The dreaded feeling in the pit of her stomach, her parents were gone, Dancia was god knows where, and now her brother had left her to complete a much needed task. She was envious or jealous, she just hated being left behind. The sky was growing dark and the stars started to peak out to dance about the night sky.

A cold breeze blew in, causing herself to wrap her arms around herself.  The tremendous amount of worry she had was burning a hole in her stomach. She was afraid for Danica, distressed about the company, nervous about letting her parents down and now she was worried for Orion. She sighed heavily taking her eyes from the harbor to the sky, rubbing her arms trying to get herself warm.

"Here." A warm voice said as she was draped in a jacket.

She smiled knowing the voice and pulled the jacket around her. She turned to see Patrick joining her on the dock side.

"Thank you." She smiled at him.

"You're welcome, staying here long?" Patrick asked her, his eyes going to the harbor.

"I guess there isn't much left for me to do here. I just saw Orion out to sea." Ariadne explained to Patrick.

"You mean twenty minutes ago." Patrick said with a playful smile.

"Aye I was...thinking as well." Ariadne said her face exposing her hurt.

"Hey he's going to be ok. Everything's going to be ok." Patrick said the look on her face caused his own stomach to pinch; he didn't want to see her hurt.

"Your crystal ball tell you that?" Ariadne asked jokingly.

"Do you like tea?" Patrick asked her, his playful smile turning into a sincere one.

"Aye." Ariadne replied.

"Well let's get warm and I'll make you a cup of tea." He said, offering her his arm.

"That sounds lovely." She said, looping her arm through his.

The cold air chilled Ariadne, she shivered inside of Patrick's jacket. The weather was changing rapidly, it shouldn't be this cold, she thought rubbing her arms. Patrick noticed and cautiously put his arm around her. When Ariande didn't shake him off he scooted her closer to his body. Shielding her from the cold breeze. She snuggled into his warmth enjoying the walk.

"The stars are so much brighter down here." Patrick said, pausing , looking up at the sky.

Ariadne leaned into him looking up. "Yeah it's because the sky is more open near the water. On the ocean you are literally surrounded by thousands upon thousands of twinkling stars."

" I would love to see that." He said still captivated by the sky.

Ariande smiled at him; she had this overwhelming need to show him the night sky out in the ocean. She couldn't describe it but it excited her. She began trying to come up with some way they could sneak off in a ship and just lay out on the deck watching the night sky. The image flashed in front of her eyes. She sighed thinking how perfect it could be.

"What?" He asked, looking down at her with a chuckle in his voice.

"Nothing, I was just thinking." She smiled walking ahead of him.

He laughed a little watching him walk to her door opening it she paused in the doorway motioning for him to follow her. He didn't need to be asked twice; he was quickly by her side following into the house. Patrick stayed in the doorway as he closed the door behind him. Ariadne walked over the stove and put the kettle on. She turned to Patrick, her eyebrow raised at him.

"I know you said you would make us a cup of tea but since this is my home why don't I do it and you go light the fire in the sitting room?" Ariadne pointed in the direction of their sitting room.

Patrick nodded and headed into the sitting area quickly. Entering the sit room he looked around. He took in the sight of it, there were trinkets and pieces of different parts of the world. He walked over to a shelf, there was a vase layered with sand, each section of sand had a name of a place. Next to it was a jade statue and an elephant. He looked about the room some more. It was amazing. The whole room felt like an adventure. He had been in here before but the situation was different. His eyes landed on the fireplace. He walked over to it, seeing the stack of wood next to it he grabbed a bundle and placed it into the fireplace. He made sure the hatch was open before striking a match and setting the wood on fire.

The fireplace came to life as the flames danced. His eyes landed on a huge map of the world above the mantle. On the map was a color chart and little dots of color covering different places. He found the key and read it. Blue Danica, Red Orion, Green Mom, Yellow Dad, and orange was Ariadne. He scanned over the map and realized that each dot matched a color. It was keeping track of the places each family member visited. He frowned a little realizing that Ariadne had the least amount of dots, the thought of asking her why  passed through his mind but he wouldn't ask. He looked over at the familiar couch and walked to it. Sitting down waiting.

Within a few seconds Ariadne entered carrying a tray. The tray had two cups of tea, a kettle, and some small pastries. She set the tray down on the small coffee table in front of the couch and handed Patrick his tea.

"There is milk and sugar on the tray if you want them." She said with a smile going to sit next to him.

 She got herself settled on the couch and then reached for her tea. At the same time Patrick went to get it for her.  Their hands crashed into each other and the tea went all over Patrick's shirt. The hot water was scolding and burning his chest. Patricks pulled the shirt quickly away from his chest trying to blow on it to cool it down. Ariadne grabbed a handful of napkins and began patting his shirt. She watched his face worriedly.

"Just take it off." She said quickly, her hands going to the bottom of the shirt and starting to pull it off.

Patrick was stunned as Ariadne yanked his shirt up over his head before he could even respond. She tossed the shirt to the side of him and then she began looking at his abs and chest area. She kneeled in front of him trying to see. She didn't see any blisters, some irritation but nothing too bad. She ran her hand over his skin making sure she didn't see or feel anything out of the ordinary. Patick was stunned as he tried to block out thoughts that were creeping into his mind or how her hand felt on his skin, how she was kneeling in front of him. His senses were overbearing at the moment and he was doing everything in his power not to reach forward and snatch her closer to him. He wanted to place his lips on hers again.

She was mumbling to herself as she inspected him for wounds. Various things about the integrity of his skin and how it didn't look like any serious burns. She felt his hand wrap around to the back of her neck. He inched her closet to him. His pelvic area is very close to her. As if she just realized that she had stripped his torso naked and now she was about to have her face against his crotch if he inched any closer.

She felt a sense of embarrassment rush though mixed with excitement. He scooped her up from the ground pulling her into his laps. One arm wrapped around her pulling her close to him, her skin brushing against this bare chest, her heart pounding in her chest. His other hand slipped under her chin steadying hers. His mouth moved to claim herself and he drew her in for a deep kiss.

Ariadne wrapped her hand around the back of his neck as he kissed her. Their tongues brushed against each other sending intense chills throughout her. She wanted to feel that feeling against her skin. She followed the motion of his kiss shifting in his lap. Her bottom grazed his area as she fidgeted in his lap. He felt himself stiffen, his grip around her waist tighten and he kissed her harder. His hand ran down her back and cupped her bottom. Her body responded to him and he wanted to see what else he could do to get her to react. His mouth began to travel down her neck. She let out a shocked but good noise from her mouth. She moved against him as he did, she saw his response earlier and wanted to continue to bother him. He growled into her neck, his teeth grazing her skin in response to her wiggling against him purposely. She giggled softly with a smile across her lips as she debated wiggling again. Her body tingled for his touch.

"What in god's name is going on!" A voice bellowed out into the room.

# Chapter Twenty

## Secrets:

Patrick didn't flinch hearing the noise, he was more annoyed than anything. He eyed the man standing in the doorway. He was an older man with bronze colored hair standing in the door, his hand flinching on the sword hanging from his side. His hazel eyes burned into Patrick's. Patrick's hand shifted from Ariadne's waist to his hip where he kept his dagger.

"Can we help you?" Patrick asked through his teeth.

Ariadne hadn't even heard the shout. She seemed confused as she shifted herself to look behind her. Her face turned several shades of red as she went to move away from Patrick. Patrick held her in place, his eyes deadly locked on the man in the doorway.

"Get your hands off my niece before I remove them from your wrist." He growled as he stepped into the room as he pulled his sword.

"Uncle Jack, wait." Ariadne said removing herself from Patrick she squeezed his shoulder as she got up from him.

Patrick stood behind her judging the man Araidne called uncle. Ariadne placed a hand on her hip as her uncle drew his sword she stepped almost protectively in front of Patrick. A small smile played at Patrick's lips seeing the gesture.

"Ari you better start explaining and fast before I can't hear reason." Jack said, twitching his sword in his hand.

Patrick didn't change his stance or back down. There was a deadly staring match going on between the two of them. Ariadne tried to search for words but couldn't find any she wanted to say to her uncle. Seconds later a curly blonde headed woman popped in behind Jack. She went to put her arm around Jack's waist but stopped feeling the tension.  The woman's sky blue eyes locked with Ariadne who was pleading for help and then back to Patrick's.

"Oh goddess." She said putting a small hand over her mouth.

"Thank god you're here Auntie." Ariadne said with relief.

"Ari what was-

"I'll tell you what was going on. His hands were all over our niece." Jack said, pointing his sword at him, steam coming out of his ears.

Claire glanced at Ariadne and saw her embarrassment. Her eyes asked her if she was ok. Ariadne nodded to her.

"Auntie nothing was-

"Ariadne don't you dare say nothing was happening. You're lucky it was me and not your father because this..this...boy might not be breathing." Jack said fuming, his chest raising and falling hard.

"Jackie." Claire said her voice could calm a wild beast; she stepped to Jack and placed her hand on his forearm.

Jack's anger seems to disappear with her touch. Jack looked at her and frowned. He growled looking at Patrick. Patrick remained calm and collected like right before a storm. You could see the flicker of fight in his eyes.

"Jackie." Claire said softly again tapping his forearm.

He groaned and put his sword away. He turned and looked at her almost frustrated but he couldn't be with her. She smiled sweetly at him and he shook his head. He sighed walking past her. He kissed her forehead before walking into the kitchen.

"Now why don't you get yourself together and come join us in the kitchen." Claire said with a smile before walking after Jack with a playful smile on his lips.

Jack was pacing the kitchen and when he saw Claire enter the room he gritted his teeth. Claire went to his side and rubbed his arm softly. Jack turned, pulled her into him and melted into her.

"Can I kill him?" Jack muttered into her hair.

"Let's see what his intentions are first." Claire said with laughter in her voice.

"But it's Ari." Jack growled.

"Aye believe me I know but I remember a girl that was about her age who met a boy about his age and they lived happily ever after." Claire said with a soft smile on her face.

"Fine, Gorgeous." Jack growled, kissing her hair.

Jack settled down in a seat at the table while Claire fidgeted around in the kitchen making her and Jack something to drink. Several minutes later a still very flushed Ariadne came out with an over protective Patrick following behind her.  Jack looked Patrick up and down trying to size him up. Patrick ignores the look from Jack.

"Ariadne, why don't you introduce us to your...friend." Claire said with a sweet smile.

"Auntie Claire and Uncle Jack, this is Patrick." Ariadne said very shortly, she wasn't about to let them know he was Patrick Smith son of Ed Smith and their rival.

"Nice to meet you." Claire smiled at him.

"Pleasure is mine Ms. Claire." Patrick nodded his head respectfully to her.

Jack was grinding his teeth and didn't care to say anything to Patrick. He glanced at Ariadne.

"Where are you parents? Your Siblings?" Jack said his voice was still full of frustrations.

"Mom and Dad went off on an adventure, Dani, well she is also off on an adventure and Ori is going to fix contracts in the east." Ariadne said, trying to summarize everything.

"What in the world? What adventures are everyone on? And why is Orion needing to Fix contracts? They left you here alone? In charge of the company?" Jack said, bolting up.

Patrick stepped forward protectively and was about to open his mouth to tell Jack his place but something flashed in Ariadne's eyes, she stepped towards her uncle, her hands at her hips and power in her stance.

"I have been running this company for the last several weeks almost months while everyone is off doing whatever the hell they like. This company is still a float because of me. Because I took the responsibility. Do you think this is easy? Do you think I want to be doing this? " Ariadne said, stepping forward to the kitchen table and putting her hands on it.

Jack blinked and glanced at his wife who seemed to be wearing a proud smile on her face. Jack was confused because Ariadne had never spoken to him like that. He frowned debating on what he was going to say next but before he could open his mouth Claire stepped forward and placed her hand on his shoulder.

"Ari tell us what's been going on so we can understand." She smiled at her as she sat down at the table.

Ariadne nodded in anger as she started to shift away. She came around the table and sat across from Claire and next to Jack. Ariadne patted the seat next to her looking at Patrick. He came silently over and sat down next to her.

"Mom hadn't been on an adventure in a long time. With their anniversary coming up Dad wanted to surprise her and whisk her away on an adventure. They left to go see places she really wanted to see all along. Mom always puts the family first but we're all grown now so it is only right that she gets to. Shortly after another trade company opened up across town. I wasn't worried at first but they quickly became our competitors. They then started stealing our contracts out from under us. I tried to petition the court but they said everything was being done legally and there was nothing I could do. That's when Dani found a map in fathers study. A map to a treasure. We were losing contracts and money. We need money for a deadline that is in less than a week away. Dani had this idea about going after the treasure. I told her no, that it was foolish. She left in the middle of the night with the North Star. Patrick has been helping us. He found out how the other shipping company is stealing our contracts. We have no time frame in them. I had to rewrite all of our existing contracts. I've sent Dean to the west and Orion is heading east to ensure nothing else happens. Without Patrick we would have never been able to find out the reason we were losing them." Ariadne said, catching everyone up.

Once finished she took a deep breath in studying their faces. She felt  something warm on her thigh under the table. Patrick reached over and squeezed her leg gently letting her know she was ok and had this. She smiled and thanks to him. Claire looked over at Ari studying her, she could see how exhausted she was. This was all so much for her.

"You did wonderful Ari. I am so proud of how you've kept everything together." Claire said reaching across the table and squeezing her hand.

"Ari, I am sorry." Jack said his frown deep, as he took in everything she said.

"It's ok Uncle Jack." Ariadne smiled at him.

"Who did Dani take with her?" Claire asked, worried filled her expression.

"Jacob and Adam are with her." Ariadne said, looking at Claire.

"Thank god." Jack and Claire said at the same time.

They both cracked a smile, at one point in his life Jack couldn't stand Jacob but it was for the same reason that Jack didn't like Patrick right now. Jack rolled everything over in his head the Ariadne had said.

"Treasure….Treasure." Jack said standing, talking out loud to himself.

"Gavin what treasure didn't you go after?" Jack muttered to himself.

"Ari, do you remember how Dani found out about the treasure?" Claire asked looking from Jack to her.

"Dani found a map in a dark blue journal." Ariadne said to them.

Jack stopped like everything hit him all at once. His eyes locked with Claire and as they did it registered in her too.

"The Treasure he never got. The one Travis wanted. The one that started it all." Claire said, staring at Jack.

"Aye Dani's going to The Hollow." Jack said, his voice eerie.

"What's the hollow and why are you saying it like that?" Ariadne said, becoming worried.

"The hollow is a small island where the treasure is supposedly hidden. Gavin, your father never went after it. He met your mother going after his first mate who was trying to take the map from him-

"Aye, I am familiar with my mother and father's love story but I don't know anything about the treasure or the hollow. Is Dani in trouble?" Ariande asked, the panic in her voice starting to show through.

Patrick could feel her becoming upset and worried he wrapped his arm around her shoulder and pulled her into him. He received a glare from Jack but he completely ignored him and waited for Jack to get on with telling them about the island.

"From what I remember there are two ways to get to the island. The long way which is safest. It avoids a passage called Sailors passage; it looks to be a short cut. However once you get to the end of it, your ship bottoms out. Your ship either becomes stuck or you wreck. I've never been there and your father never went after it." Jack explained.

"Danica will choose the short cut." Ariadna said looking at Claire panic in her eyes.

"How long have they been gone?" Jack asked with urgency in his voice.

"At Least three days" Ariandne said the wheels in her head spinning on how she could save her sister.

"We need to go after her."  Patrick said, trying to hide the worry in his voice.

"Aye we do but this is a family matter and your assistance is no longer needed." Jack said, narrowing his eyes at Patrick.

"Lucky for you it is a family matter for me as well, my brothers on that ship." Patrick said anger radiating in his voice.

"Your brother?" Jack and Ariadna said at the same time.

"I will explain later, I promise, we need to get going. The longer we wait the more danger they are in." Patrick said to Ariadne.

"No, I think we need to hear this." Jack growled standing and gripping the table.

"Seriously your niece and my brother might be shipped wreck right now and you want to continue this pettiness." Patrick said, standing and starting to walk out the door.

"Where are you going?" Ariadne called after him.

"To save your sister and my brother." Patrick said.

"That's enough!" Claire's voice echoed louder than the rest of them, she was angry and tired of the bickering.

Jack seems to back down slightly at the anger rolling off his wife. He frowned standing up straight letting go of the table. Patrick stopped just in front of the door. He paused waiting. Ariadne was confused; she wanted to know exactly why Patrick's brother was on the ship but she needed to go after her sister. She paused the thought to the side dealing with the most important one; saving her sister.

"Ariadne take The Evening Star. She is quicker than any ship in that harbor and she's always ready for battle if needed. Patrick, if there is some foul play going on here I can promise I will string you up myself by your insides." Claire said looking from her niece to Patrick.

Patrick looked at this small frame woman and her size did not intimidate him, it was the way she held herself; the look in her eye. The same look each of the women in her family got when they meant business.

"Aye ma'am." Patrick said, moving away from the door.

Jack went to say something but seeing his wife's mind made up he didn't want to argue. He cleared his throat.

" We will manage the business while you're gone." Jack said, grabbing a piece of paper off the table and a pen.

"Claire, we need to give them some type of map." Jack said, holding it out to her.

"I'm not my sister but I can create something." Claire said, looking at Jack.

"You remember the way to Raven's Peak?" Jack asked her, Claire responded by nodding.

"Start with that, Gavin has to have written more down somewhere else. Travis and he was obsessed with that treasure." Jack said heading to the study.

There were too many emotions racing through Ariadne; fear, anger, distrust. She glanced at Patrick, if she opened her mouth right at the moment she didn't know what would come out. She began walking to the stairs and started to head to her room. Patrick crossed the way to the stairs, he reached out and grazed her hand with his. Ariadne stopped withdrawing her hand, her eyes searching his face. Different emotions flashed across her face. Patrick's heart tugged watching her struggle.

"I am going to pack ,if you're coming I suggest you get your things and be back within the hour or I am leaving without you." Ariadna said coldly as she turned walking up the stairs.

Patrick was taken back by the coldness in her voice. He watched her walk up the stairs until she was gone. He glanced back at the table, Claire was drawing away and he could hear from the study Jack looking through books. He went to the door and opened it.

"She cares for you. Her being silent says that. Don't you dare hurt her." Claire said not looking up from her work.

Patrick felt his stomach tighten as he walked out the door. He had to get home and back within an hour. They were not leaving without him.

## Chapter Twenty One

## The Evening Star

Ariadne pulled her closet door open fiercely, she was confused and for some reason angry. Patrick had a brother? He was on the North Star? Why? Why didn't he say anything? Her stomach twisted with doubts. She grabbed several pieces of clothing mindlessly and shoved them in a bag. She grabbed a warm jacket and stood silently in her room, her thoughts racing. What if she couldn't trust him? What if he was a spy? Her Heart sank. A noise at her door withdrew her from her thoughts. She glanced to see her aunt leaning against the doorway. Her face worried.

"Ari?" She asked quietly.

"It's nothing Auntie, just thoughts that don't need to be addressed at this very moment. We need to save Dani." Ariande said quietly walking to the doorway.

"I think he's a good man. There's something there I'm not sure what it is that he;s hiding but I feel he's a good man." Claire said, reaching out and squeezing Ariadne's hand.

Arianda squeezed back; she wanted to believe her, her heart begging for it to be true. She pushed those feelings down and grabbed a hold of her bag.

"How did Uncle Jack do? Ariande said, walking past her aunt and heading down the stairs.

"Come see." Jack said, shouting towards the stairs.

Ariadne came down the stairs and saw several books spread open. They were some of her father's oldest journals.  In the middle of all the books were a piece of paper with a stretching on it. She immediately recognized her aunt's work. The ability to read, draw and study maps seem to be a gift in her family. Ariadne went over to it. Her eyes followed the map Claire had drawn out.

"We were able to piece together your best chance. We know the way to Raven's Peak but the rest is drawn from entries in your father's journal. So you need to be cautious. " Jack said as he watched Ariadne begin studying the map.

"Jonah will be going with you. I trust him more than any man on this planet" Jack said almost like he was reassuring himself.

Ariadne didn't say much, she just nodded. She made sure the map wouldn't smudge before picking it up. Claire came over and pulled her into a big hug. Ariadne needed it more than she realized. She wrapped her arms around her aunt and squeezed her back, Claire kissed the top of her head.

"You got this Ari." Claire whispered to her.

Ariande nodded in response before stepping back. Before she could even think about starting to move to the door Jack scooped her up into another hug. She laughed out loud and hugged him back.

"You got this kiddo. We will be waiting for you here. We won't let you down here. Go save your wild child sister. The Evening Star is awaiting its Captain." Jack said to her as he reluctantly let her go.

Ariadne laughed, stepping away, trying to ignore the tugging of her heart. " I won't let you guys down either. I love you both."

"See you soon." Claire said as she moved into Jack's side.

Jack wrapped his arm around his wife and repeated what she said. " See you soon"

It was something they always said when someone was leaving. It was never goodbye, I'll see you soon. Ariande walked to the door of her home. Opening it slowly. She took a deep breath in heading out. She had never been off on her own before. She was excited, worried and nervous. She glanced back inside her home.

"I'll see you soon." Ariande said as she started to walk away.

Patrick stood at the end of the dock where the walkway from the ship met the dock. He was waiting for Ariande. He wanted to explain everything to her but he also didn't want to make things worse. On top of their siblings sailing to their doom there was also someone on the ship who was working with his father and he wasn't sure how far that person would go to help his father make sure their journey failed. He shifted uncomfortably in his stance.

He felt a set of eyes on him from behind. He glanced behind him acting as thought he didn't feel the person staring him down. His eyes scanned the ship quickly. He spotted the person, he couldn't make out anything about him. He was covered by the darkness of the sails. As if realizing he was spotted the man shrunk away from sight. Patrick frowned, searching the ship with his eyes some more. The ship was something out of a story book. He imagined pirates sailing this dark ship. The sails were haunting and the wood the ship was made out of was almost black. He had heard about a ship like this. He narrowed his brow searching his mind as to where he had.

She wasn't sure what to do, she paused watching him study the ship. Part of her was happy he came and the other part of her wished he hadn't. She wasn't sure what she was going to say to him. She decided she was going to keep quiet if she said anything to him right now she wasn't going to be able to stop herself. They didn't need that right now, they needed to get going. She walked towards the ship, her stomach in knots as she approached the walkway.

He was to focus on the ship she hoped maybe he would stay focused and she could just walk past him. She knew it sounded silly but that was her plan. Her feet hit the walk way and she felt like a little kid trying to sneak by her parents. She walked slowly past him, locking her eyes on the ship entrance.

"Ari." His voice called out to her back.

She froze hearing it, she wished she could just pretend she didn't hear him and keep walking. She felt her shoulders sag for a second in response but she straightened herself up and turned to meet him. His eyes locked into hers and they seemed almost sad.

"Patrick, we need to get going. The longer we wait the longer it will take to get to them and who knows if we will even reach them in time." Ariadne said, trying to keep herself neutral.

"I know but  we need to talk. I have to tell you something. I need to explain." Patrick said his voice boarding pleading.

"We can later. If you're coming let's go." Ariadne said, ending the discussion and continuing to walk to the ship.

Patrick frowned and followed after her. As they stepped on to the ship. Ariadne seems to transform. She looked about the ship, spotted the helm and made her way to it. As she walked onto the upper deck she looked out over the men who gathered below waiting instructions.  There were no questions asked about a female leading the ship. A man behind Ariadne stood off to the side like he was backing her up. Patrick made his way into the crowd and waited. He locked eyes with the man standing behind Ariadne, the way he was looking at Patrick was threatening. Patrick matched the stare not sure why he was looking at him like that.

"Pull up the walkway, lower the sails and way anchor. We leave now. Jonah has already passed out your orders and assignments. Get to them." Ariadne's voice called out over the crowd, she was strong, powerful, and her presence instantly demanded respect.

The men grunted with approval and dismissed to their duties. Patrick watched Ariande begin talking to the man she called Jonah. As Jonah talked to her, he felt like he was being brought up. They way Jonah's eyes kept looking at him and almost threatening him. Patrick shook his head and decided he didn't care. He began making his way to the upper deck. If this man had something to say he could say it to him. Patrick couldn't get up the stairs fast enough, he didn't know why he was suddenly  angry, he locked eyes with Jonah as he reached the top deck. Jonah shifted looking from him to Ariadne and then back to him. Ariadne had taken the wheel and had begun stirring the ship out of the harbor as she continued her conversation with Jonah. Patrick didn't hear a word of what was being exchanged as he walked up to the helm. Ariadne eyed him out of the corner of her eye unsure of what he was doing.

"Patrick?" Ariadne asked without looking at him.

"Aye, what's the plan?" Patrick asked, his eyes locking in with Jonah.

"We're rushing to save Danica and the ship." Ariadne said like he already knew and was confused about why he was asking.

Jonah remained silent, his eyes studying Patrick. They were narrowed and disapproved of him. Jonah stood with his arms crossed across his chest.

"Aye, I was asking for more details." Patrick said, trying not to sound frustrated with Ariadne.

"Who is he?" Jonah asked quietly.

"Jonah, this is Patrick. Patrick, this is Jonah, he is the first mate of the Evening Star and a good friend of my family." Ariadne said leading the introductions.

Patrick ...."Jonah said wanting more information.

"Smith. Friend of Ariadne's."Patrick answered with a sharp voice.

"Smith." Jonah said as if he may know the last name. He looked Patrick up and down before turning slightly to Ariadne.

"Friend...You trust him?' Jonah asked her as if Patrick wasn't even there.

"Of course she does." Patrick blurted out his face turning into a scowl.

"Why don't you be quiet." Jonah said through his teeth.

"Why don't you try to make me." Patrick said, matching Jonah's threatening voice.

"Why don't you string up your egos before I do it for you both." Ariadne said her voice was more threatening than either of them'.

"Aye Captain." Jonah said but still sending death stares to Patrick.

Patrick stayed silent as he matched Jonah's stares. Ariadne sighed frustrated as she tried to focus on the horizon as she made it out of the harbor. She glanced at the sails they were partially down.

"Jonah tell them to let the sails completely down. We need speed. The wind is in our favor right now. Then I need you to rest, you're taking over when I get tired." Ariadne said, giving Jonah's orders.

"Aye Captain." Jonah said with a nodded he rounded the side of the helm, as he did he walked past Patrick throwing his shoulder into him as he did,

Patrick gritted his teeth, if it wasn't for Ariadne he would have gone off. Ariadne looked at him with a small smile on her lips as she watched his muscles in his chest, shoulders, and arms flx as he resisted going after Jonah.

"So are you going to tell me the plan and what's  his problem with  me?" Patrick said with a sigh.

"We are going by a map that is drawn from a mixture of memory and details out of my father's journals. The plan is to get to the hollow before my sister and your brother are into much trouble. Which by the way you never said anything about a brother or why he is on one of my family's ships. Oh and Jonah doesn't trust you and I am not sure where I stand on that any longer." Ariadne said, once she started talking she couldn't stop. It wook everything in her power to stop saying anything when she did stop.

Patrick frowned hearing her. She watched him take his lower lip into his mouth as he was thinking. She turned her focus from him onto the horizon, her eyes drifting upwards to the sky.

"If you don't feel like explaining, I think you should go find something to make yourself useful or get some rest." Ariadne said.

Patrick inhaled, he wanted to tell her
everything. He wanted to tell her that his father had
convinced him to spy on her and her family but once
he knew her he couldn't do it. His brother didn't know
the reason why he was on the ship but it was just to
have someone on the ship. All of this was on the tip of
his tongue but he couldn't let it out. It wasn't time yet.
He sighed exhaling the breath he was holding and
turned from Ariadne and walked away.

Ariadne watched him leave the upper deck.
Her eyes followed him as he made his way down the
stairs. Her heart sank with each step he took. She
wanted to trust him, she wanted to be close to him
once more but something was off, she could feel it.
She watched him several more seconds and then
pushed him to the back of her mind. All that mattered
was saving her sister right now. She locked her eyes
on the open sea ahead.

## Chapter Twenty Two

### Shattered:

Danica shifted slightly in her bed. She stretched searching for the warmth beside her. Her hand fell on the empty spot. It was still slightly warm from him. She opened her eyes slowly, his bare back was facing her as he was sitting on the edge of the bed. He had slipped on his pants  but every muscle in his back was calling for hand to run over it. She smiled softly as she pulled the blanket around her, shifting closer to him. She reached up and slowly ran her hand down his back. He inched into her touch in response. She smiled bigger.

"I thought I was going to have to wake you." His deep voice said to her.

"How about you forget I am awake and I'll go back to sleep; then you can wake me." She said her tone insinuating something more.

He groaned softly at her comment as her fingertips still skimmed over his skin. A trail of shivers mixed with fire left behind them. He glanced back at her over his shoulder. She was absolutely beautiful. The blanket wrapped around her, her long raven hair cascading behind her in a beautiful mess. The way her eyes begged him to come to her. He inhaled trying to calm himself.

"As tempting as that sounds and believe me I am using everything I have to fight myself to not give into your offer; I believe we are almost at the passage and I think the ship needs her captain." Kaleb said, catching her hand and bringing it to his lips as he spoke.

She shivered as his lips brushed over the top of his hand as he spoke. Her mind wandered to what his mouth was doing earlier. She felt shivers run through her as her thoughts got away from her. Kaleb bringing up the passage at the last second snapped her back to reality. She frowned slightly but sat up.

"You're right, we need to get dressed and head out there." She said scooting to the edge of the bed, keeping the blanket snug around herself.

He resisted the urge to pull her into his lap as she got to the side of him. He watched her look for her clothing. He smiled softly, reaching on the floor near his feet and scooping her shirt. He held her shirt out to him. She smiled her thanks reaching for it, a smirk flashed across his lips as he playful pulled the shirt towards him just out of her reach. She laughed slightly attempting to grab it again. She missed once more and now Kaleb was dangling it on the other side of him. She frowned, making a face at him, just as he was about to give in and give it back to her, she lunged for it. She hit the side of him and tried to reach for it. He lost balance and tumbled forward taking her with him.

As he hit the ground he shifted himself scooping his arm around her waist and pulled her into him. She landed neatly on top of him. The blanket falling away from her. She squeaked trying to grab a hold of the blanket and cover herself. He smirked, grasping the blanket tightly in his hand. Her eyes widened as she wiggled on top of him trying to cover herself. At her wiggling and flapping around his buttons were being pushed and Danica didn't even recognize it. Kaleb let go of the blanket allowing her to have it. She laughed and went to say Ha! Ha! But found her lips smashed against his. The kiss was hot, wanting and full of need as his fingers around her waist pulled her harder against him. She quickly lost herself in him, her own need and want growing. She felt him against her and the excitement in her spread. He groaned against her mouth wanting to take everything much further but he forced himself to stop. They really did need to get out on deck. He pulled away from her breathlessly, placing his forehead against her.

"Captain, you really should go check on your men." He said to her, trying to slow his breathing.

A playful smile spread across her lips. "I think I am checking on one of my men just fine, here and now. Call me captain again." She giggled.

He smirked in response, kissing her silly grin. "You're going to be the death of me, I know it." He said, biting her lower lip playfully.

Her expression changed suddenly, the goofy grin replaced by a frown. Kaleb wasn't sure what happened. He looked at her confused.

"Don't say that." She said softly.

"Dani ?" He asked, running his thumb across her cheek.

"Don't talk about death while we're out in the middle of the ocean." She said firmly.

He made a face at her, he didn't take her for superstitious but then again she did have sailor blood in her and all sailors were superstitious.

"Fine I take it back, you might drive me insane though." He said with a wink to her.

"You're right though we do need to check on things." She sighed, shaking her head. She moved away from him and he let her.

He watched her scoop her shirt up and slip it over her head. His eyes couldn't help but wander over her skin and her shape. He sighed standing. She was going to make him crazy. He began searching for his shirt as Danica finished getting dressed. If he looked at her any longer he might not be able to let either one of them leave this cabin. He found his shirt and pulled it over his head. He then turned to see her fully dressed and waiting for him by the door.

"Coming?" She asked him.

He nodded, walking over to the door. She unlocked the door, opened it and stepped out into the blinding light. As she walked out the door blinded she felt something land neatly on her throat. Something cold and metal pressed against her skin.

"Don't move." Luke growled at her.

Kaleb immediately drew his sword behind Danica, He weaved it around her and pointed his blade at Luke's chest. They were then in a standoff.

"Kaleb, I don't have any orders to hurt you." Luke growled.

Danica looked out behind him, Jacob was tied to the center mass with Adam. She could see the hatch to the lower deck had been locked; shouting could be heard coming from below the deck. The lock on the door rattled. A small group of men walked about the ship, two guards on Jacob and Adam; while another was on guard at the hatch door. They had enough men to barely run the ship. Danica looked at Luke.

"I should have gutted you." She growled at him.

Luke went to press his blade into her throat more and Kaleb countered pressing his blade into his chest.

"Kaleb, stand down, I have been instructed to take control of the ship and not have any harm come to you." Luke said, annoyed.

"What?" Kaleb said, confused.

Danica narrowed her eyes at Luke confused about what he meant. She tried to see Kaleb. What was going on here?

"Explain." Kaleb growled.

"How do you not know?" Luke said the annoyance in his voice increased.

"Explain!" Kaleb said, his voice full of anger.

"Your father placed men on this ship to overthrow it and take whatever they would be earning from this voyage. He didn't know it was some kind of treasure hunt but still. My order was when we got near where we were going. To take the ship and place you in charge. He said don't be a failure." Luke said.

Kaleb almost stepped back baffled. His father, how did he even know about this. His mind flashed to

Patrick. Did he say something? Why would he? He saw Danica's body language and knew she felt betrayed. Danica's heart sank hearing Luke's statement.

"Who is his father?" Danica said, her voice shaking.

"Edward Smith." Luke said with a grin.

Hearing the name, Danica felt her chest cave. Was this all a set up? Did she fall for Kaleb as part of his plan? Her mind was rattling in her head. She felt like she couldn't breathe. She didn't even care about the blade in her throat. Kaleb was stunned hearing everything Luke said.

"Dani I-" Kaleb went to explain to the back of her head; he was watching her body movements and was panicking himself.

He saw her shift and he knew in an instant she was going to turn, blade or no blade at her neck. He panicked fearing that the blade would slit her throat. As she went to move with his free hand; he slipped it between the blade and her, grabbing it as Danica turned into him. The blade cut his palm open as he held it.

"Explain." Danica said to him her voice shaking, her eyes tearing up.

"Dani, I had no idea this was in place. I swear. Yes, Edward is my father and my brother asked me to go aboard this ship but I didn't know anything about this. I thought they just wanted me out of the way as always. Danica, believe me, I have nothing to do with this." Kaleb pleaded.

Every part of her wanted to believe him. She was shaking. She couldn't tell what was true. He sounded so desperate for her to believe him but what if this was another scheme.

"Ed Smith is your father." was all she could say.

"Aye." Kaleb said his voice was defeated, his eyes begging her to believe him.

"Ok enough of this." Luke growled, he pulled his blade from Kaleb's hand, more blood poured out from Kaleb's palm; he didn't even act like he felt it.

Luke with his free hand grabbed a hold of Danica's hair. Luke had completely forgotten Kaleb's blade was still pointing at his chest. Danica let out a small yell as Luke pulled her back towards him by her hair. Kaleb let out a growl and shoved his blade forward. His blade plunged deep into Luke's chest. As it did it grazed Danica's arm. Luke let Danica go and she shockingly stepped aside to watch Luke begin to spit blood from his mouth.

"What?" Luke said blood poured down his chin as he tried to understand what happened.

Kaleb pulled his sword out of his chest and Luke fell to his knees. He let out a deep gasping breath and fell forward onto his face. Kaleb stepped over him and to Danica. Dropping his sword as he did. His hand went to her cheek. She looked down at the bloody scene in front of her trying to comprehend everything that just took place.

"Are you ok?" He asked, trying to get her to look at him.

"I...I.." Danica was stammering trying to process.

"Danica look at me." Kaleb ordered her.

Her eyes shot up and locked with his. His thumb stroked her cheek, his eyes searching hers.

"Aye, I'm fine." Danica said, shifting slightly.

Part of her was yelling at her to pull away from him, the other part of her wanted to curl into his arms. Her mind had no clue which was right. She looked at him trying to tell. His eyes left hers and went to look at the small cut on her outer upper arm. She watched as he looked relieved. Why would he care? She thought and a nagging voice in her mind was telling her that he would only care if what he said earlier was true. She watched him step around her and over Luke's dead body. He walked out onto the upper deck. The men below stopped and acted like they were awaiting orders. He was tense with anger. She stepped over Luke and walked out on to the upper deck hanging back watching him.

"Release them!" He yelled out the anger in his voice making hairs stand on end.

The men didn't even question the order due to the rage in his voice. Danica watched as the man guarding Jacob and Adam cut the ropes free. The man guarding the hatch unlocked it. The door to the hull flung open and her men began to climb out. Jacob and Adam were away from the mass looking like they were ready for anything. As Danica's men flooded the lower deck the small crew of Luke's men were pushed back towards the outer rail. They looked up to the upper deck looking for Danica. She wasn't sure what to do, traitors are traitors.

"Overboard." Kaleb shouted.

Without even thinking, several of Danica's men tossed the remaining men of Luke's into the sea.  The shouting of the men left in the ocean was all that could be heard. The silence on the ship was deafening.  Adam quickly rushed up to the helm taking over steering of the ship. All eyes fell on Danica and Kaleb. Kaleb looked at Danica and walked to her. She studied him, not sure what to say or do. He was now completely alone, he had just ordered the demise to his fathers plans. He walked over to her, closing the distance between them. He went to reach out and touch her but hesitated not sure where her mind was at.

"Danica, I swear on everything that I had no part in this and my loyalty lies with you." Kaleb said.

"Kaleb I-

"Captain, I need orders, we are approaching the passage." Jacob said, breaking the moment.

"Aye to the passage, have someone come clean this mess up." Danica said regaining herself.

"And Kaleb Smith?" Jacob said, nearly snarling his last name.

"I. I. Have Mr. Smith place in the first mate's cabin for now." Danica said, tearing her eyes from Kaleb.

Kaleb inhaled, his stomach knotted and he resisted the urge to try to explain himself. He said all he could say. Jacob nodded for him to begin moving. Kaleb didn't say anything else to Danica and began making his way down the steps. Jacob yelled to men on his way down to come up and dispose of Luke's body. He then shouted to Adam that the passage was a go. Danica stood in the center of the upper deck watching Jacob escort Kaleb to the first mate cabin. Her body is still involuntary shaking off and on. She wanted to believe him, she needed to think.

## Chapter Twenty Three

## Full Circle

Ariande's grabbed the wheel as she watched the horizon.She had steered most of the evening and into the morning. She rolled her head back and forth trying to get the crank in her neck out. She stood on her tippy toes stretching her calves. God she was tired. She felt like everything on her was drooping. She wanted to sink into the floor and curl up. They were making great time and the longer she kept a hold of the wheel, the longer she felt like she was making progress to get to Dani. The longer she held on meant that she was being useful, she was saving someone else time so when they switched they could press on. That way there was never a moment when someone would struggle to steer. Steering was the hardest and most tedious part of the ship.

The sun was peeking out over the ocean as it started to raise. She could see a large dark peak coming into view. This must be Raven's peak she thought to herself seeing it. It stood tall and was jet black. It would have been almost impossible to see if it wasn't for the sunlight.The peak reached out into the sky and towered over the ocean. A large yawn escaped her mouth and she heard the cabin door behind her open. Jonah stepped out onto the upper deck. He looked at Ariadne with a frown on his face as he began walking to her. He was up all night reading the very beginning journals of Gavin's try to get a better understanding of everything. He watched Ariande sway, his frown deeping he could tell she was exhausted. He started making his way towards her to relieve her. He saw Patrick starting to approach her, her gritted teeth looking at him. He didn't trust him and there was something with his name Patrick Smith he knew the last name but from where and why? He thought. Jonah ducked back inside the cabin and remembered something from Gavin's journal.

"You ok?" Patrick asked a very sleepy Ariadne.

She was too tired to be mad at him, she didn't have the energy to go round with him right now.

"Aye I am but see there. That's Raven's Peak.Once we pass that we have a pieced together map. Everything else after that point is from rumors and my father's mind." Ariadne said, yawning once more.

"Well let's hope that's good enough." Patrick said quietly.

"It will be." Ariadne said look at him from the corner of her eye.

Patrick didn't say anything in response, he just looked forward to watching the peak come closer. He glanced at her watching her. He watched her body sway slightly. He could see her eyelids getting heavy and her head nodded slightly. He reached out, placing his hand on the small of her back to steady her. She instantly stood straight and backed away from his touch.

"Sorry you need to switch out with someone.You're nodding out." He said softly, withdrawing his hand.

'Why is your brother on The North Star?" Ariadne asked, ignoring his statement, the anger in her waking her up.

"You should get some sleep and we can talk about it later." Patrick said softly, his voice still caring.

"How about you quit avoiding what I am asking before I have you locked up, we're on the ocean now what I say is law, my ship." Ariadne said, her head snapping to him.

Patrick gritted his teeth. " You won't understand."

"Well I don't now; so I guess you might as well try." Ariadne said, her face flushing red.

"Fine, originally and I repeat originally I began coming around because my father asked me to get information from you.-

"You bastard." Ariadne said, cutting him off.

"Let me finish." Patrick said, voice pleading.

Ariadne studied his face searching his eyes. Something in them tugged at her heart and the anger chipped away a little. She nodded her head letting him know to finish explaining before looking forward.

"I was supposed to gain your trust and report back with findings and inside details. Kaleb, my brother has no idea why he's on the ship. I am not sure why either but I was asked to convince him to go." Patrick said watching Ariadne's body stiffen.

"So are you here now because of your father?" Ariadne asked growling.

"No, I actually never provided him anything and started giving you information to help. That wasn't part of his plan. Once I met you and began knowing you I couldn't. I truly care for you Ari. I mean that with every ounce of me. As far as me being here, it's for Kaleb and because of ...you." Patrick said hoping she wouldn't hate him.

Ariadne was silent as she took everything in. She glanced at him, she understood the pressure of doing everything your family wanted you to do. She understood caving and doing things and missing out on things because of the responsibility. She inhaled watching the ocean tops speckle with gold sunlight.

"Ari, I understand if you can't trust me. All I am asking is to think about it. Why would I come with you now? Outnumber myself and be completely vulnerable. If I didn't mean anything I said. Why wouldn't I just lie." Patrick said stepping closer to her, he wanted to reach out and touch her but held back.

"I don't know Patrick, i cant trust you right now-

"You sure the hell can't!" Jonah yelled, stepping out of the first mate cabin.

Patrick tensed up hearing his voice and turned to see why the hell he was interrupting them. Jonah stormed over to them a journal tucked under his arm. Ariadne looked confused to Jonah. As he approached.

"Jonah explained." She said becoming now annoyed with the fact she was steering and couldn't give her full attention to anything.

"Do you know who he is?" Jonah said angrily.

Ariande sighed he must have overheard their conversation. " Aye he's Ed Smith's son. Our competition and lovely enemy. I know this already Jonah."

"No he's more than that." Jonah said, flipping a few pages into a very old journal.

"Patrick, do you know a Travis Smith?" Jonah asked, eyeing him.

Patrick stepped back confused. " He was my uncle, my father's brother. I barely knew him. He did a lot with ships and died in a shipping accident. What does that have to do with anything?" Patrick said his tone was very confused as he explained.

"Travis as in my Father's first mate Travis?" Ariadne asked Jonah.

"Aye, the very Travis that tried to kill your father and your mother. Died in a shipping accident, Gavin killed Travis." Jonah said, looking from Ariadne to Patrick.

Ariadne studied Patricks confused but shocked face. If he knew anything about it he was a very good actor. He took the information in and then looked to Ariadne. Jonah on the other hand looked like he was ready to kill Patrick right then and there.

"It actually explains a lot. I  have never seen my father so intent on destroying something as much as he is your company." Patrick said as if he was still piecing things together.

"So you had no idea. Just some innocent peon in this whole mess; following orders. You expect us to believe that?" Jonah said angrily, stepping towards him.

Patrick squared off ready for whatever Jonah was going to throw at him. He had about enough of this guy and his moods.

"Jonah, I need you to steer." Ariadne ordered cutting the tension in the air as she spoke.

Jonah stopped mid step on his way to face Patrick he blinked looking at Ariadne, who held one hand on the wheel and the other she let go for him to come take hold of the wheel. She looked at him waiting. He inhaled, changing his expression and stepped into the wheel grasping it with his hand and then the other as Ariande let go. She ran her hands over her face as she stepped away. She was exhausted and this was a lot to process. The two men sensing this didn't offer to talk.

"So you're telling me that you're the nephew of the man that tried to kill my father, your father is the brother of that man which my father killed, and that was all over a treasure map. The same treasure that Dani and your brother are sailing to their doom to get." Ariadne said out loud running her hand through her hair.

"Well isn't this some full circle bull shit." She muttered angrily as she began pacing.

Patrick glanced at Jonah and they exchanged a look of not knowing what to say or do at this point. Ariadne paced around some more like a trapped tiger. The two men kept exchanging looks, not sure how to help this situation. Patrick was about to say something when Ariadne stopped short in the middle of her pacing. She turned quickly looking at both of them.

"Patrick, you genuinely sound like you didn't know anything about this. I want to trust and I want to believe that you care for me but at this point it's too much. " Airande started and Jonah began to smirk.

"Jonah, you are not to harm him." Ariadne said, catching the smirk which quickly faded as she spoke.

"Right now all i can do is hope that what you say is true and give you enough rope to hang yourself if it isnt." Ariadne said almost as if she was talking to herself.

"Jonah, Patrick is your new best friend. Wherever he goes you go. I can't deal with anymore of this nonsense. So Patrick have a seat while Jonah steers. The minute I think something is up Patrick there will be one more less Smith in the world and you can meet the uncle you never got to." Ariadne said not letting one of them protest because at the end of her speech she turned on her heels and walked down the deck stairs.

Patrick blinked several times, she had just threatened his life in more than one way. That he didn't matter, that didn't hurt. What hurt was her saying she didn't think he cared about her. It felt like a hole was burning in his chest.

"Have a seat Buddy, you're gonna be up here for the next several hours." Jonah said with a sneer in his voice.

Patrick didn't say anything but sunk to the ground, his head resting against the upper deck railing. He wanted to go after her, he could hear her footsteps climbing the opposite deck stairs as she made her way to the captain's cabin. He was counting them as he tried to stop himself. He wanted to chase after to convince her that he did care, that he meant what he said. He knew she needed time and she needed space. He tapped his head back against the vertical rails, ignoring his urges. He heard the captain's cabin door slam and it felt like she had just closed him out. He felt his stomach twist as he clenched his jaw.

## Chapter Twenty Four

## Adventure

Dancia had to remove herself, she was shaking. She could feel the tears begging to slip out from her eyes. She shut the door pushing Luke's body from the doorway as she did. The blood had seeped into the captain's cabin but she didn't care. She stepped away from the door going to the desk and bracing herself with it. She turned facing the door and sank to the floor leaning back into the desk. Was everything a lie? She felt a warm tear slid down her cheek. She took long slow breaths in through her nose and then blew them out of her mouth. She needed to collect her thoughts. Kaleb looked genuinely surprised about Luke's plan. But that bastard is his father. She thought to herself  letting another long breath out through her mouth.

Why would he kill Luke? Why wouldn't he just take over? He just surrendered and doomed all of his men? She thought. She ran her hand over the back of her neck thinking. This was all too much; this was supposed to be a simple save the day mission. Take the ship, get the treasure, save mom and dad's company. Not steal the ship, get attacked by killer birds, have a mutiny,and fall in love with the enemy's son...fall in love... no! She yelled at herself. She cant and she wont. She needed a distraction.  She looked across the room staring at the bed. An image of herself tangled up with Kaleb flashed through her mind. Nope she couldn't stay in here. She got to her feet and shook her arms. Trying to get the feeling she had nagging pulling in her chest out. She took a deep breath in and headed to the door. They were close to the passage she needed to be out there.

She opened the door to find men scooping up Luke's body and hauling it off over the railing. The splash of the body hitting the sea seemed to echo. She walked out onto the deck ignoring the feeling the sound gave her. She felt like it was a foresight of this whole voyage. She wasn't going to let it get in her way. She began walking down the steps to the lower deck. The cold air hitting her face made her feel slightly better. She reached the other steps and quickly climbed them. Adam was steering and she could see how tired he was from where she was. He needed a break and she needed a distraction. This was perfect timing. She walked over to Adam and placed a hand on his shoulder squeezing it lightly.

"Care if I take over?" She asked with a soft smile.

"Are you sure you want to Captain? I know it's been a rough moment here. I can hang on a little longer." He smiled back at her.

"I am fine. You got to get some rest." She motioned for him to pass the wheel to her.

"If you say so Captain." Adam said, moving slightly so Danica could take over.

She nodded her thanks and stepped up to the wheel. Grasping the wood in her hands she felt instantly calm. She looked ahead at the horizon and saw the entrance to the passage. It didn't look threatening. It was a shortcut and they were taking it. She needed to get off this ship and back home as soon as possible. She pointed the bow at the entrance way and the ship leaned towards the passage.

Kaleb walked into the cabin not fighting Jacob at all. His mind racing to find something to do or say to make this right. He needed Danica to know he had no part in this. He began pacing around the cabin ignoring Jacob. Jacob stood back and studied him. He wasn't sure what to make of Kaleb. He was quick to defend Danica at every moment. He was quick to show he cared for her. Was he this good of an actor? Jacob thought watching him pace around the desk.

"Kaleb, do you honestly care for Danica?"Jacob asked quietly as he studied every movement of Kalebs.

"Aye. I swear I knew nothing about this." Kaleb said, stopping in his tracks.

Jacob was quiet for several minutes. Kaleb stood staring at him but after a few minutes he gave up and went back to pacing. Jacob watched him some more before heading to the door.

"Give her some time." Jacob said before walking out of the door.

Kaleb threw his hands up at Jacob as if to say really but Jacob's back was facing Kaleb. Jacob walked out the door. He growled, sinking into the desk. He placed his elbows on the desk, planting his face in them. Time....that's all he had right now.

Jacob walked out of the first mate's cabin and saw Danica holding the wheel. Her raven hair was down and blowing in the breeze behind her. He looked out to see where her eyes were focused, they were feet away from the entrance of Sailors Passage. Something told Jacob this wasn't the best move. He walked over to Danica standing beside her.

"Are you sure this is the way we should take?" He asked her his voice light showing he wasn't disrespecting or not trusting her.

"Aye, look it's not dark gloomy or stands out as a bad idea. Bonus points for it being faster as well." Danica said not looking at Jacob as she answered.

"Ok."Jacob said softly.

He stood silently by her as the front of the ship passed into the passage. The tension you could cut with  a knife. It was making Danica question her decision. As the rest of the ship passed through the entrance it was like the ship breathed a sigh of relief nothing happened. Jacob seems to easyup a little bit but not much. Danica didn't say anything and continued to guide the ship.

"I am going to check the cannons and the rest of the ship just in case anything turns up." Jacob said, making his way down the stairs.

Danica had just nodded her response as she studied the passage.It had cliffs on either side. So far everything looked normal. She remembered something her aunt told her about traveling closely to land. If the ocean began to pool it could be shallow. She needed someone to be watching the sides of the ship. She spotted Jacob still on the lower deck.

"Jacob!" She yelled down to him.

"Aye Captain?" He answered her.

" I need three men to watch the sides and front of the ship. Place a man on either side and then one of the front. I need them to watch for pooling of water. That way we don't hit any shallow part of the passage."Danica yelled down to him.

Jacob nodded his response and called to the men, he handed out the instructions and watched three men split up taking their orders to watch the ocean. Jacob then ducked down into the hull of the ship. Danica felt a little better now with eyes one the ocean around the ship.Being this close to the cliffs made her a little uneasy. She looked forward hoping that soon the exit to the passage would come into view soon.

Kaleb couldn't take sitting in the cabin any longer and he was becoming restless.He understood he was on house arrest but now he didn't care. He took a deep breath and decided in the worst case scenario he would just be thrown back into the cabin anyways. He walked to the door opening it and paused in the doorway. His eyes looked out over the deck, they had made into the passage. The ship was silent as all the sailors stood on end. His eyes found his way to her. She was standing resilient at the wheel. Her back was perfectly straight with her hair falling down around her. He could see the tension in her but she wore it beautifully. He gritted his teeth and walked to her side. She glanced at him but didn't say anything. They stood in silence for several seconds.

"You're supposed to be in the cabin." Danica said sharply.

"Yeah well lots of things are supposed to be that aren't."Kaleb said, shrugging his shoulders.

"Like?" Danica asked, annoyed.

"Like I wasn't supposed to be on this ship. I would have gotten into another fight with my father and then taken off doing odd jobs along the way to make my way to India. I really wanted to see India." Kaleb said with a shrug.

"Ok." Danica said confused at where he was going with this.

Silence happened again, it wasn't the awkward silence, it was the kind of silence that was comforting. Like when you had known someone for so long and them just being by you were ok. It was strange because Danica didn't know Kaleb like that but she felt it.

"So why India?" Danica asked, her eyes shifting silently to see him.

"It's one of the few places I have been. I read about the Sun Temple Konark and I thought I needed to see it. I guess that's what I want out of life. I want to see things, go places, and just live." Kaleb said, shifting his stance slightly angling his body towards hers.

She smiled softly, she loved the way he spoke about life. About things he cared for. She looked forward to the passage going smoothly, she breathed a little easier. She wasn't sure if it was because Kaleb was making her feel calm or if she was starting to believe what she told Jacob and that everything was going to be ok.

"So do you regret it?" Danica asked, her eyes still on the horizon.

"Regret?" Kaleb asked.

"You're frustrating when you want things spelled out for you. Do you regret coming onto this ship?" Danica said the frustration rolling off of her.

Kaleb smirked a little and stepped up behind her. He watched her take a deep breath in as she tried to pretend she didn't feel him. He stepped close enough that his body was barely touching hers. If he let out the smallest breath it would brush her skin. He angled his mouth by her ear. He could see the goosebumps run up her neck as he did. He watched her swallow hard as she tried to focus  on anything but him. He licked his lips and leaned close to her ear.

"No." He whispered to her.

Chills rushed through her as she fought herself not to lean back into him. Her stomach flipped excitedly inside of her as the need to be as close as possible to him grew.

"But what about your grand adventures, now you're my prisoner." Danica said a playful smile on her face, as she tried to take control of what was going on.

"Prisoner...So you want me all to yourself then." He smirked, running his finger down the side of her neck as he spoke into her ear.

"I never said that." Danica said a little breathy but not moving away from his touch.

"But you didn't not say it Love." Kaleb said not being able to help himself anymore, his hand snuck around her waist and he stepped into her.

Danica shut her eyes trying to stop her mind from letting itself go and giving into her body wants. She cleared her throat and shifted slightly away from him. She heard him grunt in disapproval.

"But I didn't say it ethier….Love" Danica said back to him.

She felt Kaleb shift slightly and it was almost like she could feel his sadness even though he was hiding it. She had hurt him slightly with what she said. She instantly felt regret.  She felt him step back away from her and her heart sank a little. She didn't say it but she wanted to say it.

"Kaleb."She said quietly but it was more of a plea.

"Danica, I promise I didn't have anything to do with what happened. I run away from my family every chance I get. And as far as regret and India."He paused and stepped towards her; she kept her eyes forward, afraid to look at him.

"The only thing I regret is not stopping my father's plan sooner. And as far as India goes...sometimes the greatest adventures life has for us is not in far off places but your greatest adventures can be someone." Kaleb said softly, reaching out and touching her cheek gently.

He took a step back and let his hand fall away as he walked over to the upper deck railing, not sure what to say or do from here.

## Chapter Twenty Five

## From The Deep

Danica watched the passing rocks of the cliff side, her body completely still. She kept trying to keep her mind focused on the passage but her eyes kept flickering to a very quiet Kaleb. She frowned slightly watching him. He hadn't said anything else to her since. The silence was no longer comforting and she felt her heart tugging at her to say something; anything to him. She for some reason deep down believed him.

Kaleb rested his arm on the upper deck looking forward. He was trying to focus on anything but the need to turn around and go to Danica. He searched the sky and then the rock walls. He narrowed his eyes. There was a crack in the continuous wall of rock. He squinted it wasn't odd for walls of cliff to shift and separate but something about this crack caught his attention. As the ship sailed past it he looked into the crack, it was deep dark, and gave his stomach an uneasy feeling. It was some type of hollow cave. He made a small face searching it with his eyes.

Danica was watching Kaleb's back, she tried to look at the horizon, focus on what was in front of her and guide the ship through the passage but she couldn't help herself. Her eyes traveled across his strong broad shoulders and then down over his back. Everything in her was begging her to talk to him.

"Kaleb." Danica said to him, giving into herself.

He was so lost looking in the cave that he didn't hear her. The split in the rock wall extended deep into the ocean. He wondered if the water had just eaten away at the inside of the passage or if something had made it. The way the darkness inside of the cave called to the ship as it passed made him nervous.

"Kaleb?" Danica asked this time louder, wondering what he was looking at.

Her eyes shifted to where he was looking and saw the large crack they had passed. It was dark and deep. She looked back to Kaleb who seemed to be thinking still. She was becoming a little annoyed. If he was ignoring her on purpose she was going to be very angry at him.

"Kaleb!" She said louder and a little angry.

Kaleb's head shot up hearing his voice, it then registered that Danica had called him. He turned to face her and that's when he saw it. A look of shock and then determination crossed Kaleb's face. His hand went to his waist grasping the handle of his sword quickly. He pulled his sword out of its holder slowly,  his eyes locked on something behind Danica.

She was confused and almost went to step back as she looked at him.

"Kaleb! What the hell?" Danica yelled at him as she saw him withdraw his sword and slowly start walking towards her.

Kaleb put his hand up as if to say stop and then put his finger to his lip as he walked towards her, Danica began to shift away from him still holding on to the wheel. She went to look for help in case Kaleb had lost it and that's when she saw it. Long black tentacles were wrapping up the side of the ship. The men below started to realize it and they seem to stop in their tracks not knowing what to do. The tentacles were wrapping around one of the masses now. The creature was acting like it was invisible creeping onto the ship. Danica held her hand up to Kaleb who looked at her confused. They could use this to their advantage. She felt like if they attacked right at the moment; then all hell would break loose. If they could somehow attack it all at once then she felt like there would be less damage and less casualties.

Danica looked down to the crew who were staring up to her waiting orders. She put her hand up in the air to let them know to hold their positions. They looked warily to her and then the tentacles invading the ship.

Jacob came up from the hull and stood in shock. His eyes quickly shot up to Danica. She put her hand up to tell him to wait. She then motioned for him to go back down into the hull and mouthed the word cannons to him. He nodded quickly, understanding. He stepped close to her so they could speak. He needed to know what she was thinking. He leaned into her so she would whisper to him.

"Kaleb, can you get to the lower deck and have the men ready to attack when the cannons go off?" Danica whispered to him.

"I'm not leaving you." Kaleb whispered back, his eyes locked on the tentacle that was slowly wrapping its way around the upper deck.

"I need you to do this, I will be fine. We need to survive this and I need you to do this." Danica whispered urgently.

Kaleb frowned but nodded. Danica felt relieved. "Once you get the men set up, have Jacob fire the cannons."

Kaleb nodded and looked down to the lower deck. He could make it in a matter of time but he needed to be quiet. He turned to leave but before he stepped into Danica his arm swiftly snuck around her waist as he pulled her slightly into him. He kissed the top of her forward head. Danica's racing heart sped up as his warm lips touched her skin. The butterflies fluttered around her stomach and she didn't care that the tentacle was only several feet from her. Kaleb stepped away from her. His worried face looked from her and to the tentacle. He inhaled slightly as he fought himself to not  stay with her.  He placed his sword in her hand before turning to leave.

She watched Kaleb creep down the stairs slowly, she was holding her breath. She could hear the tentacle to the right of her slithering over the rail. As it moved its suction cups made small popping noises as it detached itself from the ship. She looked at it, it's dark purple in color tentacles unwrapping from the rail slowly as if searching for something. She could see the large suction hooks that layered the tentacle. It began to change slightly in color turning a deep brown as if it was trying to match the ship. She watched as it began slithering towards her. She moved to the furthest point of the wheel, trying to be as quiet as possible.

Kaleb made it to the lower deck where the crew had gathered. He caught all of their eyes with his and pointed to the far corner to spears. The men near them nodded and they quietly began passing them out. The men on board with swords slowly pulled them out and the ones without took up the spears. Kaleb glanced up to the upper deck watching Danica dance away from the tentacle while still holding on  to the wheel. Kaleb needed to act quickly. He held up his fingers to the men who were armed and ready. He began counting down from five Danica struggled to keep her  distance from the tentacle. She froze as she felt the bumpy suction cups of the tentacle wrap around her leg. She bit hard down on her lower lip trying to contain the scream she had bursting in her chest. Her leg felt like it was on fire as the hooks of the tentacles crawled its way around her calf. She felt her stomach knot and her eyes met Kalebs as he dropped his last finger and stomped on the floor of the lower deck.

As Kaleb's foot hit the deck floor an instant later cannon fire erupted from the ship. The tentacles retracted but as they tried to escape the men on board began stabbing and slashing them; hoping there would only be one attack. If they could eliminate the threat now. A tentacle flopped onto the deck floor dislocated from its body. It flopped around blood spraying from it. Another tentacle was stabbed by two men with spears locking it to the deck floor. Two other men were chopping away at the stuck tentacle. The tentacle fought hard but soon it suffered the same fate as the previous tentacle. A third tentacle becoming angry began to slap the ship making it rock.

A small scream caught Kaleb's ear and he could feel the acid in his stomach  bubble as He glanced to the upper deck. Danica was being dragged by the tentacle to the railings, to the sea.

At first she held on tight to the wheel but as it started to pull her away from the helm, she watched as the wheel began to turn. She could see the ship starting to shift in its path. She inhaled deeply. The only thing keeping her to the ship was the wheel but if she held on they would all be doomed. The ship would crash into the wall of the cliffs.

She shut her eyes and let go. She let out a loud scream as her body hit the upper deck floor. She tried grabbing on to anything and everything as the tentacle pulled her to the rail. Her nails dug into the hardwood floor of the deck splintering under her fingernails. Her fingernails cracked as she tried to hang on. The rail is getting closer and closer.  She felt her legs go up over the rail and her stomach slam into it. The impact knocked the wind out of her. She wrapped her arms around the upper deck rail hanging on for dear life as she tried hard to get air back into her lungs.

Kaleb saw her in danger and rushed to the upper deck. He dodged in out of the crowd of men who were taking on another tentacle. They had it cornered and it was going in their favor. Kaleb took two steps at a time trying to get to the upper deck as fast as he could. His feet hit the upper deck and his sword was already ready. He rushed to Danica whose arms looked like they were going to give out any moment. The tentacle moving up her leg and trying to wrap around her waist. Kaleb crashed into the upper rail, he stepped up onto the rungs leaning over the rail wrapping one of her arms around Danica's torso trying to keep her with him.

"Kaleb I can't hang on!" Danica said panic and pain in her voice.

"Don't you dare let go." Kaleb yelled at her.

He tried to study her to see where he could hit the tentacle and not get her. It was getting hard to make out where the difference was.

"Kaleb." Danica said as one of her fingers began to slip off.

Kaleb gritted his teeth and swung his sword down on the tentacle. Dark, almost black blood oozed from the spot where Kalebs sword met the skin. The tentacle released for a second. Kaleb pulled on Danica, getting her mostly up over the rail. The tentacle didn't let go completely. Kaleb fumbled backwards trying to gain his footing as he held on to Danica. Another set of arms wrapped around Danica's upper torso with Kaleb. He looked over and saw Jacob.

"Grab her." Kaleb yelled to Jacob who immediately tightened his arms around Danica and nodded to Kaleb.

Kaleb let go and went to fight the tentacle still holding on to Danica. Kaleb climbed up onto the rungs of the upper deck rail. He climbed over them and on to the outer side. He wrapped his leg through the rail and hung on with one hand. There was nothing between him and the ocean water but air. He leaned over trying to reach the area of the tentacle that wasn't encased in Danica's body. He raised his sword above his head and brought it down just past Danica's feet.

The tentacle began to slowly retract, like it was in pain but still didnt let go of what it had. Kaleb repeated it a second time, this time bringing his sword down as hard as he could. Blood began squirting out a large slash this time. Kaleb's sword came back to him covered in dark blood. He quickly did it again aiming for the same spot. He made contact and the tentacle ripped away from its host. Danica went flying into Jacob. As Kaleb's sword came back to him he felt an instant rush of relief seeing the tentacle's base disappear into the ocean. Kaleb quickly threw his leg back over the upper railing and let out the breath he had been holding it. Danica was unwrapping the large tentacle off of her body.  She flung it away from her as it was still twitching. She stood rubbing her legs which were  bright red and covered in instant bruises. She nodded to Kaleb with a smile and then her eyes grew large. Kaleb stepped down onto the lower deck and whipped around. Another large tentacle was coming for him. Sword ready he was as ready as he could be.

"Kaleb!" He heard Danica yell as it came down on him.

# Chapter Twenty Six

## Creatures

Kaleb's knees hit the ground as he duck bracing himself. He used all of his strength to hold the sword above his head; praying the tentacle would impale itself. He shut his eyes and waited for impact. The world came crashing down on him and he felt warm hot liquid run over him. Looking up he saw the tentacle flopping around his bade. Within seconds the wait was being lifted off of him. Danica helped lift the tentacle off and let it flop to the side. Her sword covered in the saw deep dark liquid as Kaleb's sword. His eyes ran down the tentacle and saw it had been severed in half. The tentacle was still moving about as it hit the ground.  Kaleb stood watching the scene in front of him. Tentacles laid about the ship, some still twitching. Dark almost black blood was spread across the deck floors. He looked down at his body and he matched the deck floors. He looked to Danica who was taking it all in as well. Her eyes searched the sides of the ship for any more threat. Her eyes grew big as she realized that during everything no one was steering. The ship was heading towards the side of the cliff.

"Jacob the wheel!" She yelled to him and he instantly snapped into action.

He grabbed a hold of the wheel just in time and yanked the ship away from the cliff side as the ship began to scratch against it. Everyone on the ship lost footing and toppled over but Jacob. Hitting the deck floor Danica glanced around at the chaos trying to get her footing back. Standing she scanned the ship once more, there was no sign of more tentacles or a monster.

"How many tentacles?" She heard Kaleb ask.

Her mind immediately knew what he was thinking; she raced to the upper deck and began continuing the tentacles on the floor. 1..2...3...4...5 with the one up here on the upper deck.

" Five there's five in total." Danica said to him, searching his face with her eyes as she said it.

"There's anywhere from one to three more tentacles depending on the beast." Kaleb said locking eyes with her.

Danica's stomach sank, she looked down over the crew and she was glad there had been no fatalities this time.

"There's more tentacles if the monster still wants to fight he can!" She yelled down over the top railing.

The men nodded, choking back their fear, they stayed ready with swords and spears drawn. Jacob manned the wheel as the ship crept along the passage. Kaleb looked over the side at the eerie calm water. It was so dark you couldn't see down into it. He backed away from the rail and prepared himself as well.


Ariadne tossed and turned as she tried to sleep but couldn't, thoughts kept coming and going about Patrick. The word betrayed did not justify how she felt. She kept trying to tell herself he cared but she couldn't believe him no matter how her heart wanted it to be true. She was exhausted beyond belief. She needed rest. She flopped over once more in the captain's bed and squeezed her eyes shut.

Patrick's head hit the back rail of the upper deck. He shut his eyes trying to ignore the random glares he was getting from Jonah. It had only been a few hours since Ariadne left them but it had felt like days. The only thing he was doing was thinking about what he could say or do to make her believe that yes he intended to betray her but once he knew her he couldn't. He wanted to tell her that the weight of pleasing his father and the overwhelming responsibility his father put on him for success; the pressure of it all can cloud your moral compass. He grumbled softly to himself becoming frustrated, he picked his head forward and brought it back against the railing letting his head bounce a little bit. Jonah looked over at Patrick and went to say something to him about being dramatic but a cliff they were passing caught his eye.

At the very top of it the tree was moving. He saw little black leafs fluttering about, the ship making its way past the cliff was causing currents making waves hit the cliff and vibrating up the side of it. Was this causing the leaves to move like this? Jonah thought, squinting.

"Ay look alive mate there's something going on up there on the tree." Jonah said to Patrick wanting someone else to look.

"What?" Patrick asked, his tone annoyed.

"Look at the tree up there, there's something wrong." Jonah said to him, matching the tone of annoyance.

Patrick made a face at him but stood. He walked over to the side of Jonah. He looked upwards at the cliff, using his hand to shield the sun from his eyes.

"Leafs, they're genius." Patrick snarked at him.

"No, watch how they move jerk." Jonah said, gritting his teeth.

Patrick frowned and focused more on the tree moving. He was having trouble, the leaves couldn't possibly be moving he thought. He looked again and saw an area where there were leaves a second go now.

"That tree is strange." Patrick whispered to himself, trying to focus harder on it.

"I told you something is not right with it." Jonah said quietly.

Patrick studied the tree they were moving and too dark to be leaves. He frowned looking at them trying to see. As he tried to focus he saw something fall from the tree. He was floating gracefully down towards the ship. The wind picked it up and began blowing it towards Patrick. Ironically like it was being brought right to him. He held open his hand and it dropped into it. A black feather. Patrick held up the feather and then looked to the tree. He smiled silly.

"Look, your strange leaves are just birds." Patrick said, holding up the feather.

"I don't like it." Jonah said, looking from the feather to the tree.

"Don't like birds?" Patrick asked, confused.

"No, not the birds, this whole thing is wrong." Jonah said, shaking his head.

"Ok..so why don't we get someone to switch out with you. Maybe you need to lay down." Patrick said a little concerned and began looking for someone.

"No, I feel fine." Jonah groaned frustrated.

At that point a small black bird flew down and sat on the rail of the upper deck. It's jet black wings had a tinge of blue in them. It's beck matched its feathers and its eyes were darker than the night sky. They were lifeless.

"See just birds." Patrick pointed to the bird drastically talking to Jonah.

Ariadne couldn't deal with being in the cabin any longer. She got up off the bed and made her way across the cabin floor. Reaching the door she hesitated. She was going to have to face Patrick sooner or later, now's as good as it gets. She told herself opening the door. Walking out on the upper deck the setting sun made her shield her eyes. She looked across to the upper deck squinting.

"What in god's name?" Ariadne said, looking across the way.

Several jet black birds had perched themselves on the upper deck railing. Patrick was flapping his arms dramatically at Jonah and laughing as more and more birds joined him. Jonah looked more and more grumpy. Patrick walked to one of the birds on the rail and offered him his finger.

"Come on little guy." Patrick said, trying to get the bird on his finger.

"Patrick, leave it alone, they don't want to be bothered." Jonah said growling at him.

"It's just bird Jonah." Patrick said, looking back at him.

At that moment the bird Patrick was trying to get chirped. At the sound of the chirp the whole tree became bare. The bird Patrick was bothering reached forward and pecked Patrick's finger. Patrick let out a small yell as blood dripped from his finger. The bird looked happily at Patrick who stepped away from it. It began smacking its beak as it tasted the small drop of blood from patrick.

"I told you there's something wrong with them." Jonah whispered to Patrick who had moved over to him.

Ariadne watched the scene confused. She heard the whooshing noise after the bird chirped and followed her eyes to it.  The birds were making a bee ling for the ship. The way they were acting in the sky was not normal, They also seemed to be communicating with the birds on the ship. It made Ariadne skin crawl, something not right with these birds. She looked at them and then it dawned on here. These birds were about to attack them. Birds...birds what could chase birds that were in the air.

"Fire." She whispered out loud.

She ran back into the cabin racing for the desk. She began searching the draws, finding a bottle of rum she grabbed a hold of it. She needs something to set on fire. She looked around and couldn't find anything. She saw the desk chair and thought it was her best shot. The whooshing sound outside was growing louder and sounded like it may have started to circle the ship. Ariadne picked up the chair, raised it high above her head and smashed it on the floor. She did this three more times until finally the legs broke off. She was out of breath but quickly rushed to the bed ripping off the sheets. She grasped the sides of the sheets and ripped it down the middle. She then began wrapping the sheet around the leg of the chair. She repeated this four more times, till she now had four torches. She grabbed the box of matches sitting on the desk, the rum, and ready to go torches and walked out on to the upper deck. The birds were now forming a small dark cloud around the ship. The crew noticed and began to shrink away from the sides of it.

Ariadne dumped the rum onto the sheets soaking them in the alcohol. She began making her way down the ship. She handed a torch and a match to a crew member as she walked across the lower deck. She passed off a second one as she started up the stairs to the helm. Reaching the helm she could hear Jonah and Patrick still bantering.

"That's enough boys were about to be in big trouble." Ariadne said, approaching them.

She shoved the torch into Patrick's hand and he gave her a confused look. She didn't respond but looked out over the ship. They need to act quickly.

"Light your torches. Light the lanterns on the four sides of the ship. If you can make yourself a torch. These birds are going to attack us. On my say thrust your torches into the bird mob." Ariadne yelled over the lower deck.

Patrick raised an eyebrow but lit the torch watching as Ariadne did hers. The two men lit their torches below as others scampered to find a way to make one. The lanterns on the ship's side were lit. She was hoping after they had threatened the birds with fire, the lanterns would give off the impression that they were on fire so the birds wouldn't mess with the ship anymore. As the lanterns were lit. Another chirp was heard inside of the bird mob. The birds began to shift direction. A small group of birds branched off and went to attack one of the sails of the ship. Their beaks began to pierce the sail. Ariadne's eyes shot to this. They were trying to stop them from leaving.

"Now." She yelled they couldn't wait any longer.

She rushed to the opposite side of the upper deck and thrusted her torch into the circling bird mod. Flames caught the wings of several birds on fire. Patrick copied her and ran to the opposite side, thrust his flame into the black blur. Feather ignated on fire, the men on the lower deck began to do the same thing as well. Within seconds  the bird mass dissolved. The birds either retreated or plunged into the ocean. The birds sitting on the ledge of the upper deck rail were still there. It was just three of them. They were acting like they were watching the scene. Expressionless as they did.

"Patrick." Jonah called to him and nodded to the three birds.

"Tender or crispy." Patrick smirked, walking towards the bird that pecked him.

Patrick walked over to the upper rail, Ariadne had come back with her torch as well, she was ready and waiting to see what would happen next. Patrick waved the flames at the birds but they would leave. He became aggressive with it but the three birds sat there with no movement, no emotion, and no response. Patrick groaned and lunged the torch at the middle bird, the first bird that landed on the deck and the one that bit him. The bird didn't move as his feathers slowly caught fire. He didn't chirp or make an ounce of noise as he went up in flames.  Patrick backed away as the bird became on fire.  They watched it, he was uncertain about what was going on. The bird locked eyes with Patrick and within seconds the bird was just a pile of ashes. A wind kicked up and blew the ashes off the upper deck rail. The world was silent. The two remaining birds looked at each other and flew off.

"What the hell was that?" Patrick asked, whispering as he held on to his torch.

"I dont know I've never seen birds act like that."
Ariadne said quietly.

"I told you there was something wrong." Jonah
said to Patrick as they began to put distance in
between the cliff and the ship.

## Chapter Twenty Seven

## Castaway

Danica watched the men pick up the tentacles and drop them back into the sea. Their nerves were on edge, still waiting for another attack from the monster of the deep. Everyone was just waiting. A few men began mopping up the creature's blood trying to keep busy as they made their way through the passage. Kaleb was on guard and couldn't seem to relax. She never thought any of this would happen on this sea voyage. Kaleb sensed her guilt and walked over to her.

"You alright?" He asked quietly, his eyes still scanning the ship's sides.

"I'm ok we will be better once we're out of here and I know everyone is safe again." Danica said letting a little piece of her guilt out.

"Danica, this isn't your fault, this could have happened to any ship that came through here." Kaleb said, trying to comfort her.

"That's the thing, I am the one who chose this path, regardless of the warnings." Danica said frustrated.

"How could you know?" Kaleb said quietly, trying to make her feel better.

"Kaleb you just almost went overboard and became some sea monster dinner. You're really trying to tell me this is ok." Danica said, throwing her hands to her side as she spoke.

"No, I am saying the sea monster did this. Not you." Kaleb smiled at her.

"Yeah but-"

"Captain." Jacob said, cutting Dancia off.

"Aye?" She asked shifting to be able to see Jacob.

"Come look at this." Jacob said with a small smile.

Danica looked to Kaleb before walking over to the wheel. She looked out forward and was happy to see an opening. They were feet away from exiting the passage. Her heart skipped a beat; they were almost out.

"Look and you can see the cove and the land on the other side must be The Hollow." Danica said tapping Jacob excitedly.

Jacob couldn't help but smile at Danica's excitement. She felt like the world was instantly lighter. Kaleb came over to join them with a smile on his face as well. Danica's energy was contagious. Many of the crew members went to the side of the ship to peek and see what the three were looking at. A small cheer rang out on the lower deck as they realized the exit was minutes away. Kaleb reached over and entwined his fingers into Danica's. His heart jumped in his chest when she didn't pull away and wrapped her fingers around his. His smile grew.

"Well Captain, what is the plan for the island?" Kaleb asked, looking forward.

"We should settle just inside the cove and take the row boats to the shore. I know strength in numbers but I think we should leave men on the ship. The map says that the treasure is in a place where the moon light hits first. I figure it's gotta be a-

She stopped talking as she felt something rattle the ship floor. Danica knew that feeling, Her heart sank, she looked to Jacob before she took off to the side of the ship. Her eyes looked to the ocean water and she cringed, pooling water.

"Get the sails up now! We need to stop!" She yelled out orders.

"Anchor throw the anchor!" Danca yelled louder as she began racing down the stairs.

They were hitting the ocean floor if they kept going they would break the bottom of the ship and they would start taking in water. Kaleb raced down the stairs. Danica raced to the center mass, the largest sail and began pulling on the ropes with all her might.

The sails need to go up now. The rest of the crew scrambled about trying to get the other sails up. She heard the chain from the anchor let go and she prayed it wouldn't ruin them. It was risky throwing the anchor suddenly but they were already in trouble if she didn't do it they would be in danger. The rope stung and ripped through her flesh as she pulled as hard as she could hoisting the sail up. It seemed like forever before the sail reached the top.

She wrapped the rope around the mass to give herself some leverage before tying it off. The ship was dragging and you could hear it. The loud crunching, scraping noise of the bottom of the ship crashing into the ocean floor echoed off the cliff walls. As the anchor dropped and buried into the ocean floor, it jerked the whole ship forward. Danica crashed to the floor. She braced herself for the ship to continue to move. As the rest of the sails reached the top the ship slowly to a screeching halt. She got to her feet and rushed to the side of the ship trying to see if there were any bubbles, if they were taking in water. She didn't see any, she just to the opening of the hull and yelled into it.

"Are we taking in water!?" She called into the darkness.

"No Captain, what's going on?" A voice called to her out of the darkness.

"We're stuck on a sandbar I think." Danica's voice was low as she said it.

The ship was quiet as Danica straightened up. She looked around at the ship and the men all had a look of doom on their faces. They had no way to contact anyone for help. No one knew where they were. They were now stranded.  She took a deep breath in trying not to panic. The crew came out from under the hull and gathered on the lower deck. All eyes were on her. They were looking for instruction, guidance, and all she wanted to do was scream. She shut her eyes and took a deep breath in. She could do this. She opened her eyes and looked at the crew.

"We need to go to the island." She said out loud and waited for the backlash.

"The island!" A man called out upset.

"We don't know what's on that island!" Another echoed.

"Still thinking about treasure but now we have no way back." Another man yelled.

She stood silently crossing her arms across her chest and waited for them to stop talking so loudly. She stood there and surely one by one stopped talking and joined her in the silence.

"I know what you're thinking. That I just want to go get the treasure. I know this situation is bad and we are stuck and I honestly don't have any ideas right now on how to get the ship free.  What I do know is we were attacked in this passage. The safest place for us right now is on the island. We don't know what else is in this passage. We can use the rowboats to get to the island and set up." Danica said planning out loud as she talked to the crew.

The crew mumbled about themselves and then all kinds of grunts  came in response. She eyed them, not sure if the grunt was a good or bad thing. She waited a moment to see if someone would clarify.

"When do we leave Captain?" A man called out from the crowd.

She sighed in relief. They needed to leave as soon as possible but she didn't know what was on that island and they needed to be prepared. She looked around and there were about twenty men in total on the ship. They have four row boats. That would work five people in a boat. She began thinking about what they needed exactly. She felt someone come up behind her and touch her shoulder lightly.

"Captain you ok?" Kaleb's voice broke her concentration.

Her hand went to her shoulder touching his lightly, the simple touch from him instantly calmed her. Her touch to him sent shivers through him. Image flashed through his mind of carrying her over his shoulder to the captain's cabin but he quickly gained control of himself. Reminding himself what was going on.

"Just trying to think about what we need to bring. We don't know what's on that island." Danica said to him.

"Weapons." Someone called out.

"Pots for water.' Another called out.

"Fire, something to make fire." Another man called out.

"Rations." Jacob said coming up behind her.

"Well it looks like you all have this under control. We have five boats, four to a ship and take as much as you can of each category." Danica said, giving out orders.

The men nodded and quickly dismissed themselves heading to complete their missions. Danica patted Kalebs hand letting it off her shoulder as she began walking towards the captain's cabin.

"Dani?" Kaleb called after.

"My Father's journal and map." She called back down to him answering his question.

Danica walked quickly up the stairs to the upper deck and basically sprinted to the cabin. She wanted to get off this ship as soon as possible. She opened the cabin door and grabbed her bag from home which was laid by the door. She then walked to the desk and opened the drawer of the desk she sighed. She wished she could take this whole desk. Inside he desk there was medical supplies. She looked at her bag and dumped it upside down on the desk. All her personal belongings fell out. She left her change of clothing, little trinkets from home behind. She began stuffing as many medical supplies as she could into the bag. She began searching the desk more and her heart jumped seeing the pistol. She didn't know if they had any firearms on board but now she was happy there was more. She placed it into the bag along with the ammo to go with it. She carefully folded the map and placed it inside the dark blue journal. She then placed the journal in the bag. She was ready as she ever would be.

Danica started to walk away from the desk when something caught her eye. It had fallen out of her bag. She walked over it, the light coming in from one of the few windows in the room was bouncing off it, causing the light to dance. She moved her shirt away from it and found a necklace. She picked it up, she didn't realize she had packed it. It was a necklace her father gave her when he would tell her adventure stories. She remembered him coming home late in the evening and trying to rush to bed but she begged him for one story. He told her a story about pirates chasing down treasure and burying it on an island no one knew about. She remembered him leaving her room that night and then coming back in with the necklace. The necklace was a silver key, it was simple and looked like a real key but Dani loved it.

"It will unlock any treasure." He told her that night as he placed it around her neck.

She remembered she wore it from that day on, never taking it off. It wasn't until this whole mess with The Smiths started that she had taken it off one evening. Sad, angry, and upset with her parents for leaving. She quickly got over it but forgot to put the necklace back on. She must have packed it remembering it. Danica took the necklace and slipped it over her head. She smiled. It was only fitting she had her key necklace while she went and chased treasure. She took a deep breath, slung her bag over her shoulder and headed out. Walking out onto the upper deck she was met by Jacob and Kaleb who smiled confidently at her. They had her back no matter what.

"To the boats boys." Danica smiled as walked past them and heard down to the lower deck.

## Chapter Twenty Eight

### Storm

Ariadne stood on the upper deck watching the horizon. She stared at the spot that used to be where Raven Peak was.  A cold breeze had picked up and she wrapped her arms around herself trying to keep warm. Jonah was still staring. She couldn't get her mind off the birds. Did Dani have to face them too? Did she get through them? She had never thought about dangers like that? The more she thought about her sister, the more her stomach pitted and turned into knots. She had just assumed that they were sailing along peacefully to some island, maybe worse case getting into a little storm but bird attack no. She hugged herself deeper.

"You all right?" Patrick's voice asked, coming up from behind her.

"Aye just thinking." Ariadne answered not turning to him.

She felt something warm drop around her shoulders. It smelt like him and at first she wanted to shove it back at him but it was so cold. She pulled close around her, giving into the warmth of his coat.

"Thank you." She said quietly.

Patrick didn't say anything but just went and stood next to her looking out over the ocean. They were making good time and should be catching up to their siblings hopefully soon. He glanced over at Ariadne wanting to talk to her. He wanted to make things right but wasn't sure how.

"We are making good time, we should be catching up to  them sooner than we expected." Patrick said softly.

"Do you think the birds attacked them as well?" Patrick asked, trying to make small talk.

Ariadne sighed and glanced over at him. She was trying hard to not think about it but it was nagging at her stomach. She was also trying  her best to keep her distances from him but that didn't seem to be working.

"I don't know if part of me says that the birds do that every time a ship comes by. It was too organized to..creepy for it to just be a random act." Ariadne said, squeezing herself tighter.

"I've never seen anything like that." Patrick nodded agreeing with her.

"Dani is strong and if it happened I know she thought of something." Ariadne said to herself trying to make herself feel better.

"Aye, I feel like your family as a whole are strong people. Kaleb is different from most of my family. He's a bit of a loner, likes to travel doesn't ever really have a plan. I am actually jealous of his carefree nature. How one minute he could be getting on  a ship going wherever it's going and the next be climbing mountains. I couldn't do it. I need consistency. Security. Plus I wouldn't leave my family like that. There's too much…

"Responsibility like you can't let them down." Ariadne finished his sentence turning and looking at him.

"Aye." He smiled weakly.

" I would get letters from my brother about how he climbed this mountain or was somewhere in Europe working a dairy farm, the next on his way to India. He somehow found a way out of my fathers grip and ran. I, on the other hand, couldn't find that. I felt like it was my duty to be the son he wanted me to be, to uphold the family name and succeed in life. I wanted to make him proud. Kaleb didn't care about that. He got out and ran. I almost wish I would have gone with him. I couldn't leave our mother." Patrick said quietly.

Ariadne watched him as he spoke, her heart hurt for him. She understood the want and need of making her family proud. She wanted to take over the business, wanted to please her parents and show them she could do this. She got the press and the stress of it all but there was something else with Patrick. The sadness there and she didn't understand the piece about his mother. It was more than a son not wanting to leave home.

"Patrick, why couldn't you leave?" Ariadne asked quietly.

"I-I-

"Captain!" Jonah yelled over to her, his voice filled with urgency.

Ariadne tore her eyes away from Patrick and looked over to Jonah. When he saw her looking his way he pointed forward. Her eyes went to the horizon. She frowned deeply. The sky was turning deep green in color and it looked angry. She walked to the upper deck rail and looked down over the railing.

"Storms are coming! Fasten everything down that you can. Any loose items that can be stored in the hull. Limit the number of men on the deck. All those not needed go below. Raise the sails half way." Ariadne shouted out orders.

She glanced back at Jonah who nodded to her letting her know those were the right calls to make. She walked over to him. Standing next to him she sighed deeply.

"Poseidon getting in our way, Captain?" Jonah smirked a little bit.

"Aye, for some reason or another. You got this sailor?" Ariadne said with a playful tone to him as she nodded at the incoming storm clouds.

"Oh this is not my first dance captain." Jonah grinned as if to say challenge accepted as his eyes drifted to the skies.

"Well it's mine so try not to let it be my last." Ariadne said, shaking her head.

"Your father and uncle would gut me if I let that happen." Jonah smirked, throwing a wink at her.

The men on the lower raced about storing items and tying down what they could. The sails were placed halfway in order. Ariadne could hear the chains below the deck locking the cannons in place. They were ready. Patrick walked over to the helm standing just behind her.

"So what's the plan?" Patrick asked.

"Try not to die." Jonah smirked.

"Lovely." Patrick said, rolling his eyes at him.

"You can go hide in the cabin." Jonah said snarky.

"I don't need to-

"Enough, we don't like each other. Now shut up." Ariadne yelled as she slammed her foot down on the deck floor.

The men below glanced up at the upper deck, as they looked up they saw Ariadne's glare and quickly got back to work. Jonah and Patrick instantly stopped arguing with each other. She locked her eyes on the angry sky and watched the clouds begin to swirl. Jonah tensed up seeing the clouds' movements. The ocean itself had lost all sounds and the water was terrifyingly calm. Ariadne's eyes counted the men on the lower deck.

"All  but five get below now! I don't care how you decide but do it quickly." Ariadne yelled orders down at them.

She didn't want to lose any lives. She nervously began to tug on her pinky finger as she watched the sky. The ocean seemed to always be still right before something bad happened and she didn't know if this ship could handle it.  She looked back at Jonah and he didn't seem to be there. He was deadly still and watching the clouds. She gritted her jaw and grasped the railing. They were all waiting to see what would happen. Patrick walked over the upper deck railing and grabbed a hold of it.

"The Evening Star can handle anything. Trust her." Jonah said quietly his grip on the wheel making his knuckles go white.

There was  no sound, no thunder, and no rain.
The waves were almost non-existent. The ship sailed
through the ocean like a knife passing through butter.
Everything was still. The world was on pause as they
all were waiting. Lighting cracked across the dark sky
lighting up the ocean. In that split second everything
went to hell. It was like the lightning summoned it all.
The ocean became enraged. Waves began slamming
against the ship making it toss back and forth. Jonah
held his stance and held the ship steady. Another
lighting strike occurred and rain began to downpour
on the ship. The rain was cold and blinding, Jonah
held on even though he couldn't see. A howling noise
was coming from the ocean as if it was yelling at the
ship. The wind was causing it as it picked up fast,
wreaking havoc on the sails. The wind was adding to
the ships rocking as if some unseen force was trying
to take down the ship.

Ariadne grabbed a hold of the railing with all
her might. The rain was making everything slippery.
She watched one man fall and slid across the deck.
Another man reached out and caught him just before
he hit the outer ship wall. She watched the men below
begin tying ropes to themself to help them stay in
place on the ship.

Ariadne struggled to hold on to herself. She felt
her grip slipping; another wave rocked the ship and
she felt herself let go. Patrick wrapped his arm around
her and pulled her up against him. He slid behind her
and braced her with each arm beside her as he held

onto the rail. She could feel the heat from his chest burn into her back as she tried to hang on the upper rail. She knew she wasn't going anywhere as long as Patrick was standing behind her, he would make sure of it.

Waves began to crash up over the ship's side, ocean water flooding the lower deck as it did. She peeked around Patrick to check on Jonah. He had secured himself to the wheel with a strap and was stirring. His face is calm masking any emotion he might have. There was nothing anyone could do. They had to push on through the storm and hoped that it would end soon.

Another wave hit the ship causing Patrick to crash into Ariadne, pushing her up against the rail. Pushed back water rushing down his back trying to make sure Ariadne was ok but not letting go of her or the rail. His muscles in his forearms were bundling the veins almost seem like they were going to bust out of the as he held on for dear life. He wasn't letting her go, storm or no storm.  Ariande saw the pain Patrick was going through and didn't know if he could last much longer, unlike everyone else above deck, Patrick was the only one not secured to an object. The men on the lower deck tossed about but they were strapped in by ropes. She needed to think of something. He was her life line and he was going to give out soon.  She needed a rope or something to tie them to the rail. Another wave rocked the ship this time ocean water crashed over the sides of the upper deck, she watched Patrick tense more as the ship shifted.

Rope..rope..rope.  She was repeating over in her mind as she searched nearby with her eyes. Patrick almost slammed into her again by another crashing wave, something hard hit her in her lower back. She knew exactly what it was and it was going to save them. She began to try to move and Patricks grip tightened on her. She could see his shoulders starting to shake,

"Stop, let me move!" She yelled at him. She had turned sideways and she could see him frown.

" I can't hold on to you too well if you move." Patrick said through gritted teeth.

"Let me move or both will die!" Ariadne growled.

Patrick grunted his disapproval but allowed her to move. She turned around facing him, his face scowled at her not sure what she was doing but atleast her facing him was better for holding on to her. He felt her hand go over his wais and along his pant line. He nearly jumped when she started to undo his pants. Her hands fumbled along as she tried to steady herself. He shifted slightly trying to get away from her and then tensed up as another wave sent them both into the rail.

"Ariadne what the hell are you doing!." He
yelled at her.

"I need to get to your belt!" She yelled into his
ear as her hand undid it and yanked it from his waist.

His jaw dropped as she held up the belt like
she had won something. Another wave knocked them
both into the rail, due to the shock of having his belt
ripped off Patricks grip loosened and he almost
stumbled backwards. Ariadne grabbed him by the
collar and pulled him to her.

"Don't let go now." She yelled at him as his
hand grabbed a hold of the railing.

Ariadne slid the belt around his waist and then
pulled him close up against her and wrapped the
remaining amount around the rail. She fastened the
belt and then wrapped her arms around his neck. He
was secured to the upper rail now and she was
secured to him. She smiled proudly at her ta da
moment. A wave came up over the side of the ship
crashing into them, the belt slid but they remained on
the ship. She held tight to him, his arms wrapped tight
around her. The rain pouring down on them was
freezing and his body heat felt good against her skin.

She clung to him as the ship continued to
rock, she leaned her head against his chest to steady
herself. She didn't know how much longer the ship
and crew could take this. The ship creaked and
protested everytime a wave struck it. She was

concerned for the crew. She glanced over at Jonah who was soaking wet and was hard to see with the rain blurring everything. She could see his figure still standing tall and holding the ship. She was amazed at his strength.

Another wave hit the ship, she heard a snap and someone yell. She couldn't see what had happened, she couldn't turn. Patrick held her so tightly she could barely breathe. She prayed no one had gone overboard. She was becoming anxious; the storm needed to pass the crew couldn't handle anymore. She tried to look once more but Patrick forced her still. The sky began to lighten and the clouds went back to white, fluffy, happy ones. The crew waited silently, not sure if this was nature's trick or if the storm had really passed. A flapping sound could be heard coming from the lower deck. Ariadne lifted her head from Patricks chest and turned slightly. He let her turn the slightest bit, her body still most facing him;  his hand still tight around her incase this was a trapt. Looking down over the lower deck it was filled with silver fish flopping about. Birds began to chirp as the sun came out, the sunlight hit the fish scales and they almost sparkled in the sunlight.

"The storms passed," Jonah called out, his voice exhausted but full with relief.

Patrick's arms felt like jello as he let go of the upper deck rail but held onto Ariadne still. He let out a deep breath of relief. The men on the lower deck began to unstrap themselves. Ariadne looked up at Patrick shifting back from him slightly. She saw how exhausted he was and frowned slightly. She studied him for a second. Her heart pounded in her chest as she could feel the outline of his chest pushed up against her wet clothes. She knew that if he was this wet and his clothes were clinging to him, she knew hers were. Could he feel her like she was feeling him. She felt her face flush and tried to push the thought from her mind.

"Are you alright?" She whispered.

He nodded as he leaned forward and pressed his forehead against hers. Rain water mixed with ocean ran down his nose and dripped off his hair dropping on to her cheeks. She raised her hand to catch the drops but his hand caught her and she felt his thumb brush them away. She brought her hand up slowly to his cheek and brushed her thumb across it. A small smile appeared across his lips. She found herself staring at them. Her hand slowly traveled to the back of his neck, her fingers curling into his wet hair.  He tilted his head away from hers slightly so his lips could claim hers. Her lips tasted like salt from the ocean water spilling off of them. Her lips soft against his as his tongue parted them. His hand wrapped around her and traveled over her wet shirt. The wet fabric clinged to every inch of her  and it felt like he was touching her bare skin. Her other hand wrapped around his neck, locking him to her. He deepened the kiss, his tongue creasing hers. His other hand found the belt locking them to the railing and quickly undid it, releasing them from it. A loud coughing sound broke the trance they were in.  Patrick growled slightly as he felt Ariadne pull back, her lips swollen slightly from his kiss. He glanced to where the coughing was coming from and saw Jonah.

Patrick narrowed his eyes at him as Jonah smiled at him. Patrick was done. He pulled Ariadne to him and with his free hand scooped her up into her arms. She let out a small yell in surprise.

"The Captain is wet and needs to get out of her clothes before she gets ill. Stay the course and catch those fish. It will be better than eating the salted meat." Patrick announced loudly as he walked past Jonah carrying Ariadne.

"Jonah switched out. You're exhausted and need sleep. Have Darryl take over for a little bit." Ariadne said to him as she went by.

Jonah went to say something but saw Ariadne nodded in agreement as she placed her head on Patricks chest. Jonah grumbled to himself as he watched Patrick carrying her to the captain's cabin.

"Darryl report to the helm. The rest of you catch the fish." Jonah announced reluctantly.

## Chapter Twenty Nine

## My Captain

Patrick kicked open the captain's quarters door stepping into the cabin carrying Ariadne. Her heart was beating rapidly in her chest as she hung on to him. She could feel every muscle in his strong chest as her wet clothing clung to every inch of her. As quickly as he kicked it open, he kicked it shut. His mouth found hers as soon as the door slammed behind them. Ariadne's fingers entwined into his hair as she returned his feverish kiss. Warmth spread over her body as his tongue caressed hers. He let her legs slowly hit the floor as the kiss intensified, his hands going for the buttons on her shirt. His fingers tightly grasped the side of her shirt and tugged fiercely, the buttons ripped away from her shirt falling open to the side. She inhaled against his lips as she felt the cold air rush over her skin. Goose bumps and Excitement stirred in her as she felt his bare hands brush against her stomach. She felt them travel down to her hips and pulling her closer. Her hands went to his chest and explored down it, finding the edge of his shirt. Her heart pounding in her chest as she bravely tugged on it letting him know she wanted it off.

He broke the kiss and allowed her to pull it up over his head. A small smile spread across her lips as her eyes ran over his chest. She placed her hand on his bare and ran her fingers over his naked skin. He stepped into her, his hand reaching for her hip to pull her against him. She smirked, finding the confidence; she wanted him. She pressed slightly hard on his chest backing him into the wall. Her hand went to the side of his face as she did; pulling him in for a kiss.

A small look of shock flashed over his face but quickly disappeared as her lips hit his. He growled against her lips as she pushed herself up against him. Her whole body responded to the noise. Tingles of want raced through her. Her kiss full of desire and need. He pulled her lower lip into his mouth sucking on it. She whimpered, the small action made her knees feel like giving out; her hand wrapping around his neck. He bit her lip playful as he flipped positions pinning her against the wall. Her back pressed into the wall as his mouth moved from her lips over her neck. She inhaled as his mouth kissed and sucked slowly down the length of it. As his mouth reached the crease of her neck he bit softly. Shivers ran through her and she curled into him, her head turning outward allowing him more access as a small noise passed through her lips. He smiled against her skin, loving the noises she was making.  His lips made a trail from her collar bone over her breast. She arched into him, her body wanting to be as close to his mouth as possible. His mouth circled her nipple, taking it in between them. His teeth playfully grazed it. She arched into him more a low moan escaping her lips as she did. He loved the sound of it and felt himself becoming more excited with each noise she made. His tongue flicked across her nipple as he held it softly between his teeth. Her fingers buried themself in his hair in response.  He pulled her nipple into his mouth, sucking on it. Another sweet noise escaped her lips as chills ran over her, her desire for him growing.

His hand made its way to her pants as he began to undo them; once loose he slipped his hand inside. His mouth moved over to her other breast as his hands searched for her center. Finding it he ran his finger down the crease parting it to find her bud. She shuttered against him as his finger began to make small circles on it. Each movement of his fingers she felt her need growing. Her hips arched against his hand wanting more. His fingers made their way down to her entrance, finding it he pushed one inside. She tensed for a second. He paused, allowing her to get used to the feeling. He pressed the palm of his hand against her bud and moved it in circle motions. The pleasure of it caused her to relax and he began to move his finger. Her body quickly began to want the motion of his finger. She needed it; Her hips began to arch and met him. His mouth moved up to her lips capturing them in a kiss. She kissed him back with small moans coming out in between their lips meeting. He withdrew his hand from her center and she whimpered not wanting him to stop. His hand went to the edge of her pants and pressed on them. He watched her reaction and she nodded against his

mouth as she pulled his lips for another kiss. He
tugged her pants and they hit the floor.

Ariadne stepped out of them and kicked them
to the side. She kissed him back as her hand traveled
down over his abs. She found his pants and ran her
hand over his bulge. He groaned as her hand creased
it and moved into her. She felt him move against her
hand. Her fingers found his buckle and undid it. She
pulled his pants down slightly just enough to expose
him. Her hand found his bulge and she grasped it. He
groaned as she began to run her hand up and down
the length of it. His hand moved back to her center to
find her bud and his finger began moving over it in the
same rhythm she was moving her hand. She trembled
against him as her breathing picked up. He let out a
groan he couldn't take much more. He caught her
hand with his and placed it on the back of his neck.
He slid his hands up over her thighs pulling her leg up
and around him. She felt him press against her
center. Her body reacted and she arched towards
him. He drew her other leg around him and pressed
her into the wall as he entered her. He felt her
contract to him as her legs wrapped tightly around
him.  He held her still for a moment letting her get
used to him. He moved his mouth over to her neck
and bit playfully, sucking on it gently to distract her
from the pain.  The chills from his mouth relaxed her
and She moved against him slightly.  The pain begins
to be replaced by pleasure.She moaned into his neck
as he began to move. He moved slowly at first but
with each thrust he began to move quicker.

She felt an intense feeling building at her core. The warm rush through her body as pressure was building.  She wrapped her legs  tight around him, locking him into her. He could feel herself tightening around him and he throbbed with need.  He couldn't take much longer. She felt perfect like she was made just for him. The way she molded around him. He could feel his release coming. A warm feeling washed over her as all of the muscles in her began to contract. She let out a moan clinging to him as a wave of intensity rushed over her.  She bit down on his shoulder as she was going over the edge and she could feel her body shaking. He let out a low growl as he felt her teeth go into his shoulders slightly, sending shivers through him. He pulled her closer to him and carried her to the bed, still inside of her. He placed her down on it and began to move more. His own release coming. She arched into him heavy moans coming from her as he moved faster and harder against her. She felt him tense up as his warmth rushed into her. He was breathing hard as he braced himself on either side of her. Her legs are still locking him to her. She reached up curling her fingers into his hair and pulled his head down onto her chest. He laid there silent as she played with his hair and a small smile on her face. He looked up at her searching her face with his eyes; his eyes asking if she was ok. She tugged on his hair pulling him up to her mouth kissing him. He shifted to the side of her and wrapped his arms around her. She curled into his chest and before he could even ask the question out loud she was asleep.

He watched her chest rise and fall, her fire red hair sprawled out beside her. He gently ran his finger over the bridge of her nose, noticing the small patch of freckles that ran over it. He felt connected to her, like there was something unspoken between them. Maybe she would be the one person who understood. He thought about looking at her. He decided at that moment that he wasn't going anywhere. He subconsciously had already given her his alliance and he now knew it. He reached over, pulling the covers around her and pulled her closer.

## Chapter Thirty

## Beach

The sand was warm and gritty feeling as her knees crashed into it. Danica dug her fingers in it as she leaned over bracing herself. She inhaled deeply, she was desperately trying to catch her breath. The water from the ocean dripped off of her and puddled into the sand. She watched it turn the sand a dark gray color as she calmed her burning lungs. She had jumped out of the row boat as they neared the shore and helped pull the rowboat in. She felt a strong arm slip under hers and help pull her up to her feet.

"You alright Captain?" Kaleb said to her his hands lingering on her.

"Aye." Danica answered leaning back into him a little bit as she looked around.

The island was covered in white sand that led to a wooded area. Judging by how the tree's looked like they climbed upwards she could tell there was some type of mountain in the middle of the island. The earth seems to pull upwards. She glanced around at the crew who were getting off the rowboats and doing the same. They all seemed to look around and then their eyes slowly drifted to her. They were awaiting her instruction, her plan. She looked up at the sky and it was already dark. The jungle-like woods would be dangerous to travel in the dark, they needed to camp on the beach tonight and when sunlight hit then they could explore.

"We need to camp here on the beach tonight. The beach is open and less likely for anything to be lurking. We can start our journey into the jungle tomorrow but tonight we're staying here. Gather wood and make a fire." She called out to them.

They all seemed to nod in agreement and quickly began to set up camp. Danica felt Kaleb's hands wrap around her waist and she all but melted into his warm body. She shut her eyes, enjoying his touch for a moment. She didn't want to think about how they were stranded, that no one knew where they were, and they had no way of getting home. She felt a dull pain in the back of her neck, a headache wanting to form. Kaleb leaned down and kissed the top of her head as if knowing and all her thoughts seemed to vanish. He made everything better, he could make her feel like everything was going to be ok just by being near.

"We got this. We'll come up with something. But right now all that matters is getting you warm." Kaleb said softly to her and pointed to the fire.

A large fire was going in the center of the white sand. Several crew members had pulled over some fallen logs, they were all sitting around it chatting like everything was fine. Danica nodded her response to Kaleb and began walking towards the rest of the crew.

She stopped short and remembered she left her bag in the rowboat. She went to turn around and almost slammed into Kaleb. He raised an eyebrow at her asking what she was doing.

"My bag, I left it in the row boat." Danica explained going to step around him.

"My Lady." Kaleb smiled, holding the bag out to her.

Danica chuckled and grabbed a hold of it, slinging it over her shoulder as she turned and began walking across the thick sand to the crew. One of the crew members scooted over so Danica could have a seat on the log next to him. She smiled her thanks and sat down. She opened up her bag and pulled out the journal her eyes began reading, trying to find some type of clue as to where to go from her. The mindless chatter of the men faded out as she read. She didn't know how long she had been reading when she realized it was mostly silent. She looked up across the fire and caught Kaleb watching her as he chatted with a crew member. He smiled at her, his eyes meeting hers. He threw a small wink at her as he continued talking. She felt the butterflies in her stomach come alive. The smile he gave her sent small chills. It was a smile only meant for her. She closed her eyes, regaining her thoughts from Kaleb's distraction. She took out a small pad she had in her bag and began jotting down notes.

"Are you going to stay up all night Love?" Kaleb asked, sitting down next to her.

"Mhmm?" Danica said, lifting her head sleepy.

"Everyone is mostly asleep." Kaleb said, nudging her lightly.

"I'm just trying to come up with a plan." Danica said, running her hand through her hair with a sigh.

"What do you have so far?" Kaleb asked.

"It doesn't make any sense. The story that's written in my fathers journal about where the treasure is. I don't know." Danica said exasperated.

"Tell me." Kaleb said, looking down at her notes.

"It's like a riddle. It says the ocean is where the land meets the sea but not where you think. It also mentions something about being sky high and starlight." Danica grumbled.

"Well then it's not on the beach which would be the easiest. So maybe a river that runs through the island?" Kaleb asked.

"Rivers are usually freshwater, it says ocean. It makes it sound like it...like I feel like we need to go towards the mountain. It says to travel through the jungle till the earth meets the sky and the ocean will meet the land. The stars will tell you where the treasure is." Danica said with her hands in her face.

"Well then we head for the highest point. Maybe the mountain had a salt water lake underneath it or a cave. As far as the starlight goes, I will be there by nightfall tomorrow night and can find out then. Don't stress." Kaleb said, reaching over and rubbing her shoulder.

"It's hard not to when everyone's lives kind of depends on my plan and what happens because of my orders." Danica said not taking her face out of her hands.

"They all knew what they were getting into when they boarded this ship. They knew it wasn't a normal trading voyage. Anytime you get on  a ship you know there's a risk of sinking or being stranded or dying. The ocean is unpredictable. You can't control her. Take one thing at a time is all we can do. Right now we sleep. When the sun rises we will conquer the jungle and whatever else is thrown at us." Kaleb pulled her close and whispered into her hair.

Danica knew he was right but couldn't take any more chances with any more lives. She sighed leaning into him. Kaleb stroked her back lightly as she stared at the journal. The jungle noises around them echoed on the beach. The way Kaleb was rubbing her and the distant noises she could feel her eyelids wanting to clothes. She tightened her grip on the journal in her hand as it became heavy. Kaleb smiled softly as he felt her give in and lean completely on him. He glanced down at her, eyelids shut, hair so dark and raven in color it was almost glowing blue in the moonlight. He found himself smiling at her flawlessness. His thumb brushing her cheek. He was falling, not falling he was already hers and he knew it as he looked at her in that moment.

He sighed out loud realizing those facts; part of himself was upset. He looked out over the beach watching the waves crash into the shore line. He had never wanted anyone this close. He couldn't have anyone this close. This life that he was leading wasn't built for someone else. Wasn't built for love or companionship,or the what ifs of a family. He never planned for this. He felt her shift in his arms and as he looked down at her he felt his chest tensed. There was something in him telling him that she was his, that she was his person and he couldn't fight that no matter how hard he was trying to. He shifted slightly reaching for her bag, he had seen a blanket in there. Holding her in his one arm he reached into her bag and grabbed it. He one handed spread the blanket out on the sand in front of the log. He then shifted her neatly onto the blanket. He watched her shiver as his body heat left her. He shook off his jacket and covered  her. He watched her for several more seconds as she curled into his jacket. He felt someone watching him and looked up. His eyes met Jacobs. He walked over to him silently, reaching him and he kept his eyes on Danica.

"You can head to sleep, I'll take the next watch." Kaleb told Jacob.

Jacob nodded, getting up from the spot he was sitting in. Jacob looked back at Danica and then back at Kaleb.

"Not every man is built for an Abner woman but if you are, your life will be more than what you could ever hope. Cross one and I promise you won't have a life to worry about." Jacob said his words chosen carefully as he nodded walking away.

Kaleb smirked a little bit at Jacob's fatherly threat but he didn't doubt it. He didn't doubt any of it but was he enough for her. Kaleb sat down where Jacob had been sitting and resumed his watch. His eyes scanned the beach front as the men slept. Every so often his eyes lingered longer on Danica as if each time he looked at her he was questioning himself.

## Chapter Thirty One

### Uncharted

Danica stretched, arching her back  and raising her hands above her head. She let out a small groan as she did. Her outward hand reached into the sandy grit. Touching the sand she remembered where she was. She opened her eyes. The Sun was just peeking above the ocean and the tops of the waves were etched with its golden rays. She sat up pulling the jacket around her. She looked down at the simple brown jacket. She inhaled deeply and knew right away whose jacket it was. His scent made her feel warm, he smelt like freedom like the wind blowing in wide open spaces. Adventure. He smelt like the earth on a cold day. She found herself wrapping herself in it as she stood. She didn't realize it but her eyes were scanning the beach for him; Kaleb.

"Morning Captain, what be the plan today?" A man cradling his own coat to himself asked her.

The breeze blowing in from the ocean front was chilly. She recognized the man as Timmy. He was most often in the crows nest. He was small in stature so he was usually picked for the position and he never complained.

"Timmy, I think we may leave some men here on the beach and take a handful to explore the jungle. The treasure is somewhere in there." Danica said with a shrug.

"Aye Captain. Did you want volunteers or did you want to hand pick the men to go with you? Timmy asked.

"Volunteers will be fine if you could go spread the word and see who would like to stay and who would like to go." She ordered him with a smile.

"Aye Captain." Timmy nodded as he turned walking off in the direction of the crew.

She watched the men who were gathered in small groups. They were just getting the day started. The fire had been going all night and she now saw some men dividing up some rashings for the morning breakfast. She found Jacob in the middle doing most of the sorting. He was making sure everything was fair and that there would be enough to last them until they figured out something. She didn't see Kaleb anywhere. She frowned slightly and her stomach knotted where would he be? She began walking towards the group of men. Maybe she was overlooking him.  She moved about the crowd of men looking for him.

Kaleb came out from the jungle, sword dangling from his hip. He had ripped off the sleeves of his shirt and wrapped them around his forehead to catch the sweat before it went  in his eyes.  His hair damp sweat and almost dripping. He looked around the beach briefly. Everyone was now up and about. He had noticed that people seem to be sorting themselves. He took a deep breath in before crossing the distance to join them.

"How did it go?" Jacob asked Kaleb as he handed him a cup of water.

Kaleb nodded, taking the cup of water and taking a long sip. Jacob smiled and waited for Kaleb to finish.

"How did what go, where were you?" Danica asked, coming up from behind them.

"I cleared a path into the jungle, heading for the high ground." Kaleb said, finishing the water.

"By yourself?" Danica asked, trying to hide the emotion in her voice.

"Aye, the path I made led into another older path that was pretty easy to clear. Everyone was asleep except Jacob. He took over to keep an eye on everyone and I went to work." Kaleb explained.

Danica frowned a little bit at his statement. " You shouldn't have gone off by yourself. We don't know anything about this place or what's on it."

"It was fine." Kaleb said softly.

"Don't do it again." Danica said, her eyes narrowing at him.

Kaleb grinned seeing her reaction. He stepped towards her, closing the distance between. Danica felt her skin flush as she stood her ground. She quickly became aware of how the sweat on him danced across his muscular biceps and down to his forearms. She felt her cheeks grow warm as she tried to focus on making her point. He leaned in close; his mouth inches from hers. She felt herself inhale as her lips parted slightly. Her lips begging for his. He tilted his head sideways and whispered into her ear.

"Whatever you say ….Captain." He whispered his voice brushing her ear sending a shiver through her.

He grinned seeing her response as he stepped away from her. The playful grin still plastered on his face. She cleared her throat as she silently talked her body down in her head. She straightened her shoulders and turned away from Kaleb, ignoring him.

"Men, have you decided which of you will stay and which of you are joining us?" Dancia yelled out over the beach.

Kaleb hung back watching as the men began to shift into two groups. Danica stood in front of them waiting. They shifted into the two groups and then Timmy stepped forward.

"Ok captain, all the men on the left would like to come and the ones on the right want to stay on the beach." Timmy explained the two groups.

"Thank you Mr. Tim. All those on the left need you to gather supplies. Water, food, tools, weapons as well. I don't know what lies ahead for us in the jungle but I need us to be prepared for anything. The ones staying behind, you should probably make some type of shelter. Staying out in the open like we are is not safe. During the night hours there should be shifts where at least one to two people are awake to ensure the safety of the group." Danica ordered.

"We leave in fifteen minutes. All those coming gather at the entrance to the jungle that Mr. Kaleb was so kind to create." Danica ordered not looking towards Kaleb.

The men grunted and nodded their responses as they headed out to complete their task. Danica headed back to where she was sleeping and scooped up her bag. She glanced towards the men who had begun gathering their belongings. Others started gathering limbs from fallen trees. She figured they were going to make some type of shelter. She slung her bag over her shoulder and began making her way through the sand. She reached the entrance to the jungle and starred in. She looked at all the broken branches, you could see how there was once a natural way into the jungle but I had overgrown. Kaleb must have spent all night doing this. She thought studying it.

As she stared in the passage she got lost in it. She didn't even realize she had begun to walk into it.

She looked up at the tall trees that reached upward to the sky. The blue sky peeked down at her in between the dark green leaves. The earth smell that encompassed her right away as she walked onto the dirt. It was strange how just a few steps in the air immediately changed from the ocean air. The crunching of the leaves as she walked mesmerized her. She didn't know where she was going but something pulled her; trance like. The trees around her were so dense and overgrown that the path was just wide enough for you to walk down it. She paused looking upwards again and noticed that the trees began to entwine at the tops, almost wanting to block out the sky, the further she walked the darker it was becoming.

"Hey!"

Danica was spun full force around. She tripped on a tree root and was flung forward. Strong forearms reached out to catch her. Her hands going forward grabbing on to him. Kaleb grumbled pulling her into him as he studied her.  Danica blinked looking up at him confused why he was acting this way.

"Danica, I've been yelling for you since the beach." Kaleb said his hands gently on her shoulders as he studied her face.

"You have?" Danica said, still confused.

"Aye." Kaleb said his eyebrows pushed together as he looked at her.

"The beach isn't we...i didn't hear you.." Danica said as she looked away from Kaleb and looked over her surroundings.

The jungle came alive as she looked around. She hadn't heard Kaleb, she hadn't heard anything actually. The jungle noises rushed to her ears. The sound of bugs vibrating and clicking. Weird bird noises echoed around her. Everything was silent till now. She brought her eyes back to Kaleb who was still looking at her crazy.

"I don't know, I didn't hear you or anything actually. Aren't we just inside." Danica asked out loud but as she looked over Kaleb's shoulder she saw her answer.

They were not just inside the jungle, she couldn't even see the beach from where she was now.

"Danica, what do you mean you didn't hear anything? This isn't even the path I made, you stepped off of that path several feet back. I didn't even know this was here and I spent most of the night in here." Kaleb said, looking from her and then around them.

Danica looked about them once more, what did he mean this path wasn't his, she had just walked straight, she didn't turn or anything. Kaleb felt uneasy. He wanted to take her back to the beach, no back to the ship and lock her in the cabin. At Least then he would know she was safe. He watched her look around for answers and not finding any he saw her confusion deepen. He watched her quickly change herself and she seemed to stand taller.

"It's fine, I must have stepped off your path looking up at the trees. I was caught up in how beautiful it looked against the sky." Danica said, trying to rationalize everything.

"Kaleb, did you catch her!" Jacob's voice carried down the path to them.

"Aye we are over here!" Kaleb yelled back to him.

Danica stepped away from Kaleb as she heard several footsteps heading their way. She saw Jacob's worried face as he stepped on to the path. His brows disappointed looking as he looked at her.

"I guess when you say fifteen minutes you really mean seconds." Jacob said with a small smile.

"Sorry I got a little ahead of myself." Danica said softly.

She turned around and looked forward, something was telling her to stay on this path. She was sure what but she needed to continue this way. She couldn't see too far in front of them because of the twist and turns in it but it felt right.

"Captain, shall we go back to the other path?" Jacob asked almost leaning to leave.

"No, we're going this way." Danica said not looking at the men as she spoke but eyes still on the path.

"Captain I've already scouted the other way and just a head on it there's an old trail that's much more open then this one. Looks safer." Kaleb said his voice trying not to undermine her but held urgency in it.

"No, we need to go this way." Danica said, stepping forward.

"Danica-

"I said we would go this way." Danica said, snapping her head to him and glaring at him.

Kaleb jaw clenched as he pressed his teeth tightly into each other. He couldn't open his mouth to say anything right now because he wasn't sure what would come out. His nostril flared as he watched Danica begin walking. Jacob walked by him and patted him on his shoulder. Kaleb caught his hand and made him pause. He waited for the other men to get ahead of him.

"Watch her, there's something not right. She didn't even know I was screaming for her." Kaleb said to Jacob as he dropped his hand and walked by him.

Jacob followed after Kaleb confused by the whole situation but his gut trusted Kaleb. He decided he was going to stay close to Danica.

## Chapter Thirty Two

### Scars

Ariadne wrapped herself in the warmth next to her. She nuzzled her head into the warmth as  her toes curled. Her foot slowly rubbed against his leg subconsciously as she melted into the feeling. She could stay like this, she thought not wanting to open her eyes. She listened to his soft heart beat. The sound of it was better than any music she had ever heard. The rise and fall of his chest was begging her to fall back to sleep. She couldn't tell if he was still asleep, her eyes wanted to peek and look but she was afraid. Afraid that if she opened them and looked, the world would come rushing in and everything that she needed to handle would be waiting for her. She didn't want that, she wanted to stay in this small paradise where no one asked anything of her and she could just be.

"We can't stay like this forever." Patrick whispered to her.

"Shh.. yes we can. No one will notice. I'm sleeping, you're not talking to me." Ariadne said, squeezing her eyes tighter.

"As much as I would love to hide away here with you, like this. Especially you like this. I believe the ship will miss its captain." Patrick whispered.

"No shh. No captain here." Ariadne smiled.

"Ok well we can just wait till they come looking for us. I mean I have nothing to hide. They can see me nude no problem." Patrick smiled widely.

Nude… the word shouted in Ariadne's head. She was still naked; if someone did come looking they would definitely see her...all of her! She sighed deeply and grumbled.

"You ruined it." She pouted.

She groaned, stretching as she shifted away from him. She sat up on the edge of the bed, the blanket fell away from her exposing backside. Patrick's eyes wandered down her bare back. He felt himself grow with need. Ariadne went to stand when she felt arms wrapped around her stomach and pulled her back. She landed neatly into Patricks chest.

"I'll take it back." He mumbled into her neck as his lips began kissing her.

"No...no it's too late." Ariadne giggled playfully, pulling away from him.

"No it's not." He said against her skin, his teeth playfully biting her shoulder as his mouth began making its way back up her neck.

She leaned back into him, shutting her eyes; her body vibrating for his touch.  Her hand wrapped upwards to the back of his hair, her fingers entwined into it. She held him close as his mouth sent shivers through. A knock on the door came.

"Captain." A soft voice came through the door.

She tugged on his hair playfully, trying to pull him away from her neck although she didn't want to. She felt Patrick growl as he gave in.

"Aye?" Ariande called to the door as she swatted Patrick away.

Patrick growled, he pulled her back pinning her on the bed. Ariadne let out a small squeak as he did. He straddled her and began placing kisses along her collar bone. She put her hand over her mouth to help muffle her laughter which was quickly turning into small muffled moans, as he began traveling down her chest.

"Captain, you're needed at the helm. We're coming up on a passage and need orders." The voice came through the door.

"Go away is your order." Patrick mumbled against Ariadne's bare stomach.

Goosebumps scatter about her skin as she shivered. She wanted to wrap her legs around him and lock her body to his. She sighed deeply hearing the crew member.

"Aye I will be right there." Ariadne said, grabbing a handful of Patricks hair and tugging on it playful.

"Patrick, we need to go." She giggled, forcing his head up off her stomach.

He growled but lifted his head. She laughed at his response and leaned forward kissing the top of his head. He made a pouty face as she wiggled away from him. He watched her scoot off the bed. She hugged the blanket around her as she gathered her clothes. She felt his eyes on her and she got nervous as she tried to slip her pants on without taking off the blanket. She glanced over at him and he had a smirk on his face as he laid in the bed.

"Problem?" He asked, his smirk turning into a playful grin.

She frowned at him and then looked at him. Something flashed in her eyes and the embarrassed shy girl was gone. She smiled at him as she let the blanket go. It fell gracefully to the floor exposing her complete nakedness. Her smile provoked him. He shifted slightly wanting to cross and go to her, capture her and never let her leave this cabin. She was absolutely perfect.

"Problems?" She asked slyly as she shifted her hips side to side.

"You're perfect." Patrick said his eyes searching her body  and then locking with her eyes as he said it.

She felt her racing heart sutter as he said it. Her face felt warm and her whole body was flushed. She looked at him trying to understand. He stood and walked slowly to her. She caught herself looking down and away as he came to her. Her body wanted his touch but there was something happening making her feel vulnerable.

"You are absolutely perfect." He whispered, catching her chin and raising it up so she was looking in his eyes.

She smiled weakly but not for long. He stepped into her kissing her lips. She melted into him. She smiled, pulling away as she blindly searched for her clothes, finding them she began to put them on. He smiled, stepping back away from her, letting her gather her clothes and began putting them on. He walked over to his shirt on the floor and picked it up.

"Patrick?" He heard her voice almost whisper his name.

He went to turn to see her but her hand was on his back. He felt finger tips trace over a long scar. He shut his eyes as she touched it, pulling his lower lip in as he did. The scar stretched from his upper right hand shoulder and made its way across his back. Her finger tips found a matching one and then another and then another. She traced them, her heart hurting for him as she did. The scars were old and faded but His skin flinched under her touch as if her touching the scars were still painful. She withdrew her hand, staring at his back. The more she looked the more scars she saw.

"What did this to you?" Ariadne asked, her voice horrified.

"More of a who." Patrick answered as he slightly shifted out of her reach.

She let him leave her as her eyes were fixated on his back. He quickly pulled his shirt over covering his back. She watched him pause as if he was worried to turn around and see her.

"Who did that to you?" Ariadne asked her voice had anger and hurt in it although her tone was just above a whisper.

"I told you I couldn't leave my mother. That is why, it's also the reason Kaleb took off. " Patrick said quietly.

"Not all those marks were meant for me. My father is not just a ruthless businessman." Patrick said his jaw clenched.

Ariadne felt her chest rising and falling harshly as if she physically hurt from hearing what he was saying. She went to reach out and embrace him but another knock from the door drew her attention.

"What!" Ariadne snapped.

"Captain, I am sorry to keep disturbing you but we are now at stand still with no heading." The voice called through the door.

Ariadne bit her lip nervously. She needed to go but she wanted to stay with Patrick. She wanted to hold him and chase away the thoughts of his scars.

"Go on. They need you. I'll be out shortly." Patrick said his voice calm like nothing had just happened.

"Patrick I can't just leave." Ariadne said, starting to go to him.

"Go." Patrick said backing away from her a little, his back still facing her.

"Patrick." Ariadne said her voice held sadness.

"The men and mission need you right  now. Our siblings' lives hang in our hands. Go give out the orders." Patrick said almost sternly.

"Aye you-

"I am fine. It happened long ago. I'll be out in just a second." Patrick said, changing his voice to pretend he was ok.

Ariadne reluctantly gave in and headed to the door. Her hand shook as she reached for the handle and turned it. She felt like she was making a choice between Patrick and her duties. Maybe she can quickly give orders and come back in time to comfort Patrick she thought hopeful. Her stomach dropped as she unwillingly forced herself to walk out the door.

# Chapter Thirty Three

## Memories

Patrick watched the door shut and her fiery red hair disappear. He quickly found his shirt and pulled it over his head. He gritted his jaw thinking of his father. He said too much he shouldn't have told her. He stared down at the wooden floor. An image flashed in front of his eyes. Loud noises of yelling and dishes breaking. He could still feel the stairs creaking between his feet as if he was walking down the stairs in his old home. The yelling stopped as he reached the kitchen. He was scared, he didn't know why at the time but he felt like something bad was in the kitchen. Like there was a monster waiting for him. He was twelve and didn't believe in monsters anymore. He took a deep breath and walked into the kitchen. Porcelain dishes were shattered about the floor, his mother on the floor leaning against the kitchen cabinet. Tears stained her very red face.

"Mother?" Patrick whispered.

Her eyes grew wide as she shook her head at him and told him to go with her hands. He looked at her confused as he heard noises coming from the back door. His mother began to wave him out more fiercely but he didn't understand.

"No, I can help." He said confused and bent down to start picking up the broken dishes.

"Patrick?" He heard his fathers voice from behind him.

Panic flashed in his mother's eyes as she went to get up and go between Patrick and his father.

"Aye Father." Patrick answered, his father confused.

"Shouldn't you be in bed?" His father asked.

Patrick studied his father; His face was flushed, he had a small cut on his hand and he was breathing very hard. Patrick looked at his mother who seemed terrified. He was completely confused.

"I was but I heard something and I thought something bad happened so I came downstairs to see what happened. I was going to start helping my mother clean up. What happened father?" Patrick answered innocently.

Patrick's answer seemed to calm his father down, his father narrowed his eyes at his mother quickly before changing his expression to Patrick.

"Your Mother had an accident putting away the dishes, no big deal. You be a good boy and help her. I'm heading to bed." He said softly and ruffled Patricks hair.

Patrick smiled brightly and nodded as he went to work picking up the broken pieces. Patricks mother looked nervously at his father but quickly changed her expression as he left the room. Patricks mother scooped him into a hug and kissed his forehead sweetly before going to work cleaning herself. Patrick was confused about the whole event but soon he would understand too well. That was the first time he had witnessed his fathers true self but didn't realize it. If he had paid closer attention he would have noticed the swollen lips that his mother pressed to his forehead, he would have seen the bruises but he was just a child. He would grow up too quickly in the next few months to years.

Patrick shook the image out of his brain as he finished the last button on his shirt. He clenched his jaw tighter and prayed that his mother was ok while he was away this time. He started for the cabin door.

Ariadne walked out the cabin door and as the door shut behind her she felt regret. She should have stayed with Patrick and comforted him or something. She thought to herself. The sea air hit her face and blew her hair over her shoulder. She had to leave him, she was reasonable for all the lives on this ship and she was trying to save The North Star as well. She felt her stomach knot up as she tried to focus on what was going on.

"Captain, I am so sorry to keep bothering." He said softly as Ariande came out of the cabin.

"Kirk right?" Ariadne asked, looking at him.

"Aye Captain." Kirk smiled brightly at her.

"Is Jonah still at the wheel?" Ariadne asked as she began walking down the stairs to the lower deck, Kirk hurrying behind her.

"Aye Captain Darryl tried to take over but Jonah sent him away." Kirk explained and wincing slightly as he delivered her the news.

Ariadne frowned deeply as she began crossing the lower deck. As she reached  the stairs going up to the lower deck, her eyes caught Jonah. She sighed seeing him. He was barely hanging on to the wheel. He was exhausted and looked like he was on the verge of collapsing. After the storm he should have rested but he didn't. Ariadne marched across the upper deck to the helm stopping just short of the wheel; her hands planted firmly on her hips. Jonah glanced over an attempt of a smile appearing on his lips.

"Left or right Capt." He muttered his voice barely reaching her.

"You're relieved of duty Mr. Jonah please go to bed." Ariadne said, stepping to take the wheel.

"I am fine Captain, I just need a heading." Jonah grumbled, shaking his head.

"Mr. Kirk please assist Mr. Jonah to his cabin." Ariadne said, narrowing her eyes at Jonah as she spoke.

Kirk looked beside himself as he walked over to Jonah. Jonah frowned and as Kirk reached for him, he yanked his arm away. The sharp movement sent Jonah to the ground. The ship jerked to the right and began heading to the passage. Ariadne was quick and took control of the wheel. Her mind yelled "no passage no passage", as she quickly began turning the ship to the left. She felt relief as she steered the ship around the cliff passage. Once she was over there heart attack she looked over to Jonah.

"Kirk, how is he?" Ariadne asked, her eyes glancing from the horizon to them on the ground.

"I think he's asleep." Kirk said, his voice full with worry.

"Leave him there and go find someone to help you take him to his cabin. Have Darryl report to the helm as well." Ariadne order.

Patrick appeared on the upper deck, his face looked puzzled as he was trying to figure out what happened. She saw him coming and she tried to push the shivers that crept up the back of her knees. She inhaled slightly and blew out a long breath as he approached her. Seeing his face a small smile formed on her lips, she wanted to reach over and touch him but she couldn't. He walked over to Ariadne and gave her a look asking without saying anything.

"Jonah was a stubborn ass and decided to keep steering the ship. He passed out from exhaustion." Ariadne explained very matter of fact.

"Ah." He said quietly as he walked over to Jonah.

Patrick crouched down and began assessing him. He looked him over and checked for any injuries from the fall. He glanced up to Ariadne who kept looking over at him.

"He will be ok, he has no injuries, he just pushed himself too hard. He's going to have one hell of headache when he wakes up but that's probably it." Patrick said from his squatting position.

"Aye I told him to let Darryl steer while I...After the storm." Ariadne said, a little frustrated.

Patrick smirked a little as he glanced up at her from the ground. Ariadne cheeks flushed as she tore her eyes away from him. He watched her turn away and his smirk deepened. He glanced back at Jonah and rolled his eyes. He placed one of his arms under his head and the other arm under his legs.

"You're such a pain in the ass." Patrick muttered as he scooped Jonah up.

"Patrick there's-

Araidne started to say but stopped as she watched all of Patrick muscle tense as he carried Jonah like a baby to the first mate cabin. He kicked open the door and Ariadne couldn't help but laugh and then flush as an image of him carrying her the same way, kicking the door open the same way flashed to through her head. Patrick carried Jonah over to the bed and let him drop on it. He quickly turned and walked out of the room. Not a second glance given. Patrick came back out a few seconds later muttering to himself. He slammed the door shut behind him as he walked out. Ariadne muffled another laugh as she saw him come out still annoyed.

"What?" He asked her as he walked over to the helm.

"Do you have a habit of carrying people around?" She chuckled.

"No just people who are pains in the ass." Patrick smirked.

"Hey!" Ariadne yelled and reached over whacking him in the arm.

He caught her hand swiftly and brought it to his lips. He placed a slow kiss on it that set her skin on fire. Her eyes locking into his, he kissed her hand  like the kiss was meant for somewhere else.

"Captain...um where is Mr. Jonah?" Kirk asked as he reached the helm, another crew member and Darryl with him.

"Mr. Patrick sweetly carried him to his cabin." Ariadne said, trying her hardest not to laugh.

Kirk cracked a smile and Darryl chuckled. Patrick glared at all of them as he frowned. Ariadne gave him a silly grin before looking ahead. The path around the passage was clear, the sky looked good and she had set the ship far enough away from the cliff side so there was no chance of the cliff hitting the ship or rocks falling.

"Darryl, I am going to continue to steer for the time being. I will call for you when it's time to change out. I need you or Kirk to  keep checking on Jonah." Ariadne ordered them, her eyes focused on the sky.

"I also want the sails at half mast, we don't need to be going so fast around this cliff." Ariadne order being cautious.

"Aye Captain." They both said indusind.

"Mr. Patrick, would you mind keeping me company?" Ariadne asked sweetly.

"I would love to." He said walking forward to the upper deck rail and leaning against it.

Kirk and Darryl smiled to each other regarding
the scene between Patrick and Ariadne before
walking down to the lower deck and following orders.

# Chapter Thirty Four

## Trance

"This way." Danica yelled as she rounded another corner, the men growing tired as the jungle around them became dark.

They had been walking for hours, the jungle growing thicker and darker as they walked. Danica wasn't stopping. She was not even really with them. Jacob had called to her a few miles back asking her to slow her pace but she acted like she didn't even hear them. This was the first time she had spoken or acknowledged them since she veered off the path. She wasn't using any directional tools, no compass, no map, she hadn't even looked at the map she was clutching tightly in her fist. She couldn't see the stars the Jungle had locked out the sky.  That was it Kaleb had enough of whatever this was. He moved up in the group he had hung back making sure everyone was ok.

"Dani!" He called up to her as he began to push his way through the men.

The men did their best to move aside but the path they started on was getting smaller and smaller as they went on. Kaleb pushed by Jacob who was looking at Danica with the same look of concern that Kaleb was feeling.

"The men need to rest, we need to stop or some of them are going to start falling out. I've shouted to her twice but it's like she doesn't hear me." Jacob told Kaleb as he reached him.

"Aye I heard you, have the men slow their pace and we will try to find someplace a little bit more open to rest. I will get to Danica." Kaleb said as he moved past Jacob.

"Men, let's take it easy, the Captain is trying to find a place to rest. She's going to go on ahead and try to find a more open area, let's slow our pace." Jacob shouted trying to cover for Danica the best he could.

Kaleb moved up to the front of the group. Danica had slowed or even missed footing since they started. He picked up his pace just to catch up to her. Reaching her, he waited a second to see if she would even acknowledge him being there. When she didn't he reached out to touch her.

"Danica." He said as he touched her shoulder.

Danica jerked like something had shocked her, her eyes flickered to him. She stared at him as she backed away.She was trying to focus on him but it was like she didn't know who he was.

"Danica." Kaleb said softly, stepping towards her.

Her eyebrows narrowed at him; confusion still written on her face. He was confused about what was going on with her. Why was she acting this way? He thought as he reached out and touched her cheek with his hand. She didn't pull away and it seemed like whatever was clouding her eyes was starting to shift away.

"It's Kaleb." He whispered to her, his thumb stroking her cheek gently.

"Kaleb?" Danica whispered back her hand going to touch his.

"Aye Love come back to me." Kaleb said to her, stepping closer.

"Kaleb." Danica said, snapping out of it.

Danica looked around quickly trying to see where they were.  She remembered walking into the jungle and remembered Kaleb finding her. The rest of it was all blank. She looked back at the men who were exhausted. The jungle was closing in on them, her eyes flickered back to Kaleb asking him what had happened.

"I don't know Love, you have been leading us relentlessly and it was like you weren't here. Like you weren't you." Kaleb said his voice was still gentle as he told her.

"I don't remember anything. The last thing I remember was you catching up to me when I veered off the path to begin with and then before that I was just looking into the jungle." Danica said trying to hide her concern, she shifted herself away from him as she tried to see where the men were.

"It's ok. We will figure this out. The men need to rest, I think it's night.  It's hard to tell. We need to find a place to set up for the night . It's hard with everything being so overgrown, an open area would be best." Kaleb said half talking to himself as he tried to think of something.

Kaleb looked back down the path where the men were slowly catching up. Jacob locked eyes with Kaleb asking if everything was ok. Kaleb nodded shortly. Everything was not ok but for right now it was. He looked back to where Danica was standing and she was gone.

"Shit." Kaleb cursed.

"Men wait here!" Kaleb called as  he began almost running down the path to try to find her.

The path seemed like it got darker as he traveled further down it. It twisted and turned. She couldn't have walked this far in that short of time. Panic was starting to set in. There was something wrong with this jungle. Everything in him was telling him they needed to get out of it as soon as he could. The soft dirt path turned into rocks, almost gravel like rock. He was going so fast he nearly tripped when it changed.

The jungle opened up into a large clearing that was lit up by the moonlight. It had an outline of white gravel rocks and then opened up to green grass. In the center of it Danica was standing looking upwards. Her long raven colored hair flowed down her back in soft waves, the moonlight causing it to shimmer a blue. She looked like something out of a fairy tale and he would have been completely captivated if it wasn't for the fact that she gave him a heart attack.

"Dani." He called to her as he started walking into the clearing, he was hesitant because he wasn't sure how she was.

"You can see every star in the sky." Danica said but no emotion in her voice.

"Danica damn it, you nearly gave me a heart attack when you took off." Kaleb said, now mad hearing her talk.

"You can't just take off like that. Not in a fucking jungle." Kaleb said, stomping over to her.

Danica turned around at him, her eyes narrowing a little bit. He couldn't tell if she was there or not and it scared him.

"Don't talk to me like that." She all but growled at him.

He studied her for a second. He didn't know what was going on but it wasn't good. He finished walking the distance to her. He looked at her carefully. She smiled brightly at him and then looked back up to the sky.

"Love, you scared me. Please don't go off on your own the rest of the time that we are here." Kaleb said, reaching to take her hand.

As he touched her hand, she jolted back. The same confusion flashed before her eyes as she recognized him. She looked at him for a moment and then back up at the stars.

"Did you hear me?" He asked her not to let go of her hand.

"Kaleb." She said looking back to him, her eyes finally looking like hers and not like they were fogged over.

"Aye, stop going off on your own." He repeated once more to her.

"Aye, sorry. Hey, how did you find this place? Look, you can see every star in the sky. Weren't you just talking about an open area. This is perfect, you did a good job." Danica said to him, still looking up.

Kaleb's mouth dropped as he stared at her. He was looking at her like she was insane. She went to withdraw her hand from his and ask him what was his problem but he squeezed her hand tighter.

"No, you're holding my hand from here on out." Kaleb said not letting go.

"Ok but can you explain to me why you're looking at me as if i've grown another head?" Danica asked as she entwined her fingers back into his.

"Because you found this place, I didn't." Kaleb said, looking around.

"I found this place?" She asked, confused.

"Aye, it's ok. Just hold my hand ok. We need to go get the men-

"Kaleb!" Jacobs' voice yelled from the path.

"Aye over here, keep heading straight." Kaleb yelled back to Jacob.

"You left the men?" Danica asked him quietly.

"Aye you were gone. That was the only thing that mattered right then and there. Jacob had them." Kaleb explained.

She stepped in closer to him and he placed his arm around her. The men began walking into the clearing.They all had the same look of wonder and amazement on their faces. Jacob walked over to

Danica and Kaleb questions written all over his face. Kaleb just shook his head.

"We are staying here for tonight. Set up camp, we need a fire as well. Pair off and start getting things done." Kaleb said.

"What's going on with her?" Jacob whispered to Kaleb.

"Jacob I'm right here and I don't know. I keep almost blacking out. I'm here now thank you." Danica answered.

"Sorry Captain. You just have us worried." Jacob apologized.

"Aye thank you for always looking after me." Danica said with a soft smile to him letting her know she wasn't upset with him.

He smiled back and then looked at Kaleb as if he was thinking. He glanced back at Danica , questions flashed across his face.

"Danica, have you eaten anything from the jungle?" Jacob asked as he looked from Kaleb to her.

"I don't think so, why?" Danica asked.

"Sometimes plants can do things to the mind, like a poison."Jacob said, glancing at Kaleb.

"I don't remember eating anything, I actually can't tell you what I ate last. I don't remember much since the beach." Danica said frustrated.

"It's ok Love we will figure this out. Stay next to me until we do. Let's get you something to eat." Kaleb said with a nod to Jacob as they headed over to the main part of the camp.

They walked over to the men dispersing food rations, Kaleb holding on to Danica's hand so tight that she thought he was going to crush her bones. She wiggled her fingers against his hand to let him know. He looked over at her,  his face asking her what was wrong.

"If you break my hand you won't be able to hold it any more." She said with a smile.

He gave her a half smile and loosened his grip. He was afraid to let go. He didn't need her vanishing again, if he lost her in this jungle he didn't know if he would be able to find her. He would find her but the risk of it. He sighed out loud. As he did he felt her hand on his cheek. She rubbed it softly with her thumb.

"It's going to be ok." She said to him,

He gave in and leaned into her hand. He would make sure it was ok. He responded to her in his mind. She pulled her hand away from his face and something on her wrist caught his eyes. He reached for her other hand. She looked at him confused and gave it to him. He turned it over and studied it. On the outer side of her wrist were three small punctures.

"Danica, did you catch yourself on a vine or something?" Kaleb asked, still looking at it.

Danica looked at her wrist confused. It didn't even hurt. She didn't remember doing that. She frowned and shook her head letting him know she didn't know.

"Does it hurt?" He asked her brushing his thumb over it.

"No, I didn't even know it was there till just now." Danica said with a shrug.

The more Kaleb looked at the more the pit in his stomach grew. The agonizing feeling that something was wrong gnawing at his inside. The three punctures were so tiny and so perfectly set up it looked almost purposely done.

"Captain are you hungry?" The man handing out food rations broke the silence between her and Kaleb.

"Very." She smiled, taking her hand away from Kaleb but still holding his hand with her other hand.

"Excellent, I have your rations right here, the captain can have more if she would like. Oh and I

have a blanket setup over there if you want to use it."
The man smiled brightly.

"Thank you Jerry. I will have just my ration but I would
love to use the blanket." Danica smiled at him.

"You know my name captain?" Jerry asked with a
smile.

"Aye I try to know all my men's names. Thank you
again Jerry." Danica smiled taking her rations.

"Thank you captain. Mr. Kaleb here is yours."
Jerry said, handing Kaleb's his.

Kaleb nodded his thanks as he took it. He
walked over with Danica to the blanket. She looked at
him and his hand. It was going to be difficult eating
and holding his hand. She raised an eyebrow at him.

"Aye I was serious I am not letting you go."
Kaleb said to him his face held the same seriousness
as his voice did.

"So you're just going to hold my hand forever?"
Danica said laughing.

Her laughter filled the clearing echoing around
in a musical way. She put her free hand over her
mouth as the men looked over at her. She shrugged
lightly, a silly smile still on her face as she looked at
Kaleb who was frowning at her. She stuck her tongue
out at him as she lowered herself to the ground. He

smiled a little smile at her and sat down next to her. She rolled her eyes softly at him and began eating her food happily one handed.

"How exactly are we going to sleep?" Danica asked with a mouth full of food.

"I'm wrapping you up in my arms and you won't be able to go anywhere." Kaleb said, throwing a wink at her.

# Chapter Thirty Five

## Haunting

Danica stretched into him, Kaleb's warm body pressed against as he wrapped his arms around her. He had made them a spot in the inner part of the clearing, his eyes staring into the surrounding trees as if he was waiting for something before he actually decided to settle down. Danica's yawning was his final giving point. He had laid out a blanket one handed before laying down on it and pulling him against her. Kaleb wasn't kidding when he said he wasn't letting her go. He held her hand everywhere she went that night and when it was time to finally laid down and get some sleep. He did just what he said. He laid down and pulled her into his arms. She chuckled curling up into him. Turning over in his arms, She rested her head on his chest and listened to his heart beat. Kalebs strong arms encased her. She looked up at the millions of stars looking down on them and studied them.

"They are beautiful. More beautiful than anything I have ever seen." She whispered sleepily.

"They are beautiful but not the most beautiful thing I've seen." He smiled back at her.

"Aye, I know Mr. Wander. I bet you've seen tons of beautiful amazing things." She answered groggy.

"Aye but there's one thing that's more beautiful than anything else." He brushed a hair out of her face and tucked it behind her ear.

She wanted to pry and part of her wanted to ask if it was her. She yawned deeply and her eyes watered. She was too exhausted to start down that road. She glanced back up at the sky feeling her eyes grow heavy. She noticed something off about the sky, the stars were almost shifted out of place. She was too tired to keep her eyes open to actually explore this. She pushed it off to her being tired and started giving into sleep.

"I think the stars are wrong." She muttered into his chest before her body gave into sleep.

He had been staring at her, his eyes tracing the slight curve of her chin to her cheek bones. The way her eyes looked so peaceful shut and her mouth was daring him to kiss her. He was mesmerized by her. His sleepy voice caught his ear.

Are the stars wrong? He thought as he drew his eyes to the sky. He searched the dark cold sky trying to see what she meant. He yawned trying to remember constellations and how to find them. He went to find the easiest Ursa Major. The handle always stood out to him. He traced the stars till he found it. He felt instantly better finding it. Ok find the two stars at the end of the cup and it points the way to the north star. He thought he found them and then guided his eyes over to the Ursa Minor handle where the north star sits. It was off, she was right the stars seem to have shifted slightly. There was nothing wrong with the sky or stars back on the ship. He gritted his teeth together. There's something wrong with this island. He thought to himself looking about. He watched me awake pacing trying to keep myself awake. Another man who was on fire duty poked the fire with a long stick trying to keep it going. Jacob was resting. He knew he should too so he could change out. Jacob had already ordered a few men to take the first shift, then they would switch out with the ones asleep and so on. He pushed the stars from his mind and shut his eyes. Maybe he was just tired.

Danica shivered; she went to roll into Kaleb's warmth but he wasn't there. She opened her eyes, her hand searching for him. The world around her was pitch black. There was a white fog hanging over the ground and it wrapped around the clearing. She couldn't see anyone.

"Kaleb?" She whispered as she stood putting her hand out in front of her as she began to slowly move around.

The fog was thick and ghostly. The light from the moon and stars were gone. She glanced up at the moon and the stars were completely gone. The sky was empty as she looked up. She felt chills run up her arms.

"Kaleb!" she called out into the darkness.

She heard her voice echo out into the clearing, Kaleb, Kaleb , Kaleb. No other sounds were around. She tried to calm her heart, beating rapidly in his chest. Where was everyone? Where was the crew? Where was Kaleb?

"Hello?" She yelled out once more again the only voice she heard was her own hello echoing back to her.

She inhaled telling herself she was fine, that everything was going to be fine and she just needed to find everyone. She began to move about the clearing blindly. As she began making her way to the outer part of the clearing. Then she heard it.

"Danica." It was soft and subtle but she heard it.

She froze trying to figure out if she actually heard it or if she wanted so badly to find someone she was making it up. She paused in the fog, waiting and listening. Silence, not even the insects were making noises. No animal sounds just absolute stillness. She sighed and continued making her way through the fog.

"Danica!" This time it was urgent and shocked Danica, she immediately stopped and tried to find out where it was coming from.

"Danica."

She knew the voice, why was it so familiar. It was female, she was the only female in the crew so now she was alarmed even more.

"Dani."

The voice called switching to her nickname. It sounded like Ariadne but she knew there was no way it could be her.

"Ari?" She answered back and decided to muster up all her courage and head after the voice.

Regardless she needed to know who it was and where it was. Maybe she would have answers for her. She began following the sound of the voice. She felt the white rocks under her feet as she began crossing out of the clearing. The white rocks turned to dirt and she knew she was moving away from the clearing.

"Dannnnica."

Danica inhaled as the voice began to sing, she tried to push the thoughts of how creepy it was. Especially that it sounded so much like her sister.

"Ariadne?" She asked softly hoping that maybe somehow in all this madness her sister was here.

She didn't know where she was going but the voice kept calling to her and she knew she was getting close. She followed the sound down a twisty path. The world around her was still silent as she walked the over hanging trees that seemed to reach down at her. She was walking slowly due to the fog that was now slowly turning into mist. She was trying to remember her surroundings as she went. She needed to remember how to get back to the clearing.

"Stop!"

The voice shouted, shaking Danica from her thoughts. She halted and her eyes grew wide as she looked in front of her. An arch way of bright white flowers. They were enormous with giant white petals. Danica studied the archway wondering why she was stopping. She took a step closer.

"Take a flower." The voice was all but a whisper now.

Danica whipped around thinking that it was behind her. She stared into the mist waiting for someone. She was really hoping it was someone she knew.

"Come out." Danica said, trying to make her voice stronger than she was feeling right now.

"Take a flower." The voice said but now there was a figure coming out of the mist.

Danica stood still. She reached for her side but realized she had left everything at the campsite. She had no weapon or anything to defend herself. She waits for the figure to come into sight.

"Why." Danica whispered to the slow moving figure.

"Take a flower." The figure ordered again showing itself.

It was a woman who looked exactly like her mother but with her fathers hair. Danica stepped back away from the figure. There was something otherworldly about her. Danica kept backing away from the woman as she continued to walk slowly to her.

"Who are you?" Danica said as she backed into the flower archway.

"Take a flower!" She shouted and in a split second Danica's hand was thrown into the arch way of flowers.

Danica tore her hand out of the archway and looked down at her wrist. There was a sharp pain and she turned her hand over and she saw three tiny punctures. She looked down at them and she felt herself becoming lost. The world slowly was becoming faded. Everything went black and silent.

"Don't let the men near the cave. They'll hear it." The voice said to her as she struggled to see through the darkness.

"What cave? They'll hear what?" Danica said her arms out in front of her moving about.

"They hear the siren and then they'll be lost." The voice said again.

"Who are you? What cave? What do you mean by siren?" Danica whispered.

"I am a friend." It whispered.

"You look like my mother." Danica said.

"I know I choose the way I look." She said hauntingly.

"What are you?" Dabina said this time her voice became frustrated.

Danica felt a hard shove and as she fell forward the world came back. She hit the ground but it wasn't like the thick dirt she had been walking on. It wasn't rock ethier it was soft almost like beach sand. She stood quickly up and looked around as the woman was gone. Danica turned hearing waves, was she back on the beach? She turned and found herself staring into a deep dark cave. Her eyes traveled upwards and the cave turned into the mountain. The mountain reached high into the cold sky. She heard waves again and looked into the cave. The sound of the ocean was coming from inside the cave. She looked down at the sand, beach sand.

"Where the sky meets the sea." She said out
loud to herself; the treasure was inside the cave.

# Chapter Thirty Six

## Let Go

Danica walked slowly to the cave entrance. Peering inside it was pitch black. She went to step inside the cave carefully, something was telling her to be cautious.

"The flower." The voice called to her.

"Flower?" Danica asked, withdrawing her foot from inside the cave.

She turned trying to find the figure again but she wasn't there. She looked down at her hand and there was the white flower. Its stem had three thorns on it. She brought it up to her face looking at it. The thorns matched the punctures on her wrist. She looked at the flower; what was she supposed to do with this. She let the flower dangle in her hand as she looked back at the cave. A soft melody began flowing out the cave. It was haunting and beautiful. Danica tried looking deeper into the cave without going in but couldn't see anything.

"Alright here goes nothing." She whispered before stepping into the cave.

"Danica!"

Kaleb woke up in a panic, he knew before he even opened his eyes that she was going. His stomach was knotted and he could feel the acid creeping up his throat. He sat up in a jolt. The world around him was silent, the men laid about on the ground still asleep. Jacob was up still by the fire, his eyes looking around scanning the perimeter every so often. Kaleb got to his feet quickly, where the heck was Danica. He scanned the clearing quickly, the anxiety he was feeling increasing each time his eyes swept over the area and not finding her. He nearly ran to Jacob, he could feel his chest tightening as he reached him.

"Jacob, where's Danica?" He blurted out.

"Danica?" Jacob asked, standing and looking around.

"She's not with you. She was just literally in your arms. What do you mean?" Jacob said, turning in a full circle as he looked about.

"She couldn't have gotten far." Kaleb said as he began to walk away from Jacob.

"Where are you going?" Jacob yelled at his back.

"I don't know but I can't just sit here. You wait here and see if she comes back." Kaleb yelled back to him as he reached his stuff.

He flung his bag over his shoulder and grabbed a sword, looping into its holder on his waist belt. He scanned the woods surrounding them looking for a clue. He saw broken branches and began heading that way. As he reached the edge of the woods he didn't think twice before ducking into it. He needed to find Danica. The moonlight was bright and he could see where he was going. He looked down at the path and saw fresh footsteps in the dirt. He prayed that he was following hers.

"Danica!"He shouted deep into the woods.

He didn't care what heard at this point he would fight  anything standing in his way of finding her. He walked past several broken branches; she was just walking to them. He was nearly running as he turned down the next path. He slowed as he found the archway of flowers. He noticed a piece of cloth attached to the archway. He paused to look at it, it was a teal blue the same color of Danica's shirt. He saw a small droplet of blood on the piece of fabric as he reached for it. Just as he was about to tear the fabric from the archway he noticed the long thorns on the flowers and avoided getting pricked.

He left the fabric attached to the archway and passed underneath. He went to step on the hard dirt soil but once he passed the archway the dirt turned into beach sand. He nearly stumbled at the change in texture. He glanced back at the archway, he didn't see this a minute ago. He looked through the archway and saw the jungle. He carefully stepped back through it. He took a deep breath in and turned to face the archway. As he looked at the archway he saw more jungle.

"What is going on?" Kaleb said to himself as he carefully placed his arm through the archway.

He didn't know what he was expecting to happen but nothing did. He held his breath and stepped through the archway. Once more his feet hit sand and the jungle was no longer surrounding him. He spun on his feet and looked at the archway. It must be some type of illusion or reflection trick he thought. He knew at some point when they neared the treasure that he should except traps and tricks. Every pirate hides their treasure with the intent of no one but them being the person to get to it.  As he turned he felt a rush of relief he saw her standing in front of a cave. Her long raven hair flowing down in soft curls into her back. Her teal color shirt sleeves were tattered and torn but she didn't seem to have noticed. He watched her about to step into the cave.

"Danica!" He yelled to her as he rushed onto the sand heading towards the cave.

She withdrew her foot from the cave and turned to look at him, confused. The white flower hanging in her hand as blood dripped down her wrist from the punctures.

"Kaleb?" Danica asked not sure if he was really there or not.

He crossed the sand to her, his hand going to her cheek as he reached her. His eyes searching hers.

"You left again." He said breathlessly, he didn't realize how out of breath he was.

"How did you find me? Especially with all the fog? I tried finding anyone but couldn't." Danica asked him, still staring at him like she expected him to disappear.

"Fog? Dani, everyone is still back at the clearing. You left and no one even saw you leave." Kaleb said hsi hand going to her forehead.

"Are you ok?" He asked her as he watched her process what he said.

"No Kaleb, I woke up and everyone was gone. There was nothing but fog. It was so thick I couldn't see anything. But then this voice started calling me. It sounded like Ariadne but it wasn't. It led me here." Danica said, looking from him back to the cave.

"Ok maybe you dreamt it. We should get back and you should probably put that flower down." Kaleb said going to reach for the flower.

The white petals were speckled with little droplets of Danica's blood. As he reached for it she pulled her hand away putting the flower behind her back so he could not get it. She stepped back one foot crossing the cave entrance.

"No, I need the flower." Danica said defensively to him.

"Ok keep the flower, let's just get back to camp. Come on Love." Kaleb said, holding his hand out to her.

"I have to go inside the cave. Don't you see it's where the sky meets the sea. Can't you hear the ocean coming from inside of it and it's under a mountain that stretches far into the sky. I've found it, Kaleb." Danica said with a bright smile.

Kaleb inhaled and exhaled trying to be careful with his words. He wanted to call her crazy and scoop her up. Carry her back to camp so he would know she would be safe. He looked up at the mountain. She was right, this place did match the riddle.

"Aye Love i agree but we should go get some supplies and more men to help us." Kaleb said, stepping into the cave to take both her hands.

"No, it's fine, I can do this. I think only I'm supposed to go." Danica said, looking down into the cave.

The soft melody began to play again as they both stepped completely into the cave. As Kaleb entered the melody changed and became high pitched. Danica covered her ears. She glanced at Kaleb whose expression had gone blank. The noise wasn't even bothering him. He walked right past her and began slowly walking into the cave. She reached out and grabbed ahold of his arm. The voice had said not to let the men in the cave. Danica began to panic as she tugged hard on Kaleb's arm trying to stop him. It was no use he was dragging her along behind him. She dug her heels in and used all her strength to pull him back but he wouldn't budge. He tore his arm away from her and continued walking.

"Kaleb!" Danica shouted her voice echoing deep into the cave.

Kaleb didn't falter; he kept walking like he was unaware of anything in the world at that moment. The high pitch noise was piercing to her ears. She couldn't stand to hear it any longer. She followed after him, her hands pressed over her ears praying that something would snap Kaleb out of it. Was this what he was talking about with her episodes? She wondered as she was now basically jogging to keep up with him. His touch snapped her out of her trances but he wasn't even acknowledging hers. Catching up with him she reached out grabbing ahold of his arm with all her might. She tried to spin him to her but didn't have the strength. She anchored herself burying her heels deep within the sand and lowering her body. She was holding him in place as he struggled to move forward.

"Kaleb! Please! Stop!" She shouted at him as she held on to him with everything she had.

He kept trying to walk forward and shake her off his arm but she wasn't letting go. He then began to shake and tremor like it was causing him physical pain to not be able to advance further into the cave. She needs to get him out of there. His skin was starting to turn hotter as she hung on to him. His breathing became rapid and he began to whimper. She tried to focus on pulling him towards the exit but she couldn't move him back. They were just staying in place and Kaleb was becoming more in pain by the second. An agonizing yell rippled through him and he launched himself forward away from Danica. She was thrown forward with him as he went. He was now dragging her behind him. She tried to hang on as the sand and rocks dug into her flesh. Her ears felt like they were bleeding and if she could hear after this it would be a miracle. She could feel her grip slipping and as if Kaleb's body knew he shook her off. Danica's face hit the sand as she was left behind.

# Chapter Thirty Seven

## Trap:

Danica struggled to get to her feet pushing off the sand. She stumbled as she tried to race after Kaleb. The piercing noise was growing with each step she took. Covering her ears she pushed herself forward. She could hear a low rumble noise that reminded her of the ocean's waves crashing against the shore. She knew water was coming up soon and she had to stop Kaleb before he walked mindlessly into it.

The cave passage narrowed. The rocks lining it were dark ash color and jagged. She was careful not to brush against them for fear that the sharp edges would tear into her flesh. She was close to him now he was just out of reach. She held out her hand in front of desperately trying to touch him. Part of her was praying that he would trip, fall or collapse. She went to grab him and he moved slightly. As if expecting her to touch him. She nearly fell again trying to grab him. Her lungs were on fire trying to keep up with him, her chest was stinging from the rapid movement of her breathing.

"Kaleb." She pleaded, her voice almost broken sounding.

He didn't hear, he kept moving. She pushed herself after him, her legs feeling like they were going to buckle with each step. Just as she wasn't sure she could keep going, Kaleb slowed and then stopped. The dark shallow path opened up into a large opening. The dark ash colored rocks circled a deep shimmering blue pool. The stars danced on the water and they shimmered down from a large opening in the roof of the cave. It was breathtaking.  She slowly moved next to Kaleb, her eyes locked on the blue pool in front of them. Even though the sounds of waves could be heard, the pool was still. The piercing noise seemed to slow for the moment. She reached out to carefully take Kaleb's hand. He stood there almost swaying as his eyes locked on the pool.

"Kaleb?" Danica asked softly, taking his hand into hers; he didn't move or pull away from her.

She felt some type of relief that she was holding his hand and he was no longer moving forward. She looked from him to the pool. The pool looked endless and you could not see the bottom. Some spots seem shallow. She looked closer at the blue water and realized that in the shallow spots were rocks. Her eyes bounced from one shallow spot to the next. If the water was lowered the rocks would be exposed and almost create a stepping stone path. She leaned over looking at the water trying to determine if it was possible to still use the path with water over them. The water began to shimmer with flashes of light. Danica stepped back quickly, surprising her. She tried to move Kaleb back as well but he was glued to his spot. The water began to dance with random flashes of light. Danica stepped closer to the water trying to get a better look. The flashes were coming from something moving in the water.

"Eels." She whispered, stepping away from the water.

The pool was filled with eels. She frowned; she couldn't even touch the water now for fear of being electrocuted or shocked. She didn't know why but she knew the stepping stones were part of the next step but how could she get around the eels. The piercing noise tore her from her thoughts. It began getting louder again. As it became loud Kaleb started trying to move into the water.

The voice's warning flashed through her head: don't let the men near the cave or the siren will get them. She first thought the siren was meant as the legendary creature mermaids but no there was an actual siren calling Kaleb to his death. She wrapped herself around his waist trying to hold him back from entering the water. As if the eels knew he was about to step into the pool. The eels lined up in front of Kaleb flashing and waiting. Danica panicky looked around the cave trying to find where the noise was coming from but she couldn't see anything. Kaleb took a slow step forward the water now just inches from him. The eels seemed to inch forward in anticipation. Danica grabbed hold of Kaleb and pulled him back but she couldn't get him to budge. She dug her heels into the sand and pulled with all her might. He would stumble back shifting towards her but never moved.

"Please" She begged, holding onto him tighter.

The flower she had been carrying floated down onto the sand in front of her, brushing her leg as it went down. She glanced down at the flower with wonder. She didn't even realize she still had it . the specks of her blood against the white petals caught her eye. She glanced down at her wrist that she had tightly wrapped around Kaleb's forearm. The puncture wounds stood out to her. What if the flower was the reason she was not in a trance?

She glanced from Kaleb to her arm then to the flower. She was worried that she wasn't right but she was all out of options.  While still holding onto Kaleb she reached down stretching to try and get the flower. She couldn't reach it, she tried pulling the flower closer with her foot but lifting her foot made Kaleb able to move forward. She had to let go of him to get the flower. If she let go of him he was going into the water with the Eels who were eagerly waiting for him. She could scream, she felt like crying. The anxiety and adrenaline coursing through her was causing her to shake as she clung to him. She did the only thing she could think of. She moved herself infront of him and threw her weight towards him, as she crashed her body into his she let go of him. Hoping the weight and impact would send him back far enough for her to grab the flower.

Kaleb stumbled backwards and as he did Danica let go of him and dropped into the sand snatching the flower. Within seconds like nothing phased him Kaleb was walking towards him like she wasn't even there. She was now blocking his way to the pool. She needed to move or he was going to walk through her. She held her ground flower in hand ready. As he went to walk into her Danica snatched his forearm and pressed the flower thrones into him. He immediately froze, he let out a small groan and his head slumped forward. Danica captured his face with her hands and tried to lift his head. He was non responsive.

"Kaleb?" Danica asked, still holding his face in her hands.

Seconds passed which felt like hours as they stood like that. She looked down briefly at the flower in her hand and saw his blood droplets combined with hers were now slowly turning the white petals completely red. She looked down confused as to how three drops from her and three drops from him could do this. Within minutes the flower was now blood red. As the flower turned blood red Kaleb inhaled gasping, his eyes shot open and he reached out like he was trying to defend himself.

"Kaleb! Kaleb it's me, you're ok." Danica trying to calm him.

He froze hearing his voice, his eyes studying her as they swept over her face. Questions flowed into his face as he placed a hand on top of hers, that were still cradling his face.

"Dani what the hell was that?" Kaleb asked his eyes now looking about the cave.

"I don't know." Danica answered, relieved hearing him talk to her.

"Ugh do you hear that." Kaleb said his hands went to his ears covering them.

Danica knew he was talking about the piercing shrieking noise that was no longer luring him to his death. She smiled, thanking god that he was hearing it then she was.

"Aye but it's better than not hearing it." Danica smiled.

"Kaleb we need to-

Danica let out a loud scream as her body convulsed. Pain, searing pain radiates up from her leg and begins to course through her body. She was uncontrollable twitching. She let out another blood chilling scream as the pain began to make her skin feel like it was on fire. Kaleb went to grab her and then paused seeing what was happening. Danica's foot had gone into the pool. An eel had attached itself to her leg and his fellow friends were following. Kaleb inhaled preparing himself for how bad this was going to hurt. He grabbed a hold of Danica. As he touched her the electric shock course through his body. He fought through the unbearable pain as he pulled Danica out of the water. Wth one last yank she fell forward. As she did the blood red flower fell into the pool just as her foot was leaving the water.

Ripples from the flower course through the pool. The flower disintegrated, a flash of light lit up the cave as it did. The eels vanished, the one that had attached itself to Danica's leg let out a shriek and turned to ash, the same color as the rocks surrounding the cave. The cave was now silent, the piercing shrieking noise had simply stopped once the eels disappeared. The noise all along was coming from the eels. Danica crashed into Kaleb, both of them falling back onto the sand.

As they laid there trying to breath and recover from the pain. The sound of rocks scrapping was heard. Kaleb fought to sit up trying to see. Danica groaned as she followed suit, her cheeks wet with tears. Her whole body tingled as her skin tried to calm itself. The pools shifted and began to drain. The stepping stones Danica had seen through the water became exposed and an opening through the cave wall appeared. There was now another room in the cave. As Danica forced herself to stand she knew this was where the treasure was.

# Chapter Thirty Eight

## Step by Step

Danica went to step forward and her leg buckled in on her. She let out a painful cry as she almost toppled to the ground. Kaleb caught her and pulled her back into him. She collided against his chest. He grunted at the impact, she could tell he was also in pain but forcing it away to make sure she was ok.

"I think we need to take a minute." She whispered into his chest.

"Aye Love." He replied back as he rubbed her arm softly.

He glanced around and saw some rocks off to the side. He took Danica's arm and placed it around his neck. She raised an eyebrow at him as his hand moved to her back. Before she knew it Kaleb had scooped her off her feet and was walking to the rocks. She sighed about to argue  but she knew it would be of no use. He was stubborn and wouldn't put her down. She leaned her head into his chest enjoying the closeness of him. He settled down on to the rock with Danica still cradled in his arms like a baby.

"I could sit next to you." She half giggled.

"Aye you could but you're not." He smirked playfully as he scooted her closer to his chest.

She sighed happily and nuzzled into his chest. He instantly took all the pain and fear from her. It was insane to her that a person could do that for another. He leaned down resting his chin gently on the top of her head.

"Danica what the hell was all that?" He asked, staring at the water.

"I'm not sure, there's something about this island. From what I've figured out the flowers were some kind of antidote to the eels. The poison for the thorns of the flower blocked out the noise from the eels and I think it also killed them when it fell into the pond. Some pretty extreme trap." Danica said, piecing things together while she talked.

"The shrieking noise I didn't hear until the thorns pierced my flesh. Before that it was this soft beautiful music that I needed to know where it was coming from. My body instantly responded and searched for it. My mind had no control of where I was going or what I was doing. I could see the water but my mind didn't have a danger sign about it. Once the thorns pierced my flesh the noise disappeared and the shrieking noise appeared and snapped me out of it." Kaleb said, explaining what he went through.

"Part of me doesn't even want to continue forward. I have no clue what's waiting for us on the other side of the pond. I don't know if it will be another trap or just the treasure." Danica said her voice showing frustration and defeat.

"Come now Love what evers over there well face it and beat it." Kaleb said, kissing the top of her head.

"Aye." Danica said shifting in his lap.

"How's your leg?" Kaleb asked.

"Its o- " Danica went to reply but Kalebs hand had already started traveling to her ankle.

He  scooted her off his lap and sat her on the rock. He knelt down and nearly knocked her off the rock as he brought her foot up so he could see. He pulled up her pant leg, his fingertips grazing her skin. The burning stinging sensation left her ankle and her legs were filled with a tingling sensation every time Kaleb's finger tips grazed her skin. Images flashed through her head of them together and she could feel an ache beginning to form. She closed her eyes, enjoying his touch. Kaleb studied her leg and was relieved to see that just the top layer of her skin had been burned slightly.  There was a large red welt that wrapped around her ankle. He went to tell her but as he looked at her face he couldn't help but smile. He slowly traced his finger tips up and down her leg watching her respond. He leaned forward and kissed the side of her leg. He watched her skin get instant goose bumps. He chuckled lightly as he moved away.

"Your leg's going to be painful but I think you'll live." He smirked.

She opened her eyes, her mouth already pouting, as she made a face at him. He chuckled at her again, he leaned into her. His hand went to her cheek as he pulled her in for a quick kiss. Before she knew it the kiss was over and Kaleb was standing up facing the path to the other side. He was looking at the stone path while studying it. Danica stood her leg throbbing but she pushed the pain out of her mind as she walked over to him. She looked at the path and then to Kaleb she wanted to ask him to stay on this side to be safe. She didn't know what was across the way and she didn't want him to get hurt.

"I'll go across first and then if it's all clear I'll call for you." Kaleb said, still looking across the way.

"No, why don't I go across and then send for you." Danica said her eyebrows frowning as she looked at him.

"That's not how this works Love." Kaleb said, shaking his head.

"Still the captain, still calling the shots." Danica said her voice fierce, as she placed her arms across her chest and frowned deeply at him.

"Aye Danica you're the Captain but we're not doing this here. Not in a cave that we have no clue about. If you die, how are you going to save your family?" Kaleb asked her.

"No one is dying. I am going across the way and I might let you follow." Danica said moving from his side and going to the edge of the pond.

Kaleb shook his head following after her. He watched her study the stone path almost like she was debating with herself. He couldn't wait, he knew she was looking to see if the first stepping stone was rigged. He could see her telling herself to  just step on it. He wasn't about to let her. He went and stood next to her.

"What are you think?" He asked, not really listening.

"Well I am trying to decide the best way to get across and to see if its-

Before she could finish her sentence Kaleb took a deep breath and hopped onto the stone. Kaleb's feet hit the stone and he froze in anticipation. Danica had reached out to grab him but missed him as he jumped across. They stood in silence for several seconds waiting to see if anything happened. Kaleb looked over at Danica who was wide eye with concern. He shrugged at her.

"Kaleb, are you freaking kidding me! We had no clue what was going to happen and you just go for it!" Danica said yelling and flapping her arms at him as she did.

"Yeah why not." He said looking to the next stone.

"No yeah why not that super-

Kaleb jumped to the next stone as she was talking to him. Her stomach knotted even more as she watched him move to the next one.

"Are you crazy!" She shouted angrily at him, her voice bouncing off the cave walls.

"A Little." He chuckled back to her.

"I swear if this cave doesn't kill us I might kill you when we get out of here!" She shouted at his back as he moved on to the next stone.

She rolled her eyes and growled to herself as she jumped onto the stone. She then quickly jumped to the next one trying her best to catch up to him. She watched Kaleb move to the last stone before the entrance. She quickly jumped onto the next stone trying to catch up to him. She watched him hop onto the platform pausing in front of the entrance.

"Kaleb, wait." Danica said, jumping to the second to last stone.

He nodded, still trying to see in. Danica was becoming frustrated that he was going ahead of her. She jumped to the platform. She didn't jump far enough, her feet hitting the side of the platform and not landing on it. She let out a small yell as her hands went to grab the ledge. The sand and rock slipped through her fingers as she started to  fall. Kaleb slid on his stomach and caught her hand just as she began to fall over the ledge.

"I got you." Kaleb said to her as he grasped her wrist and began pulling her up.

Danica dug her feet into the cliff side and helped Kaleb lift her up. Pulling her up onto the ledge she tumbled into him.

"You jerk!" She shouted as she crashed into him.

"Jerk?" Kaleb asked, confused.

"Aye Jerk!" She said scotting away from him.

"What?" Kaleb asked, still not understanding.

"I was rushing because you're just hopping along and not waiting. I didn't want anything to happen to you and look what happened." She shouted at him.

Kaleb bit back a smile as he watched her yelling at him. He understood but he couldn't help but think she was adorable when she was mad. He wasn't about to tell her that. Kaleb sighed and stepped towards her.

"I'm a jerk." Kaleb said softly.

Danica stopped as she was about to go on another rant about how he was being a jerk. "What?" She asked.

"Aye I am a jerk, I should have waited. I was too busy worrying about finding any other traps to make sure you wouldn't walk into them. It isn't going to work this way. We're going to have to do it together or one of us is going to get hurt trying to make sure the other doesn't." Kaleb said, grabbing a hold of her hand.

Danica pushed her lips out making a funny face, she was fully prepared to  argue more but he just simply ended it. She sighed and squeezed his hand back.

"Together" She nodded as she looked to the entrance of the cave.

Kaleb smirked and they started walking towards the entrance. Getting to the entrance they both peered into the darkness. They had no way to light the way. Danica took a deep breath and nodded to Kaleb and they both stepped inside of the tunnel. The tunnel was so dark they couldnt see in front of them. Kaleb scooted Danica closer to him. They paused waiting to see if anything was going to happen. The stones inside the tunnel began to glow a light green hue, not all of them only certain ones creating  a light pathway. Kaleb felt Danica shrug and smirked. They stepped onto the lighted path together.

# Chapter Thirty Nine

## Missing

The long way around the passage was surprisingly calm. Ariadne had steered the whole time on edge waiting for something to happen. Patrick had stayed quiet, they haven't really spoken since Patrick had told her about the scars on his back. She had a bunch of questions, why did he stay? Why did he have this weird sense of commitment to his fathers company if he was that kind of person? What happened when he left for school? Where was his mother now? Was he upset that Kaleb went rogue? Ariadne clenched her jaw thinking of how his childhood must have been. She had nothing but loving warm memories. Her father loved her mother with every piece of his heart and soul. He loved his children. How could you hurt a child? She remembered the first time she had walked in on her mother changing. She gasped in horror as she saw her mothers  bareback. There was not a spot on it that wasn't left untouched with some scar. She remembers her mother quickly trying to get a dress to cover it. She remembered the tears that came to her eyes when her mother told her about auntie's father and how the world does have bad people in it. She fidgeted at the wheel, her thoughts making her angry. Her eyes flickered to Patrick. She wanted to hurt Ed Smith. Her fidgeting caught Patricks attention and he watched her face go from sad, to loving and to anger. He was wondering what she could possibly be thinking about.

"You alright Captain?" Patrick asked, turning away from the upper deck rail and looking at her.

"Aye." She said quietly.

" If you say." Patrick shrugged.

"No, I'm trying to understand things that I can't possibly because I didn't live them." Ariadne said softly.

Patrick knew immediately what she was speaking of. He got a little stiff and shifted slightly trying to respond with something that might change the topic. He searched his mind for anything to ask or say before she could say something else but he couldn't find it.

"Why didn't you all leave?" She whispered.

There it was, his stomach sank; he hated the question. The why didn't you leave or why didn't all of you leave? Like it was that easy. He sighed deeply.

"It's not as simple as why we didn't leave. It was more how could we survive without staying. My mother had no family to fall back on, she was young and had no skills. How could she raise two boys on her own? So she stayed suffering to make sure we were fed, clothed and cared for. Then when I was old enough I got in the way. Kaleb tried but I wouldn't let him. He tried taking us with him when he finally went off on his own. My mother wouldn't go and I couldn't leave her." Patrick said, trying to control the emotion in his voice as he spoke.

He looked at her and knew the next several questions that she was going to ask. Anyone who had gotten close to him and had seen his back asked the same. He was trying to not be upset with her but part of him was. He didn't want to go down memory lane, he didn't want to be this sad story. He could see it in her eyes as much as he didnt want to.

"The whole time I was at school being prepped to be my father's successor. I got sick daily and the nerves of what was happening to my mother back at home killed me. So much that I actually forced myself to finish school early just to get back home to her. She wrote to me telling me that everything was going great. How proud I was making her and father couldn't stop bragging about how smart his oldest was. Then she told me Kaleb had left. I knew if Kaleb had left it was because he and father got into it. More so he got in the way of my father. Kaleb would fight back. Kaleb wouldn't back down. I know he tried his hardest to take mother with him but she wouldn't go. She didn't want her kids suffering. Father would disown us from the business. We would have to start over. Kaleb wrote to me and told me what really happened. He broke our fathers hand before he left. I left school the next day. Made a deal that if I could pass every test that I would leave with my studies finished. I did and I was home within the next two days. Father was overjoyed that I was so smart I finished early. My mother was alone for four days without Kaleb or I. She wouldn't tell me what happened but she hasn't walked right since." Patrick said, angry.

"You wouldn't understand it unless you lived it…and the part I hate about all of this. Is he still my father and there is some sick twisted part of me that wants to make him proud still. I wish that part would die. No, I don't know what's happening at home. I know my mother is strong and smart. I'm praying that she is safe. I saw this as an opportunity to maybe be my fathers undoing." Patrick said his eyes flashing between anger, disgust and pain.

Ariadne's heart broke for him, she didn't know what to say to him as he unloaded everything to her. Patrick sighed seeing her look. He turned from her and looked outwards towards the sea.

"My mother lived it." She whispered softly.

"My Aunt Claire, her mother drowned saving her when she was little. Claire's father blamed her. My mother Morgan, her mother and father died from a sickness her father brought home from one of his travels. She moved in with her uncle and saw how this grown man was going to hurt this poor little girl and she got in the way. Over and over and over again.

The night Claire's father almost killed my mother was the night she decided to leave. It was almost too late. She was barely an adult caring for a little girl who was not even a preteen yet. No money, no clothes, nothing just took off. Sometimes just leaving is all you need to do and figure out the rest later. You are not any less for having any of that done to you. You are not weak and none of it is your fault. We can't always control what happens to us but we can control what happens next. " Ariadne said softly to him.

Patrick looked at her in silence; he didn't know what to say. He didn't accept that as a response. He was accepting judgment, weakness, sadness, and pity for him. All of it which he hated. He simply nodded. He never knew where Morgan Abner came from, looking at her you would not know she had a past like that. She had a wonderful life now and she was so full of love. He shifted looking out into the ocean.

"Patrick when we get back we're getting your mother. You can stay with us if needed." Ariadne said to him.

Patrick just nodded and he wasn't sure what to say. He glanced back to the open water as the ship began rounding the cliffs. You could see smoke coming from behind it. As the ship completed rounding the cliffs a beach came into view nestled in the back of a cove. The beach continued into an island, the middle of the island reached far into the sky. Ariadne stared in wonder.

"The Hollow." She whispered.

Patrick raised an eyebrow asking her what she meant.

"The island Danica was talking about. The one from my father's journal. Do you see the ship?" Danica replied, her eyes searching the shore.

She could see rowboats on the sandy shore and it looked like men had set up a camp but no ship. Her stomach was a mixture of excitement for finding them and knotted up with nerves hoping they all were ok.

"No ship, just rowboats." Patrick answered her coming to stand next to her.

"Land ho!" The call came down from the crow nest, the men on the ship came to attention and began preparing to dock the ship.

"A Little late with the land ho call." Patrick muttered.

Ariadne laughed at his comment as she began stirring the ship into the cove.

"You did it." Patrick whispered to her.

"We did it and let's wait until we see them.  I know we're so close but let's not count on anything till we're all back on the ship heading home." Ariadne said softly.

"Aye." Patrick said with a nod.

They remained silent as the ship sailed to the shore. The men on the beach cheered seeing the ship. Many of them lined up in a hurry to see who was coming to their rescue. The anchor was let go just outside of the shore line so the ship wouldn't get stuck.

"A small group of us will go to the shore. We only need as many to row the rowboats, that way we can help bring the men back to the ship. I am going, someone see if mr. Jonah is awake. If he is, he is in charge on the ship, if not Darryl and Mr. Kirk will be in charge until I return." Ariadne announced orders as she stepped away from the ship.

Patrick silently moved with her as they made their way down to the lower deck. The men were busy about the ship getting the row boats ready for departure. Patrick had a gut feeling that this was going to turn into more than just a rescue mission. He walked to the lower deck rail. He moved around and lowered himself into a row boat. He turned to see Ariadne waiting behind him. She had crawled over the upper deck railing and was waiting for him to  move out of the way so she could lower herself into the row boat. He smiled at her slightly and the little things she did always impressed him. He held his arms out to her. She made a face but stepped into them and he helped lower her into the rowboat. One man got on to the row boat with them and then Ariadne signal to have the row boat lowered. It lowered into the ocean with a bounce. Ariadne grabbed an oar to the ship and took her position. Patrick and the other man on board the row boat looked at her life and she was crazy.

"Just start rowing men." Ariadne said, rolling her eyes as plunged her oar into the ocean.

They weren't going to question her with the look she just gave them, they began rowing to the island. The ocean water was calm and still as they rowed to the shore. Getting to the shore Patrick hopped out of the row boat, Ariadne was already on her way out as she grabbed the front of the ship and began pulling it toward the shore. Patrick pushed the back end of the boat, while the man who accompanied them sat inside looking baffled. The row boat buried into the sandy beach shore and Ariande leaned against it trying to catch her breath.

"Great way to help whatever your name is." Patrick muttered to the man as he walked out of the ocean and up to the front to check on Ariadne.

"You….. all….right?" Patrick asked, he was just as out of breath as she was.

Ariadne nodded, standing up, her eyes scanned the crowd looking for her sister. She began walking towards the men gathered, her eyes still frantically searching.

"Miss Abner! We are so grateful to see you!" One of the men called out as she approached the crowd.

"Aye and I am happy to see you all! Where is my sister?" Ariadne said with a smile still searching for her.

"They've gone into the jungle and have not returned." One said cautiously

'Haven't returned for how long?' Patrick said, coming up from behind Ariadne.

"A day and half." The man replied cautiously.

"Kaleb!" Patrick shouted like an angry father who lost their child.

"Sir, Mr. Kaleb went with them." He replied carefully again.

Patrick groaned, turning and looking to the vastly dense jungle behind them. He glanced at Ariadne who was thinking.

"How many of them went with them? Did they leave you with coordinates or directions?" Ariadne said, masking her panic.

"A small number of men. Jacob went with them. No coordinates, they were following the Captain. Something about going with the sky meets the sea." The man said with a frown.

"Sky meets the sea." Ariadne repeatedly glanced at the ocean water and then the island, her eyes traveling up.

"Great, we have nothing to go by but a riddle." Patrick said, kicking some of the sand as he stared down the jungle.

"There's got to be a mountain on the island somewhere." Ariadne whispered.

"Mountain?" Patrick asked, looking at her confused.

"What else would touch the sky, we will start there. As for the rest of you, I want you to get to the row boats and start heading to the Evening star. If anyone would like to volunteer to go after the other men you are welcome to join myself and Mr. Patrick. Could some point me to the way they went." Ariadne said.

"Hang on, don't leave without me." Patrick groaned hearing the voice.

"Miss me sunshine." Jonah said walking passed Patrick.

"Jonah, are you sure you're ok to come?" Ariadne asked, surprised to see him.

"Aye Captain, D and Kirk have the ship." Jonah said with a firm nod.

"Alright then let's do this." Ariadne said with a smile as she began walking to the jungle.

"Come on sunshine, I wouldn't want to leave you behind." Jonah laughed following Ariadne.

Patrick growled as he started walking " Keep calling me sunshine and you might not make it out of this jungle."

"I Loved to see you -

"Boys! I will leave you both on this rock if you don't shut it." Ariande said, turning on her heels, both men almost crashing into each other as they stopped shooting.

"Aye Captain." They both said in unisom.

"Ariadne?" A voice said from behind her, almost confused.

Ariadne turned and saw Jacob standing in the entrance of the jungle with several men lined up behind him. He pulled Ariadne into a fierce hug and she wrapped her arms around him hugging him back. She pulled back and looked out over the crowd.

"Jacob where Dani?" Ariande whispered her heart pounding inside of her chest.

"We don't know. She's not right. This island, this jungle, some things are wrong. She kept going into these trance-like states and leading us off further into the jungle. Kaleb went after her but the fog got so bad and the jungle wanted us out. We had to turn back. I was going to lead these men to safety and go back after them. I am so sorry Ariadne." Jacob said his voice full of regret.

"What do you mean trances?" Ariadne asked if she tried her best to hide any emotion in her voice.

"It was like she wasn't there, she wouldn't respond to anyone. She was connected to something in the island and it was leading her somewhere. Kaleb was able to keep her ground but we fell asleep and then one minute she was there the next she was gone. Kaleb didn't even give anyone any time he took off after her. Then a fog rolled in and we couldn't even see where they went." Jacob answered.

"Ok, have the rest of your men follow suit with the men on the shore. Leave us one row boat to get us to the ship when we return." Ariadne said to Jacob.

"Men head out, you heard the captain." Jacob called out orders as he shifted out of the way.

"Jacob, I need you on the ship as well." Ariadne said softly to him.

"No, I am going to go with you to get your sister." Jacob said firmly.

"Jacob, I need someone on the ship I can trust. If we are gone too long the crew might get rowdy. What if they want to leave before we are back? I need someone skilled enough to defuse all of that. You're the only one Jacob." Ariadne said to him softly.

"Aye but I don't like this. Here take this." Jacob said, handing Ariadne a dagger and then she reached into his waist and grabbed a pistol.

Ariadne nodded, taking them, she smiled at him saying her silent goodbye to him. He sighed and pulled her into a hug squeezing her.

"Be safe." He ordered her.

He glanced back at Patrick hsi eyes studying him. " You, are you related to Kaleb?" Jacob asked him.

Patrick looked at him confused, Kaleb and him looked so different no one ever guessed that they were brothers. "Aye."

"Good, hopefully you're skilled like him, look after this one." Jacob said, slapping him on his shoulder as he walked by.

Patrick didn't say anything but stepped to the side to let the other men pass through . He knew his brother, he was strong, resourceful, and he could survive anywhere. They were similar but very different. He reminded himself that there was no way Kaleb would not be ok. He saw the panic in Ariadne's eyes and he reached over and squeezed her shoulder lightly.

"We will find them." Patrick said to her.

# Chapter Forty

## Illusion

Kaleb held tightly to Danica's hand as they made their way through the tunnel. It seemed like it was taking forever. They only stepped on the rocks that were glowing to be safe. Danica hadn't said one word since they entered the tunnel, her heart pounding in her chest. She was waiting for something to go wrong. Kaleb slowed as the tunnel began to widen. The tunnel opened to a large circle room. The room was made out of the same dark ash rock the cave was. The glowing rocks continued across the way to the center of the room. A single light shone down on a three pillar stand. At the top of the stand sat an old treasure chest. Danica inched forward seeing the chest. Kaleb caught her by the wrist. She raised an eyebrow at him.

"Look at the floor, there's something off with it. It looks fragile." Kaleb said pointing down at the ground.

Danica saw he was right; the ash rock looked thinner than the glowing rocks. She leaned down and studied it. She lightly ran her hand over it, just brushing the ash rock she noticed little cracks starting to form.

"We'll fall through if we step on that." Danica said standing.

" I think we can make it if we only step on the glowing rocks." Danica said, looking around.

"Look." Kaleb said, pointing to the outskirts of the room.

The out part of the room was lined with gold pieces. Danica watched as it circled the room. None of the glowing rocks went that way. Kaleb shifted slightly and she heard the floor around them crack.

"It's a trap, we weren't supposed to notice the floor, go for the gold pieces and fall through." Danica said to Kaleb.

"Aye lets get the chest and get out of here before something else happens." Kaleb said, taking a step forward on to the glowing rocks.

"We'll go slow and steady." He said reaching behind him and taking Danica's hand.

They carefully made their way across the glowing rock's path. As they approached the pillar Danica stopped Kaleb. He looked at her, his facial expression asking what was wrong. She tapped him telling him to let her go infront. Kaleb cautiously let her pass by him, his hand guiding her as she did. She ducked down looking at it. There was a disconnect in the pillar that the chest seemed to be holding in place.

She sighed loudly this was the trapt they were waiting for.

"What is it? "Kaleb asked, trying to see around her.

"Another trap, if we take the chest the pillar will shift and I don't know what will happen." Danica said defeatedly.

Kaleb looked around and there was nothing he could see to swap the chest out with. He watched Danica thinking as he was trying to find something.

"I've got it." Danica beamed.

"Ok?" Kaleb smiled looking at her funny, her enthusiasm was catchable.

"My bag, which has my father's journal, is back at the entrance. There tons of gravel around the pond. We can fill the bag with the gravel and swap the bag for the chest." Danica smiled brightly.

"Ok I'll go get the bag you stay here." Kaleb said he turned to follow the trail back he paused.

"You ok?" Danica asked, her face worried.

"Aye."

He smiled at her and stepped towards her. He pressed his lips to her forehead and winking at her he said " as long as you are."

He then walked out of the room. Danica watched him leave until she couldn't see him anymore. She rubbed her arms noticing the temperature in the room was starting to change as well. She was worried and just wanted to get this all over with.

Ariadne stepped onto the path, her feet crunching into some falling leaves. She looked around Patrick following behind her. She was looking for any sign that her sister had been on this path. Patrick was silent as he walked, studying every inch of the jungle. Jonah was focused and silent. The trio walked deeper into the jungle. The further they went the more Ariadne became unsure. She thought they were following a path but the further they went in the thick and denser the jungle became. It seems to wrap around them making it hard to see where to go. Ariadne could see the path going off to the right and it seemed to lead to an older, wider path. She paused looking to the left and there was a small almost uncharted path. She studied it for a second, she could see broken branches further down the way. Her heart was telling her to go left. She shifted and started to go left when she heard both Jonah and Patrick make a noise.

"They went this way, I know it. Look at the branches they've been cut. Go right if you want, I know it's this way." She said to them both without even looking at them and started off down the left path.

Patrick smirked a little as he pushed by Jonah. He loved when Ariadne's temper flared, she had this sharp spark that made him like her that much more.

"Come on Darling, I wouldn't want to lose you to the jungle now." Patrick snickered to Jonah as he pushed by him.

"Don't worry about me….sunshine." Jonah muttered to his back as they continued down the left path.

Danica felt like it took hours before she could hear Kaleb's footsteps finally coming back to her. She felt a small wave of relief rush over her. She turned slightly so she could see him coming. He had her bag over his shoulder as he walked slowly into the room. He smiled at her as he walked into the room.

"You took long enough." Danica smiled at him.

"Miss me?" He said playfully as he began walking on the glowing rocks.

"Yes." She said her breath catching in her throat as he tried to control her breathing from being panicked about him crossing.

As he got to her the bag shifted slightly a small amount of little pebbles spilled out of the bag. Danica inside twisted in on themselves as she watched the pebbles fall in slow motion onto the dark ash rocks. She watched the pebbles bounce and skip across the surface. It was as if the only sound in the room was the cracking of the ash rock platform. Her eyes widened as she saw the surface around them begin to crack and creek like ice on a frozen lake.

"We have to move quickly!" Danica yelled to Kaleb.

Danica moved towards the platform and balanced herself off to the side so Kaleb could approach the platform on the right of her. She looked at Kaleb and she could feel her hand shaking at her side. The cracking and shifting around them was making her even more anxious, she felt like she was going to crawl out of her skin.

"Plan?" Kaleb asked, his voice calm and focused.

Danica hated him for being so put together in this situation and she felt like she was going to vomit. She bit her lip and glanced at him. She felt like there was a clock she was racing against.

"The only plan we got. I pick up the chest and at the same time you put the bag there and we pray nothing happens." Danica said adrenaline coursing through her.

Kaleb nodded as he shifted the bag from his shoulder to infront of him. He was ready. He inhaled, slowing his breathing down and tuning everything else out. He was focused on the chest, Danica and Himself.

"Back up plan run like hell." Danica snorted as she placed her hands on the chest.

"Ready?" Kaleb asked her.

"No  but now or never." She said softly exhaling a big breath she had been holding in.

"Look at me, we got this. On Three." Kaleb said his voice was full of confidence and reassurance that Danica needed.

"Wait, wait, wait. Like one two three then pick up the chest or one two then pick up the chest on three?" Danica said, starting to overthink everything.

"Love whenever you want you pick up the chest; pick it up. I'm good.  I got my part.`` Kaleb said, stopping himself from wrapping her up in his arms; he wanted nothing more than to kiss her at this moment.

" Ok we will go with one, two, three and then up." Dancia said, placing her hands on the handle of the chest.

Kaleb nodded as he waited for her to start counting. He could feel his hands twitching as he tried to be ready. One the word echoed around him in the cave causing his heart to speed up, two he sucked in as much air as he could. He was now holding his breath not even realizing he had done it. Three he literally jumped out of his skin as he watched Danica start raising the chest. As she did he was quick and precise as he slipped the bag filled with rocks onto the platform within a second of the chest raising. Danica held the chest close to her as she stared at the platform where the bag of rocks were now sitting. She glanced at Kaleb who shrugged as they both waited for the world to come crashing down.

After several long seconds Danica exhaled. Kaleb relaxed and then motioned for her to pass him the chest. She carefully extended her arms out toward Kaleb and he took the chest.

"Ok let's get the hell out of here." Kaleb said to her as he stepped away from the platform.

"Agreed." Danica said to his back as she began following him.

They carefully began following the glowing rocks path out of the room. As they got to the entrance of the room Danica paused and looked back at the platform. She looked back just in time to see her dark blue bag filled with rocks tumble over on the platform and the rocks began to spill out onto the floor. Danica immediately felt sick.

"Run." She yelled, turning around and pushing Kaleb forward.

She wasn't sure what was about to happen but she knew it wasn't good. The floor shattered as the rocks continued to spill and bounce across the dark thin ash surface, Danica was running down the long curved path after Kaleb. She could barely see him in front of her through the darkness. There was a noise starting to echo in the tunnel. Something large was coming up from behind them. She pushed herself trying to keep up. There was light up ahead, she knew the exit to the tunnel was coming up. Kaleb kept glancing back as if he was looking for the monster that  was chasing them. Kaleb's feet made a screeching halt as he stopped short just outside the exit. His feet scraped against the platform that led to the stepping stones across the pond. Danica crashed into his back side. Almost causing him to topple into the pond.

"What!" She yelled as the noise behind him was getting louder.

"The waters are rising. The stepping stones are disappearing." He said to her,

"Go!" Danica yelled, stopping herself from pushing him.

Kaleb hopped onto the first stepping stone and began making his way across. He kept checking behind him to see if Danica was still close by. He had wanted her to go first but there was no time. As they reached the middle of the pond, the loud noise finally caught up to them. Water. Rushing water began spilling out from the tunnel into the cave. The water spewed down into the pond making the water  rise even more quicker. Kaleb picked up the pace, clearing the stopping stones in a matter of seconds and landing on the pebble shore. He glanced back to see Danica racing against the rising water. She jumped over the last stone and landed next to him. She didn't say anything but to him but grabbed his elbow and pulled him with her, racing towards the exit of the cave.

# Chapter Forty One

## Reunited

The jungle was dark and a deep green color. It held a coldness to it and it wasn't the temperature.  It closed in and wrapped around them making it hard to move through the jungle. The vines seemed to want to tangle you up and stopped you from moving. They struggled to advance even though there was already a small charted path. It looked like it had been cut through only a day ago but already the jungle was trying to erase it. Jonah had pulled out his sword and began chopping at the branches and vines around him.

"Captain let me go first, I can clear the way. Jonah called up to them.

"Aye." Ariadne agreed and tried to shift to make room for him to come up to the front.

Patrick shifted back pushing himself up against branches and vines but couldn't really make room. Jonah went to squeeze by Patrick but the dense jungle got them stuck up against each other.

"Get off of me," Patrick growled, trying to push Jonah forward.

"You need to move back." Jonah said, gritting his teeth as he struggled against Patrick.

"I am! I can't push back anymore!" Patrick said, shoving Jonah.

Ariadne almost burst out laughing seeing the two. They were like siblings fighting back and forth. She rolled her eyes.

"Jonah, move back and pass your sword forward. It's too dense here for us to squeeze around each other." Ariadne laughed.

She heard them grumble back and forth as they moved back into their original positions. Jonah shoved his sword into Patricks hand, still grumbling. Patrick made a face as he took it from him. Turning he slowly passed it to Ariadne. She was still trying not to laugh at the two.

"You would think you were brothers the way you two bicker." Ariadne said, taking the sword.

"Pass on that." Patrick muttered as he stepped back so Ariadne could chop at the foliage in the way.

"No hurt feelings here Sunshine." Jonah snickered behind him.

"Enough! Or I'll leave you too here in this jungle." Ariadne called behind her.

Patrick and Jonah fell silent as Ariadne began making progress. She managed to cut a wider path as they moved through the jungle. She could see where

Danica and the crew made their way through this path. She was relieved they were heading in the right way. They continued on in slienes and finally the path broke open into  a large clearing. Ariadne could see the impression of the campsite the crew had left. The fire ashes looked still warm. They crossed the white rocks that circled around it and ventured out into the center. Where would Danica go from here? Ariadne thought while looking around. Jonah and Patrick spread out and searched the clearing. Ariadne found herself looking up at the sky. She beat at night you could see every star. She remembered nights where Danica and her would sit on the roof of their home looking at the stars. Most of the time their mother and father would join them and tell stories to them about the constellations. She smiled at the memory. As she got lost in her memory her ear picked up a strange noise. She looked over to Jonah and Patrick who had stopped in their tracks, hearing the noise. They closed the distance to her and were staring out into the jungle. The noise was a low grumble. It didn't remind Ariadne of any animal she ever heard.

The followed the noise out of the clearing and down an enclosed path. The sound grew louder as an arch way of white flowers. Ducking under the archway a large mountain came into  view. At the base of the mountain was a larger cave. The sound erupted from inside of it. They stepped closer into the clearing beach sand in front of the cave. Ariadne peered into the cave, squinting her eyes as she did. Patrick inched closer, slowly stepping towards the cave. The sound intensified as the trio paused debating on what to do next.

"Run!" The words were screamed from the inside of the cave.

Kaleb and Danica raced out the entrance of the cave, the noise chasing behind them. Each one of them holding on to a side of the treasure chest. As they came into view Kaleb and Danica almost tripped seeing Ariadne, Patrick and Jonah standing just on the outskirts of the clearing. Ariadne looked completely shocked seeing Danica and Kaleb racing out of the cave.

"Ari! Run!" Danica yelled she didn't even think to second guess if she was here or not.

If she was making her up it didn't matter she still wanted her to run. Kaleb faulted slightly running, pausing to see Patrick. Danica got yanked back a little bit but pulled him forward.

"Kaleb!" Dancia shouted at him as they ran towards Patrick, Ariadne, and Jonah who looked confused.

Kaleb snapped out and continued to run with Danica. Suddenly behind them water erupted out the entrance of the cave. It took a second for Ariadne to realize what was going on as Danica and Kaleb reached them. Danica shoved her not knowing if she was real or not.

"Freaking run!" Danica shouted as she spun her sister around with her free hand.

The group raced off into the jungle, the rushing water closely behind them. The archway quickly came into view. Danica glanced back over her shoulder hoping the water was slowing down but it was still coming full force at them. How much water could come from the cave. It was like the entire ocean was after them. Ariadne stumbled forward catching her foot on a vine, she was falling towards the ground as Patrick hand caught her and pulled her up right. She didn't miss a step, thankful to Patrick and kept going forward. They ducked under the arch way and raced towards the clearing. They stumbled over the white rocks that outline the clearing. Reaching the center of the clearing the water reached down the path heading towards the clearing. The water hit the white stones as they reached the center. As the water hit the white rocks it didn't cross them. The water circled outwards and then was pushed back. Like the white rock was some type of barrier the water couldn't cross. The water slowly rolled back like waves hitting the shore going out to see. As they stood in the center of the clearing they looked from where the water once was to each.

"What the hell was that?" Ariadne asked out.

Danica dropped the side of the treasure chest she was holding  and turned to her sister. She stepped forward and grabbed her face in her hands.

Ariadne blinked back at Danica confused and slightly startled.

"Are you really here?" Danica whispered, squishing Ariadne's face.

Ariadne laughed out loud as she pulled Danica into a hug. "Aye! We've come to rescue you."

"How did you know?" Danica laughed asking.

"Uncle Jack and Auntie Claire. They came home early and I told them what happened. Uncle Jack knew the short cut would strand the ship." Ariadne explained.

"And I see you've brought a friend." Danica said, narrowing her eyes at Patrick.

"Well I can see that you have one too." Ariadne said back to her just as sassy.

Patrick ignored the girls and walked over to Kaleb, slapping him on the shoulder.

"It's good to see you alive brother." Patrick smiled.

"Aye. I would be more thrilled to see you if you had let me in on the whole mess and mutiny on the ship." Kaleb said a little harshly as he wacked him back.

"I wasn't aware of that completely. We can talk later. Ariadne knows everything. Patrick said quietly.

"Danica knows everything as well." Kaleb said with a small nod. " I also had my father's man thrown overboard."

Patrick shrugged, stepping back from Kaleb and standing next to Ariadne.

"Well I do appreciate a lovely reunion but if we could please get going before something else tries to kill us I think that would be ideal." Jonah chimed in.

"Aye." Danica and Ariadne agreed together.

"Come this way." Danica said as she started walking; she paused and nodded to them as if to say to follow her.

Danica reached down and grabbed the side of the treasure chest with Kaleb. Patrick came up next to her taking the other side of the chest motioning for him and Kaleb to carry it out. Danica looked to Kaleb who nodded to her letting her know it was ok. Danica still did not trust Patrick. She made a small face but trusted Kaleb. She let go of the chest.

"I am only trusting you because somehow you won over my sister. Bonus points for being Kaleb's brother." Danica said to Patrick as she let go of the chest.

"Well I hope to gain your trust as well." Patrick said, trying to show sincerity as he spoke.

"We shall see. I didn't appreciate anything that happened on my ship that your father and possibly you were involved in." Danica said to him, giving him a side look as she began leading the crew out of the jungle.

# Chapter Forty Two

## Tea

Kaleb smirked watching Danica lead the way his eyes fixated on her. Patrick glanced at him slightly as he helped carry the chest. Kalbe caught him looking at him and raised his eyebrow. A silly smile formed on Patrick's lips.

"What?" Kaleb said his voice was drawn out as if he knew what his brother was going to say.

"So did you find a reason to stop your endless roaming?" Patrick asked, his smile growing.

Ariadne squeezed by the brothers hurrying to catch up to Danica. She raised an eyebrow at Kaleb hearing the question Patrick asked him. Instead of stopping to listen she kept going. They didn't have time for endless chit chat and she needed to form a plan with her sister.

"Did you find a reason to take chances?" Kaleb shot back at him and nodded towards Ariadne who hurried to catch up to Danica.

The two stared at the two women, both men stunned at the view. One bright like the sun, constant like the day  and the other as enchanting as the moon and as carefree as the night. The two were opposites and completely what each brother needed.

"Aye." Patrick answered honestly looking fondly after Ariadne.

"About damn time. Father isn't going to be happy." Kaleb smirked.

"Yeah well it's about time for that as well." Patrick said softly.

"How do you think mother is?" Kaleb's voice was quiet, it had guilt in it as well.

"She's a survivor." Patrick couldn't say anymore, his stomach knotted.

He wanted to trust that she was ok but he didn't know for sure. He didn't know how angry father was going to be now that both his sons were missing and god forbid if he found out that they were all conspiring against him now. His stomach knotted even more.

"Aye she lived with that man before we were around." Kaleb said, trying to ease his brother.

The two continued in silence as they walked behind the sister. Ariadne caught up to Danica who was on a mission as she led them through the tightly woven path. Ariadne reached out and squeezed her arm slightly. Danica smiled at her. She wasn't sure how her sister was going to respond to her running away but she was so grateful she was here.

"You're really here right." Danica whispered, glancing at Ariadne.

"Aye Dani, I am really here." Ariadne said then smirked and pinched Danica.

"I'm sorry I left." Danica whispered, rubbing the spot Ariadne pinched her.

"I'm sorry I didn't listen." Ariadne said back.

Danica glanced at Ariadne and they both smiled. Ariadne placed her arm around her little sister and gave her a side hug.

"So what's the plan?" Ariadne said to her with a smile.

"I don't really have one. It kinda stopped when I got the treasure and went home. The North Star is stranded in the passageway and I don't think there's any way of getting out of there." Danica said sadly.

"We might just have to leave it." Ariadne said with a shrug.

Danica did not respond; she didn't know what to say. She knew that is what they had to do but she hated leaving one of their father's ships stranded behind. This mission was supposed to save her family, not place them in more debate.

"Dani, it will be alright." Ariadne said reassuring her sister with a smile.

"Aye, so what's the deal with Patrick? Do you trust him?" Danica asked to change the subject.

"Aye I do." Ariadne said with a nod.

"You're sure?" Danica asked, looking at her studying her sister's face.

"Aye not everything is as it seems. I trust him. He is a good man." Ariadne said, glancing at patrick.

"Ari…do you more than trust him?" Danica asked with a silly smile.

"Oh hush I could ask you the same thing about Mr. Kaleb back there but i dont need to ask. It's clearly written on both of your faces." Ariadne said, nudging Danica.

"Aye I more than trust Kaleb." Danica laughed as they made their way down the path, the beach exit coming into view.

Ed paced the floor of his office. He hadn't heard from either of his sons in a week. Kaleb this was expected of but Patrick. Patrick knew better. He walked past his desk and he felt a surge of anger course through him. He slammed his fist into the wood desk. The wood gave away behind the strength of his hands causing the wood to bend inward.  He closed his eyes as he began to sway with rage. This was all his wife's doing. The words echoed in his mind. He grabbed a hold of the whiskey glass that was now empty and squeezed. He felt the glass give away in his hand. Shards of glass pierced his skin and blood poured down his hand.

"Wife!" He yelled, his voice echoing throughout the quiet house.

He dropped all the pieces of glass from his hand as he watched the blood seep out of the small slices. The office door opened slowly as if she knew what she was walking into.

"Yes dear?" She said calmly, even though she was filled with dread.

She stopped letting him know years ago she was afraid of him. It made him more power hungry when it came to their encounters.

"Have you heard from your sons?" He sneered at her, not looking at her.

"No dear." She said softly.

"Those boys better not be up to anything. They better be doing what's best for this company.: He said to her threateningly.

"Dear you know Kaleb has just gone off on another one of his adventures. He never says goodbye. He will be back in  a few months." She said with a smile.

"Aye but Patrick! Patrick is a good son. He is going to do great things for this company. He has never left without saying anything." Ed said, now crushing pieces of the glass into the wooden floor.

"I am sure Patrick will come home soon with great news. He might be undercover like you wanted and not able to send a word. He always makes us proud." She said sweetly to him.

"Aye you are right. Clean this mess up for me." Ed said, stepping away from the broken glass and going to the fireplace.

"Yes dear, would you like me to make your favorite tea to help you sleep?' She said her voice was still so sweet.

He didn't answer as she walked over and knelt down, beginning to pick up the broken pieces. She gathered the shards of broken glass and was about to stand. His hand wove into her hair, yanking her up as she stood. She didn't make a sound. She had known something like this was coming. He twisted his hand deeper into his hair.

"If your son lets me down. God help you." He whispered into her ear.

"Patrick will not let us down." She said calm and firm.

He yanked hard on her hair pulling her head all the way back. He let out a small growl as he released her hair but sent her forward into the desk. Her hands holding the pieces of glass slammed into the desk. The glass pieces shattered more and cut her hands. She didn't let out a sound. She adjusted herself and stood up. Blood started to drip down her own hands. Ed looked at her hands and smiled satisfied.

"Bring me my tea." He ordered looking back at the fireplace.

She nodded and quickly made her way out of his study. She held the pieces of glass in her hands as an angry course through her, She made a fist around the glass wanting to go back into the study and unleash years of pent up anger. Her boys. She told herself. Without Ed they couldn't survive. If she could just get Ed to sign the company over to one of her boys. She would leave. They would be safe. She dropped the pieces of glass into the sink and raised the blood off her hands. She quickly wrapped a towel around them. Then she put the kettle on. She began prepping his tea. She pulled a small vial out of a drawer. It was hidden in the way back of the drawer, she smiled as she looked at the vial. She was all done with this life. The kettle whistle and she turned to grab it. She put a tea bag into the cup and poured the hot water over it. She then added his sugar and honey. Lastly she took the vial and tapped it slightly. A few little white specks floated down into the tea, they dissolved like sugar.

"Tea!" He yelled from the other room.

"Coming." She answered as she tucked the vial away, a small smile on her lips as she stirred the tea.

# Chapter Forty Three

## Almost

Danica's feet hit the beach sand and the amount of joy she felt finally being out of the jungle and nothing bad happening was overwhelming. She scanned the beach and realized the crew was gone. She could see the Evening Star sitting out just past the shallow. She glanced quickly at Ariadne , her eyes questioning where everyone was.

"They are safe. I had them go to the ship. I thought it would be safer." She smiled at her sister.

Jonah came out and stood next to Danica scanning the beach as well. His eyes found the Evening Star and he smiled seeing it sitting in the ocean waiting for them.

"Let's get in the row boats." Jonah said walking ahead to the row boats, he wanted nothing more than to be on his ship.

Danica smiled as she and Ariadne set off after him with Kaleb and Patrick following behind. They reach the shoreline. The ocean water rushed up under the rowboat as it waited for them to return. Kaleb and Patrick lowered the treasure chest into the row boat. Jonah hopped in the rowboat taking his place in the very back. Kaleb held on his hand for Danica and helped her climb in. she smiled brightly at him as she settled into her seat. Patrick helped

Ariadne into the rowboat, his hands lingering a little too long on her hips as he did. Kaleb took position in the front of the row boat and Patrick on the side as the two began pushing the row boat out of the sand and into the ocean. Patrick swung his leg up over the side and Kaleb hosted himself in. They both crashed into the rowboat at the same time just missing each other. Danica's hand caught Kaleb from falling into Patrick. She pulled him back into her and he landed against her. The back of his head landing in her lap as he stared up at her.

Danica laughed and ruffled his hair slightly, a soft look crossed Kaleb's face as he looked up at her. She leaned forward like it was second nature and kissed his forehead. Kaleb swallowed hard at the feeling of love he got through him. He had never felt anything like this before and he was scared. For the first time in years he was scared. Scared he was going to mess it up, scared he was going to lose her, and scared that he wasn't good enough for her. Danica raised an eyebrow at him as she looked down at his expression. He smiled weakly at her before sitting up.

"Can we row now please?" Jonah announced.

Kaleb sat up and grabbed the oar on the right side of the ship and settled into his position. Ducking the oar into the water he waited for Patrick to get his. Patrick and Ariadne exchanged looks seeing the exchange between Danica and Kaleb. Hey had questions but they weren't about to air them out now. Ariadne tapped Patricks hand telling him to wait. Patrick winked at her and got his oar and got situated. He nodded to Kaleb as he plunged his oar into the water. He looked across to Kaleb and nodded once more as they began rowing. The ocean was calm and still as the row boat glided over it towards the Evening star. The ghost ship looked haunting as it sat against the now darkening sky.

As they reached the ship Dancia could see her crew hustling about anxiously awaiting their return. A rope ladder was thrown down to the rowboat. Ariadne stood and grabbed ahold of it. Danica grabbed the other side and pulled. The rowboat moved toward the ship. Once it was against the ship the boys fastned it to the ship. Ariadne then looked at Danica , almost asking who should go first. Danica held her hand out to sister telling her to climb up. Ariadne smiled and began climbing followed by Danica. The girls reached the top one after another and swung their legs over the rail. As their feet hit the floor a cheer came up from the crowd. Jacob was smiling proudly in front of the crew. The girls smiled at the crew and then turned around to help Kaleb and Patrick who were handing the treasure off to each other as they climbed one handed.

"Pat Let go." Kaleb called down to him.

Danica leaned over the rail holding her arms open for Kaleb to pass her the treasure. Danica grabbed ahold of it and hosted it onto the ship with the help of Ariadne. The treasure hit the floor with a thud. The crew all stared in amazement. Patrick, Kaleb and Jonah all quickly got on board. They all seem to stare at the treasure chest in wonder.  Danica cleared her throat looking from the chest to the men.

"We need to start heading back. Jacob will steer the ship. We need a man in the crow nest. Sails down completely. I do not want to waste anymore time." Danica announced.

"Aye Captain." Jacob said to her with a nod.

"Patrck and Kaleb please take the chest to the captain's quarters." Ariadne said to them.

"Alright boys you heard the captains. Let all get about our duties. " Jonah shouted as he stepped out from behind Danica and Ariadne.

Patrick and Kaleb nodded to Ariadne and began carrying the chest across the lower deck as the men hurried about getting to their post. Danica and Ariadne followed behind them. Crossing the floor a crew member grabbed ahold of Ariadne's arm. She halted looking confused from the men of the grip he had on his upper arm. As if instinct kicked in, Patrick drew his sword and rested in on the man's shoulder by his neck. Danica glared at him as she stepped up to him, squaring off with him. As Kaleb drew his sword as well. All noise on the ship stopped.

"I suggest you remove your hand from my sister before her friend here removes your head." Danica growled.

The man glanced at Patrick and seemed to growl at him. Patrick presses the sword into his skin threateningly but it doesn't seem to phase him.

"Hey did you hear me." Danica said, grabbing the man by his shoulder.

The man swung around towards Danica. Danica narrowed her eyes at him. There was something wrong with his eyes. They were clouded over and it was like he wasn't there.

"Patrick, wait. There's something wrong with him." Danica said, looking at the man.

The man let go of Ariadne who quickly backed away. The man fell to the ground and began convulsing. Danica dropped down to the ground and helped the man hold still. Another loud thump followed another crew member dropped to the floor and began to shake. Danica looked up to Kaleb, his eyes looked just as confused as hers. Ariadne rushed over to help the other man who had fallen. The man tha Danica was holding relaxed but then went limp. He was passed out and unresponsive. Danica looked over to Ariadne and a few minutes later her man did the same. A third thump was heard as another man dropped to the floor shaking. Jacob was nearby and was able to help keep him from hurting himself.

"Jacob, were are these men with you?" Danica yelled as she began searching the man's skin for a mark, scratch or rash anything to give them a clue as to what was going on.

"No, these were the men that stayed on the beach." Jacob shouted back.

A fourth man dropped to the floor as the third man followed suit as the first two men slipped into an unresponsive coma. Patrick ran over and helped hold down the fourth man to stop him from hurting himself.

"I need someone who knows these men and can tell me about their actions." Danica shouted to the crew.

"What do you need to know, captain?" A tall thin man stepped forward.

"Did you see them eat anything or drink anything that the rest of you didn't? Touch a vine or plant?" Danica said, still searching for the man's body.

Danica pulled up the man's shirt and saw a red speckled rash all over his stomach. She had never seen a rash like this. She looked over to Ariadne.

"Ari checks his stomach for a rash, Jacob and Patrick you too!" Danica yelled out.

"Same here Dani!" Ariadne shouted back to her, she traced the splotches with her fingers, there were almost internal coming outwards through the skin.

"Dani, I think it's something they ate or drank!" Ariadne yelled back.

"Same rash here." Jacob called to them.

"Aye same here." Patrick yelled.

"Did they eat or drink anything?" Danica asked the tall thin man.

"They made some type of soup out of some plant they found. They were the only ones who ate it. We told them not to but they said they were sick of eating the same thing over and over. It was some type of plant that bore a red fruit." He explained.

"Take the man to the first mate's cabin. Keep them comfortable. Stop leaving. We need to go back to that island." Danica called out orders.

Ariadne locked eyes with Danica and smiled weakly. They didn't want to go back on the island but it was going to be the only way to save these men. If there's a poison most of the time there is a cure as well. The sails were drawn up as the ship began to idle.

"I don't want a large group coming. I am going. Jacob. I need you to stay behind and you too Jonah." Danica said out loud and then when she saw Jacob and Jonah both move she let them know they needed to stay behind.

"Well Dani I am going with you like it or not." Ariadne said, coming back to her side.

"You're not going back on that island without me." Kaleb said to her, giving her a look that said don't you dare argue.

"And of course I am coming." Patrick announced going to Ari's side.

"Well that's it then. The four of us will go try to retrieve a cure and will be back by sunrise. In the meantime keep those men comfortable." Danica said looking about.

"Mr.."Danica pointed to the tall thin man.

"Henry captain." The man smiled at her.

"Henry, did anyone else eat or drink the soup?" Danica asked her eyes surveying the crew as she spoke.

"No captain." Henry said quietly.

"Do you know where they got this plant from?" Danica asked hopefully.

"Aye they said they found it near white flowers." Henry said with a shrug.

"Oh thank god.' Danica said quietly.

"Uh?" Ariadne whispered.

"I know where we need to go." Danica smiled at Ariadne.

## Chapter Forty Four

### Flowers

The rowboat crashed into the ocean Ariadne was flung forward into Patrick's lap. He wrapped his arms quickly around her, steading her. She smiled softly at him as he helped her sit back on the seat. Danica watched the exchange and she was slowly starting to believe he might be a good guy or a very good actor. It was hard to trust him. Kaleb handed the oar to Patrick and they began making their way back to the island. The sky was now riddled with stars and the moon was the only light they had guiding them. Danica prayed that they could find the way back to the arch way with the white flowers. As they approached the shoreline Danica went to hop out but felt a hand catch her shoulder.

"You and Ariadna stay in the boat we can pull it in." Patrick said and jumped into the water before she could say anything back.

The two men pulled the ship to shoreline; their bottom halves soaked from the ocean water. Standing outside the rowboat Danica went to step into the water and walk the rest of the way to shore. Kaleb smiled and before she could protest he scooped her up into his arms carrying her to the sandy shore so she did not get wet.

"I could have walked." She said softly but enjoying being close to him.

"We don't need the Captain to catch a cold." Kaleb said playfully hsi voice vibrating through his chest.

Danica nuzzled into it as she wished the walk to the shore was longer. He held her a second longer as he waited for Patrick and Ariadne to catch up. He looked back to see what they were doing and He saw Patrick cradling Ariadne as well. The look on his face was something Kaleb had never seen before. He had actually never seen Patrick interested in any woman before but the look on his face was …love. He held Ariadne like she was the most precious thing in the world and he didn't want to let it go. Ariadne had the same look on her face as she wrapped her arms around his neck. She rested her forehead on the bottom of his jaw, her face in his neck.

Chills went through Patrick as Ariadne breath touched his neck, he could feel the instant goosebumps she gave him. He tried to push them from his mind as he tread through the cold ocean water. Even the ice water of the ocean couldn't stop the heat he felt coursing through of wanting Ariadne. Reaching the shoreline he gently placed Ariadne down on the sandy soil, she was still leaning to him as her feet touched the ground. His hand wrapped around her waist as she did.

"Alright let's get going." Patrick said as he took a step forward with Ariadne.

Danica's feet touched the ground and she nodded. Her eyes scanned the jungle boarding the forest. She prayed that she could recognize the spot with the path. She began walking towards the jungle. Kaleb close behind her followed by Patrick and Ariadne. Danica stalled in front of what she thought was the opening they had gone in before. She sighed stepping into the jungle. Please please please show me the way, she thought as she stepped onto the soft soil of the jungle. As if the jungle heard her pleas it began to move and separate.  It was different this time instead of over growing it was like it was moving out of the way for them. Danica went to walk further in and Kale grabbed her hand. She glanced back at him.

"I'm not so sure about this. Last time it wouldn't let us through, now it's welcoming us?" Kaleb whispered to Danica.

"I know but what choice do we have? Those men back there will die if we don't try." Danica said, stepping forward.

Kaleb didn't let go of her. She glanced back at him, her eyes narrowing ready to argue if he decided to continue.

"Fine but I'm not letting go of you." Kaleb said thoughts of what happened to her last time she was in this forest crept into his mind.

Touching her somehow grounded her and even though he was pretty sure it had something to do with the cave or jungle that had passed he wasn't risking it. Danica's expression quickly changed from defensive to warm as she entwined her fingers around his.

"You better not." She smiled at him as she squeezed his hand.

He smiled back at her and nodded for her to lead the way. The jungle opened up to them as they moved further into it. Danica could see that the ground and leaves were wet from where the ocean water had flooded out of the cave. She couldn't believe it had reached this far and then just disappeared. This place was so strange. The path opened up and she could tell they were at the cross point of the old path that Kaleb had originally found and the path that she had found. The jungle's trees and vines moved for them to decide.

"This way." Danica said confidently as she picked the path that she found.

She knew it led to the clearing and then she hopefully would find the path which led to the cave. That path would have the arch way on it with the white flowers.

"This place is so strange.' Ariadne whispered to Patrick as they followed Kaleb and Danica.

"Aye, I have never been anywhere where the vegetation would move and get out of the way for you." Patrick said, eyeing a vine that seemed to shrink away from them as they passed by.

"Aye I dont know if we can trust this." Ariadne whispered, trying to come up with a plan B in case everything goes bad.

There really isn't anything she could come up with other than to run. They didn't have anything to the advantage this island was bizarre. It wasn't like they knew what they were walking into and how you could fight nature. She sighed outwardly. Patrick glanced at her and saw the worry on her face. He reached down and grabbed ahold of her hand.

"It will be fine. Whatever we come into, we'll do it together." He reassured her.

She knew he was just trying to make her feel better, she could see it on his face that he was unsure of everything going on but just hearing him tell her it was going to be ok made her feel ok. She smiled softly, holding onto his hand still as they walked.

They finally reached the clearing although it looked different. The white rocks were no longer in a circle. They were scattered about the clearing. Danica looked around studying it before she walked into it.

The rocks must have been moved around by the rushing water. By how wet the ground felt under her shoes she knew the water had stayed  here the longest. Plus the rocks look like a current had dragged them about. Like the tide going out to sea does to the sand on beaches. She glanced around the clearing trying to find the right spot to walk through next on their mission. The jungle seemed to call to her from across the way. She started towards it and as she did the branches of the trees parted. This was becoming too easy. She was prepared for something to attack, not guide her. She looked back at Kaleb who was holding her hand tightly. She inhaled as they crossed the clearing and started down the other path.

The dirt was different; it wasn't the same soft soil that it was in the beginning. The soil turned sandy like the beach. The ocean waters must have washed up some of the beach sand onto the path. As they headed down the path they could hear the ocean. Danica was slightly confused; she didn't remember hearing the ocean before. Although before she was following some strange voice that was ethier in her head or some kind of toxic introduced by the plants in the jungle. Either way it had gotten her through the jungle the first time unharmed. This time the jungle was guiding them. Danica slowed as she saw the archway. The white flowers had multiplied over the short time they were away. Hundreds of white flowers covered the archway to the cave. Danica looked at Kaleb and knew he was thinking the same thing. If they picked the flowers would the jungle turn on them. Before she did that she wanted to make sure this was the right flower. They had said there was a plant with red fruit on it. That's what they ate.

"We need to find a plant that has red fruit or berries on it. If I'm right it should be near here somewhere. I think the white flowers are the antidote to it." Danica explained to them.

They all set out searching different areas. Kaleb, still not letting go of Danica, began searching with her. She figured it would be somewhere near the flowers. She looked in all the brushes but didn't find any fruit. She outwardly sighed as she was becoming frustrated. She guessed she would just go ahead and take the flowers even though she wasn't entirely sure that they were the solution.

"Dani." Ariadne called to her from across the way.

Danica looked over to where Ariadne was and she pointed up. In the far off tree hung several red fruits. This had to be it, she thought walking over. She needed one. She needed to make sure it was the right thing. She again was worried how the jungle might respond by them picking the fruit. Getting to Ariadne sided she paused looking up.

"I need to make sure the flowers are the key. I need to get one of those fruits but I am worried. The jungle here seems to be alive and I don't know how kindly it's going to react if we pick the fruit or the flowers. It let me take a flower once before but things are a little different now." Danica said her eyes fixated on the fruit.

Ariadne studied the fruit too. She could reach it. She was great at climbing trees. Whenever they were little she purposely would scale a tree and hide during most of the games they played, tag, hiding seek. She never told her siblings that's how she usually won.

"I'll get it." Ariadne said, walking over to the tree.

"Ari, are you sure?" Danica said becoming concerned for her sister.

"Aye, it's the perfect climbing tree. Its branches are in all the right spots. It's like it wants to be climbed," Ariadne said, throwing a wink at her sister as she reached out and touched the tree.

"Ok but be careful." Danica said her stomach was knotting.

Ariadne nodded and started to climb the tree. Patrick helped boost her up and she was off. Danica watches her climb the tree like an expert. She was up to the fruit in little to no time. She smiled down at Danica as she positioned herself to reach out and get the fruit.

"Ariadne, be careful not to get any of the juice on you and don't let it scratch you or anything." Danica called up to her.

They knew by eating  the fruit was how the man got sick on the ship. They were sure how else it could poison you. They also were going on a whim that the white flowers were the cure. She watches Ariadne carefully pluck the fruit and start climbing back down. As she reached the bottom she carefully passed the fruit to Danica before Patrick caught her by her waist and lowered to her ground. Having Ariadne on the ground made Danica feel a little bit more at ease. The next thing was to see if the flower was really the antidote to the fruit. She walked over to the archway fruit in her hand. She paused in front of it while debating.

"We need to know if the flowers will work but I really don't know how to see if it will work." Danica said softly looking at the three of them.

Ariadne smiled and held out her hand for the fruit. "I think I know how."

Danica looked at her sister a little confused but held the fruit out to her. As Ariadne went to grab it Patrick took it before Ariadne could get to it. He gave her a look before taking the fruit and rubbing it on his forearm. The juices leaked on to his skin as the prickly points of the fruit cut into his forearm skin leaving little cuts.

"Patrick!" Ariadne shouted at him.

"Don't yell at me, I knew exactly what you were about to do and there was no way I was letting you. So now we wait and see if it happens." Patrick said his voice was a little angry with Ariadne for attempting to put herself in danger.

Ariadne didn't know what to say he was right. She was going to do the exact same thing. Her first thought was to eat it but that would take time for it to process in her system and they didn't have time. She frowned deeply at him.

"Don't look at me like that." Patrick said, making a silly face at her.

Ariadne frowned more and walked over to his side, slipping her arm around his waist and moving close to his chest. Patrick embraced her with the arm not infected and held it away from her. Danica looked at Patrick with shock. Did he really just do that? Was he really putting himself at risk to make sure Ariadne didn't? She didn't even see Ariadne doing that but he did. Maybe he was not as bad as she thought he was.

"How are you feeling?" Danica said, walking over looking at his arm carefully.

"It's starting to burn and I think the skin is starting to get a small little rash. Look here, see the dots." Patrick said softly.

Danica nodded this was the fruit alright the rash was the same as the ones on the crew members bellies. She slowly let go of Kalebs hand who was staring down his brother. His look was uncertain; you couldn't tell if he was impressed or angry with Patrick.

"What no lectures little brother?" Patrick said, teasing him.

"No. I can't say anything. My thoughts were with you. There was no way I was letting one of the girls endanger themselves like that. I'm just mad it was you and not me." Kaleb said to Patrick, throwing him a wink.

He wasn't mad that he wasn't getting to be the hero, he was mad that his brother was now endangered and they only were hoping the white flower was the cure. Patrick knew that's what his brother was saying and he smiled at him.

"I love you too." Patrick said to Kaleb as the burning in his arm became worse.

"You fall over and start shaking. I am going to kick your ass." Kaleb said to him watching the rash get worse.

"Promise, promise." Patrick smirked.

Danica returned with a single flower. It was the same flower she had pricked Kaleb with it to get him out of the trance he was in. They had dropped it in the water to get rid of the eels. She was now praying it would cure Patrick. She went over to his arm as he held it out for her and his hand began to shake.

"Patrick." Kaleb growled as if threatening him would make the poison slow.

The juices of the fruit produced the poison, maybe crushing the flower and putting it over the wound would make the poison resend. Danica took the flower in between her hands and crushed it. Making a fist and squeezing hard the flower began to produce a thick water syrup. She then took the flower and rubbed it on Patrick's arm. The clear liquid smeared over the wounds and rash. In several seconds Patrick's arm stopped shaking, in the next second the red rash was gone and lastly the little cuts seemed to close up and disappear. His arm looked like nothing had ever happened.

"Thank god." Danica whispered at the same time Ariadne did.

"You're lucky." Kaleb whispered, still a little grumpy.

"Well that's that. Let's get some flowers and get back to the ship." Patrick announced happily.

# Chapter Forty Five

## Poisoned

They made their way out of the jungle so much quicker and faster than they did before. Their feet hitting the sandy beach soil, arms filled with flowers as they made it to the rowboat all running the best they could on the sand. They all wanted back on the ship as soon as possible. Kaleb dropped his arm full of flowers into the boat Danica and Araidne climbed in. Patrick dropped the ones he was carrying into the rowboat as well. Kaleb and Patrick began pushing the rowboat into the ocean. One the boat was floating in the water they both climbed in. They began to row back to the ship hoping everything was still ok.  The ocean water seemed to be effortless to paddle through and they reached the ship in no time. The ropes were lowered down to help capture the row boat. Patrick and Kaleb fastened the rowboat to the ropes and the crew began pulling it up. Once on board they unloaded the flowers taking them to the Captain's cabin. Jacob saw Danica and Ariadne arrive and carry the flowers to the cabin and he followed quickly behind them.

"What did you find? " Jacob asked as they entered the cabin.

"I believe these flowers are the answer. I'm not sure exactly how to use them yet but I think they will cure men." Danica said as she emptied her arm full on to the desk, followed by Patrick, Kaleb, and Ariadne.

"There are three more who have fallen ill. I don't know if it's spreading now. The three new men didn't not eat the soup the original man made with the fruit." Jacob said , his hand going to the back of his neck as he spoke.

The stress was starting to get to him. If it was something spreading they were all in close quarters so they would all come down with it. If they were all unconscious then they surely would all die. Danica looked at Jacob , her face worried. She looked back down at the flower and then to ariadne.

"      You know about poisons, can they also be continuous?" Danica asked her quietly.

"Only if they are in the air, like you burn the plant or if there's blisters and they ooze and you come in contact with it." Ariadne said, her face frowning.

Ariadne went over to the flowers studying them as Danica began pacing trying to think of something to stop the spread of whatever this was. Ariadne twirled the flower in her hand looking at it.

"Ok so we know the original ones ate a fruit. The rash is on their stomach so that's consistent with eating something. Did the new infected touch the rash of the original?" Danica asked, looking at Jacob.

"No-

"I'm pretty sure we did." Patrick said as he swayed, he grabbed ahold of the desk as he tried to steady himself.

"Patrick?" Ariadne asked, worried looking at him.

Ariadne went to help steady him and he moved away quickly, almost falling over as he did. Kaleb went to help him as well, walking up to him slowly, not sure what was going on.

"No!" Patrick shouted as  he jerked himself away from Kaleb.

"Patrick, what is going on with you?" Ariadne said coming up next to Kaleb.

"Look at my wrist and forearm. Get away." Patrick said backing up from Ariadne

They all looked at Patrick's forearm and wrist and the same splotchy red rash was there. This was a new rash, different from the one he had self inflicted. Did the antidote not work? Ariadne's hand went over her mouth. She didn't know how long they had till Patrick had a seizure and was unconscious. Kaleb took one look at Patrick and hurried over to Danica. He grabbed her hands and began looking her over. She was the first person to go to the rescue of the fall man.

"Kaleb I'm fine, I don't have the rash." Danica said to him softly.

"Jacob, what about you any signs of one yet?" Danica said her voice worried.

"As of right now no but if this continues we will all have it soon enough." Jacob said with a frown.

Ariande broke the stem of the flower and liquid began to ooze out. She started thinking about it. A loud thud happened to the right of her. She instantly felt like she was going to vomit as she looked over. Patrick was on the ground shaking. Danica went to go to his side and Kaleb stopped her.

"We can't risk you getting it." Danica frowned slightly.

"Kaleb, I need to help him." Danica said, walking around Kaleb.

"Danica no." He said, catching her wrist, as he stopped her; her hair fell over her shoulder and he saw the back of her neck.

The rash was creeping up out of her shirt line and along the base of her neck. He froze, letting her hand slip away. Danica looked back at him confused and then she realized he knew by looking at his face. She shot him a look saying don't say anything before going and kneeling next to Patrick and helping him not hurt himself. After several minutes Patrick was unconscious. Danica exhaled as he stopped seizing and sat back on her heels. She began to feel light headed as she sat there. Ariadne looked over to jacob.

"What if we make a serum from the flowers and place it on the rash and then have them drink it." Ariadne said, touching the liquid leaking out of the flower.

"I think that sounds go-

Jacob began to say before he dropped to his knees and fell to the ground starting to shake. Ariadne went to go to him.

"Ariadne stopped. You're the only one who can do this. Do not get yourself infected. Hurry, that plan sounds the best. You can do this. " Danica said to her with a smile.

"Dani?" Ariadne said relaxing her sister was going pale.

Kaleb began pacing; he wasn't sure what he should do. He knew any minute now Danica was going to fall over. He went over to the desk.

"We need to do this now. Danica has the rash too. She didn't want to tell you. How do you want to do this? Crush the flowers? Boil them?" Kaleb said, picking up a flower.

"That's perfect, we will make a drink out of most of them, saving some for a slab to put on the rash. Kaleb takes this pile here and begins crushing them. We need a bowel, a pan and fire." Ariadne glanced at Danica.

Danica was sinking further and further into the floor as the feeling she was fighting was becoming worse and worse. She felt an intense pressure building in her body. Parts of her felt like they were tingling and her mind was cloudy. She was becoming more and more confused by the second. She had no clue what Kaleb and Ariadne were talking about. She felt like she was uncontrollably spacing out. She watched Kaleb leave the room and couldn't process what or why he was leaving. She laid flat on the ground staring up at the ceiling. Why did she hurt like this? Within seconds Kaleb was back with a bowl and a pan. She watched them begin working on making the serum. Danica's vision began to shake as her whole body began to convulse. She could see Kaleb coming towards her as the world went black around her.

"Kaleb don't! I need all the help I can get and right now it's just you and me. I need you to please finish grinding those flowers." Ariadne said urgency in voice.

Kaleb nodded and stopped just in front of Danica. He was fighting himself to not touch her. He never had someone he actually cared for outside of his mother and Patrick. He gritted his teeth feeling helpless as he went back to the desk. He went back to the desk and began helping Ariadne once more. After several long and dragging minutes all the flowers were grinded and the liquid placed in a small container.

"Ok I need to take this pile here and we need to boil water. Then added these flowers. I don't know how much of the serum it's going to take or if this is even going to work. Well try it on Jacob, Patrick, and Danica first and then the rest of the crew." Ariadne said.

"Let me go find someone and ask about a heat source….maybe a lantern so it's contained and we don't burn down the ship." Kaleb said, walking to the door.

"Ok hurry." Ariadne said not trying to add pressure to him but needing him to find something quickly.

She wasn't sure what damage was going on with the unconscious as they stayed out. Nothing could be happening but it made her nervous the longer they took. She looked over at Danica. She needed her sister. She needed everything to be ok. She looked down at the serum they had collected. She pulled open the desk drawer and began searching for something. She found a small brown glass bottle and the top of it was a drop. She looked at it, it was empty. She poured some of the serum into the glass brown bottle and then inhaled trying to calm her nerves. She pulled some of the serum up into the drop and walked over to Jacob, Patrick, and Danica laying on the ground. Her eyes moved over them, the man she knew since she was a child, almost like a second father to her, Patrick the man she was pretty sure she was falling in love with, and her sister, her best friend. She knew Danica would always be there for her. She felt tears welp up into her eyes. She kneeled down next to her sister. She cradled her head in her arms, carefully trying to avoid the rash. She placed the dropper into the side of her mouth and squeezed. Two small drops of serum from the flower.

"Come on Dani." She whispered to Danica moving a strand of her jet black hair out of her face.

"You can't do this, you need to wake up and come save the day with me." Ariadne whispered to her.

"She will. She has to." Kaleb said walking back into the cabin, holding two lanterns, a jug of water, and another bowel.

Ariadne nodded gently, placing Danica's head back down. She quietly walked over to the desk as Kaleb set down the supplies.

"So I figured, we light the latens, place the water into the bowels, place the bowels on the top part of the lantern, and once the water is heated up add the flowers." Kaleb said thinking out loud as he spoke.

"I think that sounds great." Ariadne said, picking up a match.

Kaleb nodded and Ariadne lit the lanterns. Kaleb placed the bowels on top of them and poured the water into them. They sat there waiting impatiently for the water to heat up. Ariadne wasn't sure how much of the flower's serum they would need to disgust for it to work. She didn't even know if this would work.

"Hey it's gonna work." Kaleb said, reaching over and patting Ariadne's hand softly, seeing the worry in her eyes.

"Thank you." Ariadne whispered.

They watched the water for what seemed hours. It was taking so long Ariadne bean pacing. At the first sign of a little bubble Kaleb nearly fell as he became excited. Ariadne smiled slightly at him as she walked back over to the desk. They began adding a small amount of the flower into the bowel. The flowers melted into the water change the water from a clear color to a light blue. Ariadne was unsure of the reaction; the flowers were white she would expect that from a colored flower. She watched as Kaleb did the same.

"How many?" Ariadne whispered.

Kaleb looked up at her, he didn't want to tell her that when he went out on the ship that there were six more men unconscious. It seemed to be moving like wildfire, almost the crew members. With no way to isolate themselves from each other they were all doomed.

"Six more." He said quietly adding more flowers into the water, the water turned a bright blue.

Ariadne didn't say anything to the increasing numbers. She knew they would be on the rise. She was actually thinking it would have been more by now but there were now ten members of the crew infected. And three people she held closest to her. She dipped the drop she had from the old brown bottle into the blue water and drew up the liquid into it. She walked over to Danica and kneeled down next to her. She again gently took her head into her lap and fed her the liquid. Now all they could do was wait. She had given Danica both the serum and water medicine. She sat close to her sister as they waited. Kaleb continued to work on making more. They would need a bunch of the flower water to heal the crew. He tried to stay focused on working on the solution to avoid feeling helpless and lost. He hated that he couldn't help Danica or his brother right now.

## Chapter Forty Six

## Cure

Several minutes which seemed like hours passed. They began setting up a system. Each person infected would get serum followed by the flower water. Then those not infected would have the flower water as a precaution if the rash occurred then the serum. Ariadne glanced at Danica who was still out. She sighed heavily, Kaleb touched her shoulder lightly trying to comfort her.

" I don't know what else to do. I can't think of anything else." She whispered, her voice cracking as she spoke.

She could feel her hands starting to shake, she was about to lose it. She took a deep breath in trying to calm herself before she lost control. This was too much, this all was too much. The company, the pressure, the voyage, and now she needed Dani to wake up. She didn't realize it but her breathing rapidly changed. She was on the verge of hyperventilating when Kaleb pulled her in for a hug. It was the only thing he knew to do.

"Hey we got this, you got this. Everything takes time. It hasn't been that long. Breathe. Shh. Breath." Kaleb said quietly to her, rubbing her back as he spoke.

"I know but I....I..I can't lose her." Ariadne said as a few tears slipped out.

"We're not going to lose her. Shh. It's going to be ok." Kaleb said his voice was solid and firm.

He meant it. There was no way in hell he was going to accept that they were losing her, losing any of them. He glanced over to them from Jacob, to Patrick, and lastly his eyes settled on Danica. He squeezed Ariadne tightly as he prayed he was right. Ariadne tried to settle herself down but Kaleb was making it easy to break down. She shut her eyes and focused on her breathing. She was strong, she could handle this. A small noise caught her ear. It was a small moan. Kaleb tensed up and Ariadne pulled back from her eyes shifting from one to the next. Danica had moved slightly. Ariadne stepped away from Kaleb going to her. Kaleb followed, did they both make it up. Was the noise really her? Was she really in a different position before? Ariadne kneeled down next to her sister.

"Dani?" Ariadne whispered, reaching out and placing a hand on her arm.

A groan escaped Danica's mouth and Ariadne's stomach exploded with butterflies. The serum and flower water was working. Kaleb dropped to his knees next to Ariadne. He rubbed Danica's cheek softly.

"Come on Dani, come back to us." He whispered as his thumb stroked her cheek.

Ariadne watched Kaleb's face; the concern and love he had coming off of him from Danica made her heart smile. She knew this man was perfect for her sister. Danica began to move and tried to roll away from them. Ariadne caught her and kept her in one spot.

"Ari, sleep now." Danica groaned, squatting at her sister.

Ariadne lunged forward and wrapped her arms around Danica. Danica seemed to come as soon as Ariadne wrapped her arms around her. Danica groaned slightly; her head was killing her and Ariadne pulled away as she studied her sister.

"Are you ok? How do you feel?" Ariadne blurted out studying her face.

"Like I've had too much rum." Danica smiled, holding her head.

Kaleb reached over and squeezed Ariadne's shoulder. "You did it."

Ariadne smiled rightly and then Kaleb pointed to Jacob who was starting to try to sit up. Ariadne looked from Danica to Kaleb and then to Jacob. Kaleb smiled and pulled Danica into his arms.

"I got her." He said to Ariadne.

"Oof Kaleb. That was too fast my heads spinning." Danica said, resting her head against his chest.

He smiled, cradling her and scooping her up into his lap. She curled into his lap more and sighed happily. He pressed his lips into the top of her head.

"Thank god you're ok." He whispered to the top of her head.

"It wasn't painful and while I was asleep it was just darkness." She said, yawning.

Her body did hurt and the seizure was painful but she wasn't about to tell them that. She saw the guilt and worry on their faces when she opened her eyes. She was just happy to be out of the darkness. She looked over to Ariadne who was helping Jacob sit up. Patrick began to stir. Ariadne stabilized Jacob and hurried to Patrick.

As he sat up she pulled him to a fierce hug. Patrick winced slightly and hugged her back tightly. He smiled looking at her.

"See you did it." Patrick said cupping her chin with his hand and running his thumb down her cheek.

"Are you ok? Does anything hurt?" Ariadne rushed out trying to look him over but his hand kept her still.

"Patrick-

Patrick pulled her mouth into his and kissed her. The kiss was like he hadn't seen her in years. Powerful and forceful but gentle at the same time. He pulled her closer as he kissed her deeper. Ariadne wrapped her arms around the back of his heck. She was startled at first but the heat from the kiss made her forget her thoughts.

"Ahem." Danica said loudly from Kaleb's lap.

Kaleb chuckled as he resisted to do the same to Danica. He held her tightly. As she made the noise again louder this time. Ariadne pushed Patrick slightly as she heard her sister. Patrick groaned and broke the kiss. He glanced at Danica, a smirk on his lips.

"So I think we should get to fixing the rest of the infected now." Danica said, making a funny face at Patrick.

"Aye your right." Ariadne said getting up from Patrick who tried his best to not let her go.

Ariadne tapped his hand lightly letting him know he needed to let go. Ariadne walked to the desk. Danica scooted off of Kaleb's lap but her hand still had his as they walked over joining Ariadne at the desk. Jacob and Patrick slowly followed.

"So we give two drops of the serum and then the flower water. It took forever, well maybe fifteen minutes but it felt like forever. Then you all slowly came one by one." Ariadne explained, touching each item as she did.

"Ok so let's divide and conquer." Patrick wobbly announced from behind them.

"Aye Jacob will you get the ship sailing, Kaleb and I will go dispense the serum. Ariadne and Patrick you guys go get everyone with the flower water." Danica said coming up with a plan.

"Aye I think even if we're not displaying symptoms we should drink the flower water." Ariadne said as she reached for two glasses.

She poured one for herself and then one for Kaleb. Kaleb took the glass and then glanced at Ariadne. He debated, he was a little unsure.

"Ariadne let me drink it first. We know it stops whatever poison was happening but we don't know what happens if you drink it without having the poison." Kaleb said, catching Ariadne's arm as she went to drink herself.

"No, then let me drink it and you wait." Ariadne said her eyes flickering to Danica.

Danica wasn't worried until Kaleb said anything about it. She looked from the glasses two her sister and the man she was falling in love with and her stomach knotted.

"I'll drink." A voice from the doorway.

Jonah stood leaning against the doorway of the cabin. He shrugged as if to say he didn't care and began walking over to the desk. Kaleb frowned. He couldn't let someone else take the risk. He debated back and forth with himself as he watched Jonah make his way over.

"Jonah, we shouldn't be thinking about this lightly." Ariadne said to him.

"It's not a big deal, I have no family, no children, nothing that if I disappeared would miss me." Jonah said with a shrug.

"You're like family. Uncle Jack and Aunt Claire love you to pieces." Danica said, shoving him as he said that.

A glass slammed down on the table as Jonah, Ariadne, and Danica argue. Patrick instantly knew what it was. Danica slowly turned around and her eyes narrowed at Kaleb. He smiled, scooting his empty glass away from him.

"And now we wait." Kaleb announced.

"Well mate that was stupid." Jonah said, coming over to the desk.

"Kaleb-

"Now Love we got people to save and places to get going." Kaleb said, throwing a wink at Danica.

She gritted her teeth  looking at him, fire flashing across her eyes as she was getting madder at him by the second.

"Patrick, come help me start giving the serum to all the unconscious. Jonah follows us with some of the flower water so we can dose them with that right after the serum." Ariadne said, looking from Kaleb to Danica.

"Aye Captain." Jonah said gathering up the flower water and heading to the door.

"Are you coming sunshine or are we just gonna stare at Kaleb all day?" Jonah asked Patrick with a smirk on his face.

"Listen sweetheart it's not too late for me to pour some of this water down your throat and see what happens." Patrick grumbled getting the serum and following after Jonah.

Ariande chuckled at them as she shook her head. Danica raised an eyebrow at Jonah's and Patricks exchange.

"They're like that always. Like a love-hate relationship. It's super cute." Ariadne said, her smile turning into a grin.

"It's not at all cute." Patrick protested.

"Aye and there's no love." Jonah chimed in.

"Aye no love!" Patrick declared, narrowing his eyes at Jonah.

"Ok ok. Whatever you two say….Dani come find me if you need me alright." Ariadne said, rolling her eyes at Jonah and Patrick.

"Kaleb don't you dare let anything happen to yourself." Ariadne said, squeezing his shoulder as she walked by him.

"Don't plan on it." Kaleb smiled at her.

The four left with Jacob following behind them. The door closed behind them, Kaleb went to say something to Danica but when he turned to look at her, the fire in her eyes was back alive and dancing.

"Kaleb, what the hell do you think you were doing!" Danica said glaring at him.

"Well I figured it was better than your sister drinking it." Kaleb said nonchalantly.

"Seriously there could have been another way." Danica said becoming more angry at how careless he was being.

"Danica, there was no other way." Kaleb said softly.

"Well we won't find that out now." Danica said you could see the stream coming out of her ears.

Kaleb smirked and he loved the fire she kept buried inside her.  He didn't shy away from it and he loved watching her come to life. He could see that she wanted to scream at him some more but didn't have any more words to throw at him. When she went to open her mouth to say something, he was ready. He grabbed his chest and fell forward on a chair in front of the desk. He let out a small groan as he clutched his shirt tightly.

"Damn it Kaleb! I told you." Dancia said, panicking.

She grabbed a hold of him to steady him. He began to shake slightly as he hid his face from her. He was shaking because he was laughing.

"What's wrong? What's happening?" Danica asked, trying to get him to face her.

She finally was able to pull him around so she could see his face. As he turned she noticed that his face wasn't in pain but he was laughing. She shoved him into the chair. She was furious.

"How dare you!" She yelled at him as she slapped the chair with her hand.

"I thought you were going to die! That is not at all funny!" She yelled at him.

Kaleb was laughing harder and harder as she was becoming madder and madder. She went to walk away and he caught her hand. She went to yank it out of his grasp but he used her own force against her and pulled her into his lap. She began struggling and fighting to get off of his lap. He let her get up off his lap but pulled her back down to him.

"Dani, Dani I'm sorry." He laughed.

"Stop laughing!" She yelled at him, turning to look him in the face.

As she turned to look at him his hand caught her cheek and She was pulled into a heated kiss. His mouth captured hers hungrily. His lips taking hers like without them they would die. She resisted at first being angry with him but gave in her lips wanting him just as bad. Her fingers tangled into his hair keeping him close to her. He pulled her onto his lap, her legs going around his waist as he began to kiss her down her neck.

"Kaleb i really think-

He captured her earlobe in his mouth as she was talking. It sent shivers through her as she leaned down into it. She ran her hand down the front of his chest, her fingers going to his waist and teasing traced his belt line. He groaned slightly as he felt excited. She smirked as she moved her hand across his groin. She applied a little pressure as she smiled at the noise he made. Two could play this game she thought. She moved her hand in a circle against the outside of his pants teasing him. He let out a growl as his hand went to the back of her neck his fingers tugged on her hair slightly as he brought her mouth to his kissing her.

"Dani hows Kaleb-

Ariadne asked, walking into the cabin Patrick close behind her. She stopped her sentence when she saw her sister tangled up with Kaleb. Danica squealed a little as she scooted herself off Kaleb's lap.

"Um he's. He's fine." Danica choked out.

"I could be better." Kaleb smirked as he stood up slowly.

"Ok well then, anyways all the crew members have been treated that were infected. They are slowly coming too. We wanted to see how Kaleb was before we started passing out the flower water to the non-infected as a precaution." Ariadne said, looking at the floor a little.

“Aye he's fine.  I think we can do that.” Danica said her face was on fire, she knew her cheeks and ears were bright red.

“Ok. I will go make sure that is done.” Ariadne said as she slowly ducked out of the cabin door.

“I will help.” Danica said going to grab more flower water.

Kaleb caught her wrist and spun her into him. He kissed her once more, it was hot and passionate but he kept it short. As he pulled away Danica was still breathless.

“Ok I'm going to go help.” Danica said with a small smile on her face.

“Danica.” Kaleb said being serious for a moment.

“Aye?” She asked, confused , stopping and looking at him.

He closed the distance between them, his hand going to her cheek. She leaned into it as his thumb rubbed her cheek.

“I didn't know what I was going to do if we couldn't get you to wake up.” Kaleb said softly.

“Kaleb its ok i'm fi-

His thumb pressed against her lip, stopping her from talking. She raised an eyebrow at him and waited for him to finish.

" I more than just care for you now. I..I don't ever want to not be without you." Kaleb said softly.

Danica's heart fluttered in her chest as she watched him struggle to find the right words. She grabbed a hold of his hand and squeezed it softly. A small smile on her lips. She leaned up to his lips and kissed them softly.

"I don't want to be without you anymore ethier." She whispered back against his lips.

He kissed her back deeply, his arms wrapping around her and holding her to him like he was never going to let her go. They pulled back from each other's kiss. Resting their forwards together.

"I have to go help Ari." She whispered to him.

"Aye lets get everyone fixed up and we can go home." Kaleb said to her.

"Home?" Danica asked, she had never heard him call; from what he had told her he was constantly on the move.

"Aye, I'm going to be staying there for a while now." Kaleb smiled.

"What about all your adventures?" Danica whispered, kind of sad for him.

"Why would I need to go chasing adventure and beautiful things when I have the most beautiful thing in the world in front of me." He smiled, tapping her lightly on the nose.

She blushed and wasn't sure how to respond. He took her by the hand and began leading her out of the cabin. At that moment she promised to give him the biggest adventure of his life some day.

## Chapter Forty Seven

## Kidnapped

Ariadne came out of the captain's cabin, her face flushed a little. She smiled a little embarrassed at seeing what she saw. She straightened up and gained her composure. Patrick raised an eyebrow at her asking what was wrong but she just smiled sweetly in return. He walked over to her with a puzzle look on his face.

"Are you alright?" He asked, taking her hand in his.

"Aye I'm ok. Kaleb and Dani that's all. Anyways, how's it going with the rest of the crew?." Ariadne laughed, his fingers entwining with his.

"Good we're just waiting on the rest of the flower water." Patrick  said, nodding to the lower deck.

The men had lined up and were waiting to get their share of the water. Ariadne smiled, she was thankful for Patricks help and was really liking that he was taking control in some areas.

"Thank you. You've really been a great help." Ariadne smiled at him.

"Well it's kind of my family's fault we were all in this. So it's the least I can do." He smiled, squeezing her hand.

"Well, although your father is a bit of an ass. I'm glad I met you." Araidne smiled at him , moving to the side of him and leaning in.

Patrick's arm wrapped around her waist pulling her close. Jonah came up the stairs to the upper deck, rolling his eyes as he saw Ariadne and Patrick. Ariadne's smile turned into a grin. She really loved the banter that Jonah and Patirck had developed.

"All right love birds, what's next?" Jonah smirked.

"Home." Danica came out of the cabin behind them carrying more of the flower water.

Patrick and Ariadne smiled looking back at Danica, they all nodded in agreement as Kaleb came up behind Danica.

"Aye Home. Jonah let Mr. Jacob know the heading." Ariadne ordered.

Danica nodded as she walked by them carrying the water. Kaleb headed down with her to the lower deck as they began passing out the flower water to the remainder of the crew. Jonah headed off to give out coordinates.  Patricked pulled Ariadne closer to him as they were somewhat alone now. Ariadne melted into his warmth. She glanced up to him and she could tell he was debating saying something. She looked up at him confused, he caught her looked and smiled at her shaking hsi head as if to say nothing. She frowned lightly as Jonah's calling out coordinates and sail adjustments distracted her.


Orion's feet hit the dock with a rush of relief, he was home. He was grateful after settling all existing contracts they held with the new paperwork he felt lighter. The business was safer. He scanned the harbor. The North Star or the Morning Star was not yet back. His sister nor his parents were home. He frowned; he noticed that when he pulled into the harbor the candle they kept lit in the window was out. He felt uneasy as he looked up the cliff at his house. Why would the candle be out if his family's ship had not returned. He dismissed the men and began making his way slowly towards his home. The sky was dark and the stars were just coming out. The rest of the men were happily going home to their families or to the bar. He walked up the path to his home, his eyes studying the house. Maybe the candle had burned out and Ariadne had yet to replace it. She had been so busy lately, he thought. As he approached the door although he was telling himself everything was ok his stomach was telling him something was wrong.

He reached the door handle and turned it slowly. He let the door slip out of his hand as it creaked open. The house was dark, he stepped inside. He looked for the lantern on the kitchen table blindly. He tripped over something and landed forward into the table. A chair had been knocked over, tripping him. He found the lantern and the match. He struck the match and the lantern. As the light from the lantern lit the room a struggle unfolded in front of him. Chairs were knocked over, papers that were on the kitchen table were thrown onto the floor. Someone had been cooking when it happened because the food was knocked all over the counter top in the far corner. Orion moved around the table, his hand going to his side where his sword and dagger hung. He began searching the house. Each room he walked into unfolded more chaos. He stopped in front of his father's study door. The lock had several scratches and  looked like someone had made several attempts to pick the lock and break the door down but did not prevail. The frame was starting to be pulled away from the door, the wood was giving away. Someone had tried to pop the door and the door wouldn't give up.

"Ari?" Orion called hoping she had locked herself inside.

He shouldn't have left her alone here. He began knocking on the door.

"Ari? Ari is Orion. Hey are you in there?" Orion asked with each question his voice becoming more concerned.

He threw his shoulder into the door. The door didn't budge. It was solid. He backed up and threw his shoulder with a bit of more power. The door stood still.

"Ari!" He yelled loud as he rammed the door once more with his shoulder.

He heard a groan coming from the sitting room. He left the door immediately and ran. Jumping over the falling chairs to get to the sitting room as fast as he could. Getting to the sitting room the light spilling in from the kitchen he could make out someone on the floor. He raced back into the kitchen grabbing the lantern and coming back into the sitting room. Golden blonde hair was sprawled out in front of him. He rushed to the side of the confused person. Getting there and kneeling down he realized it was his aunt Claire.

"Auntie." He said quietly, rolling her over slightly.

As he rolled her over he saw a wound above her left eyebrow blood slowly leaking from it. There was another wound on the back of her head. Someone had hit her hard in the head and face.

"Auntie." He said louder.

Her blue eyes fluttered open and it took her a minute to realize who was kneeling over her. She sat up suddenly as if everything came rushing back to her.

"Hey easy. Take a minute." Orion said slowly steadying Claire.

"Jack." Claire said foggy.

"Uncle Jack? He did this?" Orion asked, confused.

'No, they took him." Claire said, holding her head.

"Who took him?" Orion said confused as he helped Claire up from the ground and onto the sofa.

"Ed Smith." Claire said, holding her head.

Orion gritted his teeth, rage forming  in the pitt of his stomach. Who did this man think he was? Orion let his aunt on the sofa he blindly walked around in the kitchen gathering a rag wetting it and returning back into the sitting room. Claire was trying to stand up.

"Auntie stop. Sit down." Orion said going to her and helping her back on the sofa.

"We need to go to the Smiths and get your Uncle back." Claire said, taking the wet cloth and holding to her eyebrow.

"Where's Ari?" Orion said not letting go of Claire's shoulder in case she wasn't steady enough.

"Ari went after Danica. Long story short Danica was sailing into a disaster and Ariadne went to save her." Claire said, holding her head again.

"Ok so what happened here." Orion said, trying to understand.

"Ed Smith came with a few of his goons. They wanted the contracts, and tried getting into your father's office. Jack got pissed off and fought off several of them with me but more came. Someone knocked me out as I saw them hit Jack over the head and take him." Claire said.

"Why would he? I understand the scheming and business shady things he does but kidnapping. Is he that desperate?" Orion asked out loud.

"He was saying something about his sons being missing. He was furious because he found out that you had gone and sealed the rest of the contracts. Ariadne and you found the loop he was using." Claire said, starting to stand.

"Claire, you need to sit. Your head is seriously hurt." Orion demanded.

"He has Jack. If I was missing an arm we would still be going. Let's go." Claire growled.

"We need a plan." Orion said firmly to Claire.

She nodded, she couldn't argue with that but they needed one quickly they didn't know what was going on with Ed Smith and what he planned to do with Jack.


"Ed! What in the world are you doing? Why is there a man in the basement?"

The shouting woke Jack. His head hung forward, the loose strands of hair falling in his face. He lifted his head slowly and the world was spinning. He remembered getting hit over the head with something and then the world went black.

"Mind your own business bitch!"

A loud smack echoed from above him as a loud crash hit the floor, making the ceiling above Jack's head shake. He recognized the voice from earlier. It was Edward Smith. Was he in his house? Jack looked around, he was in a basement. The room was dark and he could see the stone walls. The old musty smell filled the air around him. He searched for the exit with his eyes. He could make out an old wooden stairway. That must be the way out. He looked down at the chair he was strapped to and the ropes. He flexed his wrist to see how well he was strapped in. The ropes gave a little but not enough to let him slip his hands out. He heard loud footsteps stomping around up above him. They became louder as the stairs began to creak. Soon enough Edward Smith was standing just inches from him.

"Oh good your wake." Ed sneered at him.

"Aye I'm awake. You're lucky I'm tied up. What exactly is your plan from here?" Jack said his tone belittling him.

"Plan…Plan." Ed walked over to Jack and grabbed a handful of his hair pulling his neck backwards as he spoke.

"Don't really have one. I want your brother's company and I want my sons back." Ed said his knuckles turned white from how tightly he was holding Jack by his hair.

"Well two problems we have here. First I don't have any ownership in the company so I couldn't even if I wanted to hand over the company which I wouldn't. Second, you should keep a better track of your children. Maybe fire the babysitter." Jack smirked as he spoke.

Ed drew his hand back and through his first forward, it connected with Jack's jaw. Jack's teeth sank into his cheek and tongue as his hand went to go to the left. Ed's hand held his face in place as he held onto his hair.

"All you Abner's talk way too much." Ed said through his gritted teeth.

"See you're wrong again." Jack said, spitting a wad of blood on the ground near Ed's feet.

"I'm not an Abner." Jack smirked.

Ed cranked his fist back and was about to hit him again, when he heard the stairway creak. Ed let go of Jack's head and it slumped forward. He spat out some more blood as he watched Ed try to see who was coming down the stairs. A small framed woman appeared at the bottom of the stairs holding a small tray. She looked fragile and broken. A freshly placed mark on her cheek was turning a shade of purple. Jack's eyes narrowed as he knew exactly where it came from. The man was a coward.

"What are you doing down here? I told you to mind your own business!" He growled walking to the stairs; his fists curled in as he walked to her.

"I brought you your evening Tea. I know how you like everything to be on time. So I made sure that the tea was ready and brought it down to you….you…work." She said holding out the cup of tea on a small saucer.

Astonishly Ed's body softened and he walked over to his wife. He took the tea and nodded to her. She didn't say anything else and headed up the stairs. He came over to Jack holding the tea. He blew on it lightly before taking a long sip. He leaned against the wall finishing the tea and looking at Jack.

"When does everyone get back?" Ed asked, taking another sip.

Jack glared at him, not saying a word. He ignored Ed as he sipped the tea. He was slowly working on the ropes that were holding his hands in place. He could feel the ropes slowly giving. The skin on his wrist burned as he tried his hardest to get free.

"Fine dont say when. We will know as soon as they dock anyways. I have eyes all over this harbor. This harbor and all your ports will be mine shortly." Ed grinned turning to the stairs and began walking up them.

# Chapter Forty Eight

## Rescue:

Orion gathered what weapons he had in the home. He had several daggers stashed on him, his pistol and sword hung by his waist. Claire was determined to come with him. She walked back into the kitchen for the third time, Jack's pistol hanging from her hip with her sword on the other side. Orion could tell she also had a dagger in her boot. He smiled a little bit. They couldn't come up with a plan so now they were just going to storm the castle and see what would happen.

"Are you sure you're ready?" Orion asked, looking at Claire.

"Stop asking me boy, you have no idea what your aunt has done in the past. Now let's go get Jack." Claire said walking to the door.

Ariadne was nervous as she stared the ship into the harbor. She was excited to be going home. Her trip was somewhat successful. She kept glancing at Patrick who was on the lower deck helping get things prepared for docking. Danica sensed her sister's anxiousness and she walked over to her.

"Whatcha doing?" Danica asked her playfully.

"Thinking." Ariadne answered not hiding anything from her sister.

"About?" Danica said quietly.

"Probably the same thing you have been thinking about Mr. Kaleb." Ariadne said not being funny.

"Aria?" Danica asked.

"Come on Dani, you know what I mean. What if this whole thing was happening because we were stuck on a ship together? What if the ship docks and we go back to our lives. We are enemies. What if he doesn't…what if-

"Ariadne stop it. Have you not seen the way he looks at you? Have you not seen that he has defied every order given to him because of you? It wasn't because it was the right thing. It's because the minute you opened that door at our house, the minute he laid eyes on you everything changed. He was supposed to be a double agent for his father and yet here he is helping you save me and the company." Danica said, squeezing her shoulder.

"Are you sure?" Ariadne whispered.

"Aye, I'm as sure as the moon in the sky." Danica said with a smile, repeating something their mother always said to them.

"The moon changes." Ariadne smiled answering the way she did when her mother said that.

"It may change but it's always there." Danica winked.

"Besides I would kill him if that was even true. Then you wouldn't have to worry about it." Danica laughed.

"Stop that." Ariadne chuckled back.

"What about you? Are you sure he's the one?" Ariadne smirked looking from her to Kaleb.

"Aye." Danica said firmly looking down at Kaleb who was right beside Patrick helping every inch of he way.

"Well you sound very sure. Especially from the girl who didn't want a love story." Ariadne chuckled.

"Well this love story was different." Danica said, making a face at her sister.

"Approaching Dock!" Jacob's voice rang out.

"Oh look Ori's home too." Ariadne pointed to Orion's ship.

"Aye that means he managed to get all the existing contracts straightened out. So now with the treasure we are in great shape." Danica said feeling a little relief.

"Aye. Everything will be all straightened out before mom and dad come home." Ariadne smiled.

"The candle." Dancia said, her voice holding confusion.

"What?" Ariadne said looking up at their house on the hill.

"Anchors! Ropes!" Jonah's voice rang out

Ariadne drew her eyes from their home and focused on pulling the ship into dock. Danica walked down the stairs quickly. She knew something was wrong. The candle was always lit when someone was out to sea. She immediately was by the exit waiting for the ramp to be thrown down. Kaleb came up beside her and caught her hanging hand.

"What's wrong?" He asked softly.

"Somethings wrong. I need to get home." Danica said her eyes fixed on her house.

"How do you know?" Kaleb asked following Danica's gaze.

His eyes landed on a house nestled in the cliffside overlooking the water. He glanced back to Danica waiting for her to answer. She dropped his hand impatiently waiting for the men to finish up.

"The candle it's not lit." Danica said quietly, her eyes now staring at the ramp.

"Candle?" Kaleb asked.

Before she could answer him the ramp was secured. Danica didn't wait; she hopped over the railing and took off down the ramp. Running as fast as she could.

"Danica!" Kaleb called after her.

He jumped over the railing and began running after her. She was fast but he was quickly following behind her. Ariadne raced down the stairs from the upper deck, crashing into Patrick as she was set on following Danica as well.

"Woah, Woah. What's going on?" Patrick said steadying her as she ping ponged off of him.

"Somethings wrong at home. We need to get there." Ariadne said quickly, trying to move around Patrick.

"Ok lets go." He grabbed her hand and started leading her off the ship.

Danica raced up the dirt  path way to her house, tripping and falling. The pebbled in the dirt scraping into her knees and palm. She was up before she could even process the pain. She could see her house; racing there as fast as she could. Reaching the stone walkway she slowed down. Her stomach in knots. She walked to the front door and reached for the handle. As she went to touch the handle the door pulled open. Danica stepped back not sure what she was expecting.

"Dani?"

Then it hit her, her brother was standing in the doorway dressed for battle. She looked at him confused, did he come back from the ship like this.

"Orion what's going on?" Danica said, breathing heavy as she tried to catch her breath.

Before he could explain Claire stepped out from behind him. Danica was at first excited to see her aunt. She had missed her so much but then looking at her closely she saw her skin split above her eyebrow and the blood in her hair.

"Auntie what happened?" Danica asked, her hand's going into fist at her side.

"Ed smith came demanding the rest of the contracts and something about his missing sons. I see you've found the other one. He took Jack, after he knocked me unconscious." Claire said, looking at Danica and then behind her as Ariadne, Patrick, and Kaleb caught up.

"He took uncle Jack?" Danica asked, confused.

"Who took uncle Jack?" Ariadne said breathlessly as she reached them, looking at her brother and aunt with confusion.

"Your father." Danica said turning and facing Kaleb and Patrick.

Patrick let out a long breath and put his hand on the back of his neck trying to figure out what to do.

"I knew he was crazy but this. Kidnapping he may have just lost it now." Kaleb said, looking at Patrick.

"Let's go see if we can talk to him. Let me and Kaleb try before you all go kicking in the front door." Patrick said, glancing at Kaleb and then at Ariadne and Danica.

"Yeah I don't think so." Claire said moving past Danica and starting to head out.

"Auntie. I think Patrick's right. If we can get uncle Jack without any more injuries or chaos we should take that route." Orion said, speaking up from behind her.

"Orion you're lucky I'm not there slitting that prick's throat right now." Claire growled.

"Auntie, Let Patrick and Kaleb try first." Ariadne said softly, touching her aunt's arm.

"Aye Auntie, I agree too." Dancia said with a small smile.

"Fine but the littlest thing goes wrong and he will see a side of me he didn't wish he did." Claire growled, moving out of the way for Patrick and Kaleb to go.

Patrick glanced at Kaleb and began walking. As the two of them led the way Kaleb leaned closer and whispered to his brother.

"So what's your plan?" Kaleb asked.

"I dont have one." Patrick whispered back.

"Well we know he's not listening to me so it's on you." Kaleb whispered back.

"Aye I dont know if I can reason with him. Maybe he's drunk and we can distract him and free Jack. I don't know what he's thinking. He's always been manipulative but never reckless. This is reckless." Patrick said, trying to think things through.

"Well, in the worst case scenario I'll have no problem hitting him." Kaleb smirked.

"Kaleb." Patrick said using his older brother's tone on him.

"What." Kaleb shrugged.

The rest of the way they walked in silence. Danica was becoming nervous the closer and closer they got to The Smith's home. Ariadne was playing with her pinkie finger like she did when something was upsetting her. She knew stories about Patrick's past, this his father did to him, Kaleb, and his mother.

She didn't want Patrick facing any of that. She didn't know why Patrick thinks that he can get through to his father but she was going to let him try.

They got to the house and Patrick with Kaleb paused in front of the door Patrick inhaled and looked at Kaleb. Kaleb gritted his teeth before looking back at Danica and the rest of them.

"Stay here, we will call for backup if needed." Kaleb said with a wink before moving past Patrick and opening the door and stepping in.

Patrick nodded to them and quietly followed after Kaleb. Entering the house it was dark and silent. A light came from the kitchen. Kaleb's first thought was mom. He walked to the kitchen slowly. He was worried about his mother since he found out that Patrick had left her to go come save him and Danica. Patrick followed behind Kaleb, his hands clenched in fist. Each step he took to the kitchen his stomach dropped more and more. Kaleb was holding his jaw so tight that he began getting pain by his ear. Hy enter the kitchen and found their mother's back facing them. She leaned over the sink, her auburn hair down in messy waves as she gripped the side of the sink. Her hand hung low.

"Mom?" Kaleb's voice carried in the empty room.

"Kaleb?" Evelyn said, surprised, turning around to see both her sons standing in the doorway.

She smiled brightly and walked across the room quickly, her arms opened ready to give them hugs. Kaleb stopped her as she got closer.  A larger bloody bruise was across her cheek. Kaleb's hand went to her cheek touching it lightly. The Pain in his stomach grew. Patrick noticed blood coming from her ear slightly. His father must have hit her with something on the side of the head.

"Where is he?"Kaleb growled.

"He's down stairs with that man. I tried getting him to let him go." Evelyn frowned, Patrick's eyes narrowed knowing that's why she had been hurt.

"Go take care of yourself."Patrick said, kissing her forehead.

Kaleb stormed out of the kitchen, fire in his eyes as he rounded the corner in the hallway heading for the stairs.

"Patrick, Kaleb." Evelyn said her eyes worried.

"Aye I got it mom." Patrick said with a wink before following Kaleb.

He wasn't stopping Kaleb this time. He had gotten in the way of Kaleb going after his father for years. This time he didn't care. This time was enough. Patrick rounded the corner in time to see Kaleb heading down the stairs. Patrick picked up his pace.

Kaleb stormed down the stairs to the basement rage boiling in his stomach.

"Father!" He yelled as he stopped down the stairs.

Kaleb's feet hit the bottom stairs and he spotted his father. His father was looking to the stairs confused as if not excepting Kaleb.

"Boy, where have you've been? Where's Patrick?" Ed smith yelled, turning away from Jack.

"What the hell are you doing?" Kaleb yelled at him, stepping down from the stairs.

"Who do you think you're talking to?" Ed growled at Kaleb.

"You, are you insane? Kidnapping? Move out of the way." Kaleb said, walking over to Jack.

Jack's head was dropped. He had been hit several times in the face by Ed's fist. He had several slashes on his arm's from the sword Ed was holding in his hand. Kaleb threw his shoulder into his father as he walked by him. Kaleb went over to Jack.

"Hey buddy." Kaleb said, shaking his shoulder.

"Get away from him, Kaleb. Don't you dare do anything. " Ed Smith yelled.

Kaleb ignored him as he began untieing Jack. He heard movement behind him but was still ignoring his father who was making grunting noises. As if he was working himself up into being more angry. Kaleb was focusing on Jack; he seemed to be in rough shape. He needed to get him out of here.

"Kaleb!" Patrick yelled as his feet hit the floor.

Kaleb didn't see his father raising the sword above his head and coming towards him. He was going to bring his sword down on Kaleb. Ed was seeing nothing but red. Patrick didn't have any time to think. Ed began to bring the sword down towards Kaleb. Patrick ran full speed at Ed. Patrick hit Ed in his side causing him to lean away and fall as the sword came down. It caught Kaleb in the shoulder but not enough to cause nothing more than a laceration. Kaleb groaned in pain as the sword cut through his skin. He stood just in time to see Patrick and his father hit the floor. Ed's head hit the floor with a crack. Patrick stood quickly up and looked at his father. He was not moving. He was unconscious.

"Kaleb you ok?" Patrick called to him as he kneeled down to check his father.

"Aye." Kaleb said, ignoring the blood starting to come down his arm.

He finished undoing Jack's ropes. Jack groaned slightly starting to come to. He picked his head up trying to figure out what was going on. He looked at Kaleb confused.

"Can you stand?" Kaleb asked Jack.

"Kaleb." Patrick said his voice was monotone.

"Aye?" Kaleb asked, turning to look at Patrick.

Ed Smith wasn't responding to Patrick at all. He had shaken him and moved his arm. Nothing but he was still breathing. Kaleb came over to Patrick looking down at him. Kaleb shrugged and went back to Jack. He didn't care if the man was unconscious. A weird sound caught his ear. Ed began to shake and foam at the mouth. His body contoured, white bubbly spit began to pour out of his mouth. Kaleb restaurant to Patrick's side who was now holding him steady. Kaleb sighed and kneeled holding his legs still.

"Seizure?" Patrick asked out loud to no one in particular.

"Aye." Evelyn said from the stairs.

"Mom." Patrick said guilt hitting him.

Ed began to shake more violently and twist, his fingers curling in painful positions, his eyes rolling back into his head as his lips turned blue. Patrick and AKleb continued to hold him still trying to make sure he didn't hurt himself. Ed stopped twitching. Patrick let up on holding him. Evelyn made her way slowly across the room.

"Breathing?" She asked, her voice emotionless.

Kaleb's eyes went to his chest, it was no longer raising and falling. Kaleb looked at Patrick , answering with his eyes. The foam coming out of his mouth stopped. Evelyn kneeled down and turned his head slightly.

"Dead." Evelyn said her voice almost sounded happy.

"Mom I, he was going to kill Kaleb. I'm sorry I-" Patrick began to try to explain to her.

"It wasn't you Dear." Evelyn said, touching Patrick's cheek.

"What? I made him hit his head." Patrick said, confused.

"The foam, the seizure, it was the poison." Evelyn said softly.

"Poison?" Kaleb asked from the ground.

"Aye Poison." Evelyn smiled.

"Mother?" Patrick asked quietly, connecting the dots.

"Aye, I was done with being a victim.  I was done watching him hurt you boys. Hitting his head was just a coincidence. The little dose of poison I have been giving him in his tea was finally enough." Evelyn smiled.

Jack began to stand shaky. Kaleb looked from his father to his mother, and Patrick. He wasn't sure what to say about any of this. He went over to Jack, catching his arm and helping stand up. Kaleb looked around the room.

"Good. Put him by the stairs, he smells like alcohol anyways. We can just say he fell down the stairs." Kaleb said over his shoulder to them as he started to the stairs.

Patrick looked at him and realized that he was right. If the constable were to come by they would need to cover all this up. It was the best way.

"Mother why don't you go upstairs and get ahold of the authorities let them know dad fell. Kaleb we need to get Jack out of here. Patrick said, going over to the chair that was in the center of the room, where Jack was kept.

He grabbed the chair and dragged it out of sight. He then began cleaning up the blood from Jack. Evelyn came over and began helping him as Kaleb and Jack slowly made their way up the stairs. Reaching the top of the stairs Kaleb heard the front door basically get kicked open. As the door swung open the Abner's rushed in. Kaleb smirked, holding on to Jack.

"Jack!" Claire yelled rushing over to him.

Jack had been quiet trying to keep up his energy. Seeing Claire he stood up straighter. Kaleb moved off to the side as Claire wrapped her arms around him. He put his arm lightly back around her.

"Hi Gorgeous." He whispered to her with a half smile on his face.

"Damn it Jack." She whispered squeezing him.

"You guys are ruining my grand escape." Jack smirked.

"Oh hush." Claire said, taking his face in his hands, frowning as she felt his very swollen and bruised face.

"I'm going to kill him. Where is he?" Claire growled.

"He's dead." Kaleb said quietly.

"Kaleb?" Danica said, going over to his side.

"It's ok. We need to leave, we have it set up to look like an accident. I'll explain everything else to you later but we need to go." Kaleb said quietly to Danica.

"Patrick?" Ariadne asked worriedly.

"He's ok. He's down stairs with my mother arranging things." Kaleb smiled at her.

"Kaleb your arm." Danica said noticing his shirt was turning red.

"Aye, it's ok. We need to go now." Kaleb nudged Jack, who began walking forward.

Jack moved away from Kaleb walking on his own now that he regained feeling back in his legs. Claire held on to him as he walked out the door. Ariadne and Orion followed suit. Danica watched Kaleb carefully trying to figure out how he felt.

"Let's go Love." He whispered to her, clutching his arm slightly, the pain starting to bother him.

Danica nodded and came over to him, She entwined her fingers into his open hand as he started to walk out of his home.

# Chapter Forty Nine

## Treasure Chest

Danica walked silently back to her house with Kaleb. He was clenching his jaw off and on. She didn't know if it was because of the pain in his arm or of everything that happened.

"You know, I'm still so angry. He's dead and I am numb to that but I'm angry. Every ounce of me wanted him to hurt for the years of pain he put us through. The constant beatings , the be the best or else attitude pounded into us, and hurting my mother. I took off as soon as i could and still feel so much guilt from it. I never knew if I did the right thing. My mother begged me to go. He had told her he would kill me the next time he was upset or one of us failed. I was always the least favorite. I don't know if I ever did the right thing leaving. Part of me wanted him to suffer more. To feel what it felt to live the way he made us all." Kaleb said the words just falling out of his mouth.

"Kaleb, you did what you had to do to survive. No one can fault you for that. And anger is a perfectly reasonable response." Danica said her eyes were full of compassion for him.

"I guess." He whispered softly looking upwards at the stars as he walked.

"At Least my mom will be safe now." Kaleb said, his voice full of relief.

"What happened?" Danica asked.

"He went to kill me, Patrick tackled him and he hit his head. We thought that's what killed him but then mother said she had been poisoning him. He went into a seizure and stopped breathing." Kaleb said no emotion in the statement.

"So you're staging it like he fell down the stairs?" Danica asked.

"Aye, he had been drinking so it's believable." Kaleb answered as Danica's home came into view.

"I really need to look at your arm." Danica said softly as they walked up the walkway.

Kaleb just nodded, he was sort of spacing out on her. Jack and Claire walked into the house. Ariadne and Orion went towards the dock. Danica had forgotten about the treasure and that they just left the crew up in the air without orders. She was thankful her sister and brother were going to go handle that. Danica led Kaleb into the house and made him sit down at the table. Claire had gotten a rag and a bowl of water and disappeared into the bedroom to tend to Jack. Jack was exhausted and needed rest. Kaleb let out a heavy sigh as he sat down. He needed to get back home.  He needed to be with his mother and brother to make sure everything went smoothly. He didn't even realize Danica had left the room and returned with a shirt from Orion's room; she had set up a water basin, rag, and some bandage material next to him.

"Take off your shirt." Danica said, tapping him lightly trying to draw him from his thoughts.

He nodded and began trying to take his shirt off. He gritted his teeth from the pain. He felt Danica's fingers on the edge of the shirt as gently  pulled it over his head. Her fingertips lightly grazed his chest as she lifted upwards. Her touch on his chest sent shivers through him. He smiled lightly as she set his shirt down. The smile he gave her made her blush slightly, which made him smile more. She looked at his wound, he was lucky anymore force and it would have done serious damage. She took the wet rag and cleaned the wound. Patting it dry she glanced at him. He was no longer with her again, he was lost in his thoughts. She bandaged his arm quickly and before no time had passed he was all fixed up. She tapped him, handing him a black long sleeve shirt of Orions.

"Here put this on if you bleed more or through the bandage no one will see it through he black shirt. Go." She whispered softly to him, her hand rubbing his cheek lightly.

He smiled at her, capturing her hand and kissing it lightly before standing and pulling the shirt over his head. He looked at her, he could see how worried she was about him. He didn't say anything but pulled her towards him. He circled his good arm around her waist and buried his face into her neck. He inhaled slightly the smell of her calming him. He held her like that as she wrapped her arms around him tightly. After a few seconds he pulled back, placing a kiss on her forward head.

"I'll be back as soon as everything is cleared up." He said to her squeezing her hand lightly.

"Aye go take care of your family." Danica said understanding.

Kaleb smiled his thanks and quickly headed to the door. She watched his back walk out the door and stared after it as the door shut. She didn't know why but she was worried. What if he went home and decided this was all their fault and she never saw him again. Her stomach knotted in on itself.

Ariadne met Jacob and Jonah at the ship. They had dismissed the crew and were waiting for them to return. Orion followed behind her. Jacob and Jonah carried the treasure down to her.

"You alright lass?" Jacob asked her, eyeing her carefully.

"Oh you know just another day in the life of being an Abner. Uncle Jack got kidnapped but everythings all fixed." Ariadne said letting out a long sigh after.

"All right then.." Jonah said looking at her funny.

"It's a long story but I'm exhausted. Everything is fine. You men get back to your families. I will take this home and be happy to be home once everything is settled." Ariadne said, exhausted.

Jacob nodded as Joanh scooted off the chest treasure. He was sitting on top of it. Johan nodded at them as he nudged Jacob who was still staring at Ariadne as if trying to figure out if everything was ok.

"Come on, let's go get a drink." Jonah said as he started walking off the ship.

"Jacob, we are fine, I promise." Ariadne said with a soft smile.

She nodded to Orion who picked up the handle on the other side and Ariadne grabbed hers. Jacob frowned and shook his head at Ariadne as he grabbed the handle waiting for her to move.

"Jonah, I'll meet you there. I'm going to help them with this." Jacob said stubbornly.

"Aye, I'll save you a seat." Jonah said with a wave over his head as he began making his way to the tavern.

Ariadne sighed and let Jacob take the handle. She walked down the ramp ahead of them heading for home. Jacob glanced over at Orion who had extra quiet.

"What's going on son?" Jacob asked.

"Everythings ok now. Don't worry Jacob." Orion said with a small smile.

There were a few people gathered on the docks gossiping. As they walked by them, they could hear them chatting.

"Did you hear what happened to Ed Smith?" One man said to another.

"Yeah his son Patrick came home to find him dead." The man responded.

"Do you know how?" The first man asked.

"I heard he had one too many and fell down the stairs." The second man replied.

"That's embarrassing." The first man responded.

Jacob glanced over to Orion who was trying very hard to act like he did not hear any of that. Jacob frowned deeply.

"Everythings fine, huh?" Jacob said to Orion with a look, Orion looked down to avoid eye contact.

"This freaking town is so small." Ariadne grumbled ahead of them.

Three made their way back to the house in silence. Jacob kept glancing at Orion who was avoiding looking at him at all cost. He knew Orion would give if he just questioned him further but he could tell Ariadne was on the verge of flipping out on someone. Ariande noticed that someone had relit the candle in the upper window. She knew it must have been Danica. Their parents were still out at sea. Ariadne opened the door to their home. Danica was sitting at the kitchen table just staring at the wall. Ariadne looked at her slightly but she was also in the same mood. It was like the stress of everything had finally built up enough that they were numb and tired. Now that they were back home and for the most part things were ok. Orion and Jacob set the treasure chest down on the table with a thud. The table shook and gained Danica's attention.

"I had completely forgotten about the treasure." Danica said standing and going over to the end of the table.

"I guess we should open it and see what is in it." Ariadne said, approaching Danica's side.

"Aye. " Orion said, agreeing.

The three stood in front of the treasure chest looking at it. There was no lock which was strange but no obvious way of opening the chest. Orion looked to Ariadne who shrugged and they all looked to Danica.

"Well Dani this was all you. Any ideas?" Ariadne asked.

Danica stepped closer to the chest and looked at it. She noticed the groves were different. She traced the pattern and as she did. She realized the pattern mimicked the night sky.

"It's a push lock. The pattern mimics the night sky. It's a constellation. If we guess the wrong one I think it will never open." Danica said thinking out loud.

"Dani, you know all about the sky. You got this." Orion said to her, squeezing her shoulder.

Danica shut her eyes and ran her fingers over the chest. She could feel all the buttons but she needed to know which order to push them. There were so many constellations in the night sky and some were very close in shape to others. She skimmed her fingers over the buttons once more. Her eyes shot open. She glanced at Ariadne. It was perfect.

"It's Ariadne's crown." Danica said smiling to Ariadne.

They all held their breath as Danica slowly began pressing on the button making the constellation with her hands on the chest. She inhaled deeply as she pushed the last button inwards. The chest began to creak and shift, after several clicking noises the lid popped open. Ariadne and Orion shifted away instinctively. Danica touched the lid carefully and slowly opened it. Thousands of shimmering gold coins shined back at her. There were rubies, emeralds and sapphires as well. Danica looked at it in awe.

"Well you won't have to worry about how you're going to repay dad back for losing the North Star." Ariadne said, grabbing her shoulder.

"Holy shit look at all this." Orion said, reaching in and touching some of the coins.

"You could buy Dad more than one North Star replacement." Orion laughed.

Ariadne slipped her arm around her sister and squeezed her tightly. "You did it Dani." She whispered in Danica's ear.

Danica smiled softly but for some reason she didn't feel happy. She had been feeling off since Kaleb left. She hoped it was just because she was tired. She looked at Ariadne with a small smile on her face.

"No, we did it." Danica said and squeezed her back.

"Orion, let's open Dad's study and lock this in there for now." Ariadne said to him.

"Um sure but how exactly are we getting there? The door is impenetrable." Orion said glaring at the door.

"Oh here.' Ariadne said, finishing a key out of her pocket and handing it to him.

"Let's hope this works." Orion said, going to the door.

"You guys got this? I wanna head to bed." Danica said her voice sounded sad.

"Aye go ahead Dani, we got this." Ariadne said, looking at her with soft eyes.

She didn't know what was wrong with her sister but she hoped that whatever it was it would be fixed by sleep. Danica smiled at her and disappeared up the stairs.

## Chapter Fifty

### Forever

The next several days were a blur. The Smith's
had buried Edward. Patrick had come by several
times to see Ariadne. They were now official and very
out in the open. They couldn't be in a room without
touching one another. Patrick was now co-owner of
the company with Kaleb being his partner. They had
been discussing merging or being partners in the
company. Danica sat by the dock, dunking the tips of
her toes in the water reflecting on the first day Patrick
came over. He and Ariadne were sitting closely at the
kitchen table talking terms of agreement and
partnership between the two companies when Danica
walked down the stairs. Patrick smiled brightly at her.

"Morning Danica." Patrick said politely to her.

Danica smiled back at him, her eyes searching
to see if maybe he had come with him. Realizing who
she was looking for, Ariadne frowned slightly.

"How is everything going?" Danica asked,
trying to not make it seem awkward.

"Ok the Smith side of business needed a lot of
tweaking but it's fixable." Patrick smiled at her.

"That's good to hear….How's Kaleb?" Danica
asked shyly.

Patrick inhaled slightly and let air slowly out as if trying to delay his response as he pieced it together.

"He's ok. I think Father's death is hitting him the hardest. I don't know what he's going through but he told me he needed space. He's doing what Kaleb does when he needs to process. He …He left the morning after father's funeral." Patrick said cautiously, glancing at Ariadne, who bit her lip at his statement.

"Oh well I hope he finds what he's looking for." Danica said, trying to not sound hurt.

She had asked once more after that day but Patrick said he still had not heard from Kaleb. Since then her parents had returned home shocked and surprised at everything that had happened. She remembered how amazed and proud her father was. They sat up late at night on the roof of their home watching the stars as Danica told him in detail the adventure she went on.  She watched her father's face as she told her tale, he listened like a child hearing his favorite story. She smiled looking into the ocean water. She glanced back up at the house. The candle danced in the window. No one had questioned her why she never put it out when their parents came home. No one had tried to put it out ethier. They knew deep down she was leaving it burning for Kaleb.

"You ready?' A voice from behind her said.

"Aye." Danica straightened up hearing her Uncle Jack behind her.

'Are you sure you want to get back on the ocean already?' Jack asked her from the dock.

"Aye it's better than sitting around here. " Danica said, dunking her toes in the ocean more.

"All right kiddo, I just gotta go get the paperwork from your Da and we will be on our way. Whenever you are ready you can head to the Evening Star." Jack said not asking any more questions.

Danica loved that about her Uncle. He didn't push or pry. He let you do what you needed to do and he would be there when you were ready. Danica nodded to him as he headed back to the house.  She grabbed her bag sitting on the side of her. She slung it over her shoulder and slipped her shoes on. She slowly walked to the Evening Star. She had already said goodbye to her siblings and parents. She didn't want to go back to the house and risk seeing Patrick. She didn't want to tell him she was leaving, she didn't want him to think she was going because of Kaleb. Not that it matters but she just didn't want to deal with it. She saw the sails being dropped as she approached the ghost ship. She didn't even ask where they were headed; she just wanted away from here. She thought as she climbed up the ramp to the lower deck. She nodded to the men shuffling about preparing the ship to get ready to sail. She recognized several of them from before. All the men that  went with her and Ariadne the last time decided to stay behind. They had had enough of the ocean for a little bit. She leaned on the lower deck rail looking out over the harbor. Once Jack was back with the paperwork they would be on their way.

"Running from something?" A voice came from behind her.

Danica stiffened and closed her eyes. It wasn't possible. She probably made it up. She wanted so badly to see him. She didn't respond and kept looking out over the water.

"I happen to be an expert in running from things so I kind of know the look." The voice said again this time he leaned on the rail next to her.

She froze, her stomach twisting in on itself as her heart began to stutter. Turning in shock to her right. He was there, his auburn hair ruffled in  a mess, his blue eyes staring at her. They were full of regret. She looked at him confused and angry.

"Kaleb?" Danica whispered to him.

"Aye Love." He said softly back.

"Why? Where did you go? What are you doing here?" Danica asked, her tone going from confused to angry.

"I couldn't process it here. I guess everything that I suppressed as a kid came to the forefront when he died. I did the thing I was best at. Ran. I didn't

know where I was going or what I was looking for.”
Kaleb started to explain.

“You didn't say one thing to me. You just left.
Left me here to wonder. Do you know what that feels
like! “ Danica said, hands in fist at her side.

“Dani-

“No, I understand the need to think things
through and process everything but to just leave. How
can you just leave someone you care for? Or was I
wrong?” Danica yelled, her voice starting to shake.

“Danica no. I do care for you.-

“Why are you here Kaleb?” Danica said, cutting
him off a tear escaping her eye.

“I was looking for you,” Kaleb said, catching the
tear with his thumb.

The warmth of his hand against her cheek, the
intense feeling she got from his touch, stopped her in
her tracks. The anger wanted to melt away. She
looked at him confused.

“What?” Danica asked, her voice cracking as
she spoke, trying to make herself somehow pull away
from him.

“It's you. The whole time I was gone I was
looking for peace. For meaning, to stop the pain. I

was searching for something that made me whole. It's you Danica." Kaleb said, stepping closer to her.

"Me?" Danica whispered.

"Aye Love. From the minute I met you the numbness I held started to drift away. Before, running was easy. No matter what was going on as soon as I left here  I left better. This time I felt worse. I couldn't shake the feeling. The guilt from running all those years took a toll but there was something much worse. It was being away from you. All I could think about was you. I am so sorry" Kaleb said, rubbing her cheek with his thumb.

"So what do we do from here?" Danica asked quietly.

"Stay by my side forever?" Kaleb said with a smile.

"Forever?" Danica asked, her voice still just above a whisper.

"Aye Forever. Wherever you want to go, I'll follow." He said, leaning his forehead against hers.

"Honestly I don't know where the ship is going. I just couldn't stand being here and you not coming back. I couldn't wait any more. I need to go." Danica whispered back to him.

"I will never leave you again. Ever." Kaleb promised.

Danica studied his face for a second and could not see anything but truth in his eyes. She reached up and her fingers curled into her hair, pulling his face forward to hers. She pressed her lips against his. His arms wrapped tight around her as a rush of relief went through him. He kissed her hard, long and passionate. Chills rushed over her body from the heat of his lips. She was pushed back up against the rail of the ship as he kissed her like he had not seen her in years. A throat cleared from behind them and it almost didn't stop them.

"Love birds." Jack growled slightly seeing his niece locking lips with Kaleb.

Danica chuckled against Kaleb's mouth as she pulled away. She peeked out from behind Kalen raising an eyebrow at her uncle asking what he needed with her face.

"Your father said to buy a ship when we dock and sail it back in place of The North Star. If you're still coming."Jack smiled.

Danica looked from Jack to Kaleb. Her face asked Kaleb what he wanted to do.

"Wherever you go love, it doesn't matter to me as long as you're there." He whispered to her.

"Aye Let's set sail." Danica called to Jack before her lips found Kaleb's again.

www.ingramcontent.com/pod-product-compliance
Lightning Source LLC
Chambersburg PA
CBHW062101290726
48975CB00001B/64